Questioning Return

Questioning Return

BETH KISSILEFF

Enjoy this armchair visit to Jerusalem!

Beth Kissileff

[M]

Mandel Vilar Press

This book is typeset in Minion. The paper used in this book meets the minimum requirements of ANSI/NISO Z39.48-1992 (R1997). ⊗

Designed by Barbara Werden
Cover photo © Can Stock Photo / lucidwaters

Publisher's Cataloging-In-Publication Data

Names: Kissileff, Beth.
Title: Questioning return : a novel / Beth Kissileff.
Description: Simsbury, Connecticut : Mandel Vilar Press, [2016]
Identifiers: ISBN 978-1-942134-23-7 (print) | ISBN 978-1-942134-24-4 (ebook)
Subjects: LCSH: Graduate students—Jerusalem—Fiction. | Jewish pilgrims and pilgrimages—
    Israel—Fiction. | Jews, American—Israel—Fiction. | Jewish way of life—Fiction. |
    Immigrants—Israel—Fiction. | Israel—Emigration and immigration—Fiction. |
    Israel—Fiction. | Jewish fiction.
Classification: LCC PS3611.I87 Q47 2016 (print) | LCC PS3611.I87 (ebook) | DDC 813/.6—
    dc23

Printed in the United States of America
16 17 18 19 20 21 22 23 24 / 9 8 7 6 5 4 3 2 1

Mandel Vilar Press
19 Oxford Court, Simsbury, Connecticut 06070
www.americasforconservation.org | www.mvpress.org

"When one is asked a question he must discover what he is."

GEORGE HERBERT
A Priest to the Temple
Collected Works: 226

Contents

PROLOGUE—A Decisive Moment?   1

ONE—Holders of Foreign Passports   11

TWO—Walking in Jerusalem   18

THREE—Sabbath Peace   27

FOUR—Bayit Ne'Eman   45

FIVE—Centers and Margins   73

SIX—New Jerusalem?   91

SEVEN—Accompanying the Coffin   111

EIGHT—Wendy and Noah: The Aftermath of Desire   124

NINE—Shared Dreams, Shared Eternity   153

TEN—"Good Night World"   170

ELEVEN—Dr. Hideckel   183

TWELVE—Meeting Atarah   198

THIRTEEN—Purim: Until You Don't Know   209

FOURTEEN—A New Chance   231

FIFTEEN—Rituals of Incorporation   247

SIXTEEN—Confronting the Question: The Seder   260

SEVENTEEN—Self-Counting   276

EIGHTEEN—Forty-Two Journeys   295

NINETEEN—Teiku   325

Glossary   347

Acknowledgments   353

Questioning Return

PROLOGUE
A Decisive Moment?

Il n'y a rien dans ce monde qui n'ait un moment decisif. (There is nothing in this world that does not have a decisive moment.)
—CARDINAL DE RETZ, quoted by HENRI CARTIER-BRESSON in the introduction to *The Decisive Moment*

To me photography is the simultaneous recognition, in a fraction of a second, of the significance of an event as well as a precise organization of forms which give that event its proper expression.
—HENRI CARTIER-BRESSON, in the introduction to *The Decisive Moment*

"Who is asking?"

"No one's ever questioned that. I'm the one who grills the subjects," Wendy responded.

"So we're reversing it now," Jacob Lamdan added, smiling. "How did you get to your dissertation topic?"

Wendy looked at him and sighed gently, trying to suppress the queasiness she'd been feeling since the plane's takeoff in New York, still with her in the air, now somewhere over Europe. "I almost didn't. I'm studying newly religious American Jews in Jerusalem, to see how they discuss changes they've made in their lives. What they feel they've gained, what lost, what is constant, what radically new in their religious incarnation. I can't believe I'm finally on this plane; I only got a dissertation Fulbright late last spring, after being rejected from everything else. So," she said pausing, both hesitant to declare her pride in an as-yet-unwritten project and proud of her achievement thus far, "I guess it was *basherte*." Her use of the Yiddish word was forced for a third-generation American in her twenties; it was solely to impress Lamdan, a professor of Talmud at Princeton, where she was a graduate student in Religious Studies.

He gazed at her, sitting next to him, closer together than they would be anywhere other than the cramped seats of an international plane flight. "I have a hard time with this thing *fate*. If everything is so *basherte*, why am *I* here, when so many others who deserve to be alive much more, are not? I can't accept that all is foreseen. Humans have free will. Sometimes, we make terrible mistakes."

Wendy's left arm was on the armrest of the seat to his right. She could see the indelible mark of the six blue digits on his left arm even in the hazy dimness of this not-yet-morning hour. "But you're religious? Do you really mean there's no *basherte*, no . . . greater power . . . behind it all?"

He was surprised by her question; students weren't usually bold enough to challenge him. Most held him in awe and approached him with reverence, distance. Lamdan never had Wendy in class; even though she was a student in his department, she didn't have the Hebrew background to take his type of courses. Had they been somewhere else, he would probably never have thought to answer her seriously.

"No simple answers, young lady."

She decided, glancing sideways at him, not to let go of the matter. "The people I'm studying don't seem to think so. The prevailing view is that once you make a leap of faith, it's all easy."

"*Halivei*, would it were so. Listen, I'll tell you a story."

Wendy liked the soothing cadences of his voice, the soft accent his first languages, Yiddish and Hungarian, lent to his English. His voice and tone were melodic, as though he would begin to chant a sacred text at any moment. She had never sat so close to a professor; their knees were aligned, virtually touching. His frail skinny body, forty or fifty years older than hers, wasn't attractive. His stomach was practically concave, his skin pale and his clear blue eyes as sharp as the laser of his intellect, able to bore into unprepared students and terrify them, she had heard from departmental chatter. His soft smile and the crinkles at the edges of his eyes made her want to imagine what he'd looked like as a teenager, at ease, before he was taken to Auschwitz. Her qualms about being on the plane, whether she'd be able to do this project, how it would be to live in a foreign country, seemed insignificant and minor when she thought of the difficulties he had faced in life. She was ready to listen.

"There were two men, a robber and a rabbi. The rabbi was famed for his beauty, so much that he would stand outside the ritual bath as women left it and tell them to look at him and wish for children as beautiful as he."

She listened and felt entranced by the lyric singsong of his voice telling a story. But she couldn't stop her rational self from asking questions. "What kind of person would do that? It's so . . . arrogant?"

"Maybe. Or, he knew the impact of his beauty? In any case, one day he was bathing in the Jordan River, and a robber jumped in after him, an incredible athletic leap. From afar, the robber thought the beardless rabbi was a beautiful woman; perhaps he wanted to rape her. When the robber got close to him, the rabbi said, marveling, 'Your strength should be for Torah.' The robber said, mocking him, 'Your beauty should be for women.' The rabbi said, 'I'll make you a deal. You like my beauty? Come, repent, use your strength for Torah in my yeshiva, and I'll marry you to my sister, who is more beautiful than I.'"

Wendy, intrigued, asked, "Did the robber take the deal?"

Lamdan continued, "Absolutely. He went and studied, and married the rabbi's sister."

"So, the robber saw the light. That's it?"

"Everything is fine until one day in the study hall, they're discussing weapons and how to determine whether a weapon is ready to use. The rabbi turns to the former robber and says, 'Share your expertise. You're a thief; you know your weapons.'"

"But he hasn't been a thief for years now, right?"

"This is where the story gets interesting. The robber says, 'How have you benefited me? I was called "rabbi," master, among the thieves, and here I'm called "rabbi" too. You've done nothing for me.' The rabbi became depressed about the robber's anger, and the former robber became sick, physically ill. His wife, the rabbi's sister remember, asked her brother to pray for her husband so she wouldn't be a widow, and his nieces and nephews, orphans." Lamdan looked over at Wendy and added, "The rabbi refused."

"That's terrible. Shouldn't he have some responsibility for his student, his brother-in-law?"

Lamdan shrugged.

Wendy demanded, "What happened? Did the robber get better?"

"He died."

"And the rabbi?"

"He mourned him. He died soon after, grieving for his friend and student."

"But it was *his* fault; his insult led to the man's death."

"Yes, a hundred percent," agreed Lamdan.

"But . . ." Wendy was frustrated, "Why? A rabbi tried to change the life of a thief and then threw his past back in his face. I don't see a lesson."

Lamdan said, gently, softly, in his European inflected accent, "It's not simple. It seems to be a lovely narrative; one man convinces another to change. It turns tragic. Being religious, asking others to be . . . it's not simple either."

"In the narratives I've come across, subjects say, once they decide to be religious, everything else falls into place."

"Your task should be to question that." Lamdan looked at his seatmate. "Find the places where they doubt. Being a returnee is never simple. Even when someone has been religious a very long time, something can come along and disturb him."

Wendy said, "I see." She added, "That is part of what I am trying to do, to see how people talk about themselves and the changes they've made in their lives, to capture the fault lines and fissures in their identity."

"Be careful. A rabbi caused a tragedy by throwing the past at his student and friend. You are asking people to tell their stories."

"Yes?"

"Be aware of the effect you have on others."

Wendy was unsure what it was that he was implying. The passengers around them were sleeping, the plane was dark, and she was sitting incredibly close to him. He added, "It takes training to get someone to speak about his life. That's why we value psychiatrists; they help their patients create healing narratives. You aren't trying to heal people, but the power you have in asking them to tell their story, it can't be measured. You don't want to remind a person he was once a thief, in the language of the story."

Wendy shrugged her shoulders quickly. "You're making me nervous. I'm talking to people but I'm not . . . well, I'm asking their life stories, but . . ." she stammered.

"I'll tell you my story. I began life as a Hasid; I learned with my grandfather. I was a prodigy; wealthy men would come and give me a *lei*, a coin, for reciting Gemara. When I was deported, I kept learning and teaching others in the camp. My learning wasn't the same; I could never go back to what I did as an innocent child. Before the war, when I learned with my grandfather, I heard the voices of the souls who commented on the text float out of the page and fill the room. After the war, instead of the Gemara *niggun* of study I used to hear, I'd hear the screams of my grandfather and the others who were murdered. I study the same texts, but I take a critical approach now. I had to see the text differently. This helped me remain in the framework of tradition, but without the mute relationship to the text I had in my early life. I needed to be critical to stay religious, to remain accepting of a God who could create a world in which evil wields such great power."

Wendy decided silence was the best response.

"Religion is never an all or nothing proposition. There are cycles, ups and downs. The story I told you, the rabbi and the thief, things are fine until the rabbi insults the thief. Those careless words result in both their deaths. For me, religion . . . there's no *basherte* . . . there *is* something to hold on to. I have faith in God; it's a relationship. I can feel angry at God, furious, resentful. My wife has been gone almost a year now; she suffered so much at the end. I don't know how or why a merciful God could inflict a painful illness on someone who had a lifetime of suffering before her teens were over. I can't answer all my questions, but that doesn't mean I can't ask them, can't be thinking and religious. I need my faith as an anchor; it . . . I can't have faith in humans; I need another power. And Israel . . . you'll see, spending a year in Israel; every day there is truly a miracle."

"I guess. I've been thinking more about how it will be to be writing my dissertation, finally, launching my academic career. Much less about being in Israel itself, odd as that sounds," she confessed. She didn't want him to see her as ungrateful for her opportunities, so she hastened to add, "I am taking *ulpan* this year to improve my Hebrew. I've done French and German, but haven't had a chance to work on my Hebrew yet."

"A good start. Try to do some learning too this year."

"I'm a graduate student; of course I'm learning."

Lamdan laughed. "No, I mean *lernen,* in the Yiddish sense of the word, learning Jewish texts. It isn't central to your dissertation, but . . . you might find what you need, as a Jew."

"Maybe. I liked your story about the rabbi and the thief."

"There are many more where that came from. Look, you're a bright person; spend some time thinking about who you are, a Jew. You have time now, as a graduate student, without the burdens of teaching and family responsibilities." He paused, taking just a bit too long to look at her, the glance more penetrating than she preferred. She remembered hearing something about how female graduate students fared under him, but wasn't sure what it was. She tried to move away from him slightly but couldn't go far because she was wedged into the cramped seat of the plane. "You are asking things of others, but the questions may turn back to you, Wendy. Sometimes questions help you decide who you are. Or might be."

The lights went on in the cabin and an announcement about when breakfast would be served came over the plane's speaker system. Their heads had been quite close together, speaking softly so as not to disturb the surrounding sleeping passengers. They were both startled by the light and began blinking, as if they had shared some kind of intimacy that seemed less appropriate in the illumination.

Wendy was at a loss for words now, in the light.

"Do you mind getting up?" he asked. "I need to daven *shaharit.*"

"Nice to talk to you. Thanks for the advice," she said, rising from her seat and moving into the aisle.

He followed her and rose also, stepping into the aisle. "May I ask you a favor? I have a bad back and can't reach up. Can you get my *tefillin,* that blue velvet bag, out of the overhead bin?"

Wendy nodded and reached above her, pressing the latch of the compartment in. As she did, she felt his eyes on her chest, close. She shifted to the right, away from him, and reached up to find the bag. Fortunately, it was at the edge of the compartment. She plucked it out quickly and handed it to him, closing the hatch. He hadn't done anything inappropriate; maybe it was her imagination, feeling vulnerable and exposed, reaching up. *I should stop being suspicious of people,* she thought. But her musing continued, as she gazed at Lamdan. *Sometimes suspicions were warranted. Even in the Talmud, two men trust each other for years, and then with a few words, betrayal.*

"Thank you, Wendy," he said and called out in Yiddish to a passing Hasid in black hat, peyot, long black jacket, and pants. The man replied in Yiddish and nodded, as Lamdan started following the man to the end of the plane, where Wendy could see a group of men beginning to gather in the limited space, to don tallis and *tefillin.*

Watching, she felt left out, alone. Not that she wished to be one of them; but it seemed cozy, the little group of men, sharing the same activity, binding themselves with the black leather straps to God, to their faith. It was something she could never be part of, though she did see a woman in the back, standing at a respectful distance from the men. She had blonde curly hair, very frizzy and thick like a mane ringing her pretty round face, holding a prayer book and intoning her own prayers. The woman's face looked like something out of a Dutch painting, Rembrandt or Vermeer, precise but lighted well, the light from the windows of the plane landing on the white of the prayer book, which then seemed to reflect up to her face. What had Lamdan said about the Torah being a source of light, bouncing out and being reflected back? A painter would depict this scene well, she mused, showing the holiness coming off the books into the faces. Though noting the woman's loveliness, Wendy still had to conjecture cynically whether the fervor emanating from her face at prayer could last over time.

Her gaze turned to Lamdan himself. Wendy was suddenly embarrassed by the unnatural proximity to others inside the plane, seeing religious men so fervent, so close up. Lamdan looked sincere, binding himself in his *tefillin.* As he had departed with the Yiddish-speaking Hasid, he said to her, "I can't study with them, but I can pray with them. That's the most important thing." She wasn't sure quite what he meant. She wanted to connect it to what he said about his need to question the tradition, yet be nurtured by it. Critical in study, comforted in prayer; it seemed like a nice balance.

The men at the front of the plane bound themselves in their leather straps, kissing the boxes, putting them on their heads, opening their prayer books, their expressions changing as they opened the books—she couldn't tell exactly why or how. They all looked raw, exposed, like someone had rubbed off the outermost layer of skin, camouflaging true expression, and now their emotional selves were on public display. The face of a man about to come during sex came into her head. She tried to get rid of it—such a profane analogy—but she saw in the daveners the same fervor, concentration, rush of emotion—the total being in the moment so that nothing could intervene to break the focus. Usually during sex she kept her eyes closed, but sometimes she liked to see her partner's face, to fathom who he was, what he wanted.

These men did not expect to be watched. Lamdan didn't glance her way once, his frail body encased in the group of men around him. As more men from other parts of the plane gathered, it was harder for her to see him. As she remained by Lamdan's seat and stared at the men at prayer, she wondered what it was like to have that trancelike state, that connection to a higher power.

"*Dossim*, what you want with them?" said the Israeli guy with the nose stud and tattoos who had been sitting in the row in front of her as he walked past on the way to the bathroom. He didn't stay to hear her response. There were other people trying to get by her in the aisle. Finally the flight attendant with the breakfast cart needed to go by. Wendy was embarrassed both to be caught staring and to be in the way of so many people.

Wendy returned to her seat and looked out the airplane's small windows to see sunrise: lavish pink streaks extending across the sky, the glory of the sun only glancing out carefully through the clouds. The miniscule size of the airplane window only heightened the vastness of the vista. She was startled by the unexpected beauty; she wished she had her camera. She remembered something the photographer Diane Arbus wrote: "I really believe there are things nobody would see unless I photographed them." That was the essence of what Wendy hoped to do this year: see fascinating and beautiful things, and help others see them by writing about them.

What she'd said to Lamdan was true: this trip, her whole dissertation, almost didn't happen. She came to her doctoral dissertation topic in a totally meandering way, completely by indirection. Her senior year in college, she needed a thesis topic and decided to write on the changes American life wrought on the practice of Buddhism. She loved the process of writing a longer research paper—the time for rumination and digestion of facts, the ability to take the time to consider and rearrange one's work, the digging in books for nuggets of information that will encapsulate a thesis and provide it with the necessary verve and philosophical underpinnings. As an undergraduate, she had found her time in Columbia's Butler Library thrilling, exhilarating even. Writing a thesis made her certain that graduate school was the right path.

Doing the work of her senior thesis Wendy loved, but the topic itself, not so much. She felt apart from it, not quite invested in the *why* of its importance. She didn't understand entirely the schisms that led to different strands of Buddhism—Mahayana versus Theravada—and the regions of the world where the religion was practiced. It just wasn't *her*, she finally concluded, though she loved examining the impact of America on a religious group. Once finished, she had decided she would continue to work in the field of American religion, to be able to teach about the Shakers and Quakers, Jonathan Edwards and the Great Awakening, and how individualism and democracy in America impacted religious identity. She almost went to study with a historian of American Judaism at Brandeis. When Wendy went up to Boston to meet him, he told her that he himself had trained not in Jewish studies, but in American history, and that he saw his work on the lives of Jews in America as a subset of American history. So, she decided to do the same and study Judaism within American religion at the best department in the field. She went to Princeton to work with Cliff Conrad. The work behind choosing a dissertation topic was how to put issues she found fascinating into a dissertation that would position her as a saleable commodity in the limited academic job market. This made her subject to the vagaries of hot topics that students would flock to take courses on, thus increasing departmental enrollment and clout within the university. Her dissertation topic needed to demonstrate her command and understanding of the field as well as establish a base for her future scholarly work. Wendy wanted to do a Jewish topic. It couldn't require extensive Hebrew knowledge that she did not have, and it needed to equip her for positions in American religion, not Jewish studies. One day, complaining on the phone to Nina Distler, her best friend from growing up in Westchester, Nina said, "Debby. Write about her."

Nina's sister Debby was now Devorah, morphed with a vowel shift from the casual English "e" to the Hebraic long "o," from a tennis playing, roller-skating all-American kid, to a *sheitel*-wearing, Torah-studying mother of children with impossible-to-pronounce names. Yerachmiel Zvi was followed by Baila Bracha and Sheindel Menucha. In high school, Wendy had accompanied Nina for Shabbos in Crown Heights to help her friend deal with it all on more than one occasion. At Nina's suggestion, the dissertation was born, and its title was similarly lifted from the speech patterns of Devorah's newly religious cohort. Wendy's magnum opus-in-progress was titled "It Was *Basherte*": Narrative and Self-Identity in the Lives of Newly Religious American Jews." Little did Debby Distler know, back when she left for Israel before college, that she was going to inspire her kid sister's friend to spend a year studying people like her.

There was something at stake for Wendy in writing this dissertation, different from her senior thesis. Wendy was curious about whether Debby, or other returnees, had changed at all. Her scholarship came with a sense of nosiness and voyeurism, wanting to snoop into corners of belief that their adherents would prefer to leave untouched and unexamined. But still she had to know: Was there something left behind, some remainder of who Debby had been before, or was it all as covered as her naturally strawberry blonde hair? This driven inquisitiveness, the need to know if anyone can really change, went beyond the professional.

What Wendy wanted above all, what every graduate student desired, was to know whether all this effort, all this seemingly endless deferral of anything besides graduate school, would ever pay off. Would she work hard at her dissertation, get a series of one-year jobs, and then end up living with her parents and going to law school? She hoped only that if she kept going, continued on the path she'd set down—following the steps, courses, research, dissertation idea, fellowships—she would have a sense, eventually, of the rightness of it all. But if she were entirely sure, there would be no room for new possibilities. She had to hope that going forth into the unknown would lead to something good.

A decisive moment. A moment when the viewer realized she was seeing something that was there, actual, but not able to be seen without the photographer's lens. Wendy Goldberg hoped, in writing her dissertation in Jerusalem this year, to perform a similar feat.

ONE

Holders of Foreign Passports

Home is a group of people who miss the same imaginary place.
—ZACH BRAFF, *Garden State motion picture*

———————————————————————————

Wendy stepped off the plane. She was at the top of a flight of stairs, looking into blinding sunlight and palm trees.

She hadn't anticipated this: to live for a year in a place with palm trees, tall and swaying, their tops absurdly high, not necessary for a utilitarian purpose, but solely decorative, like the absurd pink crests on an exotic flamingo, sitting on one leg, rising above the water. Flamboyant—that was the word for these trees, their grandiose plumes alerting you to their presence, so different from the modest and decorous trees of the home of Wendy's parents on Raleigh Street in New Bay, New York. Foliage there blended in, giving evidence that there was a gardener in the background whose job was to contain the wildness of nature, keep botanical growth in proportion.

Were these trees, fifteen or twenty feet high, even real? Maybe they were only an exotic projection of what tourists wanted to see when they got off the plane?

What else here would surprise her? She knew intellectually that in Israel the climate and topography would be entirely different. It still felt so unsettling to actually be in this place, to realize how changed her surroundings were from what she was used to.

The heat. When she left New York last night, the summer evening had a cool undercurrent to it. In Tel Aviv, the middle-of-the-day humidity showed no signs of abating; it asssaulted her with its denseness.

The light here was different, somehow sharper, bringing objects into clearer focus. Were she in a movie, the lenses would shift now; all would be in Technicolor, highlighted, distinct from the black and white of her last few weeks at her parents' house and, after she had closed down her Princeton apartment, a short reprieve from them visiting her grandmother Essie.

This year, there were no classes to dictate how to spend her days, no students with papers needing to be graded. And no family to ask that she come home for Hanukkah or a nephew's birthday. She breathed in the humid summer air, and it actually felt refreshing.

Waiting her turn to gingerly tread the steep metal steps, Wendy began the slow passage off the plane, shuffling behind other passengers.

She looked down. It was a long way to the ground.

Wendy was seized with a sudden feeling of vertigo. *What if I fall? Can I make it down these steps?* She felt her heart constricting, the flow of blood to it getting smaller, more limited, as though fear might make it stop and harden suddenly, to become a great stone sitting in her chest.

She couldn't go down the steps. As she was panicking—picturing how she would turn around and go back to the plane with a feeble explanation that there was a mistake, she wasn't really supposed to get off—she was jostled gently from behind. She felt her feet move down the stairs with the crowd. The descent down the steps was performed only by her legs, the connection between their actions and her brain's volition entirely severed.

Abruptly, her legs brought her to the ground; now she was putting one foot in front of the other. She remembered a moment at the beginning of *On the Road*, when Kerouac's narrator wakes up in Iowa and feels a stranger to himself, his life a haunted life, himself a ghost. His temporary disorientation, this moment of blankness and bafflement, stays with him, fueling his search for a way to get at himself, who he is capable of being. Steadying herself after the steep descent, she thought, taking her first step on the flat ground, *Am I going to feel Kerouac's hauntedness and blank incomprehension this year?*

She was on the ground, the actual soil of the Holy Land, and only felt terror. She wondered whether anyone still kissed the ground, as she remembered hearing travelers did in bygone times. She didn't see anyone performing a sense of reverence for the sacred ground.

Wendy felt disappointed, seeing the travelers trudging to the waiting bus. She wished for ritual, fanfare, drama, to accompany her journey.

She took her carry-on luggage, the backpack with her laptop and her orange and green striped canvas tote bag filled with toiletries and snacks, and followed the crowd to the waiting bus, for the ride towards the airport building. The travelers proceeded to the area where they would get their passports ceremonially embossed with today's date—the modern ritual of entry, shorn of religious import.

She waited in the line labeled, "Holders of Foreign Passports." There were significantly more booths open to holders of Israeli passports than foreign ones. The five lines for possessors of Israeli passports cleared rapidly, while her queue and the one next to it had five or six family groups still waiting. Wendy felt unwelcome, like a child visiting a friend's house who sees that the mother always gives her own child more food and bigger portions of dessert. She felt the child's stunned surprise that an adult would play favorites so obviously.

Wendy finally reached the passport control booth. The young woman inside looked to be about twenty-five, her straight black shoulder-length hair dyed in reddish highlights, her skin the tawny color of Jews from Arabic-speaking countries. She asked questions of Wendy in routine bureaucratic language: "What is the purpose of your visit? How long do you plan to stay? Do you speak Hebrew? Are you visiting family? What is your address in Israel?"

Wendy looked at the clerk and thought of what Lamdan had said to her: "The questions may turn back to you." She thought about questions that would devastate her because of her profound inability to answer them. Is anything you are doing here is worthwhile or will it amount to much? Should you be here now? Who are you kidding—will you ever be able to write this kind of dissertation? How are you going to manage in a country where you don't speak the language?

"I plan to be in Israel for a year to do research on my dissertation."

"The . . . em . . . subject of this dissertation?"

"American *baalei teshuvah* in Israel."

"Oy." The clerk stared at Wendy. "Baalei teshuvah. They're crazy, *metoraf li'gamrei*. I had this boyfriend, Aharon. We travel . . . India . . . after the army. I thought we get married. He had this—I don't know how to say in English—*havayah*—at a rave. He became *dati*. I hate all the rules—it takes the . . . how do you say . . . *ta'am,* taste, from life. He in yeshiva, and his wife . . . with their second child. We were *biyahad,* em, together, seven years. *Zeh lo fair!* It should be me, his wife!"

Wendy did not know how to respond. She had never thought her dissertation topic would touch a bureaucrat at an airport. She hadn't thought about Israeli baalei teshuvah. Did the fact that they exist invalidate her theories that baalei teshuvah are merely another self-invention of the American Jew—Jewish piety inventing itself like Hollywood invented itself? Would she have to include footnotes and literature about Israelis to show she'd done her research homework? *Do I have to worry about this now?*

The clerk stamped firmly on Wendy's passport; she looked up and straight at Wendy's face. "I hope zey don't leave you when you write about them. Better luck zan me." She smiled at Wendy, but it was a smile that faded quickly and looked impossibly tired for someone so young.

"Thanks," Wendy called out, not knowing what else to say.

Wendy looked down at the date on the passport: July 17, 1996. The previous stamp, from 1987 when she'd first procured the passport, was from her trip to Israel before her senior year of high school. She hadn't wanted to go with a group from Camp Kodimoh, the Jewish camp she'd attended for three years, because for those kids the trip was a chance to drink and hook up. She wanted to do something more meaningful and productive, so chose to spend six weeks working on a kibbutz. She had barely toured the country then, and didn't know Jerusalem, where she'd be living, at all. Her parents, Sylvia and Arthur, had thought it a good plan: build the Jewish state, be around Jewish men. She'd only told them recently that the most interesting person on the kibbutz was a non-Jewish volunteer from Malmo, Sweden, whom she dated briefly. This trip, her parents were worried that she was going to follow the paths of her subjects and become similarly totally religious. It was so demeaning that it was easier for them to imagine her as a subservient woman with a wig and lots of kids than as someone capable of pursuing a professional career as a university professor. She was the youngest of three, and they just didn't take her professional aspirations seriously, assuming graduate school was just a way for her to fill time till marriage and children. They assumed that, like her sister Lisa, who quit her good job at a law firm when she didn't want to return from maternity leave, Wendy might work a bit, but only until she had kids.

At the luggage carousel, Wendy noted the household goods on the conveyor belt. All the items—baby swings, drum sets, stereos, microwave ovens, computers—were to enhance a house, the place people live with a family. She felt conspicuously alone. Looking around at the waiting families, she knew that she wanted to fall in love and have kids one day, to have someone to make a home with. It had to be in her own way, if she met the right person and wanted to, not because it was expected of her by someone else.

Her thoughts were diverted by a dull pain in her thigh as a large trunk suddenly rammed her. "Ow! Look where you're going!" she yelled at the man behind her. She spied her duffel bags coming towards her and stopped massaging the ache in her thigh long enough to nab them.

Wendy left the baggage area to go to customs, pushing a luggage cart with her two huge duffel bags, the box of books too important to trust to the mail like the other four boxes of books, and her backpack and tote bag. She made a declaration that there were no individual items worth over five hundred dollars and imagined what it might be to have diamonds or cocaine in the lining of her suitcase if she were a black market smuggler. Could *she* be bringing anything dangerous into the country?

Once she cleared customs, she came to the exit door and began to hear a dull roar from outside. The automatic doors parted and she began to walk through an assemblage of faces. All were in family groups, the mass of them appearing like a collage made with oil pastel crayons. The color was applied with smudges and blotches, light skinned ones here, darker swarthier groups there, blending in a crowd that was a microcosm of Israel. Ethiopian families darkest of all, Arab families with kaffiyehs and chadors, Hasidic families with black hats and wigs, secular families without any kind of hair covering save a baseball cap for the heat. The splotches of color blended together to greet their relatives returning home.

Part of her found the family groups amusing and made her feel relieved to be alone, with no family members to embarrass her. She thought back to the teenagers going on summer tours to Israel she'd seen at the airport in New York, whose parents kept embracing them, copious tears in their eyes, not letting the kids go. Wendy felt embarrassed by so much public display of affection, thinking it as inappropriate as the adolescent variety, something that belonged in a more concealed environment, its excrescences making her recoil. Yet, she felt a pang: of all the howling, whinnying, growling noises that were being made to attract the attention of returning family members, none were for her.

Was home only a place where you were welcomed? Robert Frost's lines about home came to her mind—that it is the "place where/ When you have to go there / they have to take you in."

Would anyone take her in this year? Who would be her friends? She knew that part of the Fulbright fellowship was meeting with the others once a month and presenting their work to each other. She always had things in common with other future academics: similar priorities and values, a shared frame of reference, even a knowledge of the quirks and flamboyancies of the most prominent senior people in each field. It was easier, Wendy generally found, to be friends with someone who shared something in common with you—someone who knew someone you knew, had been to the same school or camp, knew a place you did. She remembered one of her friends telling her as she left Princeton, "Maybe you will find the best friend you've ever had there."

She was again jostled by someone at her side. She knew that, somewhere in the airport, there was a shared cab to Jerusalem, but wasn't sure how to find it. Wendy was dazed, blinking in the bright summer sun, trying to find her way; but there were tears in her eyes. From the intensity of the sun? From exhaustion at not having slept well on the plane? Or from a larger anxiety about what she was doing here at all?

"Do you know where you're going?" a familiar voice asked.

"No," Wendy responded, turning to see Professor Lamdan, now pushing an airport luggage cart filled with suitcases and boxes of Little Tykes and Fisher Price toys, gifts for his grandchildren. She noted his six blue numbers on the forearm that carefully gripped the cart, and asked why she was feeling sorry for herself. How, she wondered, had Lamdan figured out where he was going?

She looked at him gratefully and said, "I'm looking for a shared cab to Jerusalem."

"Come, it's over here," he said gesturing. "It must be a bit overwhelming to be here for the first time. For me, every time, it's a miracle. The Gemara says the air of *Eretz Yisrael* makes one wise." He stopped and paused for breath, his intake of the molecules of the Holy Land's air slow and careful.

She followed after him, pushing her own off-kilter cart—the heaviness of the duffel bags making her progress forward an exercise in awkwardness—and marveling at the dignity in his gait. He looked weak, because he was so physically skinny, yet strong, striding in front of her, pushing his luggage cart. What did it cost him, that single-mindedness of putting one foot in front of the other? Maybe it was indeed heroic to keep going, no matter what.

Having followed Lamdan, putting his one foot in front of the other, she and he were at the end of the path from the airport to the parking area, where cars were everywhere, horns honking. He maneuvered his cart in front of the van they would share, spoke to the driver in Hebrew, and gestured at Wendy, indicating she was coming also. She stood next to him, catching only the words "*yofee*," "fine," and "*Yerushalayim*," Jerusalem. The driver yanked their bags off the luggage carts and heaved them to the storage area in the rear of the van. Lamdan gestured to Wendy to get in. There were three rows of seats—the back one had a mother and two young children in it; her older two were in the middle row. Lamdan got in and filled out that row, so Wendy sat by the window in the front row of seats. She rested her head against the window of the van and closed her eyes.

TWO

Walking in Jerusalem

Jerusalem was a place where history is not a one-way street; here the resurrection of old glories still seemed possible.
—SAMUEL HEILMAN, *A Walker in Jerusalem*

██

Friday morning, Wendy was walking around her apartment, getting ready for her day's task, to go to the *shuk*, open-air market, and buy things she'd need this year for her place. Wendy picked up the metal *grogger* on a shelf in the living room. It was a small, cheap thing with its caricatured pictures of the dense Persian king, his heinously evil advisor and rapturously beautiful Jewish queen portrayed in clashing tones of turquoise blue, hot pink, and neon orange. Was it a sacrilege to throw it away? She had misgivings about whether it was worth saving; yet it made a slight mewl of protest as it was being tossed to the garbage pile, the plastic cogs grinding angrily in complaint. Would its made-in-Taiwan apparatus be strong enough to hold up to repeated ritual protests against the evil Haman? It seemed to personify uncertainty, which was what led to her desire to keep it, unnecessary and ugly though it was.

The prohibitive cost of overseas shipping meant that each item from her Princeton apartment took on a larger significance. When she was packing that place up, she felt like, with each piece of her apartment she took apart or discarded, a bit of her identity was being obliterated, rubbed away—a bit of finger gone here, a brown eye there, now some locks of her black shoulder-length curly hair. If her stuff defined her, with less of it, she was lesser too. She remembered seeing a billboard for a real estate agency: "Nothing defines you more than the home in which you live." Despite her graduate student status and lack of both cash and the ability to reside in this place longer than an academic year, she wanted the things in her apartment to be part of her self-definition. She hoped it was a scintillating agglomeration of things. She wanted a visitor to her apartment to pick up any random item—book, poster, vase—and know there would be a captivating story behind it. It all added up, she hoped, to a picture of herself that was appealing—as a friend, or as a love interest.

She replaced the *grogger* on the shelf and tried to list what she needed. Extra kitchen items. She would use the pots for whatever she wanted so she wouldn't have to worry about using the kosher pots in the apartment the wrong way. In her apartment in Princeton, Wendy didn't cook much beyond spaghetti, eggs, and soy hot dogs. Cooking was a skill graduate students at Princeton did not hone. Friendships and parties were not focused on food— if people wanted to be in a group they went out to a bar or restaurant. If the department had a potluck gathering, people brought things from a takeout store. Cooking was not part of the life of the mind, and it brought no one closer to tenure, the scale by which all was rated in the world of graduate student priorities. As they frequently reminded themselves, mantra-like, *the work is all that matters.*

Wendy wandered around, getting ready to leave her apartment, looking for her sunglasses, keys, and wallet. She hoped, looking at the sunny space where her still-unpurchased desk would go, *this* would be where she'd begin her dissertation. There was something magical about the thought—*this* is where it would begin. *How do I really know where I came from?* Hadn't Freud written that the mystery of origin is one of the greatest to humans? Enmeshed within this city, woven tightly into this place that is the *omphalos mundi*, the absolute center of the religious world, source and foundation of three religions, would be the beginnings of the lifetime opus of Wendy Dora Goldberg, sure to be of field-changing, paradigm-shifting, earth-shattering proportions. She laughed aloud at her own grandiosity.

Before leaving, she put a small notebook in her purse, remembering the admonition of Violet Dohrmann, the anthropologist on her dissertation committee: "An anthropologist doesn't know what she thinks of a situation until she goes home and writes about it."

After going over her list of needed items, she left her apartment and walked down Mishael Street to Yehoshua ben Nun, a quiet residential street with bougainvillea framing the stone gates of the apartment houses. She admired the trees. Eucalyptus? Hopefully, she'd learn the names of the Middle Eastern flora. She noticed the cats trawling the green garbage containers for sustenance; they were beginning to have a certain charm, scrawny and disorderly though they were. The quality of the sunlight attracted her notice. Did the light somehow pierce things that normally didn't respond to its rays? But not knowing the names of the things that surrounded her, or even why she noticed the light, made her feel alien, appreciative as she was growing of Jerusalem's beauty.

There was a meow from a feral cat somewhere in the alley, and a scurrying of paws. Wendy remembered the note of caution her friend Leora Lerner gave her when she came to pick up Wendy's cat and care for him for the year. Leora had spent time studying in Jerusalem before college, and visited relatives here frequently.

Leora had cautioned her, "Do *not* adopt a cat from the streets of Jerusalem. Once they've lived wild, they can't be tamed. They don't change."

Wendy remembered asking curiously, "Why can't they change? People do. Or say they do—that's the whole point of my study."

Leora had planted her hands firmly on her hips. Wendy recalled the gesture and intonation, as Leora opined, "Animals don't."

Wendy moved away from the cat noises to see Rafi's Felafel across the street. She turned left, following the directions from her landlady how to exchange her American dollars for shekalim. She saw the money-exchange kiosk and entered a space with enough room for three or possibly four people to stand sideways and a window with a teller in front of her. Behind the teller was a blackboard with flags for different countries and the exchange rate for each currency posted. Wendy felt like she was engaging in some kind of illegal activity when she slid her hundred dollars in cash under the glass window. She felt furtive, pulling the cash out, glancing around, not wanting anyone to know where it came from or how much she had. She thought of the Off Track Betting windows she passed when she went through the

George Washington Bridge bus terminal on the way from visiting her brother Joel and his family in New Jersey back to college at Columbia. At OTB, people slid things back and forth under the glass, hoping for profit and gain. As she took her four hundred shekel notes and some assorted change, she hoped she was not being cheated because it seemed like there were fewer shekalim than she'd thought there would be. Of course, she could look at the rate and do the math, but her concern was more that she didn't quite know how things work in a new country.

Walking out the door, she decided the OTB analogy wasn't completely farfetched; this year was a bet. If she stayed here, hung around with religious people, listened, took notes, wrote it all up, she'd get material for a dissertation. Then she could get some articles out of it, get published and on conference panels, and get a job. But maybe not. She could be stuck in a series of one-year visiting positions—or none at all. Or, become so mired in the research that she'd never begin to actually write the thing. Or, worst of all, get so frustrated by the enormity and scope of the project that she'd just give up, and run straight to law school, screaming at the stupidity of having wasted four years as a graduate student with nothing to show for herself.

For now, she would just enjoy getting to know a new place, discovering the small things that pleased her in the neighborhood. There was a movie theater on nearby Lloyd Cremieux Street, and bars and cafés lining Emek Refaim, the main drag. Every other store seemed to be either a hair salon or a store offering some kind of arty accessory: clothing or jewelry or housewares. There was a grocery store, a video store, and quite a few felafel and pizza places. At all times, there were people on the street, going to the stores, hanging out at cafés and restaurants. More than either New Bay or Princeton, there was street life. At all hours, people strolled the main boulevard, sat in outdoor cafés, and enjoyed being on the street.

She noticed the street sign, Rahel Emainu, Rachel our mother. Streets named for biblical characters were so different from those in her parents' neighborhood in New York, where streets were named for cities in North Carolina: Raleigh, Durham, Charlotte, Wilmington, Greensboro, Goldsboro, Asheville, Fayetteville. Wendy had always felt vaguely dislocated by living in a place that was planned to evoke vistas of elsewhere.

She found the bus stop for Mahane Yehuda, the open-air market on Jaffa Road. She asked the driver to indicate to her where she should get off. The other passengers overheard. At her stop, Jewish grandmothers were gesturing to her in Hebrew, Russian, French, Spanish, and English that it was time for her to descend. She followed the others off the bus and watched as they fanned out through both the narrow covered stalls entirely full of shoppers and the wider outdoor area separating the two sections. She smelled fresh bread and saw a young Arab boy carrying stacks of pita on a wooden tray on his head, selling them ten in a plastic bag, which had condensation on it from the warmth of their freshness. She saw a booth that sold only spices, all with gorgeous colors: the deep rust of paprika, the bright yellow of turmeric, the fragrant green of basil and oregano, arrayed in large conical piles which the merchant scooped and weighed. There was one kiosk with just halvah, a sesame seed candy that came in a dazzling assortment of flavors: espresso, peanut butter, pistachio, and chocolate. She saw every kind of kosher fish available in Israel, arranged carefully on ice to keep it fresh. Other stalls had dried rice and beans, or all kinds of teas, salads, and meats.

Everywhere she could hear vendors hawking their wares, screaming loudly, "*Avatiach, hamesh shekel! Avatiach le'kvod shabbat.*" She paused to look around, and one of the merchants beckoned to her and offered a taste of watermelon, *avatiach*. She bought half a melon to satisfy him, placed it in her backpack, and immediately regretted having bought the heaviest item first. She passed a store with delicious-looking salads of all kinds in a free-standing refrigerated display case and ordered a number of them. When she finished ordering, she handed over her money, holding up fingers for the number of bills the vendor requested. Walking away, she did the monetary conversion and realized she had spent almost forty bucks, a large sum for her student budget. She turned to the right to one of the many alleyways inside the *shuk* and found a group of stores all selling housewares. She purchased a spaghetti pot, a soup pot, a frying pan, and two plates, two cups, and silverware for less money than she paid for the salads.

She went back outside, somehow finding the way through the winding alleys of the narrow *shuk*, all leading to the wide area between the two sides of the market, and looked for a bakery to get something to bring to dinner tonight with the cousin of her friend Leora from Princeton. She spotted the bakery with the longest line and figured it must be the best. She was usually impatient waiting in line, but somehow the smells emanating from inside the store, and the anticipation she felt seeing customers exit with looks of pronounced satisfaction on their faces, relaxed her. Her usual frustration with waiting in line was her feeling that she was doing nothing; now she was listening to the Hebrew around her, absorbing the atmosphere. On her turn to order, she chose entirely by visual cues, pointing at the items she wanted and holding up her fingers to indicate the amount.

Walking back to the bus stop on Rehov Yaffo, Wendy reflected on how much more satisfying this experience was than a trip to an ordinary American grocery store. At the *shuk*, all the food is on display; there is no layer of artificiality, plastic wrap or anything else, between seller and consumer. She remembered her grandmother Essie saying that when the A and P supermarket first opened, she was positive it would be a huge financial flop because no one would be willing to pay more for lettuce with plastic on it. Maybe that was the difference between America and Israel—people were willing to pay for barriers between themselves and their food, to obstruct their encounter with sources of nourishment.

At Mahane Yehuda, the smells of the fresh pita and spices and the alluring look of all the fresh foods enticed Wendy to spend much more than she had planned. Would this too be a metaphor for the rest of her year, becoming sucked in to something she hadn't known about, released from her usual level of detachment from ordinary things of life like food? Would she be pulled in unexpected ways to things she hadn't anticipated?

She liked the lack of pretense in the market, the obviousness of vendors yelling for customers, the pushing and shoving of the crowds of Friday morning shoppers trying to get the best bargains. Even if she didn't celebrate Sabbath, it was her Jewish culture, not Sunday, emphasized as a day of rest here. She'd never thought about being excluded by Sunday, but now that she was here, she liked this activity filled, errand-doing Friday. Wendy found her bus stop and successfully navigated her bags and bundles aboard the bus for the return trip, excited that she was able to recognize the corner stop of Rahel Emeinu and Emek Refaim.

Wendy now had a bit of time before she and her landlady, Amalia Hausman, would share a cab to Amalia's granddaughter's new apartment for a Shabbat evening meal. Wendy had heard about this apartment because Amalia was the great-aunt of her Princeton friend Leora, who facilitated the arrangement when Wendy wasn't sure how to find a place to live. Amalia was in her seventies and had lived in Israel most of her life; she was fortunate in her birth to a German Jewish family astute enough to leave their fatherland for Israel in the early 1930s. Leora's grandfather, Amalia's brother, had lit out for the States as a young man, met an American woman, and raised his family there. Leora had told Wendy the story about her great-grandfather, Amalia's father, who owned a silver factory. One day, he was asked to put a Nazi flag up over his property. He told his wife the time had come to leave, and they did, in 1933. Neither Amalia's father nor her mother had other close relatives who survived. Wendy and Leora were both fascinated with alternate possibilities and spent hours discussing what if: Would either of them have known when to leave? What if Leora's grandfather had remained in Israel? What if Wendy's great-grandparents had stayed in Poland, not come to America? The speculation made Wendy realize that there are so many plausible ways in which anyone's life could be completely different, something that she wanted to get her subjects to admit, but that many, with their belief that God was guiding them constantly, refused to.

After putting her groceries in the fridge and her pots on the shelves, Wendy had two hours before dinner at Shani's. She decided to try to do some reading. She gazed at her bookshelf. *Textual Soulmates: Professors on the Texts They Love,* was an anthology purchased out of voyeurism and curiosity, to see whether there was still ardor and enthusiasm in the ranks of the tenured. That was something that worried her—would she retain her zest for a subject, any subject, over time, or would what started as passionate interest devolve into the chore of necessary deadlines and obligations, devoid of joy or thrill? Wendy had read a few of the essays by professors she knew and knew of, but, still, it was nice to be reminded that many professors do their work out of interest and love. Holding the volume, knowing it existed and was full of excitement for its topic, reassured her somehow. She wanted to love her work and to interest others in it, get them to love it as well.

She pulled her main dissertation advisor Cliff Conrad's first book off the shelf. She had read it for a senior seminar at Columbia, and it inspired her to go to Princeton as his grad student. *Legible Promises: American Transformations in Puritan Diaries and Sermons, 1636–1740* had won numerous awards and established Conrad's career. Its title was a quote from Cotton Mather: "America is legible in [God's] promises." New England preachers saw America as a place to re-create the narrative of an errand into the wilderness of Israel by a chosen people. Her research, in the actual country of Israel, was studying members of the original elect people, also going voluntarily on their own mission of return. She felt both anxiety and excitement to know that Conrad was interested in her work for its extension of the lineage of his own, and hoped she was up to the responsibility of upholding his high standards of scholarship and writing.

Conrad's serious work on American religion at the beginning of his career had marked him as a maverick. His advisors had encouraged him, but they didn't share his interest in American religion as a subject worth a major study, particularly for a dissertation and first book. It was thought at Yale's religion department in the sixties, the time he was working on his dissertation, that to develop a body of work of any stature one must work with some kind of philosophical phenomenon, preferably something involving lots of German, which would lend an imprimatur of heft and gravity to even the most trivial of subjects. There was still the attitude that American religious thinkers were less important subjects for study than their European counterparts. Conrad had persisted, his career ascending with that of his advisor, Sydney Ahlstrom, one of the first to examine a trajectory of American religion as a central part of American culture. In the course of his career, Conrad had worked with documents ranging from Puritan diaries in his own dissertation, to New Age religious narratives in which people experience some kind of sudden revelation that enables them to change their lives and, in the process, earn gobs of money with a bestseller about the experience. Conrad's interest in these New Age narratives stemmed from his sense of them as part of the continuity of American religious expression and ideology of selfhood that has made America unique. Conrad had never looked at any non-Christian narratives; he was excited about Wendy's project because it built on his own work and extended its reach by venturing forth to unknown Jewish territory. It didn't hurt Wendy's chances for future academic success that Conrad was known across the country. Her primary advisor had even reached the pinnacle of success for a public intellectual— he had been a guest on daytime television talk shows that he and his peers in the academy are aware of but never admit to watching.

Wendy lifted a third book from her shelf. Entitled, primly, *Meaning in the Field*, she had been told it was required reading by her anthropologist adviser, Violet Dohrmann. It was about the trickiness of the researcher adjusting her or his relations with subjects to a comfortable and appropriate level. One wants to be absorbed with a culture, but not to the dreaded extent of going native. Dohrmann had told her, "Immerse yourself in your host culture; you will be changed by it too, if you do your fieldwork properly. Yet, your hosts, particularly the community of Israeli returnees, may not always recognize your outsider status. They are always on the lookout for another recruit." Then Dohrmann had told Wendy about her niece Ellen, raised in a good secular Jewish household and educated at Smith like Violet and her sister. Her niece went around the world on a spiritual sojourn in the early seventies, arrived in Israel, and became a religious Jew. It was the first personal information Dohrmann had ever volunteered to Wendy. That was the funny thing about this line of research, Wendy mused: it always seemed to elicit much more personal reactions, from questioner and respondent, than the average discussion of academic research.

Wendy started reading, figuring it would be good preparation for her first Sabbath, learning to immerse herself in the lives of religious people, at least for one Friday night dinner.

THREE

Sabbath Peace

As much as the Jews have kept the Sabbath, the Sabbath has
kept the Jews.
—AHAD HA-AM

An hour before the Sabbath, Wendy and her elderly landlady, Amalia Hausman, hailed a cab at the nearest bus stop and headed to the apartment of
Amalia's granddaughter and her new husband. After they climbed the three
flights slowly, at the apartment's door Shani, the granddaughter, and her new
husband, Asher, greeted them. Asher took Amalia's bag to the spare bedroom, and Wendy handed Shani the bakery packages of assorted cookies
and the elaborate cake with ornate sugared confections on top, tiers of cake
and parve cream within, that she had procured from the winding alleys of
Mahane Yehuda.

"You asked me to bring whatever makes Shabbos for me, so I have desserts here," Wendy uttered cheerfully. Nothing had ever "made Shabbos" for
Wendy, but she figured that any dinner could be worth sitting through if
there were good pastry at its conclusion.

Shani squealed, "Oh, Wendy, Marzipan Bakery," reading the name on the
boxes. "Did my cousin Leora tell you it's my favorite?"

"I spotted the bakery with the longest line, and figured," she shrugged
her shoulders, "it must be the best."

Shani carefully positioned the boxes, along with the homemade gefilte fish Amalia brought, on the counter of her tiny kitchen. Asher excused himself to take a shower, while Shani scuttled around the apartment, turning on and off lights, asking her grandmother what else she should remember, plugging timers and appliances in, pulling electric cords out.

Wendy and Amalia were put to work setting the table. Wendy stretched out the white cloth while Amalia tugged the other end. They arranged the apparatus of ingestion: plates, cups, forks, knives, spoons, napkins, *Kiddush* cups, salt, challah board, and cutting knife. All was arrayed for the eight people who would just about fit into the space.

Wendy walked around, laying a plate here, a napkin there, counting to be sure there was enough of everything. The rhythmic repetitiveness of this task, the assurance that there was a place for each person, felt soothing as she placed the items around the table. She felt recaptured by pleasant childhood memories, since table setting had long been marked as Wendy's chore, a good task for the youngest in her family. She remembered Friday afternoons of her youth when she and her mother set the table together before her brother Joel, sister Lisa, and father Arthur returned from school and work. These moments provided an intimacy for Sylvia and Wendy to talk, quietly, peaceably. The week over, setting the table delivered them to the relaxed zone of weekend time, unfettered them temporarily from the tensions and constraints of the week. Wendy felt nostalgic for those Friday evenings of her youth. *I should have called my parents earlier today, when it was early morning for them and they were still home,* she thought, reflecting on her own youth and home as she readied that of someone else for family togetherness. Other than calling them after her arrival, Wendy hadn't given much thought to her family, busy as she was preparing herself for her new life, figuring out what things she would need to be comfortable in this new country. Something about the onset of the Sabbath tugged at even her frayed and dispassionate feelings about her parents. It wasn't—Wendy thought, noting how Shani looked so pleased to see her grandmother, as she came in to inspect their work on the table—that she *didn't* love her parents; she did. It was that she wanted them to be people other than who they were, people who were more thoughtful and intellectual, who had opinions on things, who read the *New Yorker* for the writing and stories as she did, not for the gossipy, short Talk of the Town pieces, cultural listings, and cartoons. Wendy wanted them to love *her* for who she was and wanted to be, and it seemed currently that she was in the business of disappointing them mightily, ever since she announced that her grad school applications would be in the field of religion and not law. Wendy saw Shani hug her grandmother and speak to her in Hebrew, and so remained lost in her thoughts about whether, even though she missed her parents now, they would ever change their disapproving attitude enough to allow her to feel closer to them.

Asher came out of the bedroom, cleanly shaven, dressed in the Israeli male Shabbat uniform of white short-sleeved button-down shirt, black pants, sandals, and white crocheted kipah with a navy and turquoise-blue diamond pattern around its rim.

"Haven't you *benched licht* already, Shani?" Asher said, looking at his watch. He steered the three women to the living room corner where a small table covered by a white cotton runner with a lace embellishment held two sets of candlesticks. A third set was quickly produced. Before Wendy had time to protest, Shani said, "We'll each light and then say the *bracha* together." Wendy's impulse was to put her hands in her pockets, step away, and disengage, but the skirt Shani asked her to wear lacked a place to hide her hands. Wendy stood behind as first Amalia and then Shani lit their candles. Shani handed her a kindled match, blazing.

Holding the ignited match, Wendy stepped forward to place it on the wicks. It felt so ordinary, holding flame to wick. She remembered reading an interview in a piece she admired about the symbolism of Sabbath candles to the newly religious, which juxtaposed what women said when asked to speak about their religious observances in an essay written expressly for the school they were attending, and afterwards in a follow-up interview with the sociologist. One returnee spoke in her essay of the magic of lighting Shabbes candles: that the candle detonated an explosion of the sacred into her home. The woman said she felt like a superhero action figure. Wendy had made up a title for her, *Wonder Woman of the Numinous*, as she herself merely put the candle to the flame, no supernal power summoned. The whole account, written for the school in the article, seemed exaggerated and ridiculous— *Pow! Blam! Boom!*—an attempt to make a dull life seem more exciting.

Actually, the article, by exposing the gap between what the baalei teshuvah wrote expressly for the school and what they said in conversation, was a great model of how a researcher got subjects to speak about their feelings about religious practices. Wendy loved the section about conversation, how the speakers sounded like those who had no excitement in their lives trying desperately to seem like they did; it reminded Wendy of girls she knew in high school who were obsessed with soap operas because the thrill in the sensationalized fictional world made the girls themselves more interesting for being absorbed in it, this drama so disconnected from their actual lives. What irritated Wendy most so far about baalei teshuvah was their flatness, like the dull girls in high school; many BT's were white kids from the suburbs trying to glom on to a newly ethnic identity to give their bland lives some spice. She'd have to write about that—Did baalei teshuvah exaggerate to make themselves seem more interesting? How would she put on exhibit and showcase the various sides of the ways they spoke about themselves? Her notebook was in her bag—could she sneak off to take notes in the bathroom?

Now, Shani and Amalia covered their eyes and recited the blessing. Wendy stood to the side, having moved over after she touched flame to wick. Reluctantly and slowly, she followed their gestures and summoned her hands over her eyes. She felt like she was back in Hebrew school with someone telling her to read the foreign alphabet, when she didn't want to make a mistake or embarrass herself, hoping to be as inconspicuous as possible.

Wendy recited the blessing in an undertone, echoing Shani and Amalia, and quickly removed her hands from her eyes. She gazed at Shani and Amalia, their hands lingering over their eyes, standing in front of the candles, obviously deep in recitation of some kind of private prayer that Wendy was unaware of, though she had lit candles with her mother for her whole life at home. Shani removed her hands from her eyes and gave her grandmother a big "good Shabbos" hug.

Candles lit, Wendy felt a shift in the apartment. She couldn't pinpoint its source. The contrast between smoldering candles suffusing the room, and the last glimmerings of natural light outside, or something in Shani's mood? Now Shani hugged Wendy, all her movements leisurely and unhurried rather than her previous bustling and stress. Wendy was a bit stunned at the hug, this unprecedented level of intimacy for someone she had met moments ago, but she hugged back, mustering her gratitude for the family's trust in her as a tenant.

The four of them headed off for the synagogue after a quick glance around the apartment to be sure the food was warming properly and the key was with them. Shani held one of Amalia's arms and one of Asher's, while Wendy followed behind the threesome. As they walked through the quiet streets, Wendy was startled at how the city had shut down.

No cars zooming about the street, or bicycles careening in their lanes. No kids goofing around on the sidewalk. The contrast with the clamor and commotion on the street a few hours earlier was stark. It felt to Wendy like a Sunday morning in the suburbs, an indolence overtaking the residents, no one rushing to be anywhere. A general somnolence pervaded the streets, yet it mixed with an effervescence beneath the surface, a rejuvenation in the calm.

When they arrived at what they indicated was the synagogue, all Wendy could see was an ordinary cement box, a school building plunked down, without design consultations, in a spot where the Jerusalem municipality granted the land. Asher took Amalia's elbow and helped her ascend the steep cement steps at the school's side to the top level.

Shani turned to Wendy, "It's probably not what you are used to in a *shul.*"

Wendy, heaving herself up the narrow stairs, replied, "Synagogues in the States have to be handicapped accessible. This would never make code," she said, nearly slipping on the cramped steps.

"Adjust your perceptions. You'll see how special *Shir Tzion* is once you experience the *davening*," Shani added.

Once up the steps and inside, they faced a door, which led to a large gymnasium. They entered separately; Asher stayed to the right, the men's section, while the three women filed through the back of the men's section to the left, partitioned off by white muslin curtains on metal frames, hung by what appeared to be round metal shower hooks. There was no art or decor on the walls. Nothing in this space suggested an arena in which to access the sacred. Basketball hoops mounted on either side of the room appeared like heads of a netted animal overseeing the proceedings. The metal folding chairs were of the most clattering and uncomfortable variety.

Wendy couldn't see the men on the other side of the divider from her seat next to Shani in the middle of the women's section. She felt disgruntled and disempowered, unseen and unnecessary: *They are leading the service; we are here to answer amen and look pretty.* But she thought next, *It isn't my life, these Orthodox synagogues. I'll go to a liberal congregation, or none, next week. I need to just remember that being here is fieldwork. Violet will be proud. And strictly speaking, most of this group isn't my population since they are religious from birth like Shani. I can just see what is happening, experience it, without thinking about my dissertation.* Wendy looked around as the afternoon service wended its way through the litany of words. The prayer leader standing in front was the only man she could see clearly. Women were continuing to enter, a gentle flow of bodies filling up the space, most of them around the age of herself and Shani, though there were older women with older children and young mothers with babies in slings attached to their hips, cradling their offspring as they walked. There was also a sprinkling of women in Amalia's generation, white and gray hairs still piously covered.

The elegant and colorful dress of the women—long skirts and matching headscarves in vibrant summer prints—contrasted with the overall dinginess of the gym and the thin crust of dust on the floor. Wendy mentally compared the site to the suburban synagogue she grew up attending, Beth Tikvah, with its immaculately kept premises, never a burnt-out lightbulb anywhere. The building was in pristine physical condition, an underutilized empty shell most of the year, except during the High Holidays. Wendy liked those fall holidays, with the hullabaloo of jumbled people, the bathroom where she and her friends tried to spend as much time as possible, to not be in the sanctuary. The restroom overflowed with various excesses and smells from the massive hordes that contrasted with its top-of-the- line fixtures and carefully planned color scheme. Wendy found something about the swarming crowds irresistible; the sheer numbers of worshippers emitted an energy that the synagogue lacked during the rest of the year. The assemblage on an ordinary summer Friday evening, here in this school gym, seemed more akin to a High Holiday crowd in the States, especially in its variety.

Wendy turned to Shani and asked, "Is there a bar mitzvah or wedding? There are so many people."

Keeping her rhythmic back and forth rocking motion in prayer going, Shani replied mechanically, still poring over her prayer book, "It's always this way."

Shani handed Wendy the prayer book she herself had been using, opened at the proper page, and took the one Wendy had been clutching, closed, in hopes that the tighter her grip, the easier it would be to follow.

As Shani handed the book to Wendy, Wendy observed that a new guy had gone to the lectern at the front of the gym to switch places with the one who had been leading the weekday afternoon service. Wendy was surprised to see that both men were wearing informal clothing, the equivalent of casual Friday dress in the States: white button-down shirt, black pants, and sandals.

As the buzz of humming from the wordless tune started by the prayer leader grew from a softer and soothing to a more joyous and raucous level, Wendy found herself relaxing, feeling calm, closing her eyes. She realized, suddenly, the tune was familiar from Friday nights at her Jewish summer camp, Kodimoh.

Wendy remembered first being aware of the opposite sex at Jewish summer camp. When boys and girls prayed together each morning, there was a masculine power in those boys now wearing *talleisim*, and the sinewy wrap of their black *tefillin* echoed the newly appearing musculature in the arms of those beginning puberty. The tufts of hair above their lips, beginnings of mustaches signaling masculine growth, seemed to come at the same time they began to wear those white garments that enabled them to sway and swoop in prayer, active and in constant motion as they were in sports. Wendy's prayer time always seemed wrapped up in noticing those around her, who they were, what was appealing. She never quite understood the prayers at camp, all in Hebrew. But she liked the slowness of moments they brought, and how they enabled her to pay attention to what was around her, particularly if a guy she found interesting was nearby.

The wordless melody, the pent-up buzz of the congregation, was now set free. The prayer leader began chanting the set of psalms that culminated in the greeting to the Sabbath Bride, the *Lecha Dodi*. The man now leading the prayers had the wide shoulders yet narrow body and hips that Wendy associated with swimmers, as though his arms were more important in propelling him than his legs. As the service progressed his legs remained rooted, but his hands and arms moved. His tallis was entirely white with white stripes, and with his wide shoulders, he looked as though he might bound into the air and soar at any minute, his spiritual force powering his ascent. His voice was a lovely clear tenor, high and smooth, gliding lovingly over each note and intonation, channeling its melody outward. Enjoying his voice, she wondered, *Will I ever find myself so seduced by anything as to change my life completely?*

She settled back in her chair and concentrated on the singing around her, its twittering sounds, words rising and falling, joining, trilling a note, crescendoing, falling again. The music was now a slow aching tune of yearning. For what? The Sabbath Bride? God? A heavenly Jerusalem? Messianic times? *Was there something else to hope for, even actually being in the Promised Land?* She'd have to ask Shani later what the worshippers were yearning for.

In the midst of the congregation, crooning, harmonizing, the prayer leader's voice out ahead, creating the tune that others wrapped their voices around in a coiled helix of melodic shape, was one solo male voice. As the congregation harmonized, his voice kept originating his own harmony, echoing the others' song but in his own tuneful, melodic, and utterly gorgeous way. His voice above the others made an impression, lulling and thrilling at once. Whoever the owner of this voice was, he had finessed the dilemma of how to be in a group and be a unique individual, doing both simultaneously. Wendy was in thrall, listening, and puzzled over what type of person had the confidence required to soar above the sound of the crowd, and at the same time, the musical ability to improvise. The sound of his voice penetrated her; she leaned back in her chair and closed her eyes. She wanted to concentrate on the sound, blocking out other stimuli to let this ascending voice pulsate through her, to focus totally on her pleasure.

As she listened, a tingly, swoony, feeling overcame her. She heard harmonies from worshippers around her erupting spontaneously, sounding at once improvised and planned. She kept hearing the solo male voice, mysterious bringer of joyful melody. He was singing alone yet supportive of the communal sound, protective of the entirety of the musical montage. She speculated whether, rather than being seduced entirely, absorbed into the fibers of the entire being of another, it would be possible to have a love that was a partnership, a commingling of two voices with separate identities, which together could create a united sound?

The worshippers rose as the service built to its crescendo at the last stanza of the song to greet the Sabbath Bride. While they were standing, she tried to scan the men's section and find the owner of the voice, or who she would like him to be. On her feet, broken off from the lulling fantasy of lush sound she had been in, yet now in motion as part of the group bending towards the Sabbath Bride emerging at the door, Wendy gazed around and asked herself, *When was the last time most of these worshippers had gotten laid*? She would have liked to stay in that moment of desire and connection, but getting out of her chair had shattered her pleasurable moment. Feet on the dusty floor, Wendy reverted back to her observer self: *Is the intensity here completely a consequence of repressed sexual feelings, my own included?* She hadn't thought about the role of sexuality and its repression in her baalei teshuvah, but it definitely needed to be covered, she decided, feeling under her chair with her hand for her purse with the notebook as the congregation resumed its seats. She didn't dare write a note in it now, but just wanted to assure herself that she would bolt to get it down as soon as was feasible.

More importantly, Wendy scanned the room, trying to guess where the owner of that voice was located, even though she needed to crane to see the men's section while seated. She couldn't discern any likely candidates, but saw a man at the periphery of the men's section closest to the women; he was pacing and looking over the *mehitza*, surveying the crowd. He was looking at the women, intently, searching. He looked like he was on military patrol with the preciseness of his gait and the specificity of where he was looking. Wendy looked away; she didn't want to be a target of his stare. *Notes on sexuality and its discontents*, she repeated to herself so she wouldn't forget later as she sat and tried to follow the Hebrew prayers, with Shani pointing to the spot every so often when she became confused.

At the service's end, Shani smiled and greeted people. Wendy and Amalia hung behind. Shani introduced Wendy to a few women their age as a friend of her cousin, here in Israel to write a dissertation. Some of them asked politely what it was about and Wendy considered how many times she would have to repeat herself, explaining what she was doing in her research and why. She hated the tedium of constantly explaining herself to new people. *Could I just be back in Princeton with my grad school buddies*, she thought, feeling meager and inadequate for not wanting to retrace her life for new strangers.

The first day of classes at Princeton, after the introductory seminar required for all religious studies graduate students, they adjourned to Café Metro, all eleven of them, to detox after the stress of the first class, worries about the heft and density of the reading, and early anxieties about the final paper. Each one of her cohort had a different background and potential area of research. With this group of people who were so different, she still shared so much: basic values of intellectual inquiry and skepticism, along with respect or reverence for religious phenomena. And all of them, except Matt Lewis, a former crew rower, had been bad at gym in school, like Wendy. Had a basic disconnect from physical skills led them all to academia? With her fellow grad students, she felt so *at home*, comfortable, and relaxed. As they trained together in graduate school, reading common texts and learning from the same mentors, their modes of discourse and thought became more strongly formed along comparable lines. *Could I find a group in Jerusalem to feel at home with this year?* she asked herself, feeling alone in the crowded gymnasium, having little in common with most of the people there.

Finally, the group of four left the school where the synagogue met, the happy chatter of people meeting and greeting following them, knots of individuals in threes and fours dispersing in different directions in the Jerusalem evening. As they walked, they heard the Friday night home prayers, *Shalom Aleichem* and *Kiddush,* from the windows of different apartments, a chorus of welcoming. *But for who or what?* Wendy thought. Are they welcoming *me* here to the country for my first Sabbath? Or greeting only those who are religious at a certain level, an exclusive band of worshippers? Still, Wendy enjoyed these familiar and comforting songs emanating from apartments along their route.

The dinner at Shani and Asher's apartment was the same mix of comforting and frustrating as Wendy had experienced at *Shir Tzion* and on the walk home. On the one hand, it was pleasant: delicious dishes that the newlyweds had prepared together kept popping out. First came homemade whole wheat challah with all kinds of Middle Eastern spreads, alongside a wonderful Moroccan salmon with tomato sauce. Accompanying the main course of chicken baked with forty cloves of garlic were a bulgur salad with pine nuts and onions, redolent of some superb seasoning that Wendy couldn't name, potato kugel, and green salad. There was plenty of wine, and Wendy enjoyed the pleasant tipsiness she got after a few glasses. Her week of moving at an end, it felt good to be able to drink with others and de-stress. Wendy wasn't a big drinker, but enjoyed booze at parties, to relax, particularly when meeting so many new people. Finally, there were desserts: a variety of cookies and cakes, including what Wendy had brought from the *shuk*. She hadn't been to such an elaborate meal since Passover at Grandma Essie's.

There was pleasant conversation on a variety of topics. The other guests seemed interesting, not what she would have expected from a religious group. They were aware of the latest TV shows, movies, music, pop culture references. She thought they'd be more bookish and serious and less interesting and hip. But there was a moment when Wendy blundered. They were discussing politics, and Asher proclaimed that, now Bibi was in power, since he'd formed the government in June, there wouldn't be any more terror attacks like those on the number eighteen buses back in February and March. Wendy asked why that should make a difference and what had happened on those buses anyway? Another guest whose name she never caught but whose accent was Canadian, yelled at her, "Why are you coming to this country if you don't want to *really* know what's going on? There have been almost sixty people killed this year, Americans too. You didn't know about those buses on Rehov Yaffo?"

Shani added, quietly but in a tone that could be heard, "Americans our age. Sara was my friend. You remember her, don't you?" she said to the group as she tried not to let the others see the tears beginning to form.

Wendy just wanted to fade into the floor, but was rescued by another guest. "Guys, she just got here. When you are in *hutz la'aretz*, you don't always know what's happening in Israel. Give her a chance, would you?" He glared at her Canadian interlocutor. To Wendy, sitting across from him, he said, "Opening your mouth is risky in this country. You see what your innocent question started? But basically Asher's position is that a tough politician like Bibi won't let the Arabs get away with these kinds of attacks, that he will stop them. There hasn't been one since he took office," the rescuer, Donny, added hopefully.

Asher tried to squelch any ill feeling and changed the subject to give a *dvar Torah,* saying he had planned to do it later but now was the most appropriate time for it during the meal. The one thing she grasped was that there was a verse about the nature of God being hidden in the weekly portion from the book of Deuteronomy. The word for *hidden* somehow sounded like the name "Esther"; and the biblical Esther, even without knowing what God's plan was, was willing to act in a decisive manner. He applied this lesson to some aspect of Israeli politics but she couldn't follow the names of the politicians and parties. One guy kept making smart aleck remarks in the middle, interrupting Asher good-naturedly. She felt so clearly outside the group when he did this, as she didn't get any of the jokes.

At the meal's end, Shani and Asher asked Donny Zeligson, Wendy's fearless defender, to walk her home so she wouldn't get lost. He was walking in the same direction to Yeshivat Temimai Nefesh, "the yeshiva for pure souls," in the Old City and agreed to help get her back to her apartment.

It was strange to feel she needed someone else to give her direction. She didn't expect she would get lost, really, but there weren't that many people out on the empty streets to ask directions of, and even if she found someone, that person would need to speak English too. The way wasn't far, but there were a few turns on the way that had strange angles, perhaps remnants of some older system of navigation, an alternate logic for street layout. She acquiesced to her host's desire to have her escorted home, feeling vaguely like a teenager, dependent on someone else for a ride from one place to another, incapable of her own mobility.

Wendy and Donny walked side by side on silent streets. Wendy felt obligated out of politeness to converse, though she didn't know what to say; he had spoken little during the dinner other than assisting her. "What brought you here?" she asked.

He kept walking. She didn't know whether to repeat herself or just accept that he wasn't interested in talking to her when he began to speak. "*Hashem*. I came as part of my undergrad work in Oregon. I was a lousy student there." He gave a sad smile and tossed his shaggy bangs out of his eyes. "I was, I still am, a pretty big disappointment to my parents. They're dentists, in practice together. All they want is for me to join them."

"Two dentists for parents? Did you never get candy? Get your teeth cleaned constantly?"

Donny laughed. "Yes and yes. But they . . . they do love me, even if they were hard to take as a kid . . . or now. The worst horror I brought on them was suggesting I might leave school because I loved working as a line cook in a restaurant, something they considered working class."

"Celebrity chefs can be a pretty big deal these days."

"Not good enough for the Doctors Zeligson. So they sent me here for a summer to a program on historic preservation of buildings and objects, because they thought contact with physical objects was what I should do, something that involved learning but also the world of the physical. One weekend the program set up an optional visit to a yeshiva, to let us experience different aspects of the country. I went and just felt . . . at home; it was my place, so I went back there, and then I wanted to stay at the end of the summer. Last summer, so I've been here a year now. *Hashem*'s doing."

She wanted to ask him how he was so sure, but didn't want to pick a fight. So she stayed silent, hoping he wouldn't ask her whether she too believed *Hashem* was looking out for her.

"How did *you* get here?"

She decided to just keep it simple. "Shani's cousin is my friend and classmate in graduate school. My friend told me her family had an apartment for rent. I took it, so Shani and Asher invited me over for my first Shabbat. It was nice but . . ." Wendy paused and decided to just be candid, "I don't know, I felt kind of like an outsider there, awkward."

"Me too!" Wendy's formerly laconic companion seemed more excited by this than by anything else all night. "I mean, if you want to have guests, you need to ask them about themselves, welcome them. I was never asked one question!"

Wendy concurred. "That's what was bothering me. It was just kind of nice polite general conversation but no one *talked* to me! I couldn't figure out why I felt out of place."

"Hey, they fed us; we shouldn't be criticizing our hosts," he said evenly.

"Maybe not, but it *is* fun." She grinned at him, wondering if she had said something to offend his sense of what was gossipy speech, *lashon hara*, and what was not.

"True," he said, and smiled back.

She was surprised he would knowingly go against doing what he thought he was *supposed* to. Maybe, as Lamdan had said, it wasn't so simple: those who believed still did have their human moments of frailty and betrayal. She continued, "No offense, but I really hated that turban Shani was wearing. I felt bad for her because she kept trying to keep it on her head; *her* fiddling with it made *me* feel off kilter, you know? White women and turbans just do *not* work—you know, like white women and dreadlocks?" Wendy didn't know why she had to be so catty about the turban, except that it *did* seem way too big for Shani's head, and ready to topple off at any provocation. The other married woman there that evening was wearing a crocheted maroon hat with silver embroidered flowers and buttons to give it panache.

To Wendy's surprise, her companion laughed. "I'll have to remember that: white women —no turbans. Important fashion memo." They walked in silence for a few more moments. Then he asked her, "So what *are* you doing this year?"

"Like you, *my* parents don't approve of my path either." She looked over at him and he smiled at her to encourage her to continue. "I'm working on a PhD in American religion."

"That sounds hard. But wait, if it's American, why are you in Israel?"

"I'm looking at Americans who come here and become more religious."

"Oh, like me."

Wendy had no response.

He added, "It's okay. It's good that you're interested. You should definitely talk to the guys at my yeshiva. There are lots like me, people who just didn't quite fit in with our families and their expectations."

"Yeah?" She changed the subject, "You didn't tell me how you knew Shani and Asher."

"I don't. There is some connection through relatives, Asher's great uncle and aunt, maybe, who live in Portland and are patients of my parents. When they were coming to Israel for the wedding, my parents said they had a son here. Asher got my number from them and invited me. I don't even know his relatives, and he doesn't really either since he grew up mostly here."

"So why did you come tonight?"

"Change of pace, something different from the yeshiva."

The two had arrived at Mishael 5. Donny asked to come up to use her bathroom, since he still had a long walk before he got back to his yeshiva in the Old City.

Wendy assented. Donny insisted on leaving the door to her apartment open. Amalia was staying over at Shani and Asher's, and there weren't other occupants who might come in, so the open door at the top of a staircase where there were no other occupants made no difference either way.

Wendy plopped down on the couch in her living room in a daze. The boxes of books were gone, their volumes unpacked and settled on shelves. The apartment was beginning to look like someone lived there. She needed posters and pillows, throw blankets and knickknacks, the little things that made a place special to its inhabitant. Should she offer Donny a drink or something when he came out? All she had was water and milk, though there was some of that *avatiach* she'd bought earlier. She should at least offer.

After he left the bathroom, Donny stood for a moment in the hall outside the bathroom to say the bathroom prayer. Wendy heard him saying something quietly, in a soft whisper. She called out, "What?" confused that he was not responding.

He finished his recitation, entered the living room, and stood above her, looking down at her on the couch.

"Can I get you something to drink, a slice of *avatiach*? I got it at the *shuk* this morning."

"I should get back. It's late," he said rationally before adding, "Yeah, sure, I'll have some *avatiach* before I go."

Wendy stood, shakily, and then said, "I don't even know what to cut it with. I must have some knives here."

"Don't worry, if it's too much trouble."

"No, I'm glad you walked me home. I want to give you something." As soon as she said those words, she felt her error. He would take it as suggestive. It *felt* suggestive, though she wasn't entirely sure what the suggestion would be. He smiled at her; she smiled back, looking at him facing her. She walked over to the counter where the knives could be. She opened a drawer and found a huge knife, long and sharp enough to cut the watermelon, and a new plastic cutting board. She took the hunk of watermelon from her fridge and surrendered it to the counter. With Donny watching, Wendy started to hack at the fruit. The knife seemed powerless, or she was just not strong enough to prevail against the tough rind.

Finally, Donny stepped in. "Allow me. I have great knife skills from my time as a line cook." He expertly cleaved the chunk of watermelon in two and then dismantled it, stripping the pink juicy flesh from the rind and cutting it into even, bite-size pieces as Wendy stood back, gazing mutely. His body seemed different now with a knife, his movements confident and precise, knowing exactly where each digit and limb should go, how much pressure to apply where. He was in a zone of competency, wielding each section of his body with the same grace as the knife in his hand as he chopped. She looked at him from the side, noting the tautness of his body, the way his perfectly sized butt filled his black cotton dress pants nicely.

"Do you have a bowl for this?" he asked, stepping back, task completed.

Wendy stopped her admiration of his carving skills and opened the cabinets to find a simple clear-glass bowl. She handed it to him. "Thanks," she said. "I didn't know how to deal with the tough rind." *That sounded stupid,* she thought to herself. *Why am I worrying? I don't like him. I'm just being polite.*

He scooped the chunks of fruit from the cutting board with his hand, dripping their pink juices into the bowl. He handed her the bowl, smiling, and rinsed his hands under the sink. "You just need to know the technique. Do things as simply as possible, expend the least amount of effort. Make the fewest cuts in the rind and work the soft flesh." He dried his hands on a dish towel, fished out a piece from the bowl, and started to hand it to her. She moved closer to him, and opened her mouth. He reached to her mouth and inserted the watermelon directly in her mouth, instead of placing it in her hand as she'd expected. She clenched her teeth around the fruit and he took his hand away without having touched her, as the laws of *shomer negia*, not touching a member of the opposite sex before marriage, would demand. She put her hand to her mouth to take the remainder of the piece, and when she was done with the first part, chewed the rest. "Mmm, you try some," she said, handing him a piece. As she did, he moved close enough to take the piece in his mouth. She held it in his mouth; he made no motion to put his hand up to take it. Her hand was close to his mouth, though the fruit was between them so they were still not touching. After swallowing the first bit, he slowly reached his mouth around the fruit and her fingers. She held them there, enjoying the sensation of juices mingling with his tongue on her flesh.

She licked her lips, the sozzled feeling from the glasses of wine at dinner making her bolder than she was otherwise. She stretched another piece towards his mouth. He kissed her fingers as she positioned the watermelon between his lips.

Then, he put a piece of watermelon in his mouth and walked closer to her, close enough that she could take it from him with her own lips. They were standing so that only the piece of watermelon, clenched in both their mouths, was between them. Now, drops of pink juice were scattering the floor as they stood facing each other, watermelon between them. She moved closer, pink flesh mingling as lips and fruit met. They were kissing. He put his arm on her waist tenderly and leaned in.

Wendy felt surprised but pleased by this turn of events. She wouldn't have pegged him a good kisser, but he was, knowing when to smooth over her lips and when to apply pressure. So different from Matt, the crew rower, who, though so suave in most arenas, was totally awful as a kisser, unaware of how to hold his lips on hers. *I am going to enjoy this year more than I thought,* she joyfully intoned to herself as she leaned closer to Donny.

He pulled back. "I shouldn't. I've been *shomer negia* more than a year . . . I don't know, something happened. Having that knife in my hand . . . Part of the appeal of the restaurant was the proximity of others; I had so many girls there . . . I'm sorry." He put his head down to the ground in shame and began walking to the door. His manners got the better of his shame and he added, "I . . . you're a nice girl. I . . . can't just go kiss a girl every time I find her attractive. You . . . you're not . . . I want to find my *basherte*. I wish I could stay . . . Forgive me." He scuttled out of the room as quickly as he could in light of this confession.

Wendy stood in place, watermelon juice still dripping off her mouth. She found a dish towel on her counter, and wiped her lips and chin, still staring at the door. *What just happened here? Did he seduce me and leave, or did I seduce him and he left? Did I want it or was I playing along, flattered as always at any attention? Did he take advantage of me, thinking secular women are easy? I felt like he was weak and lacked confidence, but then something happened; he was different with the knife; he had this kinetic energy whirling about him. Were we equal participants or was I playing a game of* corrupt the yeshiva student? The rules may not have been fair, but she wanted to play. He didn't seem averse; after all, he came into her apartment even if the door was open, and drew close to her to hand her the watermelon. But still, she shouldn't have let herself play; he wasn't someone she had any interest in, and it wasn't fair to toy with someone else's feelings. *That was it: they each had an attraction for the other, but there was no feeling on either of their parts.* She wasn't religious enough for him and he wasn't academically inclined enough for her; there was absolutely no reason for the allure between them. She could say she was slightly inebriated, or disoriented from the dislocation of being in a new place, both throwing her usual restraints off. Those excuses were false; she knew the kiss happened because of the attraction, which existed like so many other things in life: illogical, irrational, preposterous, but present and enticing. Like the gorgeous male voice in the synagogue, something she was drawn to without knowing why. How many more gaffes would there be this year? How many times would she be drawn elsewhere than expected with unknown consequences? Her desire was like a surging current; once she had thrown herself into the water after it, she would be buffeted to and fro until the waters finally ceased foaming. *I want to find a guy worthy of risking the battering and buffeting of the current of desire, who would similarly want to hold on to me as we journeyed the risky course together, avoiding the shoals that could force a vessel ashore.*

She imagined a big warning sign from the anthropology department: Never kiss a member of your subject population or you will be unable to write objectively ever again. Would this kiss derail her dissertation? Wendy was determined to have a good time this year *and* to get her research done—clearly neither was a simple task in Jerusalem.

FOUR
Bayit Ne'Eman

People are walking in the counterfeit city / whose heavens passed like shadows, / and no one trembles. Sloping lanes conceal / the greatness of her past.
—LEAH GOLDBERG, "Heavenly Jerusalem, Jerusalem of the Earth"

On Sunday, after her first *ulpan* class at the university on Mount Scopus, Wendy took the number nine bus through the center of town. She was glad to have the intricacies of Hebrew verb conjugations and new vocabulary to focus on to get the sensation of Donny's kiss and her surging desire, kissing him back, out of her head. It would come back at random moments for the next few weeks she guessed. It wasn't the biggest misstep ever, or the worst, just yet another thing she shouldn't have done. Hopefully she wouldn't see him again and wouldn't have to feel like a sleaze; she'd been involved with guys in ways she regretted in high school, but not recently, and thought that was in her past.

After the bus left the center of town, it crawled down Aza Street. She asked another passenger about the stop and got off before the corner of Rav Berlin Street. The café From Gaza to Berlin was there at the intersection, as Avner Zakh, the Fulbright advisor, had told her. She was proud of herself for getting around in this new place; that only lasted until Wendy entered the air conditioned café and realized that she had no clue what Zakh looked like.

As she gazed around the room, she saw in her peripheral vision a tall man with mostly dark hair, bits of gray jutting out here and there. He was wearing a navy *kipah seruga*, knit headcovering of the modern Orthodox, and jaunted over to her athletically, bouncing as though he were on a basketball court.

"Wundy?"

Israelis couldn't pronounce her name. Her *ulpan* teacher this morning had insisted on calling her "Varda," her Hebrew name, which she'd always hated for the clumsiness of the sound. An awkward name, like Helga or Ursula, its syllables slogged together in an unlovely clump like an overweight older woman with a headscarf and heavy calves in orthopedic shoes.

"Professor Zakh?" she held out her hand in greeting.

He nodded at her without taking her hand. "Nice to meet. Shall we get some coffee?"

They went to the small counter in the back of the store and gave their orders: lemonade for Wendy, espresso for Zakh. They found a table by the window and sat across from each other. "I apologize in advance. I don't have much time today. I'm attending the *parsha* class at the Van Leer. I'd invite you to come, but I understand you don't have enough Hebrew to follow a lecture."

"Not yet. Today was my first day of *ulpan*."

"We have an excellent *ulpan* here. It went well?"

"Yes."

"Good. I want you to tell you, I find your dissertation project very interesting. We've never had faculty in American religion, but we are now cultivating a donor in American studies. They want a . . . how do you say . . . department? Not that, a . . ."

"Program?"

"Right. Americanists in all departments—history, literature, political science—to make a program for students who are interested. We'll see; these things always take time. Anyway, here's my home number." He took a small notepad out of his pocket, wrote his name in Hebrew and English with his number and address below it, and said, "Call with any questions. The bus lines, where to get good felafel, whatever. I've been Fulbright advisor for a few years. Can I guess what you need? E-mail, library privileges, pizza?"

She nodded.

"E-mail and library, go to the overseas student office, the Rothberg building. Ask for Donna. Tell her you're with me and she'll take care of you. Pizza. Where are you living?"

"Rehov Mishael, near Rahel Emainu."

"Pizza Sababa; they deliver. Burger Bar, right on Emek Refaim, has the best hamburgers, students say. *Tov*?" he asked.

"Are other students here?"

"Not yet. No one else is taking *ulpan*. Our first formal meeting is not till September, when they all arrive. I'll have my secretary send a letter. We'll be in touch." He looked at his watch. "I don't want to be late."

Wendy saved the most important question for the end. "The thing I need most help with is how to interview people. Where should I start? How should I find places to find interview subjects?"

He looked at her, puzzled. "Go to the *Kotel*. The recruiters pick you up; you'll see where they send people. Yerushalayim is a small town. You'll meet plenty of your *hozrei b'teshuvah*."

"My what?"

"*Hozrei b'teshuvah*, returnees."

"What's the difference between that and *baalei teshuvah*?"

He laughed. "*Hozer* is return, and *teshuvah* is answer, so they are returning to the answer. If someone is *dati* and stops being *dati,* we say they are *hozer b'sh'ailah*, returning to the question. You, Wundy, are questioning the returners." He got up to go. Standing, he said, "I'll look forward to working with you this year. *Naim meod.* You'll do fine."

She watched him walk out of the café with that spry lift in his step, and wasn't sure whether he'd helped her or not. Was he a jerk for cutting the meeting short or a good guy for making time for her? Funny, male academics, with their vanity about their time and how busy they were, did not change over oceans, she thought. The level of self-importance was a constant. Zakh *did* give her some advice; she'd just been hoping for more. She needed more direction: which schools would be good places to try, how to approach the administrators. What if she couldn't get into any of these places to talk to students? What if after getting this fellowship and settling in a new place she couldn't do her project? She'd have to try to get help, from him or someone else. No matter what, she just had to keep going. It was what everyone said about a dissertation: persistence was the most important factor. Not talent or ideas, just stubborn refusal to give up. As she finished her lemonade she opened up her notebook to study the Hebrew verb *lebanot,* to build, that she had started learning in *ulpan* that morning.

Wendy followed Zakh's advice to go to the *Kotel,* the Western Wall, on her third Friday night in Israel. The prior week, she lay down for a nap Friday afternoon and woke up long after dark, exhausted from six intensive hours of studying Hebrew verb forms each day.

If Mahane Yehuda was a collision with all manner of foodstuff and produce, the *Kotel* on Friday evening was a confrontation with every species of humanity. Wendy was overwhelmed by the mass spectacle as she stood where the cab dropped her off by the Zion Gate, so many others thronging towards the spot. Once she arrived at the stairwell that overlooked the Kotel Plaza, she went through the security check and leaned over the railing to gaze out at the crowd. She wished she had more anthropological training. How to categorize each group? There were Japanese or Korean tourists, snapping photo after photo, all in matching white polo shirts with carnelian red trim and red skorts for women, red shorts for men, and matching white baseball hats for their tour group, so the leader could find strays easily. On the men's side, she could see from her aerial position, there were various groups massed together, some dancing in a circle. By contrast the women's side consisted of discrete individuals, each with her own liturgy, no attempt at unison.

There was nothing moving about any of the particulars of the scene; if anything, Wendy felt sad that the women praying at the *Kotel* seemed so singular, so without the protection of a mass, but each sobbing, alone against the wall. Yet, the *entirety* of the spectacle moved her. People came to connect with something beyond themselves. This was the place Jews had been pulled and drawn to for so many thousands of years.

As she watched women praying by themselves, leaderless, each woman separate, the voice of the mysterious harmonizer at *Shir Tzion* came into her mind. How did he sing with the melody of the group, yet improvise his own sound beyond it, totally individuated? Could she find a way to do that, to feel herself part of the group, not an outsider alone and detached, yet still able to sing independently?

She listened to the group of men singing joyfully on their side of the *Kotel,* and thought back to an undergraduate party she had been to for members of a Columbia singing group and a visiting group from another college.

It was at the alumni club, a space unlike any she'd been in at Columbia, with old wooden beams in the ceiling and leaded glass windows. It exuded the solidity of a Tudor style house. She hadn't known a building like this existed on the mostly urban campus, sandwiched among much higher structures to either side on Riverside Drive. Either the singing group's CDs were selling really well, or there was an incredibly generous alumnus out there. The guests were drinking from an open bar and nibbling copious hors d'oeuvres. Suddenly, someone in the middle of the room started singing. People spontaneously gravitated—a powerful current of force propelling them—to the spot where the singing had started. Without choreography or staging, a natural grouping occurred, as though they were a flock of birds, a collusion of singers banding together, jamming. Wendy stood at their periphery. She wasn't sure what exactly was so moving about the experience, whether the talent and youth of the singers, or the way she heard individual parts but also the totality, different from what each individual brought alone. Not a singer herself, Wendy was glad to be in their presence, absorbing the joy and spontaneity she felt in the room. She remembered walking home on a silent Riverside Drive with her date, and asking what he liked most about singing. His response? "Eliciting emotions from the audience." He added, "It's what I like most about sex, making a woman feel good and watching her in pleasure." Then, he had kissed her.

Now, Wendy longed to know where Donny was at this moment. Would he go back to working at a restaurant one day? He seemed so different when he was chopping. She remembered walking with him, laughing about Shani's ridiculous turban, listening to his story of his parents disapproving of him, the sight of his adorable posterior chopping, and the kiss. Would they kiss again? Wendy fantasized that he would sneak out of his yeshiva late at night and come to her apartment, knocking on her door, telling her he had to see her again. Her rational self knew that he was embarrassed that they had kissed; the fantasy scenario was unlikely. Still, watching the others praying, seeing their sense of knowing what they were here for, what they were doing, only increased Wendy's sense of aloneness. She thought, *I guess I need to pray that I make some friends this year, to have a group of people, or even just one person, to talk to and joke with, who will understand me and listen to what I am doing and care. Donny isn't that person, but he's the closest I've come in the last three weeks . . .*

She descended to the *Kotel* and stood at the edge of the women's section, the very back but not inside, so that men were passing her too as crowds began to gather for prayers. She wasn't praying or even holding a book; her aura of being out of place caused a recruiter to spot her quickly. The recruiter was dressed in a black hat, suit, and Bruce Springsteen T-shirt on top of a white button-down shirt. He asked if she needed a place for Shabbos. On hearing her assent, he pointed to a place to wait, along with other guests of a family that hosted twenty strangers for a Shabbat dinner each week.

She waited for the father to lead the group to a huge apartment featuring a panoramic view of the Western Wall. The man of the house—she never did get the name straight—in his early sixties, was tall and fit, with the relaxed look of the prosperous man he was, a dealer in rare Judaica. His wife was at least twenty years younger. Under her wig, her face looked drawn and exhausted, her eyes had heavy circles, and she was either pregnant or lugging around extra weight from a previous pregnancy, though the youngest child appeared about four. There was clearly a kitchen staff, but the woman seemed to absorb the stress of these multiple guests while the man enjoyed playing host. Wendy felt sorry for her. It was generous of him to invite strangers to his lavishly appointed home each week, Wendy thought, but didn't he have friends of his own to ask? There was something manufactured about the set up—did a yeshiva *pay* this family to do this? Wendy wanted to ask whether he had a security system, kept his most valuable pieces at the gallery he ran at the Cardo, or just had faith that no one invited to his home would steal?

The host began the meal by having each guest say what they were doing in Israel and what made them happy about Shabbat. At Wendy's turn, she said she was taking *ulpan* at Hebrew University and writing a dissertation, and that seeing people buying flowers in the street on Friday was her favorite part of Shabbat. She was seated next to a girl named Dawn who had come to Israel to do an archeological dig and was spending Shabbat at a hostel in the Old City run by RISEN, a women's division of the RISE yeshiva. On Sunday, Dawn was hoping to try out some classes at RISEN's school, Bayit Ne'eman, in a different part of Jerusalem. Dawn's favorite part of Shabbat was being at the *Kotel*.

The Sabbath blessings were intoned, everyone washed their hands at a sink built into the dining room for this purpose, and the *Hamotzi* was said over the bread. The wife went into the kitchen to get the first course, assisted by other female guests and a maid who appeared to be some sort of foreign worker. Wendy looked down at her plate of gefilte fish and lost any appetite. She picked at it to be polite and felt similarly when a plate of food consisting of a dollop of chopped liver, a piece of chicken with paprika and oil, a mound of white rice, and green beans cooked with tomatoes was brought to the table and put in front of her and the other guests, each plate indistinguishable, without variation. She wanted to feel grateful to her hosts for welcoming her to their home, but she just felt resentment at having such unappetizing fare in front of her. She felt like she should offer to help in the kitchen, but since a number of female guests had already volunteered, she thought any aid she could provide would be superfluous. She was there to observe, she knew, but she also wanted to know, *were the observations in the kitchen as important as those at the dinner table*? She didn't want to be around the wife who looked as though all she wanted to do was go to sleep, not deal with all these guests. The father gave a talk on the Torah portion of the week as the dessert was arriving: clear plastic cups filled with red jello topped by whipped cream made from some kind of non-dairy chemical that left a film on the roof of Wendy's mouth, like the patently artificial oil it must be derived from. Wendy couldn't follow all of the talk, but it had to do with judgment, as the name of the portion was *Shoftim,* Judges. Somehow, the fact that the land of Israel was holier than the Diaspora demanded a different kind of system of judgment; it was held to a higher standard. He added that they were now in the month *Elul* in the Jewish calendar, and the initials of the month, *alef-lamed-vov-lamed*, stood for the phrase "I am my beloved's and my beloved is mine," which meant it was a time to draw closer to God. To truly do this, one must live a Torah-true life in Israel, he said. The message, to Wendy, held the same appeal as the chemically enhanced food did, both assuming one size fits all, that guests would wish to eat identical items and portions, and that, once given both food and message, the assembled would be delighted and willing to swallow them equally and gratefully.

At the dinner's conclusion, Wendy left with Dawn and asked if she could visit her at Bayit Ne'eman because Wendy was, in her spare time after *ulpan*, hoping to take some other classes. Wendy accompanied Dawn back to the hostel she was staying at before trying to find a cab home herself.

At the hostel, she picked up one of the variety of brochures listing study programs for women. The brochure read:

Do you feel flattened by life?
   Want to rise and find your full potential?
      RISEN is here!
Not sure how to access the
jewels of your Jewish heritage?
      WE have the keys to the treasure chest!
   Come to RISEN (Rabbi Isaac Shlomo Elkeles Yeshiva, Nashim/
women)
   You will learn at our women's school, Bayit Ne'eman, how to
establish a Jewish home, ensuring an eternal future for the Jewish
people!

   Call Rebbetzin B. Now to find out more about classes and
dorming options. Phone: 02 613 6334

The brochure reminded her of a bottle of Dr. Bronner's Peppermint Soap, loads of words, off base, crammed together. The pamphlet, with its large wording and simple language, made Wendy feel she was being screamed at. Who even thought women are fairy tale princesses looking for someone to give them a treasure chest of jewels? She clutched it as she made her way to the Zion Gate, where she heard there might be a cab.

On this August morning, Wendy woke with rays of the Jerusalem sun streaking into her room. She stretched her arms out in front of her and hugged herself, stretching, and feeling the warmth of the sun next to her bed mix with the overall chill of the room. She longed for the warmth of the sun, leaned out to it to warm her hands, extremities that always felt colder than the rest of her. Like the warmth of the sun, her goals existed within reach; getting to them and actually feeling their warmth was just slow. She was making up her questionnaires and working, gradually, on her first chapter, the dreaded literature review. Any sense of progress she had was in minute increments—intermittent progress, no large leaps or discoveries. Only in movies do people bound ahead, instantly.

   Wendy lay back, rubbing her hands together for warmth, and ran through her day in her mind. She liked to try to keep something of the reverie of her pre-wakeful state, and stay focused on whatever had been in her sleeping head, to hold the images with her through the day as she went to sleep so that when she woke up she could have a sense of what was on her unconscious mind. She liked to know what swarming swirling blurred visions were able to make it over the barrier of the dream state into her conscious awareness in order to tell her what was most urgent to her at the moment. It didn't always work. Whatever her dream had been was now buried in her to do list for the day. Errands: get to the bank to exchange money, buy more phone tokens, called *asimonim,* which she never seemed to have when she needed them, and do some grocery shopping to fill the practically bare fridge. She hated the state of kitchen emptiness, no food around to snack on if she felt like it. It was good to always have a reserve, something lying in wait in case she needed it. But she operated mainly without many reserves, in the cabinet and in life.

Compartmentalize, her mentor Cliff Conrad, sage as the Puritans he studied, often told her. So she lifted the notepad at her bedside and listed the tasks, a sure way to put the anxiety in its place. She wrote, "My first interview. Today's the day." Banal, and yet these words moved her. Writing this dissertation wasn't, as her parents thought, some kind of whim, a nice way to pass the time until she got married, had kids, and started what they thought of as her "real" life. She needed to do this to get a job and have a life that she was creating, of her own choosing. Even though it was a small and gradual step, she savored this thought. She would be doing a preliminary interview today, getting closer to her goal.

Wendy wanted to do some preliminary interviews to see how the thing was going to proceed. She wasn't ultimately going to use the data from these interviews in her study because she would be using them to tweak her questions.

Wendy had to see what it was like to question someone to his or her face. There was nothing the slightest bit daunting about handing a piece of paper to a person and asking him to fill it out, but the thought of actually sitting right across from another person and asking intimate questions . . . What if she unintentionally upset her subject or made some kind of faux pas, even if inadvertent? She would feel embarrassment and . . . shame. She didn't want to look foolish. More than once she had asked a friend something that Wendy thought entirely innocuous and then found out from a third party that she had hurt the person's feelings. How could she develop the insight, imagination really, to envision her way into the mind and emotions of someone else in order to anticipate how they might react to a given question? She lacked empathy, she worried, standing up finally and stretching her hands over her head to shake the sleepiness off her body. Was there an essential coldness in her nature that would keep her from succeeding?

It was a kind of occlusion between the way she saw others and what they expected of her, a barrier as real as a physical one. Wendy felt sometimes like she just did not know how to connect to other people. It worried her at times, that she would never have a truly intimate relationship with someone else, where each knew and understood the other. She had close friends, but always felt like, for each of them, there was some other friend who was closer. She was never the closest.

Wendy got out of bed and opened the doors of the wardrobe closet built in to the wall. She stared at the contents: the look she was going for was professional, yet not too formal. She wanted to be friendly yet tailored—hard to get the right balance.

That was what she needed to talk to Meryl about in this interview. How many of the things being newly religious demanded of women and how many were part of general chauvinism in the larger culture? The differences between the ways men and women told their stories was one of the avenues for her research. Her provisional hypothesis was that when men told the story of their conversion it was an attempt to take up more space in the world, to boast of what talented and resourceful individuals they were, that they found a way to change and find religious meaning. However, when women spoke of changes in their lives, it was in a humbling, demeaning, self-effacing manner to the tune of: "*Baruch Hashem*, it was the hand of God that put this person in my path and led me this way." Women always claimed less agency in their lives. It was one of the many things that annoyed Wendy about the world—this notion that women aren't supposed to want things. They were not to work at anything too hard, or appear to. Wendy had always wanted to have space and agency in her life; beginning as a little kid, when most of her friends shared their beds with multiple stuffed animals. She never liked having something else in bed with her. She always wanted to be able to roll around, take up space as she pleased. It was self-effacing—girls in our culture are given the message not to take up too much space. Share, be smaller, make room for others.

Leaving her apartment to go to Beit Ticho, where she was meeting Meryl, Wendy decided she would make her way up Emek Refaim and window shop as she walked.

Wendy took one brisk step in front of the next and thought about why Meryl was a good test interview subject. Miriam now—she had to respect that—had been at Brown with Wendy's childhood friend Nina Distler. Miriam was a talented artist whose parents wouldn't let her go to art school; she chose Brown because she was able to take classes and hang out at the adjoining Rhode Island School of Design, known to most as RISD. Brown was Wendy's first-choice college and she didn't get in, while Meryl didn't like being there. Wendy was trying to not resent her. Wendy sighed and, spotting a bench in the park above Yemin Moshe, decided to sit down and go over her notes for the interview one more time. Meryl had a one-woman show at an avant-garde public school showcase gallery two years after college. It was given a review—a scant paragraph or so but an actual review—in both the *New York Times* and *Art World* magazine. Then, something had happened. It was Wendy's task to elicit the narrative of how Meryl had gotten from the hip art world of Brooklyn, to its religious Jewish section, and then to Beis Mushka in Jerusalem.

Wendy could hypothesize—Miriam's parents divorced and she wanted some of the stability that Orthodox Judaism seemed to provide its adherents? Or, she'd had a series of non-Jewish boyfriends and felt betrayed when they didn't understand her dismay over their thoughtful Christmas gifts? Maybe Miriam had a drug or alcohol problem after college, and starting over with a new group of people was a way of removing herself from a druggie circle of friends?

For Wendy's dissertation, the actual reason was irrelevant. That was for a psychologist. For her, it was how Miriam *recounted* her transformation. The biographical reconstruction of the life to account for the role changes that new religious commitment demanded, yet remained on a continuous plane with other aspects of the subject's life was, Wendy contended, the most important of the rituals of incorporation that enabled individuals to be fully part of their new group.

Miriam was the perfect person to test her questionnaire, and ideas, out on, because Wendy had known her before and knew how she talked, how she thought about the world. Wendy needed to ask her questions in a way that would elicit a story. The trick was to ask enough questions to get a subject to talk and then get out of the way and listen. Wendy wasn't sure she was enough of a listener to do this well. Or that she could ask the question well enough. If she couldn't get the subject to produce relevant information . . .

Then what? She couldn't write a dissertation if she had crappy data . . . Then? Back to law school or her parents' house. She needed to do this right.

Hitting the benches by the windmill in Yemin Moshe, Wendy decided to sit for a minute and look over her list. She opened her bag and took out her list of questions, and felt her anxiety dissipate. Now, she felt the same sense of excitement, anticipation, even exultation, as she had when she first opened the envelope from the Fulbright committee.

"It's really happening," she said to herself. The excitement at having an idea and now really beginning to carry it through, to prove to others that something of the way she, Wendy Dora Goldberg, saw the world really was true. She wanted to run all the way to Beit Ticho, with this burst of energy: she was *really* on the way to a scholarly career, going where she wanted to go. Nothing else in her life was so exhilarating as this possibility—she was creating something that was her own idea and would go out into the world. It was beginning. She wasn't going to be like her subjects, humble and self-effacing: *Oh it was nothing; the dissertation really wrote itself, you know. I didn't really intend to do it; it just happened because I still wasn't married.*

She placed the folder gently back into her purple canvas messenger bag, put it back over her shoulder, and broke into a run towards Beit Ticho. After a few blocks, she stopped and continued at a walk, hit Jaffa Road and turned left, then made a right onto Rav Kook Street and went past the cabstand and up the street. She breathed more slowly, winded from fast walking. The nineteenth-century stone Arab-built house was at the end of a narrow path, right next to the house where the first chief rabbi of Israel, Rav Kook, lived. The Ticho House was a museum and café, willed to the city by artist Anna Ticho and her eye doctor husband. It housed many aspects of the history of the city: the historic house, the paintings of Jerusalem and its wildflowers by Anna, which were displayed, and the eye doctor's diverse collection of Hanukkah menorahs from many countries and epochs. The food in the café was quite good too, even though it was too hot this summer day to sit outside on the terrace.

As Wendy entered, she spotted a woman with a big purple scarf wound around her head. Couldn't be—Miriam wasn't married yet. The woman did look artistic, with large turquoise earrings and a necklace to match, and a serene gaze. There were some older people sitting in a group at a table, taking advantage of their status as *pensionaires*, retirees, to get a discount; a young couple, both in jeans and sweaters; and a third table with three women. Wendy sat down to order some tea while she waited.

As she was looking at the menu, she heard, "Hey, you're Wendy Goldberg," and looked up. The woman who said this was wearing a black close-fitting ski cap with blue, green, and orange stripes, a bright orange puffy ski jacket with tags from various lifts, and an ankle length denim skirt paired with Doc Martens black boots. Wendy looked up and said, "Meryl. Thanks for meeting me. I really appreciate it."

"Oh, no problem," she said, sitting down and taking off her coat and hat. When Miriam removed the hat, the dreadlocks originating from her scalp flowed out, asserting themselves. Wendy thought, *I do believe you are from Syosset, not Jamaica. What's the deal? Dreadlocks on Caucasians are just too pretentious.*

Miriam sat down and said, "I remember you. You visited Nina Distler at Brown. Your boyfriend was at Brown and you were studying . . . Eastern religions?"

Wendy blushed. It had been a short-lived relationship, that one. She met him at a party there, visited a few times, he visited her, and it never went anywhere.

"I've totally forgotten his name. Rob? Rich? Ray? I did visit Nina like once a semester. You were on her floor?"

"Sophomore and junior year. I was into the art scene and she was pre-med but we had friends in common; we all knew each other. Same here in Jerusalem. It's nice to see a familiar face. No one will visit these days."

"Even my most adventurous friends have bailed on their promised visits." Wendy thought of Matt Lewis from grad school.

"You need *bitachon* and *emunah* to come now. My parents were really pressuring me to come home after that American got killed on a bus last month. So sad," she said, clucking her tongue to emphasize her melancholy. She gave Wendy a serious look. "Do you ever think, even if everyone has a *basherte*, that you might somehow miss yours? Like if he is killed by terrorists, or in an accident? Or if you meet, but don't realize it's him?"

Wendy decided to use this opportunity to move into professional interviewer mode. "Good question. I don't know. Hey, order something, my treat, and I'll explain what I want to ask you."

"Sure," Miriam said, and perused the menu. She gazed over its top to ask, "I've never eaten here. Is the soup good?"

"Order anything," Wendy said liberally.

Miriam continued, "It's strange for me to be in a museum now. I got here early and was looking around since I really haven't been in a gallery or museum since I came to Israel in August."

"What'd you think? I know you've done more avant-garde stuff, so this must seem . . . old-fashioned."

"I like the site specificity, that this family lived here from 1924 to 1980 when it became a museum. It really gives me a sense of how people in Jerusalem lived years ago. The menorahs are amazing, the creativity and variety of ways Jews find to fulfill the same mitzvah. You know the idea of *hiddur mitzvah*, that every mitzvah you do should be as beautiful as possible?"

"Sure," Wendy lied.

"I loved the menorahs. The paintings . . . I don't know. They didn't move me."

"Maybe Anna Ticho wasn't such a talented painter?"

"No, it's me, my opinion. My priorities have shifted. I want to use my talents for a purpose, to channel them, not just to shock people or display an emotion. Art should be in service to *Hashem*."

"I see," Wendy said, adding, "How does your yeshiva encourage you to channel your talents? Do they have a studio there for you to paint?"

"No, I need to be learning now. It isn't time for me to go back to the studio yet. I was reading in the explanations about Anna Ticho that when she first moved to Israel she didn't paint. She lived here from 1912 until World War I and left with her husband to serve in the war in Damascus. Away from Jerusalem, she started painting again, and continued when she came back. I don't have to do it all now; I want to catch up on my learning first."

"Your career?"

"Not now. It's not the most important thing. I just want to lead a good Jewish life."

"Isn't using your talent and developing your potential part of leading a good Jewish life?"

Meryl paused and looked at Wendy. "Depends. I don't want to spend my whole life in the studio. I want to have kids and spend time with them, even have outside interests. Being religious will give me a better shot at a balanced lifestyle, I hope. I don't know of any super-successful women artists who have more than one kid."

Wendy thought and said, "That photographer who uses her kids . . . Sally Mann? She had three."

"Exception proves rule," Miriam assented, slapping her hand down on the table.

"Are you giving up on having a career?" Wendy continued, leaning back in her chair and crossing her arms over her chest.

"Why are you hostile? I thought this was an interview?"

Wendy sighed. "Okay, sorry. I am totally screwing up here." She waved her hands to demonstrate that she was letting everything go, and added, "I wanted to start by talking to a friend, but I'm not doing this professionally enough. I want to get you to talk about yourself, and how you view your journey, and I just keep putting myself in. I have to step back. I'm sorry."

"*Mehilah* granted." Miriam added, "Pardon," in response to Wendy's quizzical look. "You? How will you do family and career?"

"I'm not worrying about it now. Men don't. Why should we?"

"They don't have biological clocks."

"Let's change the subject. What drew you here?"

The waitress brought their food. "Emm, *blintzes givinah metukah.*" Wendy pointed at Meryl and the sweet cheese blintzes were set down before her. "And *marak batzel*"—onion soup for Wendy.

Meryl said, "I have to go wash."

Wendy felt annoyed at Meryl's compunction to wash before eating bread. Wendy bit spontaneously into the warm rolls the waitress had just placed on the table with their orders. She was in the process of putting soft butter with small flecks of dill in it on the warm rolls when Meryl returned and recited the *Hamotzi* in an ostentatiously loud voice.

Wendy watched as Meryl cut her blintzes neatly into small bite-size pieces, not eating anything until the entire portion was pared down. As Wendy watched her she thought to herself, *It's so unnatural to cut up everything and parcel it out. Eat the damn thing?* She remembered, watching, that Meryl had been anorexic. Was this some kind of ritual she created for herself around food?

Meryl eased a piece of blintz into her mouth and chewed before she began: "How did I get here? I can tell the story so many ways. I could start with my parents' divorce when I was five and my intense desire for a more intact family. Or I could talk about having my show at the gallery and feeling, afterwards, this big . . . letdown. After the opening night party thinking, *That wasn't so great. That's it? I'm still not happy.* I thought ahead of time that if I work hard enough and have this show and it's successful, I'll be happy. I could talk about my grandmother who wasn't super religious, but lit Shabbos candles and made special foods. Food was her way of giving me love. When I was a teenager, I wanted to cut myself off from my family and not accept anyone's love; part of that was denying myself food. Now, I want to open myself up to the love in the world and reconnect with my grandmother and her candles. But I could just as easily say it was all *basherte*." Wendy pretended to look puzzled just to see how Meryl would interpret the phrase for her.

"Hey, I see you need to cut the food into all those pieces. Has your eating disorder gotten better since you've been religious?" Wendy wondered as soon as the words were out whether they were going to sound insensitive somehow when it was meant as just a friendly question.

Meryl glossed it over: "Thanks for asking, but yeah, I've been fine. I do love all the rituals though. They create more meaning than my own personal ones, you know? But I'm not sure you understood what I was saying before. *Basherte* is "meant to be." I was *meant* to be here in Jerusalem and learn and heal from all the pain in my life. That's what religion is, a balm; you know the Psalms talk about God as the healer of shattered hearts. I mean, isn't that an amazing gift from *Hashem*, to be able to mend our broken hearts through doing mitzvahs?"

Wendy nodded and listened, then worried. How to account for multiple versions of the narrative? There was never only one way to tell the story; all the things Meryl was saying were true. How could she accommodate this in writing her dissertation?

Trying not to sound too anxious, she said, "Was there a turning point for you when you knew *for sure* you were going to become religious?"

Meryl glared at her. "That's the problem with ivory tower academics. You see life . . . needing to be reduced to symptoms, diagnoses. For everything there is a pathology and a cure. One Friday night last winter, I was going out to an opening for someone I knew from Providence; he'd gone to RISD. I was in a black, short leather skirt, heels, fishnets, and as I was going down the stairs of my walk-up apartment, I passed the Kaminetskys' door—they're Lubavitch, and lived below me. I heard laughing, voices, adorable toddler squealing. I thought about what it would be like at the opening, having to make witty allusive conversation, to name drop, to do things to get people to notice me. No one at that opening would like me just for myself the way the people in that apartment, or that toddler Chaye Mushke, would. I thought, I'll just go in to say hi. I went in and was greeted so warmly, and Shmuel made *Kiddush* for me, and Leah showed me how to wash my hands and gave me two rolls to make *Hamotzi* on, and they said just stay and have some soup with us, and I thought, okay, I'll have some soup and go a little later. But I never went to the opening, and I started going to them Friday night more and more often. I felt so accepted and loved just for being myself, dreadlocks, fishnets, and all. They were so unjudgmental, especially compared to the scene at the opening where you have to *be* someone to be noticed. I was meant to be religious and was born into the wrong family. It took me a quarter of my life to figure out a true path and now I'm where I belong."

Wendy looked at her, "You're lucky, Meryl, if you've found your true path after only a quarter of your life. It takes most people much longer."

"There is one true path for all Jews, Wendy. It's called Torah. If you follow it, you'll find everything."

Wendy decided not to debate her. "I suppose. So, look this is outside the interview, but I'm just curious. Do you miss art?"

"I do, but I don't feel it's compatible with a Torah lifestyle. I could see, as I was telling you earlier, making ritual objects, trying to beautify mitzvot, but not what I did before, no."

"Aren't you limiting yourself?"

"The rabbis have an expression, *liphoom tzara agra*, according to the suffering is the reward. I need to give up things I love to gain a reward for mitzvot. I'm eating now, so I need to give something else up. I don't know if a non-anorexic can understand that."

"Do you think you'll be religious in the future, five or ten years down the road?"

"God willing."

"You changed to become religious. You *can* change back," said Wendy provocatively.

"I don't know the future. I hope, with God's help, to continue on this path."

Wendy decided to try another tactic to get an answer reflecting the thoughts of Meryl herself, not just a repetition of her teachers' ideas. "What is the hardest thing for you about religious observance?"

Meryl put down her fork and knife and set her palms flat on the table on either side of her plate. "Hmm. Maybe that things are so prescribed: one must say this prayer at this time, feel this way on this holiday, feel that way on Shabbat. I wish I had more room as an individual to do my thing. But I like that on Shabbat there is a shared sense of time. Everyone is resting; no one has other plans and will blow you off the way people did on weekends in college, always going elsewhere."

"What do you like most and least about the yeshiva?"

"I love learning Hebrew, learning new things. It's exciting, this whole new world that is *my* world but that I really knew next to nothing about until recently. What is hard is being back at the beginning, like a little kid, learning Hebrew, learning things religious kids know from day one. I don't want it to be so difficult for my kids. Least, well, I don't want to be a snob, but not everyone at Beis Mushka went to Brown, you know. Most of them went to Queens or SUNY Stony Brook and don't have the . . . sophistication that we have. I'm not sure how to explain it."

"More provincial? Or more sheltered?"

"Maybe. It's just . . . most of them just aren't the type of people I would have been friends with before. But I am changing too, so I don't know what type of people I should be friends with now. I used to be friends with people who I thought were cool, or thought I was cool, or were also artists and we would all sort of inspire each other."

"Can you be inspired about doing mitzvot? Who observes more or better?" Wendy added.

"Competition isn't the only basis of friendship, Wendy. You and I were never friends in the States, yet here we are, sitting here, in Jerusalem. I don't think either of us would have imagined it a year ago."

"A year ago I was still finishing the applications for fellowships so that I could come here. I wasn't sure I'd actually make it."

"And I was getting ready for my show—it was last January. You know it's really very postmodern. If I were to do a collage of my life story, or my return to Judaism, I'd have to find some kind of shape where all these different paths and influences led to the center, a sort of swirling vortex, where Jerusalem is at the center and all these things lead to it. As we're talking, I'm thinking maybe I will do some kind of piece chronicling my return."

Wendy smiled at her. "Why should you give up art?"

"I have to find a way to bring things together. To use my experiences and express them, to move people to teshuvah. The teachers at Beis tell us we have to integrate who we were before. I'll talk to one of my rabbis."

"Okay," said Wendy, sort of annoyed that, though Meryl was embarking on an artistic endeavor, she felt she needed to ask permission.

Why can't you make decisions on your own? Why do you need a rabbi? What about individuality? she thought, but was proud of herself, this time, for not saying anything.

Tuesday, after morning *ulpan*, Wendy got on a bus and went to a nondescript religious neighborhood on the western edge of the city, *Nofe Tzedek*, views of righteousness. There was something about neighborhoods on the fringes of cities, an emptiness at being so far from the center. Getting off the bus, Wendy didn't see much of a view, righteous or otherwise. Her sight range included Jerusalem stone apartment buildings, fairly close together, and women and children, all pushing baby carriages, some with real babies and some with dolls. There was nothing else on the walk from the bus stop to the Bayit Ne'eman campus.

After she walked through a gate, empty of occupants but ostensibly constructed to house an absent security guard, Wendy saw a cluster of buildings ahead. There were signs for dorms, classrooms, and a cafeteria, where Wendy had agreed to meet Dawn from the Friday night dinner after the *Kotel*. The buildings were on the newish side, she observed as she followed the signs to the cafeteria. On her way, she saw a woman wearing a housedress, with a mop and bucket cleaning the floors, but noticed that the windows did not appear to have been washed in the ten years since the facility had been built. The uniform streaks of dirt covering the glass made it impossible to see out with any clarity.

When Wendy entered the cafeteria, she scanned the crowd of women to find Dawn from Friday night dinner. Seeing the students assembled to gain nourishment, Wendy viewed them all as her prey. She felt odd to think of them in this rapacious light, since she hoped she would also be genuinely interested in them. But then, she thought, seeing these women as her quarry was probably no different than the way the teachers and rabbis here saw them. The faculty's stated goal was to hunt down ignorant and soulless Jews and bring them into a Torah lifestyle, to capture them away from the corruptness of Western values. Wendy's investment in the students, by contrast, was merely catch and release, without attempting a hold.

Wendy found Dawn in the cafeteria and joined her in the line to get lunch. Dawn handed Wendy the coupon she got for a meal as someone wanting to try out classes. The school was generous with these, to encourage students to bring in recruits.

Waiting in line, tray held passively in front of her, made Wendy feel like a kid in elementary school, waiting for an adult to give her lunch. Once the food was on their trays, Dawn and Wendy joined a group of students who were, like herself and Dawn, from the New York-New Jersey-Pennsylvania tri-state area. Wendy told the others they sat with that she was at Hebrew University's summer *ulpan* and she might want to take some additional classes. The group told her in unison how wonderful it was here, how warm and caring the teachers were, how they loved the other students, that she should definitely come here right away. There was intensive Hebrew here too, but at Bayit Ne'eman a student could learn so much more than just language.

"Torah makes people happy," they kept repeating.

To Wendy, there appeared little happiness in the physical surroundings. The cafeteria was dark, and the food adhered to an institutional hue, greenish meatloaf astride graying potato kugel. Vegetables, which could usually be expected to provide colorful variety, had their nutritive value blanched out by being overcooked to a mushy green. Wendy thought that when she got back to her apartment she would make a cucumber and tomato salad. She wanted to let the vivid red and green colors of the food peek up at her from the plate, and to enjoy their tang with a squeeze of pungent lemon juice and a bit of salt that would just punctuate the intense freshness of the vegetables in Israel.

Picking at the featureless food on her plate devoid of appeal to her sense of taste, sight, or smell, Wendy focused on the conversation of her tablemates. Their desires were simple: stay in this neighborhood, marry *frum* Mr. Right, and have parcels of children. Wendy thought of other researchers she knew of who sat and collected anecdotes. She remembered learning in college about Henry James going to dinner parties, waiting for his données, the kernels of stories casually heard, which could become the gold ore he would mine to create his fiction. Looking around, Wendy thought that James's soirees at grand English manor houses, being served turtle soup and oysters, were impossibly far from Bayit Ne'eman's cafeteria in *Nofe Tzedek* in Jerusalem.

"I agree with Rebbetzin B. that all the problems in America are because women don't spend enough time with their children. If only everyone could see that, and stop trying to be men," said the girl across from her.

"I hate that Hillary Clinton. Barbara Bush, she's a real woman," came from the left. Wendy, from a pure blue Democratic family, gritted her teeth to refrain from arguing with them. The girl on her right said, "If we all lived a Torah true life, *Moshiach* would come. Wouldn't that be amazing?"

How did they get to this point so quickly? The summer program had only started three weeks ago, Dawn had told her. Wendy sensed that they were competing to see who could become scrubbed most clean, most pure in her devotions and Orthodoxy, with the least residue of her previous life. Would these women, trying to scour themselves of pieces of their earlier identities, show any fault lines to an outsider? From this casual chatting she would see what they thought. Listening without expressing an opinion was not natural to Wendy but she remained quiet. Only through listening could she formulate her questionnaire, to get the information that would be the nucleus of her dissertation, the main hub for her theoretical notions to circulate. She would never be able to theorize if she didn't have informants who trusted her with their life stories.

Was she using them? Running this through her mind as she tried to digest the conversation gave Wendy a jolt of discomfort. Letting them speak openly without telling them that she was here to write a dissertation, was it dishonest? If they thought she was posing as one of them to gain their trust, wouldn't they be furious on finding out? Wendy was on the verge of confessing that she had come to write about baalei teshuvah when the recitation of the Grace after Meals swept over the room, voices surging in unison, a mob of piety joining together in Hebrew. When the chant ended, the students got up from their tables, bussing their trays to the back of the room. Wendy followed Dawn and the others to class without having revealed herself as a hunter sniffing out her quarry.

The classroom was of the same ilk as the rest of the building, not very old, but seeming older, with unwashed windows and junior high school-type desks with attached writing arms. The blackboard too was streaked, as though only hastily cleaned, never thoroughly erased of the jottings of previous teachers. The students waited, whispering and gesturing among themselves, for the teacher to enter. They were talking as though about a celebrity, trying to glean small pieces of information about the teacher from the droplets he gave off in the classroom, where he lived, how many children he had, how long he'd been married.

Rabbi Pavlov entered the room, placing his black leather briefcase, with shiny silver buckles, on the desk. He stood in front of the class, looked at the floor, and paced back and forth, as though using up restless energy. He began, "The Ethics of the Fathers teaches '*aseih lecha rav*,' make for yourself a rabbi. One must always ask a rabbi a *shaila*, a question. Even if you think you know the answer, there may be intricacies of the law you can't grasp. Nothing is too obvious or simple for your *rav*. He wants you to ask. The whole system of *halacha*, Jewish law, is based on *mesorah*, the transmission of the chain of tradition. You, *women*"—he put the emphasis on this word and finally looked up directly at his female charges rather than the floor— "can't know what a rav does, so always, always"—here he paused in his pacing—"ask your rav a *shaila*. If you think for yourself, you won't be connecting to our heritage, only your own thoughts. Never make that mistake. Ask, ask, ask."

Wendy, stifled by this train of thought, daydreamed back to her favorite college class, Contemporary Civilization, known as CC, her first year at Columbia. She had started college with plans to be a history major, Columbia's most popular undergraduate field of study, because there were so many outstanding professors, particularly in her domain, American history. History was supposed to be good preparation for law school, which she assumed she'd do because her father, brother, and sister had. Her interests shifted when she took CC with Caroline Van Leeuwen, the religion department's first female tenured professor. In class, Van Leeuwen often closed her eyes while speaking, as though she were possessed. When the teacher spoke with her eyes closed, she appeared as though in a trance, reciting knowledge gleaned from an otherworldly source. On leaving the classroom, if someone asked Wendy what had been discussed, she might not be able to define it with certainty; yet she knew something revelatory had occurred. What made Van Leeuwen's classes special wasn't just seeing the teachers' eyes closed in a state of apprehension outside the immediate realm of the students' grasp, but also what she was able to elicit from the students themselves.

Often, at the beginning of class, Professor Van Leeuwen would come in and tell the class that she had been up all night reading the assigned text and listening to jazz. She would stroll to the classroom's large picture window and gaze out at the statue of Rodin's *The Thinker* resting on one of the few small swaths of green on the city campus, waiting for students to respond. These moments of classroom silence were scary. The students were never sure what would come next. As the silence grew more oppressive in the classroom, someone always gave an answer. One day, Wendy spoke first. As she answered a question about the role of art and passion in Plato's *Republic*, she felt enchanted, as though there were a magic spell over her, making her more articulate than she had ever thought herself capable of being.

After that class, Wendy was captivated by the power of the question. That's what she would spend her life doing, she decided in the semester with Van Leeuwen: asking questions. She loved the ways in which questions of religion were concerned with issues of meaning and significance in the world. Her teacher's passion for her subject was palpable—Van Leeuwen, in late middle age, stayed up all night reading. Yet, with the rumors of the teacher's instability and frequent breakdowns leading to the nickname Van Loonen, her path seemed risky. Wendy doubted she could live as her teacher did, swayed by passion for books and music, putting the minutiae of daily life aside to be fully absorbed with ideas. Yet, Wendy loved to watch someone living in this exalted state of rapt absorption with her own ideas and those of her students. Over the next two years, Wendy declared herself an American religion major, instead of an American history major. She wanted to sprinkle magical thoughts into the minds of her future students, she decided as she filled out the graduate school applications. She wanted to both live in this world and connect to things beyond it, larger than it; the study of religion seemed like a good choice.

Wendy had to elbow herself to suppress a laugh, squeezed as she was in the tight chairs made for smaller people, as she thought of how different the classroom at Bayit Ne'eman was from the one in Philosophy Hall. These students too were drawn by ideas. They wanted to have an idea of their path in life, to be less lost, to connect with others, to find love, and to be a more ideal version of the self they had been. But the ways in which the questions were asked and the types of answers given in the two places were so divergent: one encouraging active thought and the other active obedience. But still, she knew, feeling small in the junior high-sized writing desks, that she was as needy and lost as the students around her. Though she had chosen a more intellectual approach to solving life's problems, she was still facing the same ones the others in the class, she understood, as she continued to half listen to Rabbi Pavlov.

A few weeks later, she went back to Bayit Ne'eman. She had an appointment with the dean of the school, Rabbi Dr. Lifter, who specialized in getting even the most difficult of returnees to rise.

Wendy dressed in a below-the-elbow-length T-shirt this time, with the same modestly long wrap-around skirt she'd worn before, and found Rabbi Lifter's office on the second floor. She had made an appointment with a secretary and was on time, but there was no one there. She wasn't sure whether to wait in the office or the hallway, but since the door was open and there were no chairs in the hallway, she entered the office.

She sat on a metal chair with an attached cushion, marking it as a grade above the absolute cheapest metal chair. She looked at the desk in front of her, overflowing with papers and with more stacks of paper behind it. To her side were bookcases whose contents were mostly English, a bit of Hebrew in a title sprinkled in. One case had a sign: "Rabbi Lifter's lending library. Sign out and return." A diploma, she thought from a rabbinical institution— though it was all in Hebrew or Yiddish so she wasn't sure—and a degree from Brooklyn College were hung on the walls along with an inspirational poster of the kind found in office supply stores. It was a garishly colored picture of a caterpillar and a butterfly, all neon pink lettering and green background, cheerily accompanied by the caption *"Keep rising!"*

Wendy waited, and after a minute took out some of her work from *ulpan* to review so she wouldn't be wasting time. Twenty-five minutes after their scheduled appointment, a man came in, saw her, and said, "Can I help you?"

She rose to be polite and began to hold out her hand to shake his before stopping herself midair and lowering her arm. "I'm Wendy Goldberg, I had a two o'clock appointment with you. I wanted to talk about some research I'm doing."

"Research? None of our classes require research. We want you out doing works of *hesed*, kindness, in your spare time. Not research."

"I'm not a student here," she said.

He strode in, seated himself behind his desk, and asked, "Who are you then?"

"I'm a graduate student at Princeton. I'm writing a dissertation about American baalei teshuvah and I'd like to speak with some of the students here. I sent you a letter about my project."

He waved his hand in dismissal. "Absolutely not. We are here to mold souls. No interference."

"I won't interfere. Perhaps I can help. I want to understand how baalei teshuvah tell their stories, how they put their journeys into words. You might be able to use my work in your promotional material. Or your fund-raising?"

"Hmm."

"Did you get the letter from my advisor at Hebrew University, Avner Zakh? He asks your permission to let me do this work?"

"Avner Zakh? How do I know that name?"

"He told me you are related through marriage. A nephew of his, I believe, is married to a niece of yours. The last name is different, but I think his nephew is Shmuel?"

The rabbi stretched out his arms in front of him. "Yes, of course. The *hassana* was before *Pesach*; the uncle is at the university. I remember now. Good family, quite *frum*, direct descendants of the *GR"A* and the *Hassam Soifer*." Wendy nodded, pretending she knew what he was talking about.

He looked and her carefully and continued, "What kinds of questions will you be asking?"

Wendy pulled out a copy of her questionnaire and handed it to him.

He glanced at it and said, "Seems harmless. You," he pointed a finger, "you are *dati*?"

"Well ah," she thought quickly. "There's a reason I am drawn to the subject. I like the atmosphere here in Israel, the Yiddishkeit"—she was proud of herself for getting the lingo down on that one—"and . . . I think I'm growing. My grandmother keeps kosher." She didn't know why she blurted out that last part; he'd surely see her as an idiot now.

"A religious grandmother; you'll come back. Religion skips a generation in *galus*. Make yourself right at home; sit in on any classes you like; I'll send a note to the faculty. Of course you'll be sure you dress modestly while you're with us."

"Absolutely, I'll be very careful. Thank you so much, Rabbi Lifter. I can't tell you how I appreciate your kindness."

"Anytime. Come for Shabbos."

Wendy went out the door feeling jubilant. Stage one accomplished. She had access. *Whew, that felt close, but I did it. I talked my way in. Kind of funny that he let me in because he assumed that the school would impact me, without taking me seriously enough to believe I might have my own motives.*

As she left Lifter's office, she made a note to herself to call Zakh and thank him. He told her the only way things happen in this country is through *protectzia*. It was amazing how quickly Rabbi Lifter's tone changed when she used Professor Zakh's name; Zakh had told her that was the way to do things here, to know someone who knows someone, the smallness of the country operating in favor of the ease of these connections. Wendy definitely needed to revise her view of Zakh; he *had* helped her now despite his lack of time at their first meeting. The problem was, she wanted more specific guidance on the steps of a dissertation. He *had* helped her, it just wasn't exactly the way she still wanted assistance.

Leaving the building, Wendy approached a few students she saw in the hallway to ask if they would fill out her questionnaire. She had attached stamped self-addressed envelopes and figured that if she gave out fifteen she'd get five or ten back, to give her an idea of how to start. She wanted to see what kinds of questions they would respond to, and which ones would lead to the most revealing responses. At this stage, she just wanted to give out surveys anonymously, not for data, but to develop her questions and tweak them as necessary.

Please respond to these questions as honestly as possible. Do not put your name on this—all responses are anonymous and confidential to protect your privacy.

This will not be used for any purpose other than my own information. I will be giving out a more detailed version of this questionnaire as part of my dissertation research on how baalei teshuvah tell their stories. This is a sample to help me figure out which types of questions are most useful.

If you have any questions, feel free to email me at wgoldber@
princeton.edu.

Thank you so much for your time.

Wendy Goldberg

QUESTIONS FOR RETURNEES

How long have you been at this yeshiva?

How did you get here?

What aspects of religious observance are hardest?

What aspects of religious observance are easiest?

What are you working on changing about your observance?

What do you think you'll be working on six months from now?

A year from now?

Can you pinpoint one particular event or point in time that made
you realize that you were becoming more religious and would not
return to your former life?

As a follow-up, do you think you will still be observant in one year?
Five years? Ten years?

What has guided you in your journey to observance?
Teachers?
Friends?
Books?

What aspects of your life have changed most since you became
observant?

Is there an aspect of your life that is unchanged?

Is there an aspect of this lifestyle about which you are uncertain?
Why?

Have your career or family plans changed since your involvement
with the yeshiva? If so, how?

The students took the papers obediently, as though Wendy herself were Rabbi Pavlov. She was curious whether they would be honest or merely give her stock answers. She fervently hoped there was a way to get at what really disturbed them, under their veneers of certainty.

FIVE

Centers and Margins

But life can be interpreted in so many different ways . . . Perhaps there the novelist has the advantage and he can let his imagination go where it will . . . Haven't the novelist and the anthropologist more in common than some people think? After all, both study life in communities, though the novelist need not be so accurate or bother with statistics and kinship tables.

—BARBARA PYM, *An Unsuitable Attachment*

The Fulbright group had its first unofficial meeting a few weeks later, at the end of August. The occasion was a discussion, "Center and Margin: A Writer and A Critic Discuss the Diaspora and Israel Today," at Mishkenot Sha'ananim. That evening, a leading Israeli writer and public intellectual would debate a visiting lecturer from Europe. The postcard invitation to the event, the first item to be posted on Wendy's fridge, had a big circle with smaller circles of color inside it, reds, oranges and yellows, like a Josef Albers print, only circular. There were Hebrew and English words, microscopic, encircling both the inner sphere and the outer loop. It had been on Wendy's refrigerator for over two weeks now and she was excited to finally be going, and hopefully to be meeting some new people.

In the summer evening, Wendy walked to the Yemin Moshe neighborhood. She passed the landmark windmill that had been built to anchor the neighborhood at its inception in 1860, and tread over crooked stone steps built to reach Mishkenot Sha'ananim. She saw a plaque outside it stating that it was the first building constructed in modern Jerusalem, to persuade Jews to live beyond the walls of the Old City where they dwelt huddled and cramped at the time.

She entered the room where the talk would be; it had seating for seventy-five to a hundred people. Stackable metal chairs with black plastic backs were the only amenities for the audience. A small podium was at the front, with a lectern to one side for the speaker, a table containing three microphones, a pitcher of water, and three glasses for the two discussants and a moderator. In Wendy's mind, this place, to which the Jerusalem municipality brought visiting artists, writers, musicians, and intellectuals from abroad, should be more impressive and distinguished, with wood beamed ceilings and stone fireplaces, overstuffed chairs and small portable microphones that could be clipped to the speakers' clothing. There should definitely be better chairs for the audience. Those are the amenities that would be in a room for a talk like this at Princeton, Wendy thought. She looked around, dismayed at having to sit on the hard plastic for the duration, an hour at least, probably more.

Most of the audience in the three-quarters-full room were in their forties and beyond. Wendy felt conspicuously young. The visiting speaker didn't know Hebrew, so the proceedings would be in English. Perhaps that limited attendance? Wendy could see someone she thought was Avner Zakh at the front of the room. There weren't a whole lot of kipot in the crowd, maybe five or six, and two or three women were wearing berets. The man she thought was Zakh was in front chatting with those around him, and there weren't seats up there anyway. Wendy started to walk forward to be as close to the front as possible. When she reached the middle of the room, she saw a woman about her age, reading an English language magazine. The woman, who had long black curly hair, tawny skin, and dark brown eyes, was sitting in the middle of the row. There were two empty seats near her.

Wendy decided to try to get to the middle of the row, to sit near the English magazine reader. She said to the man on the aisle, "Excuse me? I'm trying to get to those seats."

He stood up and allowed her to pass.

"Thanks," Wendy said, stepping past the first few people in the row to sit one empty seat from the woman her age.

Once seated, purple messenger bag on floor, Wendy asked the woman reading the English magazine, "Are you here on a Fulbright?"

"Excuse me?"

"A Fulbright? Are you in my group?"

"I'm a journalist. Orly Markovsky. "

Wendy looked at her. "Orly Markovsky? Camp Kodimoh?" she said, stunned.

Orly looked at Wendy and replied, "Wendy?" with an upward quizzical lilt in her voice. She added "Wendy Goldberg?"

"When did we last see each other? At thirteen, so . . . 1983?"

"You were the only person I liked in that bunk," Orly said. She paused and added, "This is so weird. What are you doing in Israel now?"

"I'm writing my dissertation. My fellowship group of graduate students was invited to come tonight so I guessed you might be one of them. The only person in the group I've met is my advisor. He's up front."

"I'm a freelance journalist, working on a book. I'm hoping to get a piece about this debate in a hip publication."

The participants were assembling on the dais, not seated, but still standing and chatting, even though it was ten minutes after the lecture's scheduled start time. Finally, a preliminary rustling and settling in emanated through the room, as Emma Fletcher, the chair of the Hebrew University English department, tapped the microphone to get the audience's attention.

"We'll talk after. I'm glad to see you again," Orly whispered to Wendy across the still empty seat between them.

On the podium, Fletcher began: "Welcome to the fall 1996 Van Leer Lecture of the Hebrew University English Department. We are pleased to have Phillipe Berger with us from Palo Alto"—she paused for the polite applause—"and Yedidya Hartheimer with us from Jerusalem." The stronger applause from the hometown crowd necessitated a longer halt. "The format we've devised is that each panelist will speak for fifteen minutes. Then, I will pose a few queries addressed to both speakers, and finally I'll accept questions from the audience. Yes?" She looked around to be sure her audience concurred with her ground rules before continuing.

"Our honored guest will be first. Phillipe Berger was born in Zurich in 1930. His family sent him on a *Kindertransport* to England during the war. He stayed on to matriculate at Oxford, where he received his undergraduate and graduate degrees. He has taught European literature at the Sorbonne, Oxford, the University of Turin, and Harvard, and is currently Percy Stanford University Professor in Palo Alto. Professor Berger has received every major award for his writing, including a National Book Critics Circle Award and a Prix Médicis. This is his first visit to Jerusalem and we are honored and pleased to welcome him. Professor Berger."

To the sounds of mild applause, Berger rose from his seat and stepped to the lectern. He began: "Our eternal homeland," and was silent a long moment.

"The fixity of the text is the only place the Jewish people can truly be at home. The longing for perpetuity can never be found in a fixed physical abode, only on the page, the permanence of the black ink burnished by the whiteness of the space around it, the blank space a flame in which burn for all time the passions that created the writing. The word is where the Jews, the *lecteurs de durer*, enduring readers, belong. Only in the margins, in the disputations with what is around us, can we truly fulfill our destiny as individuals and as a people. We must remain there, on the margin, never in the center, never allowing ourselves to be trapped in what *is*, only what is in formation, in becoming. The margin is flexible; it yields," he continued. Somewhere in this message, Wendy's mind had begun to drift off for a brief snooze.

Wendy was roused by the polite applause marking the end of Berger's presentation. She opened her eyes to hear Fletcher introduce Yedidya Hartheimer. "The writer Yedidya Hartheimer needs no introduction to this audience. We are all aware of his two novels and his penetrating book of journalism, *Victims in Power: Children of Survivors Serving in the Territories*, which has won many prizes, including the PEN Writers of Conscience Award, the Prix de Rome, and the National Jewish Book Award. We are fortunate to have you with us. Yedidya."

"The *aron hesafirim hayehudim*, the bookshelf of Jewish texts, is ours. We who live here in *Eretz Yisrael*, speak its language, the language of the Torah, the prophets, daily, as we wander on these eternal hills. Without the land the Bible is . . ." he made a cutting off gesture with his hands, "*zeeffft*, nothing. This place is for me, *eretz hakodesh*, the holy land. Not because I am a religious person—I cannot take the privilege to claim that for myself—but because it is ours, the place we have yearned for, these centuries. Now, we are like dreamers and have returned. It is ours, to bring our Jewish ethos into every stone in this country.

"Moshe Rabbeinu stood *benikrat hatzur,* in the cusp, the cleft of the stone, to behold God, *ahorei,* literally, from behind. But those who are intimate with the language know *ahorei* can also mean belatedly. Moshe sees God belatedly. And that, I am afraid, my friends," Hartheimer said with an air of prophecy and sadness," is what will happen to us if we do not realize the miracle. I am purposely using this word 'miracle' with religious overtones. In this wonder that is the modern state of Israel, with Jewish sovereignty, we have Jewish culture in all its glory and grossness, from Hebrew hip-hop and Jewish whores and drug dealers, to high art, Hebrew opera, and epic poetry. If we do not understand the treasure of our miraculousness, of our permission to be at the center once again, if we continue to only see ourselves as outsiders, as victims, we are in grave danger. I want us to stand in the stones of this place, not belatedly cognizant of our power like Moshe, but grasping it fully. I want us to take it with each and every stone, to use it to create a place with a fully Jewish ethos, to be the moral creatures we can be, created with the possibility of being divine, *b'tzelem Elohim.* We can overcome our mortal flaws, even to make peace with our enemies. That is the possibility we have been permitted here in *Eretz Yisrael,* to fully be at the center."

The applause died down and the questions from the audience began. Wendy had not thought that any audience could be more certain of the uncontested significance of each of its utterances than the ones at Princeton. In a moment, she saw this assemblage as able competition. Each question was *not* a question, but a disquisition on the work of the questioner, and the grave mistake the speaker was making in not paying more attention to its significance, imperiling his ability to draw proper conclusions. After a number of these, Emma Fletcher cut off further discourse and thanked the audience for their attendance.

Wendy rose and gathered her belongings, and so did Orly. As they waited behind the others in their row to file out, Orly asked Wendy, "Shall we go for coffee? I know a good place near here."

They left Mishkenot Sha'ananim and walked up the hill, through Yemin Moshe, out to David HaMelech Street. Orly told her, "I'm taking you to Café Florence. They have amazing Italian food."

They walked through the pleasant air of the late summer evening and sat on the patio on the street outside the restaurant, stepping over the ropes separating the restaurant's seating from the street. They didn't need to enter the restaurant since they were going to sit outdoors, on the patio. The décor was minimal: an awning overhead, black iron tables and chairs with lattice work, white linen table cloths. A waitress brought them menus. The summer night, with a bit of a breeze, was perfect for sitting at an outdoor café.

Orly spoke confidently, "The crepes here are amazing, and they make their own gelato. Want to share one?"

"Sure."

"You won't be sorry," Orly said as she turned to the waitress who reappeared to take their order. Orly spoke to her in fluent Hebrew.

When the waitress had departed, Wendy asked, envious, "How do you know Hebrew so well?"

"My mother is Israeli. She spoke Hebrew at home, and I spent some summers here growing up. It's helped my career—I only write for English language periodicals, but I interview people in Hebrew. They trust me because I speak the language."

"I have a question. If you get Israelis, can you explain that Hartheimer? I'm confused. He's not religious, but I've never heard someone speak of the land of Israel with such . . . I don't know . . . intensity? It seemed religious to me. Am I missing something? And, he looked, so . . . how can I say it? Did you notice something almost translucent about his skin? If he were an insect he'd be missing his carapace, whatever it is that protects him from outsiders. He just seemed . . . those bug eyes, so large and like they can't create a barrier between him and anything that might hurt him in the outside world. He looks shorn of ordinary protection, you know?"

Orly picked up her knife and stabbed menacingly at the air, "Yedidya Hartheimer is not protected," she intoned.

Wendy laughed, "I'm not explaining myself. I guess . . . I was surprised by what he said."

"How so?"

"I haven't really heard anyone articulate this notion of Israel and its potential to be miraculous and at the center. I mean . . . on the plane here I bumped into this professor from my department who's a survivor and religious, and he told me how miraculous it was to be in Israel, but . . . I was surprised to hear an avowedly non-religious person speak of the place in such unabashedly sacred overtones."

Orly placed the knife down and turned serious. "Wendy, how many of the people in this country would not be on this earth, just wouldn't exist, if this place were not a haven? I wasn't shocked by Hartheimer, but by Berger. A guy who spent his childhood away from his family, who didn't *have* a family by the time he was an adult, to say that we shouldn't have a homeland because Jews don't belong at the center, but on the margins? To me, and I hope I'm not offending you, that position is completely not intellectually or morally defensible. What did this guy learn from history?"

Wendy said, "It isn't about him, personally, it is about where the religion belongs in the world, what kind of space it occupies in the public sphere. Is Judaism a religion for the world, to be on the periphery, or for ourselves to be at the center?" Wendy mused. "I've taken classes on the role of religion in public debate, First Amendment issues and how they play out in America versus Europe versus Moslem countries. Each country has its own code of what works for that place. Israelis are, by and large, willing to put up with Sabbath restrictions to create some kind of common shared culture. Americans are freaked out when the Ten Commandments are posted in courtrooms. The French don't like seeing little Muslim girls wear headscarves in a public school."

"What do *you* think?"

"I just got here, Orly. I'm not ready to formulate an opinion—very un-Israeli of me, I know. Having said that, if I'd gone through the Holocaust I'd be more Hartheimer than Berger. And Berger . . . his appearance. No one in Israel wears sports jackets, and his whole getup—the Hermes handkerchief in his jacket pocket, the tortoiseshell glasses that he kept taking on and off as he spoke—something about him was too . . . polished? I'm not sure what I'm getting at."

"Wendy, the man is legendary as a womanizer, who beguiles and mesmerizes, enthralling the ladies them until they succumb to his charms. He just separated from wife . . . number four? Three? I agree, there is just something . . . unctuous about him."

Wendy smiled. "There was this guy at Princeton who was a grad student in literature. He kept propositioning my friend Leora. He would tell her things he wanted to do with her, like "cunnilingus" in eight languages. He confessed to another friend that he got all the words from an article by Phillipe Berger, which bragged about how he seduced women in different languages. *That's* how I know his name." Wendy guffawed, loudly and unabashedly, proud of herself for recalling the source of her knowledge of Berger's name.

"Glad to know tuition dollars are being put to such good use, multilingual seduction. I knew a PhD had some practical value."

"Yep." Wendy looked at Orly, more thoughtful. "Can we reduce this Diaspora/Israel thing to Berger's need to prove himself desirable to as many women in as many places as possible, and Hartheimer's apparent monogamy?"

Orly looked up as the waitress approached with their chocolate crepe with dollops of both cinnamon and espresso gelato on top and an extra plate. She thanked the server in Hebrew and said to Wendy, *"B'tayavon."* Wendy gave her a look of incomprehension and Orly translated, "With gusto, good appetite. *Ta'avah* is, literally, passion, so when you say 'eat with good appetite' you are saying 'eat with passion.' To passion."

Wendy raised her fork to dig in. "To passion," she said and bit into the delicious combination of hot sweet chocolate and cold bitter espresso gelato. "Ohhhh," she moaned, "you were so right. This is . . . superb." She dove her fork back for more, smiling at her friend.

Orly smiled back, chocolate sauce dribbling lazily from her chin. "From the Holocaust to the sex life of Phillipe Berger. This is good. I need friends who can have meaningful conversation and also talk about sex, you know?"

Wendy laughed. "We're going to be good friends this year."

Orly responded, "I'd like that. I don't have many friends who are serious about their careers. My boyfriend, Nir, he's fun to be with, he's in a band, he works in computers during the day, but he doesn't really understand when I have a deadline and can't go out. Or my passion for my work; he just says I work too hard, wants me to party more."

Wendy sighed. "I have the opposite problem. This guy in graduate school, Matt, we're compatible intellectually, he's good-looking, we get along. I like to *talk* to him, but there's just something . . . not quite there. He doesn't *excite* me. We keep saying if we're both single at thirty we'll get together."

"How unromantic," Orly sympathized.

"Exactly." Wendy carefully swooped up a piece of crepe draped with chocolate and swathed with the bitter espresso ice cream, now puddling as it melted. "Maybe I need to improve my Hebrew, try seduction in different languages. My chances to land a guy will go up statistically if there are more guys to cast my potential net for."

"Phillipe would be proud—why don't you write him a fan letter and tell him what you learned from his article."

Wendy smirked.

"No, seriously, I had a professor in journalism school who made it the capstone of our class to write fan letters to writers we admired. People appreciate them, and mostly write back."

Wendy wiped her mouth with her napkin and intoned, "I'll pass on that assignment, thanks, Professor Markovsky. Currently, I'm limited to English. That's why my dissertation is exclusively on Americans."

"What's it about? You haven't told me."

"American baalei teshuvah in Jerusalem. How they tell their stories."

"They're nuts. What else can you say?"

"For starters, why? Why of all the possible nutty paths there are do they choose to do this, not radical veganism? Or Buddhist asceticism?"

"Big deal. There are a variety of ways to be a nut! As we say in journalism school, where's the story here?"

Wendy put her fork down and said, "American kids, from American families, most of them in the US for a few generations. Now, they are taking on this different identity, Jewish in a way no one in their family has been in over a century. Why? What does it say about the role of religion in America? Dormant for a few generations and then, voila, coming to the fore. Does the behavior of baalei teshuvah compare to other American religious groups or is it sui generis?"

Orly chewed thoughtfully, and said calmly, "Wendy, I'm not your professor. You don't have to use jargon or situate your work within the field as a whole. Just tell me why you're doing it, as a friend."

Wendy put down her utensils and laid her palms flat on the table, splaying her fingers. "My best friend growing up, Nina, had an older sister, Deb, now Devorah, who became religious when we were in high school. It was weirdly fascinating, how this person who'd been a lifeguard and competitive swimmer started wearing these long skirts and shirts, and looking indistinguishable from other women dressed that way. I wanted to know, had she really changed? Was she different, or was it all in the externals, just an overlay?"

"Alright, what was it?"

"I don't know. I couldn't just *ask* her. Now I'm asking a whole population of people like her. It started with my interest in whether someone truly changes or whether certain core parts of the personality are the same. I also wanted to do a Jewish dissertation in American religion. I wrote my undergrad senior thesis on Buddhists in America, and how the process of immigration changes religious practices. That semester, my grandfather died, and I felt this urge to . . . connect? I guess that's it: grow closer to my own family, my own past. Make sense?"

"Totally. I was just curious."

"No problem. What got you into journalism?"

"I've always liked to write, and I'm naturally nosy. I love to ask brash questions and get in a person's face, and figure out how to unsettle them if I sense they won't tell the truth otherwise. I wrote for the newspapers in high school and college, and decided J-school was a natural fit."

"Trying to unsettle people is one of the things I like about my project. I'm trying to get them to tell their stories to see where they are uncertain, what kinds of hesitations creep in even while they are embracing this religious path."

"The thing is you shouldn't unsettle them too much, just enough to get what you need. One of the most important things is bonding with your subjects, and knowing how to write with both objectivity and compassion. It's a hard balance to strike, but good writing demands both, in different measures at different times. If you want advice on journalistic interviewing techniques, I'll be happy to tutor you."

"Only if we meet over crepes here."

Orly lifted her fork again, and Wendy lifted hers to match. They clanged together and then both forks made their way from the plate to their owners' mouths to finish the rapidly dwindling dessert.

True to her word, Orly printed out a copy of something from one of her journalism school courses on interviewing techniques and dropped the article off in Wendy's mailbox one afternoon when she wasn't home. Oddly, the piece mentioned, in addition to some journalistic ones, the two that Violet

Dohrmann had specified she should get: *Interviewing: Its Principles and Methods* by Annette Garrett, and *The Social Work Interview* by Alfred Kadushin. Wendy was reading it over for the umpteenth time, making sure she was following its suggestions.

Of course, she had her questions written out—that had been done long ago, and she had checked them with Dohrmann to get the order right for best flow. She knew that, if there was a slowness or a lack of response, she could vary things, try to empower the interviewee by asking something about his ideal vision of being religious, or just be silent and force the interviewee to keep talking and break those awkward silences. Her favorite part of the article was carefully highlighted now and also copied out and stuck on the inside cover of her interviewing notebook along with Post-it notes saying, "Be sneaky," "Be annoying," and "Work your subjects up." All these were dream commands for the shushed and silenced youngest sister, the one who wanted to be listened to and taken seriously, but was always relegated to the kids' table, to watching cartoons on TV, to being told the matter wasn't something she could understand: "Not for you now, dear. One day when you're older." Finally, this was Wendy's chance to make people respond to her, to be in charge of the conversation, to direct it and get them to say things she was interested in. Orly's piece was about techniques for journalists, and it talked about having a sense of the shape of the article you want to write and how the quotes from this person would fit, knowing what you wanted the subject to say. For Wendy, of course, the interesting part was *not* knowing what her subjects would say, getting them to say the things even they didn't expect to say, the wholly fresh astounding honesty with which she hoped to get them to peel off their masks of piety and say what they genuinely felt, not what their teachers would expect from them.

Wendy took the tape recorder out of her purple canvas messenger bag and put it on the table along with the orange Princeton notebook she'd purchased specifically for all her interview notes. Most notes were in her computer, but she didn't want to lug it around to interviews or put a screen between herself and her subjects, so she used the notebook at the interviews themselves, to log themes or ideas, or be sure she had a quote down that she knew she'd want to go back to. She was pleased to think about how she had rattled the first subjects she'd deployed her set of questions on, for practice.

It had been a bit tough to get her first guy, Reuven, to open up. She did try the annoying technique, once the endure-awkward-pauses method failed. Some guys like that—to be challenged and provoked, pushed to say something that is under the surface but that they need assistance to articulate precisely. Using the work-them-up technique, she'd finally asked about the turning point, when he knew he'd stay religious.

She turned on the tape recorder to hear him describe it: "I was home, visiting my parents for the summer, and spent a Shabbos in Lakewood." There was a pause for him to say to her, "You know Lakewood," and her nod—though she wasn't entirely sure, she wanted him to continue—"and I went to the *shul* there Shabbos morning. We are all standing, about to take the Torah out, when there is a guy there, with his son—the kid must have been about eleven or twelve—and all of a sudden the father falls down, sinks to the ground. People rush over, there are doctors there, they assess, someone runs to the office to call an ambulance, and someone calls out at some point, 'Cohanim, leave the room. All *cohanim*, clear out.' People were sitting with him; someone went home to tell his wife and walk to the hospital with her, and someone else went to watch the younger kids so she could leave—all this bustle to take care of this man who had just had this collapse and they were still concerned about the *cohanim*. I just found it"—Wendy heard the sigh on the tape recorder—"unbearably beautiful, that in the midst of this tragedy there was concern for this other group in the community."

She heard her own voice, tentative and out of interviewer mode break in. "Please forgive my ignorance, but can you explain why the *cohanim* had to leave? I don't get it."

Reuven added, "The man had almost died on the spot, and they didn't think he could be revived. On the possibility that something could be done—there was a pulse still but barely—they broke Shabbos and called an ambulance, but knowing the man was near death, they wanted the *cohanim* to leave so that they wouldn't come in contact with a dead body if he did pass away. The man died before the ambulance came. His son was so brave, sitting and talking to him, singing, until the ambulance got there."

"That's . . . just to die like that in front of everyone . . . How awful, right in front of his son." Wendy heard herself turn into annoying mode: "But tell me, some people would lose their faith over this kind of thing; I mean here is a guy coming to synagogue, praying, keeping the Sabbath, with his son, and then he is struck down?"

"Apparently, he had this brain tumor, and they had done all they could and knew it was just a matter of time; his days were limited. They had all prepared for it, knew that it was coming, so yes, of course it is horrible, but not as sudden as my first pass at the story made it seem. Anyway, for me the point was that there was this concern for every person in the room, not just the man and his son, but the cohanim, that the humanity of each person was considered."

"Do you really think so? I mean, pardon me for saying this, but it seems so uncompassionate and legalistic to have some people leave when this happened; it's demeaning to the dead man, isn't it, that his calamity is less important than the status of the cohen?"

Reuven looked at her, trying to assess how to respond. She heard his glare in the pause on the tape. "If you don't get it, you don't, but here's my take and why I'm religious. Each person has a role and a value; we aren't the same: a Cohen isn't a *Yisrael* or a *Levi*, but each is valued. Women and men aren't the same. I like the segmentation. You don't have to understand."

Wendy had gotten defensive. "It's not that I don't understand; I do get that there are these roles. I just don't like it, that's all."

"But who are you to question it? That's how it has always been in Judaism. If you don't like it, that doesn't make it less valid."

"We don't have to agree, I am just asking questions. Look, I appreciate your making the time to do this. Thanks." Wendy sounded smug, even to herself listening. She thought, *I've got to work on saying things in a less abrasive way and not telling people everything I think so that it can be less about me and more about them. Of course I have ideas and opinions, but broadcasting them during an interview is not my task. My task is to put them at ease and let them speak about themselves, not to argue with them. I need to learn to back off and give them space to speak or I could get into trouble. What if Reuven tells his rabbi I'm arguing with him—they could bar me from interviewing people. I've got to be more careful about how I speak . . .*

A few weeks later, Wendy had sent more surveys out to additional girls' yeshivot. Orly told Wendy that, as a reward for her good behavior, she deserved to go out. Orly had decided that her mission was to take Wendy to a new place each time they got together, a Jerusalem coffee shop of the month club. This time they were meeting at Worlds Beyond Words, a bookstore and coffee shop opened recently on Emek Refaim, five blocks from Wendy's apartment. It served organic foods with as much locally grown produce as possible; the big seller was its fresh fruit and vegetable juices with nutritional supplements like ginseng and spirolina. The wares it housed were among the most multicultural in the city: Chinese homeopathic remedies alongside vegan Passover cookbooks, texts on the lives of Sufi mystics and the works of Rabbi Nachman of Bratslav, bracelets whose beads gave off good energy centers, yoga books and multicolored mats and healing crystals. The clientele was both religious and secular, Israeli and foreign—mostly Jews, though there were Christians and Moslems too, and occasionally Thai and Filipino workers came in to obtain particular herbs and spices hard to find elsewhere in the country.

The tables for the café were in the back. There was a full dinner menu, and liquor as well, making it an increasingly popular Thursday night destination. Orly's boyfriend, Nir, would meet them here later. The menu was as eclectic as the merchandise. There was Indian food: spicy curries, samosas, and masalas, with yogurt and mango lassi drinks. There were also Asian stir-fries, as well as at least two entirely raw entrees to cater to devotees of raw food, and a selection of homemade yogurts. The tables in back were surrounded by bookcases with free books, many in English, that patrons left behind because they were moving or leaving the country.

Wendy and Orly entered the store, passing the bulletin board at the front advertising environmentally friendly diapers, qigong classes, Reiki and Rolfing treatments, and all manner of hemp-based products. They walked through the display tables with books: a cross-cultural survey of ideas about luck coexisted with *Jewish Healing Wisdom: Folklore and Fancy* and *The I-Thou Guide to Opening your Partner*. Wendy stopped to browse and picked up a book on *Dreamwork: Using your Unconscious Mind to Achieve your Goals*. Orly flipped through *Love Around the World: Global Secrets of Intimacy*. Wendy didn't like general interest books; she preferred the rigor and precision of solid academic work, knowing that a jury of peers had reviewed and vetted an idea or theory. To her, the writing in the books here was airy and frothy, insubstantial to anyone other than the writer. Each book seemed based solely on itself, to call out, "I'm right. Read me and I'll tell you how to live by tarot cards, or astrology symbols, or Turkish palm reading."

Wendy said to Orly, "Let's eat. I can't take these books on positive thinking and the guilt they put on you if you don't affirm well enough."

"Lighten up," Orly said, holding her book and skimming intently. "Listen to this. Malawi tribes send a newly married couple off into the woods, with only an axe, a cooking pot, and scented oil believed to be an aphrodisiac to see how they fare in the world. Isn't that romantic?"

"An axe?"

"To chop trees for fire wood? Or kill animals?" Orly guessed. "Maybe, to see who would have control of the relationship."

"Violence is necessary to intimacy?"

Orly said, "There is always a certain degree of violation, and exposure, that has to occur to achieve intimacy. That's why we're all so afraid of it."

"It's hard to find a guy you want to expose yourself to completely. I've never felt that way about anyone."

"You never know," Orly said, putting her book on global intimacy back on the table and leading the way to the back where the tables were.

"Hey, there's Dara Glasser. We went to college together. I'll introduce you," Wendy said as she spotted Dara with a group already seated in the café area.

Wendy and Dara had bumped into each other Wendy's first week here, but hadn't seen each other since. Dara was someone Wendy knew casually at Columbia who it was fine to bump into but never to make intentional plans with.

Dara rose from her chair to hug Wendy more effusively than Wendy felt their connection deserved. Wendy returned the hug with less fervor than it was given, then disengaged and said, "Good to see you. This is my friend Orly Markovsky."

"Nice to meet you," Dara said. "How do you guys know each other?"

Orly said, "Camp Kodimoh, many moons ago."

One of the men at the table looked up and said, "Camp Kodimoh. My sister went there. How old are you?"

Wendy and Orly said, "Twenty-six."

"She's twenty-nine. Shelley Stern. Ring a bell?"

"Don't think so," Orly said. To the man, she said, "Orly. Hi," and reached over to shake his hand.

"Julian Stern. Nice to meet you."

This seemed to be the cue for going around with introductions. Next to Julian was a guy who introduced himself as Jason Lessing, then Talia Blaustein from Michigan, Robin Shearer from Ohio, and Noah Lazevsky from Long Island.

"How do you guys know Dara?" Noah asked, looking at Wendy and Orly.

"Undergrad at Columbia. You?" said Wendy.

"I went to Oberlin, but I know Dara from classes at Wisdom of the Heart Yeshiva. I just finished *ulpan* at Hebrew U."

"Really? I did that *ulpan*," said Wendy, noticing him more carefully now. He was fairly cute—brown wavy hair, nice eyes in an indeterminate shade that she couldn't decide was more blue or more gray. Noah's smile was unusual, the gap between his two front teeth giving him a certain kind of innocence, untouched as he was by an orthodontist's hand. As she started a conversation with him, Orly, who had been an undergrad in Ann Arbor, started trying to play Jewish geography with Talia from Michigan.

"What level?" Noah asked.

"Oh . . . Gimel. You?" She wasn't sure whether it would be good if his Hebrew was better or worse than hers.

"*Vov.* That's why I've never seen you. The advanced classes met in different places from the others. What are you doing this year?"

"Writing my dissertation." This was always the awkward moment in a conversation, how to say enough about the topic to keep it on the level of general interest and not too technical.

"On what? I'm in grad school too, Kabbalah at NYU."

"Religion at Princeton."

"One of my professors from Oberlin is at Princeton now."

"Mark Sokoloff?" Wendy guessed. "He's on my committee."

"Watch out. He's a dick."

Wendy laughed. "I thought it was just to me. I didn't know that was his general reputation."

"*Oh yeah,*" Noah said emphatically. "I can't tell you how many people got screwed because he forgot to write their recommendations, or missed deadlines. He just didn't care."

"He's only a reader on my dissertation, not my main adviser. Still, I would like to have someone on my committee who was . . . well . . . less of a dick, as you articulate so clearly." She laughed again. Noticing Noah's navy blue crocheted kipah with his name in light blue with white edging, she said, "Wasn't he nicer to you because you're religious?"

"I didn't wear a kipah then. I don't always even now. Most of the time, but I'm not quite there yet." He gave her a smile with that disarmingly cute gap between his two front teeth.

"I'm not religious either. I study religion, but I prefer observing to participating." She smiled back at him, uncertain what was next.

"Do you want me to get you a chair? I see some extras at that table," he said.

"Sure."

He walked a few tables over to get a chair and brought one for Wendy and one for Orly. After Wendy was seated, he said, "I hope you don't mind my asking, but why study religion if you aren't part of it?"

"I won't say I'm not part of it, I'm Jewish," she added defensively.

"I mean, why this? Why not Zulu rituals or Brazilian martial arts?"

"Israel is the Jewish homeland. I'm curious about how ideas of home and return shape people's lives and narratives. Even in the short time I've been here, I've seen this place, this city, exert this tremendous hold on people. Shabbat here is . . . special. I like it—but that doesn't mean I'm not going to check my e-mail or turn a light on or off." She looked at him and saw that he was listening, so she continued, "What interests me is how individuals see themselves and their lives in relation to it, so I'm writing about American baalei teshuvah in Israel and how they discuss their path of becoming religious."

"Smart way to get at the question—doing oral interviews and finding out how they see themselves forging these connections?"

"Exactly." She looked at him again. "Noah?" This was the first time she'd addressed him by name and she wanted to be sure she had it right. "You're the first person I've talked to here who actually gets what I'm doing. Thank you."

"It sounds wonderful."

She wanted to shift the conversation to him, so she could give him a compliment too. "Why do you study Kabbalah?"

"I have some conflicting passions, you know?" Wendy wasn't sure, but nodded politely, noting favorably his use of the word "passion." He continued, "Shabbos is really important to me. I want it to be the center of my week—looking towards it, planning for it. Learning, trying to grow in Torah, being an ethical person."

"Where's the conflict?" Wendy asked, curious as to what would make those lovely gray blue eyes clouded.

He looked at her, unsure what to divulge. "I don't know if I'm committed to grad school. Maybe I should go to rabbinical school, but I'm not sure. Which one? Hopefully I'll resolve it by the end of the year."

Wendy felt sorry for him, in his confusion. It gave her a tremendous sense of relief that, at least for the next two years, she knew what she was doing: writing her dissertation. "I felt the same way, not being sure about grad school till I got my Fulbright."

"You have a Fulbright?" he said, impressed. "That's amazing.

SIX

New Jerusalem?

Its members renounced the pleasures of this world, for the earth and all that it held to them was but a kind of illusion, and the true reality was the New Jerusalem toward which they were longing.
—ISAK DINESEN, *Babette's Feast*

Wendy was in the office of Rabbi Gibber at Yeshivat Temimei Nefesh, the men's division of the RISE yeshiva network. It was patterned on the model of the office of his counterpart at the women's yeshiva. Piles of papers everywhere, bookshelves, a lending library. The only element missing was the colorful inspirational posters proclaiming, "Keep rising." Did men *not* need images to encourage them to rise? She would have to make a note about that. The rabbi was sitting behind his desk across from her, tapping the tips of his fingers together, the door behind Wendy ajar for modesty.

"This is a highly unusual situation," he said.

"I'm giving you an opportunity. You can turn a negative into a positive. That's a mitzvah, right?" she said hopefully. She didn't want to say more than she had to about Donny because she didn't want to get him in trouble or kicked out of the yeshiva, but also so that she wouldn't be viewed as a threat, a potentially provocative and available young woman, disrupting everything the yeshiva stood for. She had already given the rabbi a hint of a suggestion that one of his students had acted inappropriately with her and that she could make this public and besmirch the yeshiva's name if he didn't cooperate. Though not in so many words, she was muting her naturally blunt personality for this, trying to speak ever so delicately and subtly, to hint without stating outright.

"Explain to me what you're doing here," Rabbi Gibber said.

"I am writing about the ways baalei teshuvah tell their stories when they understand themselves as religious people." She saw that she hadn't yet blundered and she had his attention, so she continued, "My survey can help you two ways. You can get quotes from students to use in your promotional material. And, you can learn what a student won't tell you but will write in an anonymous survey about having trouble with his, ah . . ."

"His *yetzer ha-ra*, evil inclination," the rabbi said euphemistically.

"His *yetzer ha-ra*"—Wendy was proud of herself that she got the inflection down pat—"must affect other students too. You could find out and try to help them if you knew the problems they were grappling with. I could even let you add your own questions and give out forms with yours and mine together. That way, you could find out what you want."

The rabbi looked straight past Wendy at the back wall of his office, his eyes focused in thought.

"Hand out your sample questionnaires today. I'll have someone get back to you about our part in the next few weeks. It's more complicated, the second section of your project interviewing students . . . Even if there is no *yichud*. It's too close to *ma'aras ayin*, looking improper."

"What if the interviews are in a public place, like a hotel lobby?"

"It might appear you are on a *shidduch* date. That wouldn't look acceptable."

"If I interviewed students in the offices here with the female secretaries outside?"

"Unmarried men and women shouldn't be spending time together."

"Don't you want to be able to say on a brochure or other promotional material that this is such a fine institution that people come from Ivy League schools in the States, from Princeton, to observe the students? Isn't that something you'd like to tell your supporters?" She saw him nod. "Can't we find a way to make this work? I . . . like being in Israel, the Yiddishkeit. My grandmother keeps kosher." She pulled out all the stops saying this last bit, in the hope that it would work again.

He began, "Rabbi Lifter is permitting it." She did not interrupt but gazed at him hopefully. He continued, "If you interviewed students in these offices, with open doors and others present outside, yes, it could work. Dress modestly. You've already seen how easily . . . distractable . . . our students are. If your grandmother is religious, G-d willing, you'll find your way back too. I'm glad you spoke to me—our work here is too important to let one student's *yetzer hara* distract us. Your project should have much *hatzlacha*, success. It's good for you to be around religious people."

Wendy was too jubilant to be annoyed that he seemed concerned with helping her so she could be around religious people and perhaps return herself, rather than because she actually had serious professional ambitions. *He would not be so patronizing with a male graduate student,* she intuited. No matter, the patronizing might just be his personality; for herself, she was getting closer to her research goals and that was the most important thing now.

She left a stack of questionnaires with self-addressed and stamped envelopes on his desk for Rabbi Gibber to distribute

Wendy had been looking forward to this date at the Jerusalem Cinematheque with Noah for the longest time. They hadn't seen each other in over a week, since she was spending her time at the seminaries and yeshivas, passing out questionnaires, and doing reading at the university library on Mount Scopus. Noah was taking classes on Mount Scopus and at Wisdom, but somehow their schedules didn't jibe and they weren't ever at the university at the same time.

Wendy had seen a poster in the neighborhood for a ten-day film festival, A Moveable Feast: Food on Film, and walked over to the Cinematheque, descending into the Hinnom Valley, next to the Yemin Moshe neighborhood where she had been to the lecture with Orly. On a whim, she looked over the film schedule and bought two Thursday night tickets for *Babette's Feast*, picking it over *Eat Drink Man Woman* and hoping Noah would come, and figuring Todd from her Fulbright group or Orly or even Dara would be her alternatives. Of all the films in the docket of showings, this one interested her because her grad school friend Matt Lewis had written a paper on it for his Religion on Film class. She remembered Matt's explanation of cinema and the sacred, as she stood looking around the fancy lobby, much nicer than many other public buildings due to its foreign patrons and the support of Mayor Teddy Kollek.

Compared to other art forms, film was one that had an ability to disclose the holy since it directed viewers' attention to the vividness of reality and the ineffable mysteries in the presence of concrete persons, places, and events. She was annoyed with Noah for not being here yet when the movie was going to start shortly. Thinking about what Matt had said, Wendy found his rhetoric pretentious and even slightly bogus, but she was still curious about this film, with what he said were the most gorgeous shots of exquisite food, as well as a story line about the transference of the physical to the spiritual realm. Glimpsing the poster for the movie on the wall opposite, she saw a huge shot of one flaky round pastry shell with a rich velvety brown sauce encasing and enveloping the head of the quail, impossibly delectable looking. The note at the bottom of the poster pronounced it "Cailles en Sarcophage." Wendy remembered proofreading Matt's paper as a favor to him. One of the things discussed was the symbolism of this central dish, the quail, which were positioned to look as though they were rising up out of their pastry shell tomb, being resurrected there on the table. The delicacy of the food in the photo certainly convinced Wendy that eating this food could effect transformation.

Glancing at her watch, pacing, Wendy decided she would give him two minutes and then give the usher Noah's ticket to give him when he arrived.

She was walking to the usher when she heard her name, pronounced properly and with an American accent. She turned to see Noah, and even with her annoyance at his late arrival, liked what she saw: the raffishly boyish gait, extending up from the ground with the white Converse High Tops, broadening up to his nicely faded and soft jeans—the kind that take time to get that way, not purchased already faded—and blue V-neck cotton sweater over a maroon T-shirt, up to his face, with a bit of a five o'clock shadow—always a sexy thing though it could be an annoyance when kissing—and that wavy hair, definitely on the longish side and in need of a cut, but she hadn't been his girlfriend long enough to have the sort of possessive attachment that gave her the right to tell him it was time for a trim. They hadn't kissed yet—could she consider herself his girlfriend? Once he looked at her with those bluish grayish eyes and gave her the gap-toothed smile, she was putty in his hands, lateness or anything else forgiven. *He was just so damned cute,* she thought to herself, and was glad to walk into the theater with him as he put his arm around her after they gave the usher their tickets.

But once seated, Noah didn't put his arm around her again, much as she desired the coziness of his touch, the comfort of being encased in his arms. When she did put her hand over his on the armrest between their seats, he removed it almost instantaneously, saying he had to go to the restroom during the ads before the movie began. When he returned, no intimacy was resumed.

For Wendy the movie was wonderful. She wondered to herself why she didn't go to movies more, why she didn't take more interest in this medium capable of creating something so astounding, so rich in imagery, the focus on reality able to call up some kind of inner depth. The cook in the story refocuses all those who partake of her meal. She has a chance to do her utmost as a culinary artist, to become the "great artist that God meant you to be" in the words, she remembered, of the opera singer in the story.

There was a moment in the movie when the large tortoise who would become the delicacy of turtle soup made his entrance, appearing at first like a "greenish black stone" until his "snake-like" head jabbed out from his body, appearing, on the face of the woman who sees him, "monstrous" and "terrible." Seeing the actress's face registering the extent of the horror of this animal, the theatergoers heard a loud boom from somewhere outside the theater. Wendy was so engaged in the action on screen that she thought nothing of it; Noah shot out of his seat without saying anything to Wendy, who didn't notice his absence until she turned to her left a few moments later to notice the empty chair. He returned, and when she asked him what had happened, he said no one was sure yet. He didn't tell her that the sirens of ambulances were heard outside the very well soundproofed theater, money from abroad having been pumped into the local economy to make such luxuries as thick walls possible.

Wendy left the theater sated with pleasure at the film, excited to discuss it with Noah. When she and Noah were in the lobby she stretched out her arms, flinging them wide to her sides as far an expanse as they would reach, and said, "Whoa, that was an amazing cinematic experience. Didn't you love it?"

Noah looked at her. And kept looking. What had she done wrong? Why was he so stone-faced and unresponsive?

"Wendy, I heard ambulances after that boom."

Her arms were at her sides now, their soaring buoyancy of a few moments ago replaced by a dull weight too heavy for breezy motion. "Noah, you don't always have to think the worst. Stop having such a negative imagination, that something awful has happened. What did the general say in the movie: 'For tonight I have learned, dear sister, that in this world anything is possible.' That's the world I want to live in, one in which anything is possible." She frowned at him. "Orly told me the café here has an amazing view. Let's get some coffee or something."

Noah didn't know exactly how to argue with Wendy's assessment of his character. "I don't have a 'negative imagination.'" He put quotes in the air with his fingers, sarcastically. "I *heard* ambulances." He smiled wryly. "You haven't been here as long as I have. Things happen." He planted his hands in the pockets of his jeans and gestured with his elbow. "We'll have coffee. You got the movie tickets, so this is on me, okay?" he softened. As they walked toward the café with the view of the walls of the Old City, he said, "I think there was a *pigua*. I was almost in one this summer."

His close to whispered statement didn't enable Wendy to hear him, as she was walking ahead, towards the café, and hoping that this little tiff wouldn't affect her chances of finally getting a kiss tonight. She hoped he liked the way she looked, walking in front of him, trying to put a bit of a sashay in her step, her skirt on the short side, significantly above her knee, paired with leggings and clunky clogs on this cooling fall day, but she hoped still giving her a provocative look. Noah was looking around, trying to see out the windows to get a sense of what might be going on outside.

They seated themselves and Wendy asked Noah whether he was hungry, had he eaten. "You know, I can't remember. Have I?" he looked at her puzzled.

She didn't see his look, but kept looking at the menu, wanting to order something nice but not wanting to go over his limited student budget when most of the items listed were on the pricier side. Not looking up at him over the menu, she said, "Should we split something if you aren't sure if you're hungry or not?" not unkindly, just being practical.

Impatiently, he said, "Don't you want to know what happened outside, Wendy? Don't you care?"

She put the menu down in front of her, laid her hands in two balled up fists on top. "I just saw a really incredible movie. The fun of going to a movie with someone else is to discuss it with them, and I'd like to have some fun tonight. Why do you think Babette did it? Was she doing the right thing?"

Noah too balled up his hands and leaned his body forward over them to talk to Wendy across the table. "And fun for me is to share what I am going through with the person I'm with. I told you before, I was almost in a *pigua* this summer, and I think this is another. I'm worried and want to go outside and see what's happening."

Wendy startled, sat up straight. "What? You never told me anything like that," a sense of anger that he had never revealed such a critical part of himself to her masking her guilt for not somehow knowing or intuiting that something had happened to him to upset him and make him grimace as he was now doing. She felt guilt for all kinds of things; she thought that somehow if she were a more sensitive, caring person, she would have been able to intuit this even if her feelings on the matter logically made no sense. How could she not have realized something was going on with him? All she was thinking about—as usual, she rebuked herself—was her own need.

Noah leaned back away from her, a look of anguish coming over him. "It never came up." He ran his hand through his hair and said, "Really, what is there to say? I . . . it's too painful to talk about."

Wendy was silenced. "I'm sorry?" was the limit of her conversational creativity in the face of the tragedy Noah had experienced.

"It's not your fault. You didn't plant the bomb."

"No, but I meant . . ." Wendy put her fingers unconsciously to her hair and began to twirl it girlishly, "what I want to say is . . . I'm sorry it happened to you."

He sipped the water in front of him. "These last few months have been hard, really hard. I think about Sam so much; it's just so . . . wrong . . . that he's no longer alive. I've never had a friend who died."

"When I was little, I had a friend who went sledding and hurt her leg somehow, twisted it. She got a fever and her parents took her to the emergency room. The whole thing on her leg somehow developed into an embolism, and she died in the hospital. It was really hard to understand. How could my friend not be there anymore?"

"That's about where I am. Just . . . unfathomable. I think that's it. And Sam . . . he was such a special person. I know people always say that when someone has died, but in his case . . . His dissertation? 'The Kisses of God's

Mouth?' Just from the title you get a sense of what kind of provocative and brilliant and wonderful person he was." Noah shook his head. "I was the last person to see him really alive and vital. We were at this bookstore, Berger Books, on King George. Have you been?"

Wendy nodded no.

"Oh." Noah's sigh oozed with pleasure. "I'll have to take you. It's key to the intellectual history of this city. Gershom Scholem had a list there of books he was looking for. It was called 'alu leshalom,' which literally means 'go up in peace' but also 'go up to Scholem.' The Berger family who own it came from Germany in the 1930s with whatever merchandise they could bring. The joke is that you never know the provenance of the oldest books; they could still be from the original shipment they brought from Germany. Really.

"Sounds sort of like the Ideal Bookstore in New York, over the office at Amsterdam and 115th, if you know it."

"Yeah, same vibe. So Sam was showing me these books and he read me something from this book *The Divine Kiss: Mystical and Rabbinic View* that talks about this idea that death by divine kiss is a death that is a climax, a sharing of God's breath, physically painless, being raised up to the world of entirely spiritual perceptions . . ."

"That's what he was writing about?" Wendy shook herself. "It's just too . . . I don't know. Intense? What was he like? I mean as a person, not a dissertation topic."

Noah thought for a minute. "Yes, intense, and" he thought for a minute how to say this, "noticeably handsome, to those of both sexes. I mean, he just had this look that would turn heads. Do you know what I mean? There is a sort of classical beauty that, when you notice it, you say, 'Oh, that is a person who is beautiful.' And then there is heart-stopping beauty that literally made drivers stop when he was crossing the street, just to stare at him. It happened when we were on our way to the bookstore. Seriously."

"What a guy." Wendy had no idea how to react to this information.

Noah looked straight at her and said, wistfully, "Yep, what a guy." He looked at his watch. "You know, maybe if the waiter doesn't come we should just go. Is that okay? Can you take a raincheck for coffee?"

Wendy stood up, annoyed. "Yeah, sure, let's go. You're right, I have things to do tomorrow." She thought to herself, *Why isn't this working? Did I say something wrong? Do I have bad breath? What is it that he just doesn't seem to want to connect with me now?*

They walked out of the theater and, in an effort to patch things up a bit, Wendy asked, "What was your favorite scene in the movie?"

They walked slowly up the hill towards Keren HaYesod. "I think the moments when we are aware that the table Babette has prepared and the feast itself are a kind of grace that comes over them, that there is this dissolution of what came before and a new reality being shaped in front of them. It was so beautifully done, the filming. What was the line—'That which we have chosen is given us, and that which we have refused is, also and at the same time, granted us. Ay, that which we have rejected is poured upon us abundantly.'" He turned to look at her. "Your favorite part?"

She kept pace with him, hearing his breath close to her, and replied, "I think when Babette reveals to us her true nature, that she is indeed an artist, a cook at the Café Anglais, and that as an artist she will never be poor because an artist has something of which other people know nothing. That was so beautiful." She added, "And then, when she said that the cry of the artist is 'Give me leave to do my utmost.'" Wendy started getting choked up without knowing why.

Noah didn't notice the quaver in her voice and her emotion, and suddenly both of their attention was diverted by the incontrovertible sounds of sirens, followed by their appearance, zooming by them, a convoy, a roaring fleet going to conduct the injured to safety.

Wendy felt utterly defeated by this. Noah had been right.

Noah took her hand suddenly, grabbing it roughly, as a scared child would hold a rope that will allow him safe exit. Wendy was pleased despite the harshness of the grip. Was she getting somewhere with him?

The ambulances were all going to the right, and Wendy's apartment was to the left so they turned that way. Noah kept holding her hand; instead of reassuring her with his presence by her side, he seemed to weigh her down, his hand pressing her, making it physically harder for her to walk.

Wendy wanted to be helpful and comforting, and asked, "I guess this must be hard for you, bringing back what happened this summer? You can tell me if you want."

Noah didn't respond, and they walked on with the blast of sirens detonating in the background. In the window of a flower store, Atelier Delphine,

Wendy spotted tulips in a sharp yellow, a canary yellow, glowing out, their beauty filling the window. Its display area revealed other arrangements, all in yellow: flowers in tall white teardrop-shaped vases with a curved bottom, flowers in silver buckets and peeking out of wooden birdhouses, all in extravagant profusion. Wendy hadn't noticed this store before and wanted to call Noah's attention to loveliness even in the midst of tragedy, but she knew that he wouldn't have an interest. Maybe he feared the realm of the physical somehow, and did not want to give in to it.

"I don't think I can explain it to you, Wendy. I'm sorry. It's . . . excruciating. Just hearing the sirens. I went to the hospital to find him after they took him in an ambulance . . . I sincerely hope you never have to see anything like it."

Wendy felt like an insulated kid, someone who hadn't experienced tragedy, naïve, untouched by the things that matter in this world. So, glumly disappointed in the failure of the date, in Noah's inability to rouse himself out of thoughts of the past and pay attention to her, she trudged on, thoughts of the extravagant food in the movie and flowers in the shop providing cheering ballast to the grim pictures forming in her imagination every time an ambulance filled with victims whisked past them.

She wanted to tell Noah just to go home, that she didn't need him to walk her, but didn't want to insult him or hurt his feelings, so she continued, plodding hand in hand.

"'The vain illusions of this earth had dissolved before their eyes like smoke and they had seen the universe as it really is.' I thought that was so true. I wish all the pain and suffering of the world could dissolve and only the good true things could be here." Wendy startled herself by speaking.

"I . . . I'm afraid of the physical world, of its dangers, how harmful it can be, of seeking beauty for the wrong reasons, for pleasure only, not for love or creating something of lasting value. I"—he stopped and then started again— "I know you are impatient with me and with my feelings, Wendy. I just need . . . a little bit of time to figure everything out, about the *pigua*, about Sam. I like you . . . it's just hard for me to be with someone else now, to be in a relationship. I hope you understand."

"Noah, that's fine. It's okay to . . . want to have some time. I like you. I'll wait. Do what you need to do for yourself," Wendy added, she hoped generously. She felt reassured. All this didn't have to do with her and her desirability but with the trauma he had experienced, seeing a friend die.

At Mishael 5, they parted, hugs exchanged.

As Wendy entered her gate, she realized the news on the radio was only in Hebrew at this hour, and she'd be hopelessly lost if she attempted to listen. She had no TV in her apartment. She knocked on her landlady Amalia Hausman's door.

Amalia looked through the keyhole to see her visitor. Amalia didn't cover her hair at home as she did on the street, and she wanted to check whether the visitor was one for whom she needed to don a head covering. Amalia opened the door and said in her German-accented English, "Vundy, I'm so glad to see you safe, yes? Come in, please. You heard about the *pigua*, not so far from here? I vas on the four bus yesterday . . ." Amalia gave an involuntary shudder. "No matter, we'll manage, *yiyeh tov.*" She looked at Wendy as she closed the door behind her. "You're not going back to the States, are you?"

"I wasn't planning to, no. I need to finish my research. Do they know what happened at the *pigua*?"

"Ve'll vatch the news together," Amalia said, leading the way down the hall into her living room and gesturing for Wendy to follow her. The screen was projecting images of a deconstructed bus, its insides splayed out on the pavement.

"Do you vant tea?"

Wendy wasn't ordinarily a tea drinker, preferring the stronger caffeine of coffee. "Thanks, Amalia. Tea would be nice," Wendy assented.

"Sit. I'll be right back." Amalia gestured to the sofa in front of the TV. While waiting, Wendy tried to follow the Hebrew of the news, but mostly read the English captions at the bottom of the screen and veered between averting her eyes from grisly scenes of mangled human body parts and staring at the gruesome visions on the screen with voyeuristic fascination. Wendy's vocabulary was now enriched with new Hebrew words she wished she didn't need to know—for *injury, serious, stable, to be hospitalized, bomb, explosion, terrorist.*

Amalia called out, "Sugar? Milk?"

"Both, please," Wendy responded.

Amalia returned with the tea and a plate with a few cookies.

They looked at the TV together.

"It's not the first time, " Amalia said, still gazing at the reporter standing in front of the ultra-Orthodox men gathering human remains at the scene.

Wendy turned her head to look at her companion. "Sorry? What?"

"This . . . destruction and devastation. It has happened before; since the Bayit Rishon, the first . . . em . . .Temple . . . was destroyed, people have wanted Jews to leave. We haven't."

"No, I guess not." Wendy was sipping her tea carefully when she saw something in Hebrew on the bottom of the screen that made her hands unsteady. She spilled tea all over her lap. "Amalia, do you see that name there, at the bottom? It says Binyamin Margolis, twenty-seven, residence Scarsdale, New York, United States. Why is his name there?"

Amalia looked again at the screen. "The *niftzaim* . . . em . . . injury? People with injuries?" she added. "You know this Binyamin Margolis?"

Wendy gulped down hot tea to brace herself. "He is in my fellowship group. I don't know him *well,* but I know him. Our families in the States know each other too. I . . ."

"He's injured. Ve don't know how badly. Maybe it is light?"

"Maybe." Wendy was in shock. Someone she knew was injured.

"These bombings are a terrible thing . . . any time, anywhere. My husband, he was killed . . . twenty-seven years ago. At the Supersol Grocery, here in the neighborhood. A bomb. He'd been in an antiterrorism unit in the army, and went closer to try to stop the bomber. He couldn't stop it, but he prevented greater loss. He was the only one killed. All others were saved."

"I'm sorry."

"Thank you. I still miss him every day. But life goes on. I'm most sorry for the grandchildren, who didn't know him."

Wendy wanted to go back to her apartment to change her tea soaked skirt. But after Amalia's disclosure about her husband, Wendy felt it would be rude to leave her alone. She had to stay a few more minutes and she also craved more knowledge about the *pigua*, what exactly happened, and how many were injured.

Amalia shook her head at the screen. "*Oof, nora. Mashehu. Mamash nora* . . . Terrible, awful. At least seventeen injured, perhaps more; that's what they know. We got through the siege of '48 in this city, the Gulf War a few years ago. This too, you'll see, it'll get better, *b'ezrat Hashem.*"

Hearing about these losses made her want to talk to her parents, to make sure they weren't worrying, even if Amalia were to think her rude. "Thank you for the tea, Amalia. I'd better go upstairs and call my parents. I don't want them to worry."

Amalia took the teacup and said, "Any time you vant to vatch the news, feel free to come down. I alvays vatch. I'll help with Hebrew."

"Let's hope the news is better next time," Wendy said, standing up.

She went up to her apartment and started calling her friends. Once inside, Wendy called Todd to vent. "The *matzav* in this country is totally screwing me over! It ruined my date with Noah tonight!"

Todd laughed appreciatively, "*Mon Cherie*, start at the beginning, *je ne comprends pas.*"

"So I planned this great date with Noah. We saw this incredible movie, *Babette's Feast,* at the Cinematheque, very romantic; but there was a boom in the middle of the movie and Noah ran out to see what it was. We didn't know anything about what happened, and tried to go to that really nice restaurant there and have coffee, but the waiter never came and Noah was antsy to find out the deal with the noise, and we left. As soon as we got up to Keren Haye-sod, we saw the ambulances."

"But," Todd said, his voice imitating a therapeutic professional, "you feel guilty that you aren't concerned with the injured, only with the fact that your date is flipped out."

"Exactly! He said it's hard to be with someone else now. I don't know what he meant."

"Um, Wendy dear, are you sitting down?"

"Yes, why?"

"I'm going to tell you something you may not, no probably don't want, to hear, but I am going to tell you for your own good. I don't want to see you get hurt, so forgive me for not saying this earlier but . . . I wasn't quite sure how to."

"What? Now I'm worried. Just tell me."

"Okay, Sam was gay. You didn't have any way of knowing that since you weren't in the country when he was alive. So, this is who Sam was. He was incredibly gorgeous—thick black curly hair, carefully cut to an appropriate length, dark brown eyes, almost olive-toned skin, smooth and perfectly unblemished, lithe runner's body, with muscles evident but not overly large.

He took advantage of his looks to be incredibly promiscuous. There have been Shabbat dinners when I've looked around and realized that every person there had slept with him, except me, sadly. I don't think I was beautiful enough for him. So your Noah may not be entirely on your team. I think you need to know that."

"Oh." She thought for a minute and added, "Hmm. This does change things a bit. It definitely isn't about me if he's not on my team." She stopped again and said, "So why is he bothering to date me? What's that about?"

"I can't tell you—must be that *you* are irresistible, my dear. Maybe he isn't ready to switch sides entirely and you're his last try to play for the ladies? I don't know."

"I have no interest in dating a gay man, that's for sure. What's the point if he can't desire me? Strangely, I feel much better now."

"Whatever floats your boat."

"You are *the* most amazing friend, Todd. Coffee Friday? Your favorite waiter's table?" Todd had a crush on one of the waiters who worked at Caffit on Fridays.

"Sure thing."

Wendy decided to make herself some warm milk to relax, and went over to the fridge. She got out a saucepan she'd bought at Mahane Yehuda, poured the milk into a mug to measure it, and poured it into the pan. As she stirred the milk over the flame, she thought about how comforting it was that she had people to speak with, friends who cared about her—or cared enough to fight with her, Wendy thought idly, scraping scalded milk from the bottom of the pot. Would she too be scorched by her year here, singed by getting too close to the heat? She poured the milk into her mug, sprinkled some cinnamon on top, and went over to her dining table, piled with books and papers. She put the milk down and found her diary. She began to write, and to sip, comforting herself that, since violence had hit her circle once, it wouldn't again. She would be okay this year, she told herself as she wrote it to confirm her hopes.

Finally, it was one in the morning, so it would be 6:00 p.m. in New Bay and at least one of her parents would be home. She dialed and listened, the long pauses between rings on international calls signaling the vast distances between the speakers.

"Wendy, so nice to hear your voice. Everything okay?" Wendy usually called on a Saturday or Sunday, so her mother, Sylvia, was surprised to hear from her now, a Wednesday evening, knowing it was one in the morning in Israel. "What time is it for you?"

"I'm fine, Mom, no need to worry, but there was a bomb on a bus here. A boy from my Fulbright group, Benj Margolis, was injured."

Wendy could hear an audible gasp. "Joanie's son? I just saw her at the hairdresser—you know Aunt Gail was her bridesmaid. Oh my God, Wendy, we'll send a ticket right away," she heard her mother say, "Let me call the travel agent. I'll be so relieved to have you back, sweetheart."

"I'm not coming back. I just called to let you know I'm okay."

"Wendy, it's dangerous. You don't have to stay—I'm sure you would be allowed to keep your Fulbright money and do research here. It's a government program—they'll probably tell all of you to come home."

"My research is here; my life is here. Don't tell me what to do."

Sylvia cleared her throat audibly. "Wendy . . . honey . . . no one wants US citizens in a danger zone. Tell you what, I'll have Daddy call Nita Lowey, our congresswoman. She went to junior high with him, you know."

"Mom, I don't care what Congresswoman Lowey or anyone else says, I am staying here."

"Darling, no one wants you in danger. I'm sure the government will decide that's what is best."

"Nita Lowey is known as a strong supporter of Israel. It won't look so good if she encourages people to leave. You know, I *am* an adult. I can decide what to do. By the way, I just started dating someone, a nice Jewish boy. Happy?"

"Come home with him. I'm sure his parents want him back also."

"Mom, I love you and Daddy and don't want you to worry. I'll be back in June. In the meantime, you're welcome to visit."

"Sweetie, you know we can't leave your Grandma Essie, and she isn't well enough to travel. Especially to a dangerous place like Israel. Be realistic."

"She could stay with Joel or Lisa. Or Uncle Richie or Aunt Gail. You're not her only child."

"Joel and Lisa have families of their own. They couldn't have Essie with them day and night with their own little kids. Gail and Richie . . . I don't know. We just can't visit this year." Her mother paused. "I hear someone in the driveway. Let me see if your father is home." There was stillness on the line as Sylvia walked over to the door to the attached garage and opened it. "Arthur, quick. Wendy's on the phone. She's okay but there was a bus bombing and Joanie Margolis's son was injured."

Wendy could hear her father's steps quicken as he came to the phone. "Wendy, honey, are you okay? We'll send a ticket if you want to come back."

"Hi, Daddy, I'm okay. I feel . . . I don't know . . . a bit shaken, but I like being here. I didn't expect this."

"We'll bring you home. Anytime. Just say the word, sweetie."

"Honestly, Daddy, I'm okay."

"Your mother and I only want what's best for you. You need to consider how important this research is against your need to be somewhere dangerous. You could do what you are doing right here in New York. Go up to Monsey, or to Borough Park," he added, and then continued. "I have a cousin, Kenny. I haven't stayed in touch, but he became baal teshuva. He lives in . . . Flatbush somewhere?"

Wendy started pacing, holding the phone to her ear, trying not to get angry. "I know you're concerned, Daddy. I need to stay here. I'm sorry to worry you but I need to finish this research."

"I know how hard you've been working on this degree, but your safety is more important. If, God forbid, something happened to you, this project would not be worth more than your life."

Wendy took a deep breath. "Dad, you're right. No project is worth more than a life. This is important and I want you to respect that. It feels to me like you and Mom really don't care about my career. Maybe that isn't true, but it feels that way."

"No career is more important than anything else. I work long hours, but it is for my family. I've always put you first, even if you don't realize it. Family first—and your life. *Pikuah nefesh*—you know that?"

"I do, actually. Saving your life comes before almost any other mitzvah. The person I just started dating, Noah, is sort of religious. He's teaching me things."

"Why don't you and Noah both come back to America?"

"I haven't asked him, Dad."

"After this, he'll be ready to come home."

"I wouldn't be so sure. It might make him want to stay more. Anyway, I just want to let you and Mom know I'm fine, I love you, I'm having a good time, and working hard. I like living here, you know. Shabbat, it's just . . ."

Her father called to her mother, "Syl . . . steel yourself. Buy some new dishes. Wendy's starting to be religious. I can tell. This is what happened to my cousin."

"I'm *not* becoming religious. All I said is that I like Shabbat, seeing people relax, few cars in the streets, everyone buying flowers to bring home. It's a nice feeling, everything slowing down . . . I wish you and Mom wouldn't see me as your baby."

"Okay, okay." Her father paused and called to her mother, "Do you want to add anything, Syl, or shall I say good-bye? We have to meet the Fischmans at the restaurant."

She heard her mother call, "Just tell her to be careful, Artie. I have to finish getting dressed."

"Hear that, sweetheart? Your mother says to be careful. You'll do that, okay?"

"Yes, Dad. Think about getting a ticket to visit me here, but if not, see you in June."

"If you want to come back, we'll foot the bill. And Noah too. Keep calling. It's so good to hear your voice."

She hung up, relieved that she had kept her temper. She hated that they assumed they still had complete jurisdiction over her life, even though she was twenty-six. Would that ever end? Her own mother had already given birth to her oldest brother, Joel, at twenty-six; did Grandma Essie treat her as a grown-up then, or assume she still needed help? She wanted them to treat her like an adult, whether she was married and had kids or not. They could say they wanted her to come home, but now that she was an adult, had a fellowship and the financial independence it brought her, they could not force her to come back. She would be able to do this project, with or without their support. This last thought was comforting to her as she got ready to go to sleep.

When Wendy got to the Har Hatzofim Library the next day and installed herself in her carrel, she opened her literature review file and tried to work on it. All she could think about was Noah and Sam. And was she even allowed to be mad at him for misleading her since Sam was now dead?

Maybe they were just friends and Noah happened to be with him at the end? No reason to assume being friends with a gay man or woman makes you gay; that is just silly. But, what did he say last night? She racked her brain, and Noah's voice floated into her consciousness. *"I like you . . . it's just hard for me to be with someone else now, to be in a relationship."* Why did he say that? Someone else? Was he trying to tell her there *was* something between him and Sam, that Sam had been a *someone* to him? Couldn't be . . . Todd had to be wrong, not about Sam—sounds obvious what his proclivities were—but Noah . . . He seemed so interested and charming when they first met, that adorable gap-toothed smile and those lovely eyes. He definitely had eyes for her; no one in the room could have missed the heat generated when they met. They sat the whole time, speaking only to each other, at a table full of people. Noah was *not* gay, Wendy was certain, and he wouldn't pretend to something he didn't feel. Would he?

Oh, this was useless, sitting in the carrel, the grand view of all of Jerusalem from one of the pivotal elevations of the city, always important strategically, which the panorama made clear. She could see everything but her own work. Justifying her procrastination, something she seemed to be getting better and better at, Wendy decided that, sometimes, it was more valuable to let your mind drift off and go elsewhere so that when you returned to the task you could focus better. It was true, she knew; it wasn't just an excuse. Anyway, until she knew more about the Noah/Sam thing she wasn't going to be good for much else.

So she trudged over to the reference librarian's desk and said that she wanted information on a *pigua* that took place over the summer in which an American student, Sam Handelman, was killed. After a solicitous question about whether Wendy had known him—as the librarian knew a number of students who had—she pointed out something that oblivious Wendy hadn't noticed before, a column that appeared to be a book, in the corner. The librarian told her that the artist had donated it here; he specialized in public art and had made it in Sam's memory, and knew the library where Sam had spent the most time in Israel would be the right place for it. One was going to be installed in his memory at Yale too, cast in bronze and placed outside the Beinecke Library. The column appeared to be a huge book, frayed edges, bindings jagged as the whole apparition twirled this way and that, looking unstable, though there was a metal rod at its center, securing it. The librarian explained that the title, *Yad va'shem* "a monument and a name," had come to the artist while hearing the speech that Sam's dissertation advisor gave at the airport send-off for his corpse. Wendy shuddered, and as they walked to the microfilms, the librarian said that the pages were printouts of the dissertation that had been handed in thus far, the uncompleted work cut off, as the ragged edges of the pages were never to be finished.

"Never to be finished," echoed in Wendy's mind as she followed the librarian.

At the microfiches, she rolled the *Jerusalem Post* to the date in the summer that the *pigua* had occurred. They found the front page article, "Beautiful life of scholarship and friendship shattered by bus bomb," about the death of Samuel Handelman, twenty-five, of Scarsdale, summa cum laude graduate of Yale, who had studied at the Sorbonne his junior year and was writing his dissertation in Kabbalah at Department of Near Eastern and Judaic Studies at NYU. The librarian left Wendy, telling her to be sure to ask again if she wanted anything else, and Wendy read hungrily. She read what the professor at Hebrew U. who was supervising Sam's work had said about him. Avishai Or, Wendy knew from the Fulbrighters who were working with him, had a reputation for being an impossible hard-ass, nothing ever good enough for his absurdly high standards. The newspaper article actually mentioned that Or was "putting so much emotion on such open display when he was normally so carefully regulated, grief seemed to tear Professor Or out of being the person he usually was," as he spoke of Sam's work. He told the crowd, according to the article, about "the phenomenon of death by divine kiss in his dissertation, 'Dreaming of Kisses: Ecstasy and Death in the Mystic Tradition.'" Or's explanation was that "the kiss provides the occasion for the entrance into continuing ecstasy that medievals predicted was the fate of the martyr." The reporter added, "The professor's tear-stained face looking out at the crowd, he continued, 'This is a terrible reversal. Usually, a student gives a *hesped* for the teacher. I wish it could be so. We've lost a brilliant young man. This loss of Sam's ideas and work is a tragedy for the scholarly community, for the universities he studied at here and in the US, and for *am Yisrael*, the people Israel. It is my plea to all of you to remember Shmuel Handelman. With our *zichronot*, memories, Shmuel will be given, as the prophet Isaiah says in chapter 56, a *yad vashem tov mibanim umibanot*, a monument and a name superior to sons and daughters, *shem olam etain lo asher lo yikaret*, an eternal name I will give them that will never'—Professor Or began to sob as he said—'be cut off,' and left the podium racked with sobs." Wendy too found tears in her eyes reading about the death of someone that could just as easily have been herself, an ordinary person taking a bus in Israel.

Then, her eyes moved to the photo below. It was of two men, one stretched out on the ground, obviously injured, the other leaning over him with a look of concentrated devotion in his eyes. The devoted one leaning over—Wendy couldn't explain it, but there was something almost otherworldly about his look, like the lighting in a photo by a master photographer, Atget or Steiglitz maybe, an artist who knew how to control the light streaming over a face. Noah's face looked so given over to what he was observing, like he had never seen anything else in the world and nothing else was worthy of his gaze. The stricken man was Sam, and there was nothing else Wendy needed, to know that Noah had feelings for the person in the photo. Still that look could be from the anguish of seeing his friend suffer; it didn't have to be what Todd suspected. There was something primal about the scene, a man leaning over his fallen comrade, a battleground trope. What was the story of the robber and the rabbi, the beautiful rabbi that the robber leaped towards in desire. Noah was the robber leaping, wanting the beauty of Sam, the rabbi. Or was he? It didn't quite square. Wendy, agitated, clicked the microfilm machine off sharply—too sharply—and drew stares from the other library patrons near her. She walked quickly back to her carrel, determined to forget about all this by throwing herself into her work. She did that successfully until she looked up to see a darkening city as night was falling on her panoramic view, and she gathered her things to get the Nine bus, the same bus Noah and Sam were on that day last summer.

SEVEN

Accompanying the Coffin

There is evil, I do not deny it, and I will not conceal it with fruitless casuistry. I am, however, interested in it from a *halakhic* point of view; and as a person who wants to know what action to take. I ask a single question: What should the sufferer do to live with his suffering?
—RABBI JOSEPH SOLOVEITCHIK, *Kol Dodi Dofek* (Listen—My Beloved Knocks)

That same afternoon, hours after Benjamin Margolis's death, there was a ceremony at the airport to send the coffin back to the States. Wendy looked around at the crowd. Since Benj had been a student at Wisdom of the Heart a few years ago, the yeshiva had canceled classes and chartered buses to bring the students and faculty for this ceremony.

She and Noah came on the bus Hebrew University had chartered. For Wendy, looking out at the crowd was surreal. The entire graduate student population of the third floor of the library, Wendy's hangout spot, had emptied itself onto the bus. She didn't know all of them, nor had they all known Benj, but there was a sense of fear, framed by the grim knowledge that *it could have been any one of us.*

Every young American she knew either by name or by face was here. People from the Hebrew University library, American and Israeli, whom she didn't know by name, but knew things about, like who smoked because she saw them outside the library taking a smoking break, or which library carrels they favored. Of the huge collection of people, Wendy guessed that most of these people did not know Benj personally, but were gathered in solidarity.

Wendy, clutching Noah's arm as an Israeli government official spoke in Hebrew, was astounded to see how many people had dropped everything to be at the airport in the middle of the day.

The terrifying randomness of the unplanned was socking each of them, pummeling them, demanding that they do something for the deceased, at least accompany the coffin to the airport. Wendy wanted to scream, *We shouldn't be here. We should be assembled for an award ceremony, or bent over our laptops in a library carrel. Not accompanying a body to a funeral.* She kept silent, red-eyed, and pressed herself next to Noah by her side.

The American ambassador spoke first and presented an American flag to be draped over the coffin. The funereal container itself was a hulk on the dais where the speakers were, a visual reminder of the life that was missing. The odd thing was that there was no name for this event, no formal ritual. There were hordes of people, and speeches, but it wasn't a funeral as the body was being sent off for burial abroad, not being buried here. There were cameras from all the Israeli and foreign news media. She hoped her parents and their friends would not see her in the crowd. They would be anxious anyway; they didn't need to see her on CNN. If this were a movie, she could imagine a camera panning over the crowd. She hadn't spoken to her parents again since Benj passed away, but she speculated they might attend the funeral in New York since her aunt was a friend of Benj's mother. She decided her mother would go, if only to tell Wendy that she had, to try to make her come home.

On the chartered bus back to Jerusalem there was mostly silence. Seeing one of their peers, who had done nothing more exotic and dangerous than ride on a city bus, being sent back to the States in a coffin, did not create a jovial mood in any of the riders. Glum silence reigned.

Wendy, sitting on the aisle, wanted to whisper something to Noah at her side looking out the bus window, oblivious to her presence. Wendy wished she could say something profound and connecting, like, *I want to appreciate what I have,* or *I feel lucky to be alive.* Trying out phrases in her mind, they were all too tinged with banality. She would have read a book were she alone, but even that distraction didn't seem proper now. It would remove the somberness of the moment to partake of anything ordinary. She sat and tried to look out the window with Noah at the overcast sky.

Noah turned to her and suddenly kissed her passionately on the lips, saying nothing. His lips massaged hers, testing, probing how she felt. Reflexively, she kissed him back, but being caught off guard, her emotions weren't in tune with the physical sensation. Maybe that was best—the awkwardness of the first kiss gotten over with, later there would be a more private one, to savor and delight in? This kiss, though it augered more and deeper in its contours and sensations, still lacked the spark of Donny's hungry and desirous kiss. Wendy *had* wanted Noah to kiss her. Before their date last night, her head was full only of when and how and what, and what her feelings in response would be, and how far she would go with him now. She hadn't anticipated their first kiss would be on a bus, a public and impersonal space, with everyone they knew from the library.

Wendy didn't know what to say to the kiss, or what Noah was thinking. The stillness in the bus didn't invite any kind of communication, since anything she said would be overheard completely in the reigning silence. Noah looked at her with those beautiful gray-blue eyes and smiled. She smiled back. She took his hand and held it, looking into his eyes. They continued to look at each other until she put her head on his shoulder and he put his arm around her and stroked her hair. It was comfortable, sitting like that. Feeling his hands on her hair, she contemplated whether Sam's death would be a good thing for their relationship, speeding things up because they felt a sense of urgency, of necessity to live life, be alive, say what you feel without hesitating to be sure. *Would Noah have kissed her less ardently before Benj's death?*

Then she wanted to know: *How had being with Sam in the hospital changed Noah?*

Sitting on the bus, looking out the window, she decided she liked feeling in sync with Noah, his body next to hers, his hands reassuring. They would get through this together, she thought as she leaned happily in towards him for the last portion of the hour-long trip.

At Jerusalem's Central Bus Station, the bus released the first group of passengers, before it continued back to the university campus on Mount

Scopus. As Wendy and Noah started to file off, the rain, which had threatened earlier, began. The sky disgorged its moisture in a fury, quick and fast. Wendy and Noah ran the twenty feet from where the bus had stopped, to the shelter for the buses that would take them to their respective apartments. When they got to the shelter, they were both sopping wet.

"Noah, I promised my parents that I wouldn't take public buses from now on. If you want to share a cab, that would be great." She wanted to ask him if he was hungry and wanted to get a bite to eat, felafel or pizza, but it seemed profane to have eating on the mind after returning from sending a coffin off.

"Refusing to take buses gives terrorists a victory. *I'm* taking the bus."

Wendy was surprised by the vehemence of his response. "I don't want to go down in history as a girl who would be alive if only she'd listened to her parents about the bus." Wendy shuddered, both from being cold and wet and being scared. "I'm going to hail a cab."

Noah looked at her beseechingly, with his mouth open as though he were a baby bird waiting for his mother to fill it. He put his hand on Wendy's arm and squeezed, appealingly. "Let's not fight. I'm tired. I don't want to be alone. Come back to my apartment? Please?"

"Okay." Wendy didn't need to think to respond. Still, she wasn't quite sure of the nature of this invitation. Was it *Come back to my apartment to continue what we started on the bus,* or *Come back to my apartment to talk and keep me company.* Either one was fine; she realized that she would feel odd alone in her apartment now also. Not going home meant she could prolong seeing whether her parents had left a rant on her phone machine about the necessity of her instantaneous return to the States. "I'll hail the cab."

Noah shivered and nodded his head as Wendy trudged outside the meager space of the shelter to get even more fully drenched in the attempt to get the attentions of a taxi driver.

After a number of occupied cabs passed by, one stopped. Wendy gestured toward Noah with her arms and he dashed over quickly. He told the cab driver, "Rehov Mesilat Yesharim 15." The cab driver nodded and was silent, navigating the roads at the usual ultra-rapid Israeli cab driver pace, despite his limited visibility from the pounding rain. Noah and Wendy huddled next to each other, too wet to want to put their arms around each other or hold hands, but bunching up at each other's side in the back of the cab.

Wendy paid the driver and they walked up the stairs to his studio apartment on the fourth floor. Noah unlocked the door and pushed Wendy gently to indicate that she should enter ahead of him. She went in and stood in the middle of the apartment's one room. There was a bed and a dresser in front of her, and a small kitchen nook. The other furniture was a desk and chair in the corner and a small bookcase, filled and topped with piles of books, most of them bearing small white tabs with call numbers from the Hebrew University library. No couches or comfortable chairs, and no dining table shared his dwelling. It was a place to sleep and to work; there were no other functions this room could perform. There was something sad to Wendy about the sparseness of the place. At the same time, she found it enticing because it was Noah's. She was curious about the revelations his dwelling would furnish.

She and Noah both kicked off their wet shoes, reflexively. She wanted to look at his books, to see what fascinated him and try to connect what it was that drew him to the subjects he was studying. Wendy was always fascinated by the personal aspect of scholarship; her favorite parts of scholarly books were their prefaces, the places where there was a listing of the ideas, experiences, and motivations that impelled their authors to devote time to the study of a particular topic. Wendy was always looking for what it was that could draw her in, whether to a person or a topic. With Noah too, she realized, looking around for a place to put her coat, she was waiting to see if he would pull her in, make her want him. She found him attractive, but didn't like the way the kiss on the bus seemed . . . not about *her* somehow? The lack of communication before or after, or an attempt to ask how she felt about it? She didn't feel . . . desired. That was what she wanted.

"Is there a place to put my coat?" she asked.

"I'll put it in the bathroom," he said, reaching out to take the garment from her. He removed his own and went into the bathroom to put them over the shower rod.

Even though her coat was off, Wendy was still sopping wet, her skirt, shoes, and stockings soaked as well as her hair. The thin windbreaker wasn't at all effective as a deterrent to dampness; her shirt too was soggy with rain. She didn't want to sit on the bed or chair in her wet clothes.

When Noah came back from hanging the coats and saw her standing, he asked, "Do you want to sit down? I can make tea."

She smiled at him. "I'd love to sit but I don't want to get your blankets wet. Maybe you could lend me some sweats or something?"

"Sure." Noah gave her the smile that showed the gap between his two front teeth. Once she moved her gaze from his teeth up to his eyes with their clear pools of color in the middle, looking more blue than gray today, she was immersed in him. He opened the third drawer of the dresser and rummaged among the jeans there to produce a pair of maroon sweatpants emblazoned "Oberlin Physical Education" in yellow letters. He tossed them over to Wendy.

She got up and walked toward the bathroom to change out of her skirt. Wendy returned to see Noah still standing in his wet clothing.

"Aren't you going to change?"

"If I stay wet, I'm connected to taking Benj's coffin to the airport. I . . . it will seem less final, for him and for Sam. Does that make sense at all?" he said, still standing looking down at Wendy now seated on the bed. "I was one of the last people to see him alive. It's just so . . . overwhelming . . ." he sank down, soaked, next to Wendy on the bed and put his face in his hands, sobbing. Wendy put her arms around him to try to comfort him.

He looked up after a moment and said, "My tears won't help. Let's get warmed up." He smiled at her, and she smiled. He got up, burrowed in the same drawer with his hands, and found a pair of navy sweatpants emblazoned "New York University" in white and went to the bathroom to change.

Wendy walked over to his bookcase. She picked up one of the few non-library books, an advice book titled, *Now Decide: How Indecisiveness Is Ruining Your Life (whether you know it or not)*, with a price tag on the back stating that it was from Worlds Beyond Words. From the author bio, it seemed the writer himself wasn't the world's most decisive person, having had a career as a psychologist, Buddhist practitioner, journalist, and now Orthodox Jew.

Noah emerged from the bathroom barefoot and in sweatpants, still wearing his white button-down shirt, holding a very thin white towel, the kind found in cheap hotels. "This floor is so cold on bare feet. Come, I'll dry your feet and give you some sweat socks. Then I'll make us tea," he said, beckoning her to where he was seated cross-legged on the bed.

She walked over and sat next to him, leaning forward slightly, her hands at her sides. Her curly black shoulder-length hair was still dripping onto her long-sleeved white cotton shirt. Would he kiss her again? Should she make a move? He carefully reached down for her bare feet, caressing them in his hands, and brought them to his lap. He was focused, methodical, starting at the tops of her toes, drying them, the spaces between them, the tops of her feet and finally her soles and heels. Once he had dried both feet, he began to stroke them, massaging carefully with his warm hands. Wendy liked watching him, his focus on her and her comfort. Suddenly she closed her eyes, to just have the physical sensation. She felt stimulated, wanted to be touched everywhere by those hands, have them comfort, probe, explore, caress. She heard Noah softly humming a *niggun*, a wordless melody, and was transported back to the *Shir Tzion* synagogue her first Friday night in Israel, and the voice she heard there, soaring above the others, yet harmonizing at the same time, distinctively, gorgeously individual while still contributing to the sound of the group. Noah's *niggun* pulsated in her ears; his massage of her feet aroused her, but the other voice was echoing in her mind.

"Mmmm, feels so good," Wendy said looking down at her feet on Noah's lap, in his hands. "You're . . . tender. I see you as a great dad one day, giving your kids baths, drying them off." She smiled into his blue-gray eyes.

"I've always wanted kids. Now I just feel, they're lucky, not aware of how awful a place the world is."

"Let's shut the world out and dry each other off, you and me, nothing else," Wendy said, surprised to hear herself speaking so lubriciously, seductively.

"Sounds good." Noah smiled at Wendy, showing his beautiful clear eyes and the irresistible gap between his top front teeth. He handed her the towel, now slightly damp from drying her feet, and swung his legs onto the bed. She crossed her legs and took his bare feet onto her lap. She stroked carefully each of the toes and then ran her finger over the middle of his foot, playfully from the end of his heel to the top of his toes. She encased all of one foot, then all of the other in the towel and then her hands. His eyes too were closed; she could see from the relaxed tone of his face the pleasure her hands were giving him. He opened his eyes and looked at her, and then shifted so that he was next to her on the narrow bed. He leaned over and kissed her lips delicately and sweetly. Wendy felt swollen with want. She kissed him back, hoping he would satisfy her desire. She put her hands on his wet hair and held him closer, her fingers threading through his unruly brown wavy hair. He played with her limp, wet, still-curly locks, clustered around her head.

She moved away to take her shirt off. "I'm hot now." He smiled at her and unbuttoned his white cotton shirt. It revealed a chest with more hair than she'd expected, curly and virile.

Noah got up to place both of their shirts over the shower rod in the bathroom. She looked across the room to see their clothes on the rod, their expanse of whiteness fluttering limply, like a bird beating its wings yet too frail to move its limbs high enough to fly.

Noah returned to his seat next to her on the bed and, with a new scrawny towel from the bathroom, began to towel her dry, starting with the crown of her head, carefully moving his hands in circles over her. Finished, he gave her a quick kiss on the top of the head. He continued his *niggun* all this time. Another time, Wendy might have found the humming annoying and pretentious, an act of spiritual showmanship, a sign to others: "Look at me see how spiritual I am." Now, she felt like a child being cared for by a sensitive parent, gaining comfort after a difficult experience. "Mmmmm" came out of Wendy's mouth spontaneously.

He toweled off her right arm, gave her shoulder a careful kiss, toweled her left arm, again letting her know with his mouth that he cherished each part of her. He reached to her back and rubbed the towel over her bra strap.

She could feel him bending closer to her, and he gave her another kiss on the top of her head. He moved delicately, first her forehead, then the tip of her nose, her mouth. After her chin, he paused.

"May I go lower?"

She didn't want the magic soothing of the singing to end. She didn't want to open her eyes, and murmured, "Please." As he reached both hands around to unhook her bra in the back, he fumbled upon not finding the proper hardware in the expected place. "In front," she said.

He quickly changed positions and found the way in. He removed her bra and lay it down on the bed. He kissed her chin and her collarbone, and then her cleavage. Wendy held his head in place and hugged it to her chest.

He fondled her rounded peach-sized breasts, kissing the tips of each and suckling them, first one and then the other. Her nipples were standing on end. She liked seeing his face at her breast and feeling his thick mop of hair against her chest.

"Your breasts . . . I want you, Wendy."

"I want you, Noah." Wendy pulled his head away from her breasts and looked at him full in the face as she said this. Then she kissed him, thrusting her tongue into his mouth, searching for and meeting his tongue, wanting to go as deep into him as she could, and then pulling her tongue out to caress his lips with hers. His taste was both salty and sweet, a combination of what she had expected and what she hadn't.

"I want to stay here, like this, and melt our warmth together. Will you be with me when I need you?" Noah queried, searching her eyes.

"I'll be with you now." She felt the throb of his penis against her thigh. "Something else you might need," she said as she bent her face down to it, pulled down his sweatpants and underwear, and took him, fully in her mouth. Her mouth went up and down over the circumcised tip while she stroked the bottom half of the shaft with her hands.

"You're so good," Noah moaned, "Baby, keep going, don't stop. Ohh . . ."

A minute later, he cried out, "I don't know."

She took her mouth off him, kept her hand around the shaft, and looked up at his face.

"I . . . I don't know what I want. Is that okay?"

"You don't want me?" She didn't know how to react to him.

What was happening here? Had she done something wrong?

"No, you're amazing." He stopped, "I . . . I want you, but I just don't know what else I want."

She removed her hands from his cock and propped her head on her hand on her side in bed.

The relationship discussion. Wendy would have preferred just to continue the fondling, but Noah wanted to clarify things first. Wendy could be impulsive, doing what felt right, sorting it out later. It had gotten her in trouble in past relationships when things went too fast, too suddenly. But he wanted this; he invited her up.

Noah began, "I want to be glad to be alive, to feel all the emotions, to continue life. I would love to create new life now. To prove we are going forward, embracing life." He looked at her and smiled, "The best revenge."

"If things were simpler and we didn't have to finish our degrees, and publish and get jobs and get tenure . . . if we could have a regular life without footnotes and analysis and thinking, and have a baby . . ."

She smiled at him. "We could pretend we're trying to have a baby?" she added helpfully.

"If we had a baby and got married and lived in Jerusalem and proved Sam and Benj's deaths weren't in vain, would you be happy?" Noah's gray-blue eyes gazed at Wendy. He was training the whole of his attention carefully on her face, as he had so carefully dried her feet and kissed her nipples. It was a powerful gaze, his eyes on her, investigating, exposing.

"If you're looking for someone to marry and have babies with and live here, I have lots of contacts among very lovely newly religious ladies. Not me."

"I wish I could just get answers. Go to a rebbe and find out: Was Sam taken young because he already fulfilled his purpose?"

Wendy gazed back at Noah. "Life isn't a group of mathematical problem sets that you work on and get totally confused by and go to the teacher and know he can give you the correct answer and teach you how to work it out. It's never that precise—that there's one answer, one clear and elegant way of working the solution like my high school physics teacher Dr. Stern used to tell us. There are some things you just have to figure out on your own. That's why I'm writing a dissertation—I need to figure it out on my own. If you want pat answers, go to Yeshivat Temimei Nefesh; they specialize in personal guidance."

"I wish I could have that simple faith," he continued.

"If you had that faith you wouldn't be allowed to be with me."

"I wouldn't trade it for being with you."

"Good. You know, Noah . . ."

"What is it you want to figure out? Something I can help you with?"

"If we're done with the conversation, I'd say that's possible. How about seeing how far you can take me?" Her clitoris was still throbbing, feeling like it took up the entirety of the space between her legs. She wanted to get to that point where her entire body was centered there, the tips of her fingers, the tips of her toes, and if she were stroked there she would feel it everywhere in her body, and finally explode in pleasure.

"Mmmm, I wonder. Interesting conundrum," Noah said as he began again to put his mouth on her nipples.

"Yes, yes, now would you start with your fingers . . ."

Noah reached his hand down to her vagina and rubbed the outside of her underwear, gently and slowly, rhythmically, feeling her pubic bone underneath the flesh.

"Take it off. Touch me."

Noah removed her panties with his hands while still leaning over to kiss her breasts.

Wendy moaned, "Rub my clit, please."

"Don't give me instructions. I know what I'm doing," Noah said in mock annoyance as he bent down to graze her with his tongue.

"Oh, I want you. Noah . . . Noah, yes, oh . . ."

"Is that what you like?" he asked lifting his head from between her legs.

"Ohhh . . ." The sensations were beyond words, the pleasure coming over her in waves. "God, yes, yes, oh. Yeah . . ." Wendy had raised her head off the bed in ecstasy and suddenly flopped it back with a thump. "Do you . . . ?"

"Are you . . . ?"

"I'm not on the pill. My sponges are in my apartment."

"I have some condoms. I wish we didn't have to use them."

"Hurry up, I want you."

He walked over to the dresser and opened the top drawer. "Help me out first."

He returned with a condom.

"Let me make sure you'll fill it."

She knelt on her haunches and placed her hands on his hipbones as he stood over the bed. She placed her mouth on his already erect cock and moved it up and down.

He moaned, "Oh . . . I'm ready."

"I'm just getting started here, give me a chance."

"I want to be inside you."

Noah handed her the piece of coiled rubber in his hand. Wendy took it and tried to place it over him. It was sticking. "Vaseline?"

"Drawer of the night stand." Wendy crawled over to the top edge of the bed and opened the drawer. She located the tub of Vaseline, scooted back quickly, and began to slather it on him. Now, she was able to fit the condom.

Noah lay down on the bed next to her and began kissing her, greedily, tonguing her, and holding her tight. Wendy was surprised at the intensity of his ardor.

She said, "I want you, Noah."

He looked at her with the shaft of light in his gray-blue eyes focused on her, stiff like the rest of him.

"I'd love it if you were on top."

He has ways he likes sex. He's had sex and thought about it. I'm liking this more and more, perhaps even falling in love? It was the first time that thought had occurred to her.

Wendy mounted him—she couldn't remember being in this position before. Had she? He said from underneath her, "Let me in?" and gave her an incredibly winning and radiant smile, the kind of smile a child gives a parent who he knows will indulge all whims because the parent finds the smile so endearing. She took his cock and gently slid it into her body, to absorb some of him into herself.

She liked being in this position, on top, controlling the motions and their frequency, looking down at Noah, his eyes closed. She didn't generally view herself as particularly sexy. She didn't associate herself with the type of tawdry clothes, hair, and nails that many women seemed to think was requisite to be thought of as sexy. From the little miniskirts to the acrylic nails with designs on them, Wendy had always found the preoccupations of women trying to be attractive to men trivial, shallow. Not that she didn't want to be attractive. But she wanted to do it on her own terms, as a serious person who could be sexy for who she was, not just her looks—Susan Sontag-type sexy, where looks were only one part of the package.

She patted Noah's curls and gazed down at him as she moved her haunches to her own rhythm. Usually men wanted to be on top to control everything, do all the work of motion. Here was a guy who got off on her control. Why? Just to lose control, or was he used to being with older women who taught him things? She too closed her eyes to better concentrate only on the physical sensations, block out the visual. Did someone teach her that? Or was it one of those things you just figure out for yourself?

Wendy felt with each breath that she needed to take in as much oxygen as possible, to remain alive. Enjoying each other's bodies—she felt *this* would keep her alive, gasping at air she knew would sustain her. They both climaxed, quickly.

Wendy always enjoyed the aftermath of sex, the lying in bed, spent and pleasured, cuddling, with the knowledge of having been joined in ecstasy, the closeness still apparent. Neither of them said anything, but lay on the bed, with the covers over them, looking at each other, Wendy taking in Noah's gray-blue eyes and delicate lips, Noah taking in Wendy's deep brown eyes and thick curly dark brown hair, stroking her hair with care.

Finally, lying in silence got strained. Neither wanted to use mere language to break the spell their physical communication had engendered.

"That was . . . wow! Wendy, you're . . ." Noah began.

Wendy did not want her mystic vision of gasping the air, of feeling sustained by him, to be dissolved by the banalities of speech. She said, "Shhh. No talking. Just be." She rolled closer to him and put her head on his shoulder. He put his arm around her, and she kissed his cheek and said his name: "Noah."

He said hers: "Wendy." She didn't reply. "Wendy, I think I'm falling in love."

She murmured, "Shhhh . . ."

Wendy called Orly the next day. "Orly, this is a crazy country. Death can get you laid! Noah and I . . ."

Orly laughed uncontrollably, "Seinfeld had prison furlough sex, and Israel has the post-*pigua* shag. How was he?"

"It's weird. He was much better than I thought he'd be, ardent, tender, sensitive, just . . . By far the best sex I've ever had."

"Sounds good. Why weird?"

"I don't know . . . too intense. Does that make sense? He had been with Sam at this bookstore, and then Sam died, so Benj's death brought it all up again, but . . . I'm just not sure about Noah. I *so* want to sleep with him again, and it would be so convenient to be with him this year, but . . ."

"You're not head over heels. If the sex is good, it's worth it."

"I wish I felt that way. Maybe I'm too much of a romantic, wanting to be with someone I just feel utterly, passionately, completely intense about. Maybe that's unrealistic," Wendy said sadly.

"Don't stay with him if he isn't what you want. Your guy is out there. Of course he could be married already by the time you find him . . ."

"Enough. How's Nir?"

Orly started laughing, "Mr. Right he's not. But he has some redeeming qualities."

"Nu, details?" Wendy said laughing.

EIGHT
Wendy and Noah: The Aftermath of Desire

By this time, indeed you know that in the worship of the Creator, blessed be His name, it is most important that the heart truly yearn after Him and that the soul feel a longing for Him . . . The best advice for the person in whom this desire does not burn is that he consciously enthuse himself so that enthusiasm might eventually become second nature to him. External movement arouses the internal, and you certainly have more of a command over the external than the internal.

—MOSES HAYYIM LUZZATTO, *Mesillat Yesharim*

Friday morning a week later, Wendy and Noah were lugging bags of groceries for Shabbat dinner down Emek Refaim. As they arrived at the corner of Hananya Street, where Wendy's favorite coffee shop, Caffit stood, there was a red light. They couldn't cross Hananya. Cars were turning from Emek Refaim onto Hananya, the cross street. Wendy and Noah put their grocery bags down and leaned against the street sign.

"It's crazy. This is Hananya Street, literally the street of God's grace, yet God can't be merciful! I've lost two friends this year already!" mourned Noah.

Wendy didn't know how to respond, so remained silent.

There was now a crowd waiting to cross the street. When the lights changed, the pair began to cross. There were a few cars on Hananya, now stuck behind a red light, waiting to turn onto the larger street of Emek

Refaim. The third car in the line was a dark blue sedan, of indeterminate year and make but certainly over ten years old. A man with a black hat, white shirt, and dark pants, and a beard not too long, dark with a bit of gray in it, got out of his car, holding a white pamphlet with black lettering in his hand. He did not scan the crowd at all but walked in a straight line towards the group of pedestrians crossing the street. Wendy and Noah were among a crowd of perhaps fifteen people crossing Hananya Street.

The man did not appraise the crowd but headed straight for Noah.

The man moved past the others, looked Noah straight in the eye, said, "I want you to have this," in perfectly inflected English, and handed him a pamphlet.

Then, the man turned around and walked back to his car, without making eye contact with any of the other pedestrians. He got back in his car and shut the door. The light changed. All the cars moved quickly to turn onto Emek Refaim and became absorbed in the flow of traffic.

"That was strange," Wendy commented. "He seemed to know he should give it to you, no one else. I've never seen that before—usually leafletters just give their stuff out to anyone, indiscriminately."

Noah said, "When he looked at me it was, like, this powerful gaze." He shuddered involuntarily. Wendy asked if she could see the pamphlet.

Noah began to hand it to her but then started reading himself.

It is time for you to do
TESHUVAH!
Have you done something you regret, deeply, in the last few weeks?
You can repent!
Change your life—see how inside.

"Some crackpot religious thing. It seems personal, but it's just a generic message. Totally phony," said Wendy. "Maybe I should do a chapter on people recruited that way?" she mused both to herself and to Noah.

She looked at him again. "Are you okay? Do you want to get something warm at Caffit? We're here."

Noah responded, sounding distant, "Fine. We need to cook."

Wendy and Noah picked up their bags, crossed to the other side of Emek Refaim, and turned toward Wendy's street.

When they crossed, Noah told her, "You shouldn't have said the flyer was phony."

"That guy probably does the same thing all day, driving around and stopping and giving his flyer to random people to make them believe they have been 'chosen.' It's bogus."

"I felt a chill when he looked at me and when I read those words. And," he glanced shyly at her, next to him on the street, "I have done something I regretted over the past few weeks."

"You're human. It happens."

"I'm serious."

She looked at him. "Okay, so?"

"I don't want to talk about it here. Let's wait till we get to your place."

"Have it your way." Wendy said, annoyed. *What could Noah have done that he regretted so?* She told herself, *It must have something to do with Sam. He didn't help him as much as he could, or should have stopped him from getting on the bus, something like that?*

They walked in silence, down the street, the crowds of Friday morning shoppers and café patrons swirling past them. Noah could just be a speck in the crowd, surging, going nowhere, while Wendy walked with determination. At Mishael they turned right and entered Wendy's courtyard. They went up the steps on the outside of the house, up to her apartment.

Inside, they took the groceries out of their bags and put them away either on the counter for immediate use or in the practically bare cabinets and the fridge. Wendy asked Noah, "Before we start cooking, something to drink? Water? Juice?"

"I like that Mango Spring."

Wendy opened the bottle of carbonated juice and poured some into two separate glasses. She moved her laptop and papers so she could sit at the small dining table across from him. She placed the glass of juice in front of him as she sat. "Are you going to tell me or make me guess?" she asked with a laugh, trying to set a jocular tone, despite her earlier annoyance.

Noah took a sip of the auburn-colored liquid and began, "The night Sam was killed this summer. From the beginning. I was waiting on Mount Scopus for the bus to town. Sam was waiting too. I knew who he was; he was legendary in the department for his brilliance and being a favorite of our advisor, Joseph Levi. He asked if I'd been to this bookstore and I said no, and if I wanted to get felafel and I said sure. We took the bus downtown and had felafel and walked to Berger Books on King George."

"What's terrible?"

"Listen. We got to the bookstore and he took me to the back where the Kabbalah books are. He showed me this book with an inscription. It was . . . suggestive . . . by the male author to another man."

"I still don't see what is so wrong."

"Then, Sam kissed me."

"Oh." Wendy looked at him and waited. Her mind was blank.

"I wasn't planning to. I never kissed a guy, or thought about kissing a guy, but when his lips were on mine, I kissed back; I didn't run away the way most straight guys would. Sam wanted me to go to the park—you know Independence Park is a gay meeting place—and I said, 'I can't do that.' I . . . didn't know what I wanted; he came on so strong. He was mad I turned him down. He left the store. I left a few minutes later. He took one bus, and I took the next one. Now he's gone. If I'd gone to the park with him, he'd still be alive."

Wendy had fury in her eyes as she recovered her thoughts and lashed out at him. "You totally lied to me, Noah. I thought when we slept together last week it was about us, our relationship. You said you were falling in love. I felt guilty I couldn't make some kind of equally strong declaration. But it was about Sam the whole time, not me. Not me at all." She stared at him. "You should have told me about Sam before you slept with me. You can't be in love with one person when you've kissed another."

"You're . . . jealous? He's dead."

"No. No, not jealous, Noah. Furious. I'm furious at you," she yelled at him. "You lied to me."

"No!"

"You said you were falling in love with me."

"It was true."

"You said it *to prove you're not gay.*"

"Sam . . . aroused feelings in me, yes. I don't know what to do with them. I'm not sure." He put his face in his hands and started sobbing. "I'm sorry, Wendy. I didn't mean to hurt anyone. This is such a mess."

They both sat at the table, silent. The anger and confusion each felt was compounded by the knowledge that their time until sundown, when they had to stop cooking and their guests would arrive, was limited.

"Noah, leave. Call people and tell them the dinner is off. Or do it at your place. Take the food. I thought this was going to be our first dinner party, working together, shopping, cooking, having fun, sleeping together after the guests go. I don't want to be in the same room as you right now."

"Shabbos is in a few hours. We can't disinvite people. We have to do this dinner."

"We don't."

"It's embarrassing to invite people and then tell them they can't come, don't you think?"

"You're the one who lied to me."

"I didn't have to confess."

"I don't want to be with you."

"Please. Look at all this food. We have to do something with it." Noah got up from the table to start readying to cook. "That pamphlet . . . don't be so contemptuous. I may take some classes at this yeshiva. Why was I spared and Sam killed? I need to do something worthwhile."

"Work harder at your studies; serve food in a homeless shelter—you don't have to have religion to have meaning in your life."

"You don't understand."

"Don't tell me I can't understand because I'm not religious. I *know* what it's about—I'm *studying* religious people."

"You can't. You're positioning yourself, even in this conversation, as an observer, an outsider. You'll never know what motivates someone religious if you don't understand Shabbat."

"A person can understand a group without being part of it—in fact sometimes there is a better perspective if one has distance. I'm not going to be defensive about my religious feelings or lack of them—you're the one who lied, not me. I like Shabbat here but I'm not sure I'd want to totally change my life for it." Wendy then asked, "Would you rather be with a religious man than a woman who isn't?"

"Until Sam kissed me, I never thought, really, about being with a man. But . . . I felt something when he kissed me. It was just . . . electrifying. Different from what I feel with you. I don't know whether I prefer one or the other—maybe it was just Sam, and the whole experience, the book he showed me, the conversation about ecstasy . . ."

"He gave you Ecstasy? Then it *was* date rape."

"Not the pill, religious ecstasy. He showed me this book, *The Divine Kiss*, about mystical ideas of death with ecstasy—that was his dissertation topic, and he told me that's what he yearned for, to be in pure ecstasy with God, continually."

"He showed you this book and talked about God and kissed you. What an operator."

"He wrote a fake inscription by the author in it."

"How did you know it was fake?"

"He confessed after he was injured. Now I'll admit something else." Noah looked at her across the kitchen counter where they were both standing now. "I kissed him, before he died. Then, he said, 'I've had the kisses of God's mouth.' I don't think he knew it was me. I'd like to imagine I gave him some comfort."

"Touching," Wendy said with sarcasm.

He looked at her with a glint of bewilderment in his gray-blue eyes.

She continued, "I'm serious. I can't believe you could kiss him knowing he lied to you about the book. I wouldn't be so generous."

Noah looked at her, this time with more conviction. "I *didn't* think, Wendy. I just did it. Sometimes the most important things we do aren't the ones we obsess and agonize over, but what we instinctively feel. I couldn't not kiss him. I had this sense that he was dying; though there wasn't external damage, I knew there must be something internal, he was just so weak . . ." Noah began to sob. "You don't know what it is like, Wendy, to see this transformation—someone so tough and self-confident, riding around on his red Vespa in his black leather jacket, so smart and sure of himself, stared at by every man in Jerusalem—when I walked down the street with him to the bookstore, men were staring at him; a guy even stopped his car in the middle of the street to tell him something, he was just . . . so beautiful . . . and now . . . he's gone." Noah kept sobbing. "I'm not sure I'm cut out for academia with all its intellectualizing. I like learning things and writing papers, but I'm just not sure if I want it to be the only focus of my life. I might like a yeshiva more—I loved Wisdom of the Heart . . ."

"Decide. Why be in graduate school if you don't want a career? You may as well start doing what you want. Why waste time? If I don't get a job, I don't know what I'll do. That's why I'm working as hard as I can to write an incredible dissertation so that I'll have a shot. What do you want besides grad school?"

"Rabbinical school?" he added. "I'd like to work with people, help them, listen to their stories. Or teach, maybe at a Jewish high school. I don't know what kind of rabbi I'd like to be. I can't be Orthodox if I'm gay. I'm confused. Wendy, I know you're angry—you have a right to be—but I just need some stability now. I need you—the sex the other day was so intense because we needed to be with each other."

"I'm not your security blanket. I had hoped this relationship would make my year less lonely; we could do things together, talk about our work, sleep together, pleasant but not too serious. Now, I feel *more* lonely: you're here but you're not. You want me, but not *me*, any woman, to prove you like women."

He looked down at his hands. He wept again. "Wendy, this has been the hardest week of my life. Do you know that? My only moments of happiness all week were when I was with you —especially at my apartment. I wasn't lying, about anything I said, including that I want to have kids with you. I've always wanted kids—just someone to give to and educate and really pour myself into nurturing. I felt this passion with Sam, but I don't want it to take me away from my desire to be married and have kids. Or from the Jewish community. I love learning and *davening*, Shabbat is the highlight of my week. I always imagined myself around a table, filled with children and grandchildren, guests and friends, singing, learning, being part of a community. How can I have that if I'm gay? I'll have to revise my entire life. But can I give up what I felt for Sam? I just don't know," he said hanging his head.

"Why are you doing this to me, Noah? When you tell me how tortured you are, I feel bad for you, really. But . . . I'm in shock too. I mean, you've just told me that our relationship isn't what I thought it was and I'm hurt. I have sympathy for you, but I'm upset. I'm confused about what we should do too." Wendy paused and sipped her juice before looking at him and continuing, "Listen, I'll do this meal with you, and then we're done."

"Wendy, that's . . . I need you now."

"You might have thought of that before you kissed Sam. I can't. I don't even know why you are asking. You're lucky I'm agreeing to go through with this meal; that's my concession to you. Look, Noah, it's almost noon. We have work to do. Shabbos is coming!" Wendy said with a brightness in her voice, echoing the many times she had heard it from her interviewees. Noah laughed, knowing she was speaking in parody.

"You're right: Shabbos is coming. We need to get ready."

Wendy and Noah went from the dining room table where they had been sitting into the kitchen and started their preparations. Wendy was going to make her Grandma Essie's famous apple chocolate-chip cake, though the rest of the food would be Noah's recipes, since the cake was at the outer limits of Wendy's culinary repertoire. Noah had cooked many Shabbat dinners, beginning the year he was at Wisdom of the Heart, then continuing at NYU and here in Jerusalem. Noah was planning chicken soup with matzah balls, orange chicken, noodle kugel, and roast vegetables. They got through this time, each maneuvering around the other, feeling how sad it was that they weren't really doing this together, but going through the motions in the same room. They kept the radio on to a station that had some English language programs, and managed to get the food cooked. Wendy even played *sous chef* to assist Noah once she had made her own recipe.

Once finished, Noah went back to his apartment to shower and change for Shabbat. He was going to the *Shir Tzion* synagogue by himself, though Wendy would have met him there were they still together. The guests were set to meet in Wendy's apartment after *shul*.

After Noah had left to go home and shower, Wendy needed to set the table and ready the apartment. Had they not broken up, maybe they'd be snuggling together now, catching a nap and a cuddle, and maybe a quickie before the guests came. Now she was alone, and needed to find a suitable tablecloth and dishes for the table. If the point of a dinner was to bring people together, how could she do it so alienated from Noah, feeling deceived and angry? This dinner was a total sham—no coming together around food, a unity of purpose and conversation as at the most successful dinner parties. Wendy thought of Mrs. Ramsey in *To the Lighthouse*, producing a radiant effect with her triumphant Boeuf en Daube, bringing the disparate diners together with her golden haze. Yet, Wendy was lacking in servants to set the mood and table, even if she used her grandmother's recipe—Essie's Bronx-based to Mrs. Ramsey's grandmother's French cuisine.

After smoothing the white tablecloth purchased at the *shuk* that she found on the bottom shelf of the linen closet, Wendy brushed past her bookshelf and paused, looking at a row of paperbacks. She wanted to find that scene in the novel, the meal ringing people together to say, "Life stand still here," with Mrs. Ramsay. Was that what Shabbat was, an attempt to create a moment of illumination, a making of the moment something permanent, the "cathedral in time" that Heschel described in his *The Sabbath* she'd read in Intro to Religion? Wendy thought of her LitHum teacher at Columbia, Anna Dalgrav, and how she read the dinner party passage to the class one winter afternoon, almost as a performance, in her soft yet mesmerizing voice, enabling them to hear the words of Woolf's vision as the winter sun descended in the sky through the window of her late afternoon classroom. The spectacle through the window of ambient light crowning the red sunset saturated the students' perception of the passage that day. The book still had her underlinings, and Wendy easily found the scene she wanted.

"Here, inside the room, seemed to be order and dry land; there, outside a reflection in which things wavered and vanished, waterily.

"Some change at once went through them all, as if this had really happened, and they were all conscious of making a party together in a hollow, on an island; had their common cause against that fluidity out there."

When Wendy read this, she began to sob. All *was* fluidity in her life—she had no common cause with the guests, they could never feel something together as a group. Her aloneness seemed more palpable with every one of the eight plates she placed on the table and accompanied with their silverware and glasses, napkins and a Kiddush cup Noah had brought from his apartment. This Shabbat dinner, a failure before its inception, would provide no bulwark against any piece of the outside world. Table set, she went to lie on her bed and sob. The Sabbath siren went off while she was prone, clenching her pillow and kicking her feet in the air like a schoolchild. "No lights tonight," she thought, not wanting to offend the Sabbath observers by lighting after the prescribed time, thus profaning the Sabbath. She remembered that she didn't have candles anyway. Noah had been planning to bring them when he came back to walk her to *shul.* So much for the change Mrs. Ramsay had produced with her command to "Light the candles," Wendy thought as she dragged herself to shower and dress.

When the first guests—the non-synagogue-going Isaac Babel scholar Todd, followed quickly by Orly and then Nir—rang the bell at the front gate of 5 Mishael, Wendy was composed enough to greet them with a semblance of cheer.

"Where's Noah?" were Orly's first words, once coats were hung up, and they were sitting on the couch waiting.

"Still at *shul* I guess," Wendy replied to Orly's arched eyebrows.

"You didn't go with him? Have you returned to our dark side now?" Nir added.

Todd put his arm around Wendy and said, "She'll always be on the dark side, *n'est ce pas?*" in the French of his Montreal childhood, an affectation that could be annoying when Wendy wasn't charmed by it despite herself.

Wendy returned the arm around Todd, enjoying his familiar solidity, the warmth of his itchy wool sweater, and said, "If you have your way, Todd," laughing for the first time all day. Did he have to be gay? Life was so unfair, she mused, when boyfriends who were suitable might be gay, and gay men who might be suitable couldn't be boyfriends.

Noah arrived next with Jason and Dara. Even though they hadn't been at the same *shuls,* they had met up at some point on the walk and arrived together. She had given Noah the key to let himself in with the groceries and told him just to keep it till he returned so she wouldn't have to be bothered with going out to the gate on a chilly night and he wouldn't have to ring. Wordlessly, he handed Wendy the key once inside.

Orly cheerfully called out, "Do I have to ring a bell or something? Noah, give Wendy a Shabbat Shalom kiss?" Wendy heard this from her bedroom where she was depositing the key in the drawer of her nightstand. She gave Orly a look upon returning to the room, and Orly said no more. Miraculously, the notoriously unsubtle friend seemed to realize that she had spoken out of turn; no one else commented, though Todd patted Wendy's back and asked what he could do to help.

Noah replied, "We're just waiting for Yehoshua, but maybe we should start without him. The *davening* and dancing at the *Kotel* can go on so long, and it's a big walk."

Jason added, "He wasn't sure he could come anyway. He thought there might be a *farbrengen*, and he wanted to be close to the Old City. He said if he got an invitation closer by, he'd do it."

Wendy pouted, "But . . . that's so rude. We invited him. He should have told us if he's not coming. I set a place for him!"

"Well, maybe Elijah will come eat, now," added Orly helpfully.

"Until then, we should start," Noah said, with what Wendy noted as an overtone of harshness. It didn't quite set the tone that she would have wanted to welcome people to her house. This was the first time she was having a dinner for anyone and she had seen it as a milestone of sorts, a path to adult-hood: the cooking and organizing and inviting details that others generally did. Usually, she was a passive participant in these affairs, a guest. Now she was actively trying to create this dinner in her own home. And the whole thing sucked, despite all her efforts, because she didn't want to be around Noah.

"So why doesn't everyone find a seat?" Wendy asked, gesturing to the table.

Dara asked helpfully, "Where are the hosts sitting?"

Without glancing at Noah, Wendy said, "I'm here at the head, and Noah will be down at the other end," *where I can glare at him and inquire why he put me through this,* she thought, hoping he would notice the hostility in her glare. Noah did not seem to notice and cheerfully gestured to Jason to sit on one side of him and Todd on the other. This annoyed Wendy since she had wanted Todd next to her, as her friend. Orly sat next to Todd, and Nir between her and Wendy. Dara sat next to Jason, across from Orly, so the seat next to Wendy, intended for Yehoshua, remained empty. Wendy's nearest dinner companions at the table were Dara, who still annoyed her, and Nir, whose main point of interest was his hulking body, not his conversational skills, which were at best limited in English, though he understood what others said, so Wendy would not be finding much to engage her with these companions at her sides.

Since it was her apartment, Wendy believed she should have jurisdiction over the portion of the evening devoted to religious ritual. Noah, on the other hand, believed that his having cooked the vast majority of the dishes to be eaten should give him an elective sway over the religious proceedings. Noah said, "Let's do *Shalom Aleichem,*" and Wendy immediately started to sing the tune she knew, the only tune she could sing for this song, from her days at Camp Kodimoh. No one joined in. Abruptly, she stopped.

Then, Noah started from the beginning with another tune that all joined with.

Wendy sat, listening to the others sing around her own table.

She did have to admit, Noah's tune was snappier and peppier, and the singing was more interesting with the repetition of each verse three times unlike hers where it was sung once. It made her mad that even religion-defying Nir was unafraid to join in to what she thought of as a tune from the enemy faction. Orly looked at Wendy and shrugged as if to say, *Okay, so you lost that round. Your tune wasn't as nice, but let's get on with it.* Wendy knew Orly would feel guilty later when she realized that her singing meant she was on Noah's side and Wendy had been hurt. When the song was over, Noah immediately began to sing Proverbs 31, the hymn to the "woman of valor." Growing up, Wendy's father always read this in its entirety in English to all the assembled at the table. She liked the maze of Byzantine archaic phrases in an old-fashioned English that was quaintly unfamiliar—"who considereth a field and buys it," "who looks well to the ways of the household," "girds her loins with strength," "who eats not of the bread of idleness." She knew exactly what the Hebrew was saying, but it was still an unfamiliar song and tune. Before launching into the melody, Noah and the others—for she was beginning to see them all as more his allies than her own—could have asked her if this was how she wanted it done. Out of defiance, she decided she would recite it in English after they finished, even if it lengthened the proceedings.

"*B'sha'arim ma'asekha.*" The last words of the hymn concluded and hung in the air.

"My father always read 'the woman of valor' out loud to my mother in the English she would understand on Friday night. Since this is *my* Shabbat table," she intoned with a glare at Noah though the others did not seem to note her emphasis on the "*my*" not "*our,*" "I'd like to do that."

Here, Nir balked. "*Oof,* what is this, Wundy? You said the prayer already. *Nu,* aren't we going to eat tonight?"

Dara, the Reconstructionist rabbinical student, came to Wendy's defense. "Nir, this is Wendy's family tradition. It may not be meaningful to you but it is part of her way of connecting to Judaism and creating an evocative panorama to look out on through her lens of Judaism." Wendy could not believe she would ever be so grateful to Dara, pretentious though her prattle might be—panorama?—but *she* was going to win this round. Wendy began to recite from memory, "A woman of worth who can find?" and closed her eyes to concentrate fully on the words and block out stimulation from her other senses. It was eerie; she felt as though she were channeling her father, reciting his words in his voice. She also thought, oddly, of her college professor Caroline Van Leeuwen, who would close her eyes when making a crucial point. Wendy liked the feeling of leading others, instructing them, that she sensed in reciting this passage out loud, trying to project her voice as sonorously as her father's. She liked this sense of continuing something that surely her parents, so far away, were also doing now. She was connected to them and giving something of her family to the others in the room.

When she was finished, Noah again took on himself the prerogative of doling out the ritual parts. "Jason, do you want to make *Kiddush* for us?" Noah asked. Before Jason could answer, Wendy said, "I'd like Dara to do it." At this point the guests were clear that Wendy and Noah were either like a much-bickering long-married couple who are together for the pleasure of being in an argument, or that they really were arguing and not together. None of the guests were interested in watching the argument play out or in taking sides. Watching the arguments of other couples was like accidentally coming across a dead mouse in your kitchen; you knew it had once been alive with a beating heart and blood coursing through its veins, but saw it now unnaturally stiff. You did not want to have to bend down to remove it, but just wanted it to be gone, for someone else to take it away, without your having to get near it and actually touch the petrified body.

Todd jumped in, saying, "I'd like to do *Kiddush*, if that's okay with everyone?" Wendy nodded at him gratefully, and Noah passed him the full cup of wine he'd been holding, about to give to Jason on his right, now given over to Todd on his left. Todd added, "Can I have a *bencher*?" and Noah handed him a small booklet with the blessing for the wine and Grace after Meals, which he had in his apartment from a wedding of one of the teachers at *Wisdom of the Heart* that students had been invited to. Wendy often forgot that Todd was a rabbi's son; though he wasn't currently religious, he was great at filling in these socially awkward moments. Todd began to chant, knowing the prayer by heart, not needing the book, but wanting to read it so as to be sure to emphasize each word. Nir drummed his fingers on the table to visibly demonstrate his impatience with this religious ritual, until Orly surreptitiously reached up to clasp his hand and hold it still so the drumming would cease. Todd finished the prayer and took a sip from the cup, took the bottle of wine from in front of Noah, and poured more of it into the cup he had blessed. Then he took the cup and poured some into the glasses of each of the guests near him, and gave the cup he blessed to Orly to pass to Nir and Wendy farthest away. Wendy smiled at Todd with immense gratitude, wishing she had a smile like that to give to Noah because she was pleased with something he'd done. All were sipping quietly until Noah broke the silence by humming a *niggun*. Jason and Dara joined in. The others sat at the table until Orly said, "I brought the challah from that amazing bakery behind the gas station, and I have been dying to eat it all day. Can we say *Hamotzi*?"

"You lead us, Orly." Wendy was particular to specify, mentally tallying the score, two for her side with *Kiddush* and *Hamotzi*, "but I think some people want to wash." Thus signaled, Noah, Jason, and Dara got up to ritually lave their hands. Wendy did not want to wash, to distance herself from Noah, but she knew that as hostess she needed to fetch a clean towel for the washers, so she went with them to the kitchen and foraged in a drawer until one was located. The three began to wash their hands, and as Wendy was going back to the table, Todd got up to join the washers.

Wendy wanted to cry out, "Todd, stop, please don't. I thought you were on my team," but instead patted his arm in what she wanted to be a gesture of appreciation that she hoped he would recognize as such. She returned to the table and said loudly and pointedly to Nir and Orly, "Sorry this is taking so long. We'll be eating soon," and Nir said, "I've experienced worse; don't worry. Anyway, it's not your fault *dossim* have all these . . ."—Orly completed his sentence—"rituals."

"'*Poolhan*' okay, ree-tu-al," Nir added, exaggerating how ridiculous he felt the word and action to be.

Noah, Jason, and Dara had come back from washing and seated themselves at the table. Dara started a humming tune, slow, soulful, full of melancholy, and Wendy was again annoyed, this time at the change of mood it brought. At least the other tunes, with the exception of the one she herself had initiated, were upbeat and peppy. This was like a dirge. Mercifully, Todd returned to the table hastily, and Orly raised the cloth napkin from the challot and intoned the blessing. She broke off pieces and even sprinkled salt over them as she'd seen others do at this ritual countless times, and placed the pieces on her own plate, which she passed around. The whole loaf was dismantled within moments. Orly returned her plate to her place; there was now no other serving dish to put the pieces of the remaining challah on. All wanted another piece; no one wanted to tear into the next loaf. Noah said, "Wendy don't you have a tray to put slices of challah on if we slice it up?"

"No, I don't. But why don't we just pass this around?" She lifted the loaf and ripped off a hunk of the braid. "I'll get the hummus from the fridge. Sorry, I forgot to put it out." Wendy went to get the condiment, and when she returned the formerly large braided loaf had been reduced to a few shreds and pieces. She felt saddened, the whole golden shimmering loaf gone, devoured, only crumbs and lopsided chunks remaining behind. All were passing the hummus around, trying to get some on their challah. Orly asked, to the table, "So how was everyone's week? In my house we used to do a 'highlight of the week,' Friday night, sharing whatever was most exciting or meaningful." She looked around and said, "Noah, you're the host. Why don't you go first?"

He looked at Wendy and said, "We should serve the soup before we start since there isn't much else on the table now." They had both forgotten to get more *salatim,* the *de rigueur* first course in Israel; Noah wanted to serve the soup to cover for this omission. Wendy wanted to make him squirm, so threw out, "Noah, I'll serve the soup, and you start," in what she hoped was a sweet enough tone to mask the hostility she felt. She wanted to talk not about her high, but her low of the week, having Noah tell her he was passionate about someone else.

As she went to the kitchen to get the soup, Dara followed. They weren't far enough away from the group to really have a conversation, but Dara said, "You know, Wendy, whatever is going on with you and Noah, you've invited us as guests. I'm sure what you are dealing with—I'm not going to pry"—she took the laden bowl of steaming yellow broth with the round matzah balls drifting on its surface along with slices of carrot and parsnip—"you can do without an audience. Try"—Dara started walking to the table retaining the precious liquid—"to make sure your guests are comfortable, that it's not awkward for us." As her back was almost to Wendy she added, "Just saying." Wendy continued to dole out the soup, and Dara returned to fetch the bowls, along with Todd. She was annoyed with Orly for not getting up, but it was probably for the best. There was no door or privacy between kitchen and dining room, and Wendy did not want to start crying in front of Orly, which she felt she was in danger of doing.

When all had been served soup, Wendy returned to the table, not having heard what Noah had said was his highlight. Orly turned to Wendy and asked, "So you were with Noah when he got this pamphlet?"

"Yes. Was that the highlight, Noah?" she asked in a tone she hoped wasn't too laden with the animosity she felt. He looked and her and nodded, embarrassed, and his face went back to studying the soup, probing the best place to position his spoon to cut into the matzah balls which were on the hard and solid side, as his family made them, not fluffy and airy, as from Wendy's Grandma Essie's recipe. Wendy added, "Yeah, this guy just got out of his car and made a beeline for Noah. Do they just go around all day doing that, picking out random people and handing them pamphlets to get them convinced there is something unique about the experience?"

"Yeah, that happened to my friend; waiting for a *tremp* in the army, some *dos* walked up to him and gave him a pamphlet," Nir commented.

Jason asked, interested, "So what happened?"

"*Klum*, nothing. He kept waiting for a ride."

"So what's the point of the story?" Dara asked, perplexed.

"He got a pamphlet, *zeh huh zeh*, that's it."

Noah let his spoon rest on his bowl and said to the group, "It was a message to me, and it meant something," looking pointedly at Wendy. "Seconds on soup anyone?" Nir raised his bowl to signal yes, and Jason said, "Please." Wendy added, "Me too if you don't mind," and Noah came around to ceremoniously take her bowl from her, giving her a sweet smile as he did so. Jason got up to help Noah serve.

"I don't know. Even if it is part of a ploy, Noah was still the one selected out of the crowd. That should mean something," Dara said, but added, "but I can see how rationally it doesn't make sense if it is a plan to give some people the sense that they are being singled out. Still, we're in this spiritual city. I'd like to think there is still some mystery in the world."

Todd, with his spoon in the air added, "That's the point, no? We have things we want to think, that Noah has been singled out, and those that are true. We don't know whether or not this is a technique of recruiters or a real phenomenon." He took a mouthful of soup and said to Wendy, "I didn't know you could cook; this soup is awesome."

Before Wendy could disclaim involvement in its manufacture, as she wished to, Noah said, "I made it; thanks Todd," and gave him a big gap-toothed smile and the most charming facial expression he could offer. Wendy was not in the mood to watch this and would have to warn Todd that he would be banished from her sight were he to take up with this guy. She didn't see anything getting that far, but still. Noah went back to his host role and said, "Let's continue highlights of the week." He turned to Jason on his right. "Jason?"

Jason, spoon in mouth, looked startled and then, spoon removed, pleased. "Okay, I'll try not to make this too long but"—he looked at all assembled and Wendy somehow felt she was looking at him for the first time, noticing his excited brown eyes, the pale porcelain skin that set them off by contrast, his delicate hands. She wasn't interested in him—he was Dara's guy—but she just hadn't spent any time studying him in detail until now. "So I am privileged to be learning full-time this year," Jason said, as he looked across the table at Orly and Nir, "and I do realize it is a privilege, not something I take for granted, and my highlights are those of students, learning things that are really . . . just make you connect. In Atarah Hideckel's *parsha* class this week, she talked about duality in Jacob. This portion of Toldot, generations, concerns itself with the question of whose values will prevail, those of Isaac or those of Rebecca? Each wants to see the way he or she wants things to be: Rebecca, that Jacob should be blessed, and Isaac, rooting for team Esau. But more, whose values—those of Isaac and his Abrahamic heritage, or Rebecca the Aramean, which means 'cheater'—will prevail in the next generation? The question is really, Whose child is this? Abraham's or Laban's?

"What is it about Jacob that enables him to be the fit recipient of his father's blessing? When asked by his mother, Jacob is capable of donning a costume and impersonating his brother, taking on his characteristics. Jacob is someone who is prepared for what comes his way. He is not fixed and static, but able to change in response to the demands of a situation. Jacob, as a result of his disguise and gaining Isaac's blessing, prepares years later to encounter Esau for the first time since their separation twenty years earlier. Jacob procures a gift offering for Esau, prays, and gets ready for battle. Yet what happens with Esau? There is not a confrontation, but a kiss and Esau's acceptance of the blessing Jacob offers. The real confrontation comes the night before when Jacob is alone and a 'man' comes to him. The text states clearly that it is an '*ish,*' a man, yet the angels who come to Abraham earlier are called 'men' as well, though they are clearly angels. In any case, Jacob wrestles not with Esau but with this unknown and unnamed entity. So, though he prepares to confront Esau, what he ends up struggling with is *not* Esau. Commentators suggest it might be a messenger of Esau, Jacob's conscience, a dream projection. Whatever it is, Jacob is able to confront it, though it isn't what he prepared for.

"That insight is my highlight of the week, a sense that if we prepare for and approach a problem from a variety of perspectives, we will be able to prevail over it. For most of us, what we may ultimately have to deal with is not the thing we prepared for. And the results are not what we would expect either. Jacob is *shalem,* whole, only after he has injured his thigh in the wrestling. Jacob, like all of us, is a character marked by duality, with qualities of both Abraham and of Laban. Yet, Jacob is able, ultimately, to listen to both his parents; '*vayeshma Yakov el aviv vi'el emo,*' the *parsha* ends by telling us; he listened to them both, his father and his mother. For Jacob to take on some of the characteristics of Laban to continue the Abrahamic line was a hard but necessary step. In obeying both his parents, he has proven, with his ability to access aspects of each of their heritages, he is truly theirs together."

Noah jumped in, "Jason, wow. That is such an important message: to be willing and able to cope with what life throws you in order to be ultimately *shalem.* Don't you agree, Wendy?" Noah looked at her with pleading in his eyes.

Wendy coolly said, "I don't feel like I know enough about the text to make a comment but,"—she paused—"you know"—she looked around the table—"I can identify with Jacob, becoming wounded from his unexpected encounters, confronting an adversary he did not expect." She stood up. "Noah, let's clear the soup and serve the main course."

Dara's injunction to make the guests comfortable had not been heeded; they all felt awkward now. As one, each person got up, bowl in hand to help clear the soup. No one remained seated and they went into the kitchen as a group.

While they were finally clearing the table at the meal's end, Wendy and Todd were alone in the kitchen as she rinsed off the dishes and put the food away. Wendy handed Todd a rinsed dish to dry off and asked, "Do you think you could walk Noah home tonight?"

He looked at her with a puzzled frown, taking the dish in his toweled hand. "He's not sleeping over? Isn't that the deal with a dinner party—once you successfully cook and entertain, the hosts seduce each other doing dishes, licking the food residue off each others' fingers?"

"Noah is . . . we're not together. We had a big fight today. I wanted to call off this dinner, but he insisted that it was too close to Shabbos."

Todd looked at Wendy with concern as he laid the plate on the counter. "Are you okay? Do you want me to stay so we can talk?"

"No. I'll call or e-mail my friends in the States after this." She glanced at her watch. "Someone should be home by now, it's afternoon there."

"Why do you want me to go with him? Just to be sure he is out of here?"

"If you offer to walk with him I won't be alone with him. Also . . ."

"What? Wendy?" He looked at her again, serious. "Does this have anything to do with Sam?"

Wendy didn't know how to comment, so waited for Todd to cover the conversational standstill.

Todd added, rinsing a bowl in the sink, "It's tough to be a survivor. The Biblical Noah was never the same either—after the flood, he drank and let his children see him naked; some commentators even say the sons molested their father." He looked at her. "*Was* there something that happened between Sam and Noah? I never saw Noah as Sam's type."

"I'm not at liberty to talk about it—he is very confused right now." She started to get tears in her eyes. Todd was busy drying and didn't see them, so she was able to wipe the salty liquid away quickly.

He looked up. "Done. Dessert?"

"Grandma Essie's apple chocolate chip cake. Every time it is served, someone asks for the recipe. See it over there?" He started walking over to where it was sitting on the counter.

She said, "Hey, take the plastic wrap off? Thanks. I'll bring the bowl of fruit; you take the cake. Okay?"

When they delivered the desserts to the table, Dara asked, "Do you have tea, Wendy?"

"I can heat up some water."

"I only wanted it if you had hot water already made," said Dara.

"I want coffee. You have?" Nir asked. "I'm a *goy*. I'll make it."

Wendy was fairly sure he wanted the drink only to annoy the Sabbath observers, and was waiting for him to ask whether they could put on the evening news at nine, not realizing that Wendy didn't have a TV.

Wendy answered, "I can make it." This statement provoked a raised eyebrow from Orly to Wendy. Wendy knew that by saying she would make the coffee, she was proclaiming herself for the secular team. Wendy had told Orly beforehand that, in deference to Noah, the evening would be *shomer Shabbat*. "I only have instant, though."

"I don't drink bullshit instant coffee. We'll grab a cup afterwards." He turned to Orly and she nodded, assenting. Wendy assumed he said this not because he cared either way about the coffee but to continue to irritate Noah, Dara, and Jason by reminding them that he was planning to be *mehallel shabbos*, to transgress.

Todd broke the awkwardness by saying, "Shall we cut the cake? It smells great and it's Wendy's grandmother's recipe."

After the guests left, Wendy wrote in her journal: "I'm so angry about Noah, but strangely touched by his story of kissing Sam. He comforted someone as he lay dying, even though the dying man had tried to deceive and seduce him. Noah didn't think about that, just comforted him. Kindness. But then he told me he loved me when he didn't, or wasn't sure, but needed to prove something to himself, not to me. That was selfish. Odd, someone who can be so generous, which his kiss to Sam was, could also be so deceptive.

"The pamphlet—what is that about? Maybe there is such a thing as *basherte*? It was so strange that the man just walked up to Noah in all the crowd and handed it to him."

She looked up from her desk at her bookshelf and saw a pamphlet-sized paper on top of some books. She opened the pamphlet—this time to see what was written inside.

Teshuvah tefilah and tzedaka are all paths to transformation.
We each have a neshama tehorah, a pure soul, inside us waiting to emerge like a butterfly from a chrysalis if only we will rid ourselves of the outer filth and let the inner radiance shine through.
No matter what your aveirah (sin), you can repent.
Come learn at the RISE yeshiva and our teachers will introduce you to true happiness and purity.

Call Rabbi B. at (02) 613-6333 to schedule a visit.

Wendy crumpled the brochure and threw it in her kitchen garbage on the way to the bathroom to wash up and get ready to fall into a long exhausted sleep. She didn't need to turn on the bathroom light, as Noah had taped it so it wouldn't be shut off by a negligent non-observer by accident and force the Sabbath observers to do their business in the dark. Wendy ripped the tape off the light switch with fury and cast it in the trash. She grabbed her tooth-brush and forced the toothpaste to spurt out. As she began to brush her teeth ferociously, she looked clearly in the mirror at her exposed white teeth, so sharp and hard, ready to tear into whatever necessary to provide her daily sustenance.

How could he prefer Sam to me? I've never had sex like that, so intense and furious. But then he is so . . . Oberlin wishy-washy—now I'll be religious because I got a random pamphlet; now I'll be gay because a beautiful man came on to me. She brushed the backs of her molars. *I really wanted to start building my life, being in a relationship, having dinner parties, being a grown-up. Now I'm back to being a miserable teenager, alone in my bedroom.*

That is what hurts: not being wanted. I liked him—she splashed more water on her face—*and he doesn't want to be with me. I thought it would be something ongoing over the whole year.* Wendy squeezed her apricot facial scrub out of the tube and onto her hand and started rubbing the cleanser, filled with small pieces of apricot pits, into her face, enjoying the abrasive feeling of the mushy exfoliant, light brown flecked with darker brown pieces. *I'd have a companion to do things with, go see movies, take a break, go to the museum, take long walks and talk. Now, it's just me and any friends I can corral.*

She splashed more water on her face to wash off the scrub. *I don't want to be alone forever. I want to have a boyfriend and eventually a husband. I am interesting, attractive, well read, fun to be with—I hope. I think about others— I'm not too self-centered, am I? What feels so*—she looked up at herself in the mirror and now started crying, staring at her face with the tears pouring down—*unfair. Noah just handed this down to me.* "We can't go out anymore. I'm still thinking about this guy Sam, and I want to be more religious so I'm breaking up with you." *It was so unilateral; I didn't have any say. And I guess that's what hurt most. I thought the sex was so good because it was Noah and me; but it too was lopsided, him wanting to be with a woman, and I was there, but it wasn't me that he wanted. It hurts retroactively—is that possible?* She gave her face a few more splashes of water for good measure and, looking in the mirror again, said, out loud this time, "Why didn't he give me a chance instead of thinking he was in love with someone else? He's going to change, but I'm glad I don't have to."

Three weeks after the Shabbat dinner, Noah had called Wendy and asked if they could speak. She assented and they planned to meet at a newly opened café on Emek Refaim, Café Mystica.

Thursday night was generally a big evening out for Israelis, but the hour was early, and Café Mystica not yet full. The dark room smelled faintly of incense, and each table contained candles in perforated candleholders to create an effect of shadows on the walls. The walls were a deep shade of blue, a protective and mystical color. A note on the menu, also the same shade of cerulean blue, stated that the walls matched those of synagogues in Safed, the spiritual center of Jewish mysticism. There were low tables and large pillows on the floor, a combination of India and the Middle East. There were also higher tables with conventional chairs for those patrons not willing to sit so close to the earth of the Holy Land.

When Wendy entered Café Mystica, she was looking for the Noah she dated who wore hooded zip-up sweatshirts, T-shirts of various vintage provenances, jeans, canvas Converse sneakers, and a crocheted kipah.

As Wendy glanced around the room to seek out Noah, she saw a woman laying her hands across a man's body, moving from the head down, kneeling in front of him and concentrating intensely. It seemed odd and sexually suggestive, yet this was a public place and the man was wearing a kipah. She later found out from a waitress that it was Reiki, a Japanese system of healing powers that concentrates the body's chakras to strengthen the immune system and accelerate spiritual growth. She remembered one of her interviewees mentioning it. She spotted two couples sipping herbal tea in another corner, two women wearing short skirts and tight sweaters on regular-sized chairs, and a man near the end of the room sitting by himself, reading a book. The man was wearing a black velvet kipah over his dirty brown hair, cut short, though showing traces of its former unruliness by poking up in short waves in various directions. He was wearing a clean white long-sleeved shirt with tzitzit (ritual fringes) showing underneath, black pants, and canvas high-top basketball sneakers. When Wendy entered, he looked up from the book he was reading and smiled, showing the gap between his front teeth. His gray-blue eyes gazed at her. As she was about to turn around and wait outside for Noah, he waved at her. She realized that it *was* Noah.

She walked over to the table and seated herself across from him.

He said, "Wendy, you look great. I'd forgotten how good you looked . . . wow."

Wendy was wearing a cream colored long-sleeved scoop-necked sweater, fitted though not tight, and a black velvet skirt that went to her knees, tights, and black lace-up granny shoes with a medium heel. Her clothing could certainly be worn by a woman trying to be fashionably modest in dress, but did not match the clothing of a companion with a black velvet kipah. She was wearing earrings and a bit of makeup, dressed for a night out, after a day spent with books and computer in the library.

Wendy began to blush a bit, and then saw Noah hesitating, realizing that maybe he had spoken beyond what are acceptable bounds for an unmarried religious man and woman.

"I didn't recognize you, sorry. I see you're dressing the part." She really didn't know what to say to the person sitting across from her, the one she'd been so intimate with previously.

"Not completely." He grinned at her and stuck his foot out to the side of the table, showing her the pride of his wardrobe: his white Chuck Norris Converse hightops. "I still have my sneakers," he said.

Wendy grinned back. "I'm glad."

"Some things need to change and some don't. I've been wearing these since high school. They're my trademark. I buy a few pairs at a time so I always have a replacement when one gets worn. I brought five pairs to Israel, and these are my third," he said with the pride of a kid showing an achievement that he wanted an adult to notice.

"Lots of my baalei teshuvah find ways to stay connected to their pasts, while they adhere to the rules of their new way of life."

"Am I a baal teshuvah? Do I fit with the others?"

"It hasn't been long enough, Noah." She gazed at him, feeling so estranged from this man she'd once had great intimacy with. "How are you doing, really?" He looked close to tears, and Wendy said, compassionately, "If you don't want to talk about this in public, we can go to my apartment."

He looked at her, stricken, as if she had just bitten, blissfully, into a bacon cheeseburger. "I can't. *Yichud.*" When she looked at him blankly, he explained,

"An unmarried man and woman can't be in a room alone together. It's one of the many fences around the Torah."

"Really," she said looking down at her hands. "I didn't know desire for women was your problem."

Noah smiled appreciatively. "I don't know. I had desire for you. I had desire for Sam. I feel like I can't trust my desires because they might be forbidden. I'd like to live at the yeshiva so my life could be totally structured, but I can't get out of my lease. I'm getting a stipend from NYU so I can't just blow off my university classes. I'm confused." Noah looked as though tears were about to enter his eyes.

"Isn't the yeshiva's structure the answer to your problems?"

"I don't want all of my life to be the *dalet amot*, the four walls of *halacha*. I want the structure, but I have to stretch beyond their perimeter. Does that make sense?"

"What's most difficult now?" Wendy was proud of herself for shifting into professional interviewer mode and away from anger at being deserted by a boyfriend. Her mind started whirring: *I can use this to learn something about the teshuvah process I can't from regular interviews with people who've overcome some of these initial conflicts and stayed in the yeshiva environment. A section on initial qualms and difficulties, what observances were easy or difficult to take on and what was most challenging to give up?* She began to rummage in her purse for her pocket notebook to jot down these musings.

"Do you mind?" Irritation was evident in the tone of normally calm Noah. "I'm trying to do teshuva. Put the notebook away and just be my friend. Please." Noah accompanied these words with a beseeching look.

"Just thinking in writing. You know how obsessive you can be when you're working on a project. I had an idea for my questionnaire," she said as she slipped the small wire-bound pad back into the purse slung over the side of her chair, and casually pressed her hair behind her ears to expose them to him, "All ears now. Really."

"What's hard at the yeshiva is that I don't fit in; there's no class on the right level. I'm not a beginner—I spent a year at Wisdom of the Heart and I have knowledge from university courses. But I didn't go to yeshiva high school and can't go into classes with those guys. That is kind of the yeshiva's focus, beginner and advanced. Today, I talked with Rabbi B.—I don't even know his full name; everyone just calls him Rabbi B., the *rosh yeshiva*. He tries to get to know all the students, so he can have a personal influence on their rise. He told me I should quit grad school, and the yeshiva would give me the same stipend I was getting from NYU. He has a PhD himself, American history maybe, and taught at Yeshiva University before making *aliyah,* but now says academia is a dangerous place, full of *narishkeit.* I hope the structure of the yeshiva will keep my passions, my illicit ones, at bay, at least temporarily."

"'Passions are true heathens.' My favorite line from *Jane Eyre.* Those heathens will stick around even at the yeshiva. If you're around guys all day, are you attracted to anyone?"

"Honestly, I haven't had many sexual feelings since I started going there. I'm tired when I get home after ten at night after being both there and at the university."

"You can't repress yourself forever. You'll have to deal with these issues eventually. I'm telling you this as a friend."

He replied, "Hmm."

"Let me tell you a story. When you told me that word, *yichud,* I remembered where I heard it before. Did you ever want to know how I got access to Yeshivat Temimei Nefesh? It is rather odd that they'd let a single woman talk to their students, isn't it?"

"I did, but I guessed they liked the prestige of being written up in a dissertation. What is the story?"

Wendy decided there was no reason not to tell all, so she began, "Well, you're not the only guy I've kissed in Israel, Noah." He winced at this, which she was glad to see because it meant he still could have jealous feelings even if he was the one who'd broken up with her. "The first Shabbat I was here, a guy, a baal teshuvah, who'd been at the dinner I was at, walked me home. He came up to use my bathroom, and . . . One thing led to another. I went to speak to Rabbi Gibber and told him, not about a specific student or what exactly happened, but kind of hinted that I knew personally that students who are on the path may veer from it and not be able to talk to their rabbis. So . . . if they let me do an anonymous survey but with follow-up interviews with randomly selected students, they might learn things. Find out what they couldn't otherwise."

"Do students know the rabbis might see their responses?"

Wendy hesitated. "Well, no, we haven't discussed it. It just says on the form that it is for me, but I agreed to show it to the rabbis. I guess I'll have to decide what to show and what not to."

Noah crossed his arms. "Isn't that, like, unethical, to tell someone you are doing something that only one person will see when really others will too? Aren't there, um, protocols, for research on human subjects?"

Wendy crossed her arms too. "Noah, it's *my* dissertation. Let me figure that out. It also has to get done, and in order to do that I have to get to my subjects, you know," she said with obvious exasperation in her voice. "Whatever it is I need to do for that, I will. Okay? I need to write this thing for my *career*, remember?"

"Just be careful when dealing with people, Wendy." He looked at her. "They have feelings. You're asking questions of human beings, not of your *career*."

"Like you are such an expert on feelings. Come *on*, Noah." She was weighing the cost in humiliation of admitting to him the depth of the sorrow and anguish his breakup with her had caused. She decided to tell him: "Noah, I was really hurt by you. I . . . don't think I would ever be in love with you, but . . . I liked what we had. I didn't want it to end." She breathed out. "I just wanted you to know that."

"Wendy . . ." he exhaled and then inhaled. "I really *am* sorry. I wish it weren't this way. I . . . I just don't know what I want. I shouldn't have told you about Sam."

"But then our relationship would be a lie."

"I didn't want that."

Wendy looked at him and said, "Time to figure it out, Noah. You know, *baal teshuvah* is literally 'master of the answer,' and the opposite is *hozer be'sha'ailah*, returnee to the question. Leaving the security of the answers."

"That gets at my problem. Do I want the security of the yeshiva or the unknowns of the academic world, a life of questions?"

"Strange. I had almost this exact discussion with some one a year ago, in Princeton. He also had an issue of living with freedom or security, though in a totally different context."

"Really," said Noah.

"Yeah, my friend Jay, a grad student in Talmud, was offered this position as the editor of a well known rabbi's papers. It was a guaranteed position, with a good salary, but he was starting his dissertation and wanted to do his own work. The logical thing to do would be to take the secure job. He didn't."

"Okay, so?"

"He told me this story from the Gemara, about two people in the desert with only enough water for one to live. What to do? Do you both drink and both die, or let only one drink and live? I thought they should both drink so neither of them has to watch the other die. But the Talmud says, if you own the water, you are entitled to drink it. For Jay, it meant he was entitled to use his efforts and abilities for his own work. It was a hard decision because he gave up a good salary and security."

"Where is he now?" queried Noah.

"Penned up in a tiny carrel in Firestone Library writing his dissertation."

Noah looked at Wendy. "I know it is my life and I can live it the way I want; I'm just not sure what I do want. Do I want to be gay and have intense passions and be an academic and write, or do I want to be in the yeshiva and know for sure that I am living my life properly, doing mitzvot, maybe be a rabbi and teach and help people?"

"One of my professors once asked, when I went in having no idea what to write my paper about, *What is most compelling?*"

Noah looked at her blankly.

"Not in a sexual way, just what excites you, moves you. For instance, for me, the idea of trying to understand why some people change their lives and become baalei teshuvah and some don't and why some are attracted to one type of community and some another is just fascinating. I've always wondered: can people change? This is my chance to find out. I have this friend Nina whose sister Debbie, now Devorah, became religious. Debbie was always worried about her looks and what people would think of her. When she became religious, she was still the same, except now she worries about how her *sheitel* looks and if her sleeves are long enough. That's what fascinates me—people can make radical changes and yet retain a certain core personality."

"I'm worried about whether I'll be good enough or write a decent dissertation. You're lucky you have this Fulbright. People think your work is good. You'll get a job. I don't know what I want or if I'm good at it."

"The only way to find out is to keep trying. Your department gave you funding this year. They could have just said, 'You're on your own; go get this background and come back when you're ready,' but they didn't; they're supporting you."

A woman wearing an Indian print shirt and skirt came over to the table and spoke in Hebrew too rapid for Wendy.

When she left, Wendy asked, "What was that?"

Noah explained that the woman was offering palm and tarot card readings. She wouldn't be able to work in a few minutes because there would be a speaker on the connections between healing herbs and descriptions in rabbinic literature of the plants used in the Temple for incense in the back of the café. He added, "Are you sure this place is kosher? Tarot cards and palm readings?"

"There are other guys wearing kipot here, and . . . oh, over there, by the cash register, the *t'eudah*, the *kashrut* certificate," she confirmed, proud of herself for this knowledge she'd gleaned from her baalei teshuvah.

"*Heshbon, bvakasha,*" Noah said as the server came toward them. She brought them their bill and they paid. As they left, they saw a crowd on the other side of the restaurant, gathered in rows of chairs. The owner began to introduce the speaker. The crowd was mixed, religious and secular, and almost all young, though there were a few singles in their forties and fifties, of both sexes.

Wendy said, "It's too bad my Hebrew isn't better. I'm curious. I haven't seen many places for secular and religious to mix in Israel."

"You and I are mixing," Noah added, as they walked out the door and down Emek Refaim towards Rehov Mishael, Wendy's street.

" Noah," Wendy said when they were in front of her house, "if you want to come in, you're invited," she said. "We can keep the door open."

"I can't."

"Your decision. Let's get together and talk again; you can help me understand the teshuvah process from a different perspective."

"I have to learn to use my strength for Torah."

Wendy looked at him blankly.

Noah explained, leaning against her doorframe, the light from the bulb above the door illuminating his clear gray-blue eyes which were more prominent in his face now that his hair was so much shorter. "You know the story of Rabbi Yohanan and Reish Lakish? Reish Lakish leaps into the Jordan when he sees Rabbi Yohanan. Yohanan tells him, '*Haileich laTorah,*' your strength should be for the Torah. So Reish Lakish does teshuvah, marries Rabbi Yohanan's sister, and becomes a rabbi. One day, another rabbi has been kidnapped by a group of bandits who demand something impossible. Reish Lakish says, 'I will kill or be killed.' He is the only one of the rabbis not afraid to confront the kidnappers. He uses his knowledge of criminal activity to preserve life, to the point that he is willing to give up his own life for another."

Wendy tried not to feel a surging of desire, which intensified as she listened to his gentle voice, the magic of attraction still at work with her, despite all she knew about him. Passions really are true heathens, still at work, Wendy grasped, though their breakup had hurt her.

Wendy looked at Noah, sadly. "The culmination of the teshuvah process is the willingness to be a martyr?"

Noah tapped the ground with his foot impatiently, but also with passion. "No, he has found a way to bring all of himself, every aspect, to serve the Torah, to serve God. He is using every fiber of his being to save the life of this other rabbi. It is something he, and only he, of all the rabbis, is uniquely qualified to do."

She looked at him meaningfully. "I know you won't let me hug you, but I'd like to."

Noah stretched out his arms in the air in front of him, "Consider yourself hugged."

Wendy did likewise, hugging the air in front of her.

NINE
Shared Dreams, Shared Eternity

It is a day on which we are called upon to share in what is eternal in time, to turn from the results of creation to the mystery of creation; from the world of creation to the creation of this world.
—ABRAHAM JOSHUA HESCHEL, *The Sabbath*

As she walked with Orly and Dara through the Friday night hush of Jerusalem's streets on the way home from the Hallel Yah synagogue, Wendy reminded herself how startled she'd been her first Shabbat, at the way the Sabbath overturned the usual bustle of the city's streets. No cars zooming about, or bicycles careening. No kids playing. Silence permeated the streets.

"I've interviewed people who decided to stay in Israel, change their lives around completely, after one Shabbat," Wendy told her friends. "They just wanted to continue having Shabbat here." They were coming from Hallel Yah to the apartment of Dara's boyfriend, Jason, where they were joining a group of other Americans their age in Israel for the year at a Sabbath dinner. It was the end of January, and they had to walk carefully to skirt the puddles from Jerusalem's rainy season.

Dara said, "I wish I could do that, just let myself be swept away and say, okay, Shabbos. I want it and will change everything else in my life to have it."

Orly asked, "Can't you?"

As they entered the apartment building on Be'erot Yitzhak Street, Dara said, shaking her head sheepishly, "I'm too practical. I want to support myself. I hope as a rabbi I can fuse my passion for Judaism with making a living."

Inside the building, the stairwell was lit by lights that remained bright with a Sabbath timer until later that evening. Conversation stopped as the three walked single file up four flights. The door was ajar and they heard voices inside.

Dara called out, "Jason, it's me and some guests," and a man with an apron ran out to give her a Shabbat Shalom hug and a peck on the cheek. "Good Shabbes, welcome. Can't shake hands since mine are a bit of a mess," he said, looking at the tomato seeds on his own hands.

"Thanks for having us," said Orly.

Jason added, "Make yourself at home. Dara, can you help me finish the salad?"

Orly asked, "Do you need any help?"

"If there was room for more than a person and a half in our miniscule kitchen," he laughed. "Go, mingle while we wait for the everyone."

Dara followed Jason into the cubicle-sized kitchen while Wendy and Orly continued down the narrow hallway of the apartment.

The hallway ended in a dining room. The entire space was anchored by a table with a white cotton tablecloth and surrounded by metal folding chairs. There was no standing room, as there was barely room between the chairs and the wall. The table had piles of paper plates, cups, napkins, and plastic ware on top but hadn't been set. In the center, a large bulge was covered by a tie-dyed cloth. Wendy and Orly heard people talking but couldn't see them until they carefully stepped into the room and saw an open doorframe leading into a sitting room. There were two chairs and a couch big enough for two small-boned individuals. Conveniently, all three people in the room were standing anyway. Wendy didn't know them, but as she walked in, one of the two men said heartily, "Shabbat Shalom."

"Hi." Wendy gave a generalized wave to the three. "I'm Wendy and this is Orly. I went to college with Dara. How did you get here?"

The woman, with masses of curly red hair swept off her face with a headband but tendrils still clinging to her face, laughed. "It's complicated." The two men with her laughed as well. "Do you want to know?"

Wendy was used to hearing Americans in Jerusalem talk about odd meanderings having brought them to a particular spot, usually by the hand of God. Would this story be of that ilk or would it have a different nuance, coming from someone in a more liberal community? Were the stories the same, just the places people chose to end up different? She wished she had some paper with her to jot that down. Must remember, *Narrative arc—how does it vary? Do they all reframe things so their lives fit a particular narrative pattern?*

"Sure."

The redhead began, "Short version. I was living in Australia. My father died in the States. I was in my thirties and single. Both my parents were dead. When I was little, I used to ask my mother to give me something to dream about as I went to sleep every night. I decided I wanted a baby in my life, to create someone new, to give someone else dreams. As I was pregnant, I needed others to nourish me and began to get really involved in the Jewish community. Then, I decided to go to rabbinical school and learn how to lead a community like the one I found. I came here in August, four weeks after I gave birth."

"Where is the baby?" Orly asked.

"Right there." The woman pointed at a baby carrier with a handle that was sitting in the corner enveloping a sleeping infant. The baby's hair was a blonde fuzz, and the lashes of her closed eyes were dark against her porcelain skin, each feature etched carefully.

"She's beautiful. What's her name?" Orly asked.

"Eliana. It means 'God has answered me.'"

Wendy wanted to ask the woman about mechanics. *Who was the father? Did it happen the natural way or with a turkey baster? How did she manage to be in school, study, and write papers with a baby?*

One of the other men began an introduction, "Hey, I'm James, this is Rich. How about you? How did you get here?"

"I'm here to write my dissertation," said Wendy.

"I'm a journalist, working on a book about immigration and my family," Orly added.

"Family. I wish mine would visit. I wanted to show them Israel. They won't come; we're meeting in Europe in February. It's just another way they are putting down my career choice. All they say is, 'Why can't you just go to law school and then be synagogue president? You won't have to worry about how to pay the rent.'" James sighed.

"Don't complain; you're lucky you still have parents," Amy the redheaded mom said, gently rocking her daughter's baby carrier.

The five of them heard noise as the door was opened and more guests entered the apartment. Dara and Jason were saying, "Noah, Bonnie, Shabbat Shalom, come in. Are we ready now?" Wendy tensed as she thought, *Noah—it couldn't be Noah Lazevsky; Jerusalem isn't that small.* But she listened and it sounded like his voice. Jason must have invited him, not realizing that Dara invited *her* and that it would be awkward to have the two of them together. Why would they do that—or was it on purpose, to get her back together with him? Why wouldn't one of them have told her?

Jason and Dara came into the living room, and Dara said pleasantly, "We're all here."

Jason ordered, "Everyone find a seat and we'll introduce ourselves once we're seated. Dara and I will sit here"—he indicated the chairs closest to the kitchen—"and everyone else sit wherever."

"If no one minds, I'm taking this spot so I can hear Eliana when she wakes up," Amy said.

Orly and Wendy moved out of the sitting room to take places at the table. As she walked, she and Noah caught each other's eyes. Noah looked good, Wendy noticed. He was wearing a knit sweater, with a geometric design in different shades of blue that set off his blue-gray eyes, and navy dress pants. His hair had gotten longer and looked not unruly, but curly and pliant. She was surprised to find she was happy to see him. He gave her a broad smile. She nodded back. What did he see looking at her? Shoulder-length black curly hair, brown eyes, pleasant smile, passably attractive but not a face that would stop traffic on the street. Wendy was wearing a pink turtleneck sweater, paired with a tan and pink paisley print scarf, a long darker-pink wool skirt and brown leather boots for Jerusalem's winter rainy season. Did she want him to notice her? She wished she'd put on some makeup.

Seating assignments complete, Jason began, "Before we start, let's introduce ourselves. Say your name, how you got to this Shabbat table, and what you're doing in Israel this year. I'll start: Jason Lessing, and I'm at Wisdom of the Heart Yeshiva for a second year. Trying to figure out what's next. Dara?"

"I'm Dara Glasser. I'm also at Wisdom and I'm going back to finish up at the Reconstructionist Rabbinical School in Philly next fall."

"Noah Lazevsky. I came to Israel to improve my reading of kabbalistic texts for a degree at NYU. I'm not sure whether I will go back and finish or stay here in yeshiva. I know Jason's roommate, Yehoshua, from RISE, my yeshiva. Where is he anyway?"

"Where he wants to be," said Jason. "He never wants to commit in case he gets a better invite."

The introductions continued: "Rich Rosensweig, I'm a first-year rabbinic student, and Dara and I are in the rabbinic social justice network. My journey to this table started when I was working in New Mexico for an art dealer who sold Native American pottery. When I met artists on their reservations, I kept getting asked what tribe I was from. I decided to learn about my own tribal traditions. Here I am."

"James Glatstein, also first-year Reform rabbinic student, and I know Dara from the same place. I'm from Manhattan originally."

There was a knock at the door. Jason went to get it and came back with another man bearing a beard that was scruffy and looked newly grown in. When the man removed his black bomber jacket, he was wearing a white shirt with tzitzit showing underneath, black pants, and nicely styled black shoes. Wendy couldn't decide whether he was attractive or not, as the beard obscured his features.

"This is Yehoshua, everyone," said Jason. "He lives here when he isn't at RISE or the *Kotel*."

"Sorry I'm late. Do I get a chair?" he said to Jason.

"I'll get my desk chair," Jason said as he went down the hall to fetch it. When he returned, they all reshuffled chairs. The chairs repositioned, Yehoshua was seated at the end of the table where Rich had been, so he was between Noah and Rich, facing Amy at the other end.

Dara said, "Shua, introduce yourself. Say what you are doing this year."

"Yehoshua Hendon. I came here to go to Wisdom, but I switched to RISE a few weeks ago. I'm from Detroit."

At her turn, Wendy wasn't sure what to say—*I came here to study people like you? I have a tape recorder under the table so be careful.* But out of respect for her friend Dara, she didn't have a notebook or tape recorder; she was trying to be off duty. "Wendy Goldberg. I'm here to write my dissertation. I'm from New Bay, New York, and knew Dara at Columbia."

"Orly Markovsky. I'm a journalist, and I know Wendy from Camp Kodimoh and here, and Dara through Wendy."

"Amy Ross, from Australia and New Jersey, mother of Eliana Chaya, and student at Hebrew Union College, where I met Dara."

"Bonnie Gardner. I know Dara from home, Elkins Park, Pennsylvania. I'm a junior at Bryn Mawr, and at Hebrew University this semester. I just got here a few days ago."

Wendy felt relieved that Bonnie was a younger friend of Dara's from home and just got here so probably hadn't met Noah before tonight. It bothered her that she had thought, when they walked in together, that Bonnie and Noah were a couple.

Before Wendy had time to contemplate any further, the singing started. It was a bouncy tune, peppy like some kind of revival music. *Why was everything always so cheerful? Wasn't there any music that was more inner-directed, more serious?* She looked around the table and saw that all were enjoying the singing, engaged. Dara nudged Jason and nodded at Wendy and Orly. He turned around and found a pile of *benchers*, books with the songs and blessings sung at the Sabbath table, in the corner of the room. He opened the small pocket-sized book to the proper page and handed it to Wendy and Orly.

Wendy thought, *Why are books and papers always thrust into one's hands— read this, believe that. Can't we just enjoy the experience of the words and music, their beauty, without labels?* She remembered going to a museum endowed by a wealthy society woman in Boston. The philanthropist had created a carefully constructed building, which contained beautiful objects: statues, paintings, handcrafted laces, china, furniture, hand-tooled leather books. Isabella Stewart Gardner did not want labels on any of the items because she wanted visitors to experience her things for their singular magnificence, without getting bogged down in categorizing and classifying. Wendy wished she could go through religious rituals like that, absorbing their beauty and grandeur, not worrying about the minutiae like getting the words right, pronouncing the foreign syllables. When she went to that museum, she remembered sitting in the courtyard, being surrounded by elaborate displays of orchids, mosaic tiles, and intricately carved stones, any spot her eyes gazed on yielding an object of beauty. All she had to do as an observer was take it in, hear the fountain, smell the flowers, look at the art. Couldn't the rituals in Judaism be less elaborate and confusing, not *stand up, sit down, take steps back and forth, bounce on your toes,* but as simple as cultivating the peace and wholeness one experienced with the plash of a fountain?

Obediently, she pointed at the book for her friend Orly, who knew the Hebrew but not the unfamiliar tune, to the verses about the angels of Sabbath. It was nice imagery, angels coming and greeting, blessing and leaving. The tune had a sort of drumbeat to it, da da-da *da* da, da da-da-da da, and it repeated each of the four verses three times. By the end, Orly was humming along. Then there was another Hebrew song, from Proverbs about the woman of valor, and finally blessings over wine. Jason opened a bottle of wine and poured it with a flourish into a large wooden cup, which looked like it had been painted in a Russian style with bright purples, oranges, and greens. He stood up, then Yehoshua stood up, and then everyone else stood too as he declaimed the blessing over the wine, remembering the creation, God's completion of creation in six days and resting on the seventh. Jason drank, poured more wine into the large cup, and then from that cup to thimble-size plastic cups.

Everyone passed the cups around the table to the person next to them. "Go ahead, drink when you get it, don't wait," he said heartily. It was white wine, not high quality, what student budgets could afford. Orly started coughing after she drank because she didn't like it. Wendy hoped no one noticed the cough and gave a small cough herself in sympathy, so Orly wouldn't be so noticeable.

Yehoshua said, "L'chaim, l'chaim" as he drank his. "Who brought this? It's nice," he commented.

"Anyone who wants to wash, in the kitchen," said Dara.

"Wahhh. Wah, wah," came the sudden cry of a baby. Amy jumped out of her chair to soothe her daughter. Everyone else rose and converged toward the hallway to go to the kitchen and wash their hands. Amy went to the living room to pacify her daughter. Partly because she didn't want to deal with the ritual washing and partly because she was curious about what it was like to have a baby, Wendy walked over and asked, 'Can I help?"

Amy looked up and said, "Sure, take this," handing her a diaper filled with thick dark smelly poop. "Find out where to put it? I appreciate it," she added as she returned to wiping Eliana free of the sludgy substance and putting a clean diaper on her. "I just started her on solid food now that she is close to six months, so the poop is a little smelly." The baby was still crying, the volume lowering as she realized she was being cared for.

Wendy was disgusted as she took the diaper from Amy. She thought, *This woman wanted to create the possibility for dreams and all she is getting is poopy diapers. Ugh.* She went to find Dara or Jason. As Dara came towards her in the hallway, Wendy held up the offending item. Dara saw it and pointed to a door without a word. Wendy went into the bathroom and placed it in the garbage can. *This is going to be worse than the airplane. Ten adults and a baby, a tiny bathroom and a stinky diaper . . .* she thought as she placed it in the proper receptacle and washed her hands, with soap, in the sink. She prayed she would not need to use the bathroom before the evening ended.

When she returned to the table, about half the guests were in their places and humming a wordless tune. When everyone was seated, Dara, with a flourish, swiped the tie-dyed cloth off the mound in the center of the table. Two large whole-wheat challah breads appeared, and Dara grasped them in both hands, looked around the table at each person individually, and intoned in Hebrew, "Blessed are you, Shechinat Yah, the indwelling Holy Feminine who brings forth bread from the earth." Dara broke the challah into pieces, dipped each piece in a small bowl of salt, and passed the large chunks around.

As she was doing this, Yehoshua got up and went into the kitchen. He came back holding two white braided rolls and said loudly in Hebrew, "Blessed are you, Lord our God, King of the Universe, who brings forth bread from the earth." He took a piece of his roll and passed one to Noah next to him. Noah took it and chewed noisily. Dara said, "Yehoshua, not into gender free language?"

He said, "Its Shabbes; we're all Jews; let's not argue. God is my king; it's all for a reason. Leave it at that."

"That language doesn't work for all of us anymore," Dara retorted.

Noah said, "I need some mystery in my concept of God. I like the indwelling nature of the feminine, the Shechina. It's all over mystical texts, but I want to pray to a king. I want certainty in my God. The Shechina is just too . . . unstable for me."

Wendy was coming up empty for a comeback line. She couldn't let such a reductive statement go, but was too mad to let her wiser self work on a good line. Orly said, "That makes no sense, Noah. Why is a feminine divinity inherently unstable? Women are all hysterical? Haven't we moved past that?" she said with sarcasm. Wendy, next to her, squeezed Orly's arm in gratitude for her quicker wit.

Dara nudged Jason and said, "Let's get the salads."

The hosts departed for the kitchen. No one broke the ensuing silence until Yehoshua, sitting at the other end of the table from Amy, who was holding a cooing Eliana on her lap, said, "Your daughter is adorable. How old is she?"

"Five and a half months. She's just starting solid food. She can turn over and is really beginning to be playful. I'm so proud," she said, as Eliana yanked at her beaded necklace. She asked Bonnie to hold the baby while she took the necklace off and put it in her pocket.

"Is her dad away for Shabbes? He must miss her," Yehoshua queried.

"He's always away," laughed Amy. "In Australia. It was a donor situation. I wanted to do this on my own."

Yehoshua blushed and stammered, "Oh."

"I wasn't in a committed relationship and this was the best way to have a family. Eliana has brought so much love into my life. People in my congregation were so caring, coming to doctor's appointments, bringing me food, checking up on me. Having her completely changed the direction of my life."

"Why didn't you get married?" Yehoshua said gruffly.

Dara and Jason returned with the salads. They put out hummus sprinkled with chick peas and pine nuts and spritzed with olive oil, a tomato and cucumber salad, guacamole, tabouli with fresh mint, and a carrot salad with raisins and walnuts. They also brought out a plate of warm pita bread.

"Amy isn't criticizing your life choices, so why are you attacking her? Does it threaten you?" said Dara.

"I'm not attacking her, just saying that it would be easier to have a baby with a partner. It's for sure a mitzvah to bring life into the world. Women just aren't obligated." Yehoshua gestured, making a silly face and waving at Eliana who cooed as he added, "She's a cutie."

"Amy is amazing for choosing to bring love into her life by having a baby. I'm jealous—it isn't as easy for men," Rich said as the others laughed.

People were helping themselves, salads being passed around. No one spoke as plates were filled. Finally Jason said, "Words of Torah?" He hoped to find a unifying topic before another quarrel broke out. There were generalized nods, and he began.

"This week's reading ends the book of Genesis with the death of Yosef," he continued, "Joseph the righteous. It's odd to end this book with bones in a coffin. It began with the grandeur of the creation of the universe, and now the last image Genesis offers us is the bones of Joseph. I want to focus on how this image gets us to the next book, the book of Exodus.

"This portion contains dreams and memories, certainty and doubt. Don't we all wish we could have certainty, and tell those who have harmed us, "Am I in the place of God?" as both Jacob and Joseph do at different points in their lives?

"Dreams aren't tangible. They have no monetary worth, no substance to grasp and acknowledge. Yet, Yosef was able to take the currency of dreams in all its slipperiness and indeterminacy and convert it to win the trust of the cupbearer and the baker, and eventually the Pharoah himself. My hope for all those gathered round the Shabbos table tonight is that you too can convert your dreams from indeterminate agents to bearers of something solid, meaningful, material. The cupbearer was, as his job requires, receptive, able to capture and contain the slippery liquid that is liquor, that bears the possibilities for dreams, for realms different from ordinary life, both for good and ill. The baker was too proud of the solidity of his own creations, and they were destroyed as he was. Yosef was able to praise God for what God had given him: the ability to decode, to interpret. The Egyptian name he was given by the Pharoah, 'Tzafnat Paneach,' literally means 'revealer of hidden things.' Yosef is mysterious because God has given him that ability to decode lives, both his own and others.

"At the very end of this week's reading, Yosef tells his brothers that he is dying, but God will surely visit them. These words, *pakod yifkod,* he will surely visit, recur again in the book of Exodus as a sign that will help the children of Israel decode the hand of God in the future. These words reassure the people that God is behind their salvation. Each individual is now entrusted with that task: to decode a life and to find that God has given each of us a way to be fertile even in our lands of affliction. We don't always know why God puts us in narrow places. *Mitzrayim,* Egypt, literally means narrow, constricting; but even when God puts us into these places, God allows us a way out. Even though Yosef is in this place of immense constriction, he is able to say, on naming his son Ephraim, 'God has made me fruitful in the land of my affliction.' That paradoxical fertility is the crux of the human condition. For who can say he is in an ideal setting, a place that is not in some way an affliction? Even we who are privileged to be studying in the land of Israel this year, we are not in a place without afflictions. Sam Handelman and Benjamin Margolis, *Hashem yinakem damam*, may *Hashem* avenge their blood, our fellow American students, were killed for being Jews on an Israeli bus.

"Genesis ends with a coffin containing the bones of Yosef, yet Exodus begins with births, the swarming and teeming masses of Jews being born—a multiplication on a vaster scale than the fertility amidst affliction of Yosef. That is Shabbos too: the ability to sit back, to celebrate the bounty and fertility of the week, to make time to rejoice in the midst of the misery and affliction of the human condition. Yosef was able to get to that certainty, that feeling that God was with him, that despite the bad, God made it good, through his dreams. He is different from his father Yakov, who had the dream of the ladder of connection with heaven in Bet El, but lived without prophecy, without divine connection for the many years Yosef was absent from his life. Yakov's dream and connection wavered but his son's never did.

"One of the differences between father and son is in a chance Yakov has to retell his life story, his personal journey. At the beginning of the portion he blesses all his sons, and then the sons of Yosef. As he is blessing Yosef's sons, Yakov does something peculiar. He switches his hands so that his right is on the head of the younger and his left on the older. In essence, in this moment, Yakov is re-enacting the primal scene of his life, his wresting of the birthright from his older twin. Yakov's blessing of his grandsons retells the struggle between himself and Esau as a smooth transition with acceptance by both parties that the younger son of Yosef, Ephraim, should precede the older, Manasseh. In Yakov's new version of his life, there is no enmity between the brothers. He gives the blessing to the one he designates, and they both accept the verdict, without hatred or bloodshed.

"The beauty of history is that it can be shaped with hindsight. Shakespeare, in *Henry V*, speaks of the ability to "remember with advantages." In reviewing his life, Jacob reshapes his primal scene of impersonating Esau to gain his father's blessing and removes the violent urges of the shunned older sibling. Jacob is given the ability to re-envision his life, re-enact it in a new form, much as Joseph is able to tell and retell both his own life and the lives of others through dream interpretation.

"This portion itself is closed—it is the only unit of the Torah that does not contain a space between itself and the previous section. Yet, it encodes another opening. The eighty-five verses in this section are a sign for the word "*peh*," mouth, because the numerical value of the letters "*peh*" and "*heh*" is equivalent to eighty-five. The mouth with which this portion speaks is the possibility of re-envisioning and transforming the past. Perhaps the ability to use advantaged memory of past knowledge can make possible an enhanced future, as Jacob suggests in the blessing he bequeaths to his grandsons.

"We don't know what that future is, or how to ultimately decode it. But when the future comes, when we are able to decode our dreams, I hope we will say with Yosef, 'God turned it to good.' The ability to say, whatever happens, God turned it to good, is my *bracha* for each person here. Shabbat Shalom."

When Jason finished talking, there was no sound but the breathing of the Shabbat guests. The ill will of the disagreement over the gender to address God seemed temporarily dispersed in the silence of quiet breathing rather than stunned awkwardness. All the listeners were involved in what Jason had been saying, each with his or her own thoughts and concerns about what their narrow place, their Egypt, might be and how—or whether—they would get to the point of feeling that what had happened to them in life had not been for bad, but for good.

"Jason, thank you. That was just . . . words of Torah are so . . . sustaining," said Amy, looking down at Eliana nourishing herself at her breast. Amy had a blanket draped over herself, but Wendy felt awkward seeing a woman nursing her baby even if no anatomical parts were outwardly visible. The baby was making suckling noises, greedily lapping provision from her mother.

"I love decoding things, thinking about a text. I was an English major," added James. "That concept that Joseph was able to take something insubstantive like a dream and convert it into a useful currency is so . . . cool. I loved *Joseph and the Amazing Technicolor Dreamcoat* as a kid, but I never thought of that," he blurted.

"'To be fruitful in the land of affliction.' I really like that idea," echoed Wendy. "It is what each of us struggles with, how to be productive, despite affliction. The idea that each person has to decode life in a particular way; that's what I'm writing about. I'm also thinking about what Amy said earlier, that she had a baby to hand down her dreams, to enable them to go beyond her, as her parents gave her things to dream about," she mused.

Jason responded, "Thanks. I can't take personal credit for most of the ideas since I'm echoing the ideas of the *meforshim*, the commentators."

"The cool thing is," Rich added, "Jews all over the world are reading the same section of text every week. We are coming from different places, going different places, but still reading the same text, right, Yehoshua?" He grinned.

"We do read the same Torah, for sure. But, *I* believe in it as God's word, revealed as a code for my life, and you see it as a myth with sacred overtones, but no real influence."

Removing the baby from her breast—still covering herself with a blanket and propping Eliana on her shoulder to burp her—Amy added, as she gave the baby gentle pats on the back, "We'll see what happens. We need to add other words to our cycle of sacred readings. Words of women, of gays and lesbians, of different groups so people feel they can hear their own voice at sacred moments. I'm not saying we have to replace the Torah, but we need to find other words too. That's going to be our task as liberal rabbis in the future."

Puzzled, Bonnie responded, while twirling her hair, "But what else is there besides the Torah? It's sacred text."

"That's the question," replied Amy. "We'll have to see where people find value and sacredness. It may be that there are contemporary poets who make their way into the liturgy, or songs, like the one Rabin was singing when he was killed."

"Get real," Yehoshua replied. "Some singer can replace Torah? Ridiculous!"

"Why not?" Amy said defiantly. "It's the will of the people. We've decided women and gay people can be rabbis. We can change our sacred orientation."

"Then it's not Judaism any more," Yehoshua added.

"Judaism is what Jews say it is," Amy continued.

"Why study Torah at all then?" Yehoshua continued with growing anger in his voice. "Why not just study the works of Philip Roth and say, 'Jews read it, so let's make it our sacred text!'" Yehoshua exclaimed.

"More American Jews *have* read *Portnoy's Complaint* than, say, the book of Lamentations," added Noah.

"We *could* make Philip Roth or Debbie Friedman our sacred text," Dara interjected. "In *my* branch of Judaism, the past has a vote and not a veto. We have to consider that texts have historical resonance. After Jason's words, I think we can agree that the Torah is probably much richer than anything even the most talented author can write." She gave Jason a broad smile, which he returned. "*Yasher koach*, Jason. That was a really nice *dvar Torah*."

"You're admitting the Torah is a divine product," Noah said triumphantly.

"Divinely inspired. There's a difference," Dara finished.

"Everyone had enough salad?" Jason interjected. "Dara, let's get the main courses."

Yehoshua stood up. "I'll help."

"You know," Orly stated, "every Jew at this table has a completely different opinion, but here we are, eating together, celebrating Shabbat, talking to each other through the squabbles. We do still have shared dreams, like the dream of creating a land together."

"It's a family dynamic kind of thing," said James. "We might dislike each other, but we need to come together. So we do."

"Yeah," said Bonnie. "I have lots of great aunts and uncles and, even though they are all in their seventies, they still fight like they're kids. But they want to have holidays together even if they fight about who brings what food, whose house it should be at, when . . ."

"My family too. All these arguments about what, when, where—yet we do ultimately get together. I remember hearing a definition of family as a group of people with whom you imagine a non-existent home," said Wendy.

Dara returned bearing a rice, nut, and cheese casserole and chimed, "Wendy's right. That could be a definition of the modern Israel. An imagined home—no one is satisfied with what it is, yet we are all in process with it."

"I'm not sure," said Noah. "Wouldn't it be better if we could all agree on what home is and what values we want in it?"

"Noah, you don't even know who you want to make that home with, much less the 'values' you want there," Wendy said sarcastically, her face contorted with annoyance. *Maybe I shouldn't be so publicly mean,* she thought once the words were out of her mouth. *There was no going back now,* she realized. She had drawn the battle lines and put herself and Noah on opposite sides. Even if the evening had been an attempt to get them back together, it was not happening.

Jason and Yehoshua came out with full platters. One held a baked eggplant dish with cheese and tomatoes; the other was a sort of stew with potatoes, barley, carrots, zucchini, and tomato. The dishes appeared straight out of the *Moosewood Cookbook*, a gift from Jason's mom, who was concerned about his getting proper nutrition as a vegetarian.

Amy continued, "That's the nice thing about having a baby—I know who I want to make my home with."

"I'm glad you've found the right balance, Amy," said Noah with sincerity. "I wish we all could. Wendy, maybe you'll find the right person to make your home with." She felt sad hearing him say that. Even if she hadn't been entirely sure about him, the finality of these words ruled out anything between them in the future.

"It isn't the only thing I want. I'm looking to have a career. Family comes second," Wendy said, helping herself to the rice casserole and passing it to Orly on her left.

"You can have both," Orly chided.

"I need to reach my own dreams first, before I can pass them on to someone else," Wendy responded.

Bonnie said, "Isn't having children part of the dream? I wouldn't mind working for a while, but when I have children I want to be with them. Family first."

"I'm with you, Bonnie," said Yehoshua. "The traditional way of doing things, getting married and having kids right away, is the best. That way you grow and develop with your children, not wait till everything is settled and you are forty. That's my plan."

"Plans are great, but dreams don't always adhere to plans," said James.

"What do you mean, buddy?" Rich queried, looking at James next to him.

"Dreams are so . . . diffuse. There is this clear image; but then you wake up, poof, it dissipates. Like cotton candy, which looks so solid until you put your tongue on it, and it just becomes nothing, colored sugar. It used to disappoint me so much as a kid—it looked so good and then it wasn't there. Then it is gone completely. Being in Jerusalem this year is like a dream for me. I . . . I don't know if I want to be a rabbi any more. I wanted to do it because I love being Jewish. Now, being here, I see all these other ways to be Jewish, not just as a rabbi. I love not driving on Shabbat, the connectedness to the city I feel walking, not having to worry about spending money. I don't know if I'd even like it if I just stayed on, outside the school framework."

Amy said, high-pitched, "You can't leave the program; I'd lose my best sitter. I'm counting on you to see me through."

James gave her a smile. "As long as I'm in the program, I'll always be happy to watch Eliana."

Wendy realized, watching James, that what irritated her about Amy was that both of these guys, younger than Amy, were infatuated with her. It may have been their admiration at her boldness at being able to go ahead and do something that she wanted, which they envied, being more-insecure twenty-three- or twenty-four-year-olds in comparison to her early-thirty-some-thing age. Amy seemed to revel in their attention without noticing its nature. Did motherhood turn flirtatious signals off?

Dara said, "I agree with you, James. I love Shabbat in Jerusalem, people to share meals with, going for walks, relaxing. I don't know that it is enough to make me change my dream of being a rabbi. I'm just . . . Not willing to change so much of myself."

"Is that a good thing or a bad thing?" Jason challenged her.

"I hope it's a good thing. I don't want to become a radically different person than I was when I came," said Dara.

"Isn't there something wonderful about finding a passion and yielding to it?" Noah queried.

"I think so," said Amy. "James, if you feel passionately about life here, stay. Leave rabbinic school. I give you permission," she said, smiling and pushing the coppery strand of hair that Eliana had yanked in front of her mouth away from her face.

Jason said, "The Torah warns us about giving in too much to passions in the story of Nadav and Avihu, the sons of Aaron, who offered strange fire to the Lord and were killed for it. The commentators are perplexed by the story—what did they do that was so wrong? Doesn't God want us to serve with joy? Some say they tapped into the passion and joy felt by the high priest on the Day of Atonement, the joy at being forgiven, but inappropriately. Not all passion is acceptable."

Orly said, "Wendy, you're writing about Jewish returnees. Do most follow their path out of passion or for other reasons?"

"Some didn't like their lives before and wanted something completely different. Some fell in love with Shabbat or Torah study. Some don't have rational explanations, or will say, it just made sense to me. I guess I have to consider a space for passion," she answered, surprised at her words.

"Maybe we have something to add to Jason's *dvar Torah*," added Noah. "That just as we hope we can achieve certainty, we hope we can find and pursue our passions appropriately."

"I'll second that," said James.

"Dessert anyone?" said Jason. He and Yehoshua cleared the uneaten food platters off the table, while Dara went into the kitchen to get a garbage bag. She returned and everyone passed paper plates and cups and plastic flatware into the trash. Then, the three hosts returned to the table bearing the desserts. There were cookies from Marzipan Bakery that Wendy had brought, a bowl of pistachio nuts, and a large elaborately decorated cake.

"Ooh, that cake looks good. Who brought it?" Bonnie asked.

"I did," said Rich. "Angel Bakery, best in Jerusalem. Everyone has to try it."

"You won't find me saying no," says Yehoshua. "One should enjoy what is permitted. We have to give an accounting in heaven for denying any permissible pleasures."

Wendy found herself annoyed by his logic. "Doesn't it take the fun out of everything, if you are only doing it because it is permissible, not because you really want to?"

"Depends on your attitude."

TEN

"Good Night World"

Death destroys a man, but the idea of death saves him.
—E. M. FORSTER

At the beginning of February, Wendy was strongly engaged with her oral interviews. She'd done the preliminary questionnaires and analyzed them. Now, with the permission of the *roshei yeshiva* at RISE/Yeshivat Temimei Nefesh and RISEN/ Bayit Ne'eman, she was speaking with students individually, getting them to tell their stories. This was the part of her work she loved: getting her subjects to the point of revealing something, eliciting a particular detail that marked a moment of certainty for them. She loved to hear them articulate a turning point when they knew their path was leading irrevocably in one direction and not another, and to understand something new about themselves and their journey, to consider themselves in a fresh way in light of her questions. It was thrilling to watch insight come, seeing the glistening on a face as though the fairy dust of understanding had just been sprinkled upon it. Of the fifteen interviews she had done so far, each subject had had a moment like that.

And then there was this most recent one.

Standing at the place where the cabs stopped for passengers outside the Dung Gate of the Old City on her way to meet Orly for dinner in the center of town, Wendy thought about her last interviewee of the day, Shaul Engel. Like her, he was from Westchester—the town of Larchmont, not her New Bay—and a year or two younger. If she'd tried, it would not have taken long to do the Jewish geography thing; he would have known friends of hers who had younger siblings or belonged to his synagogue or went to his summer camp. The interview seemed to take its course, she remembered, fingering her backpack to be sure the tape recorder and computer were in there, until she got to the question about the irrevocable moment, when he *knew*, for sure, what his direction was.

He could not answer.

She needed her data. She challenged him, and cringed now in retrospect. What did she say? Something like, *Maybe you* won't *stay religious. Everyone else could answer it.* After her remark, Wendy saw shame in his eyes. She shouldn't have said that; she was supposed to *hear* them tell their stories, not to shape and control what subjects said. Configuring the information, finding the patterns and motifs, that was all for *after* the interviews, when she was writing. During the interview, Wendy was just supposed to listen. *Ask open ended questions; induce the subject to tell his story so you can obtain information*—that was the key interviewing technique, her anthropology advisor, Violet Dohrmann, had instructed. Maybe she could somehow do something to let him know she regretted her conduct? What? Apologize? Tell him. She wanted to let him know she was unnecessarily rude—it had been the end of the day, she was tired, now she realized her behavior was inappropriate. *I'll do that,* she decided.

Once she got back to her apartment, she'd send an e-mail. She and Orly were planning to have dinner and catch a movie. She made a note to herself in her planner, so she wouldn't forget, before a cab came and she went off to her destination.

Later that evening, Shaul Engel strode into his room at Yeshivat Temimei Nefesh. He crossed the room, over piles of *Jerusalem Post* newspapers, kicked a Wilt Chamberlain regulation basketball away from his feet, and reached the bookcase with his personal possessions. There were two other bookcases and three beds for the three students who shared this dormitory room at the yeshiva. Everyone else was *davening* Maariv, the evening prayer. Shaul reached for morning prayer accessories, *tefillin*, on top of the shelf. He took the heavy plastic case, which held both a tallis and a velvet pouch containing the *tefillin*, and sat in the chair at the desk intended as a place for students to write letters extolling the virtues of the religious life. All he had to do now was adjust the *tefillin*, recently purchased so the leather would be strong. He had written his letter. He removed it from his jacket pocket and placed it unmistakably in the center of the desk.

He removed the *shel rosh*, the headpiece, from its blue velvet case and began to undo the knots. The amulet part of the *tefillin*, the heavy black box, was supposed to rest on the forehead, between the eyes. The leather strap ringed the head and held the box in its place at what the ancient rabbis believed was the seat of the intellect. The knot fitted the nape of the neck. His hands were practiced at adjusting the knots. New students at the yeshiva came to him to adjust *tefillin* that they had never worn, items that had belonged to a father, grandfather, or brother who had probably never worn them either. Shaul could tug and pull the knots so the amulet fit naturally on someone who was trying on this ritual item for the first time. Once the *tefillin* fit, other practices would too, he would tell new recruits.

Instead of helping others now, Shaul was helping himself. The headpiece was loosened to fit around his neck, a noose with an amulet. The knot was tight. It would hold against the weight of his body, he thought, snapping the leather. He knew he would succeed.

>   Good Night World
>   by Yankev Glatstein
>
>   Good night wide world
>   great stinking world.
>   Not you, but I slam the gate.
>   With the long gabardine,
>   With the yellow patch—burning—
>   With proud stride
>   I decide—
>   I am going back to the ghetto.
>
>   Good night. It's all yours world. I disown
>   My liberation.

I return to the daled amot
from Wagner's pagan music to niggun
I kiss you, tangled strands of Jewish life.
Within me weeps the joy of coming home.

This was the opening of the letter on his desk, the poem by the famous Yiddish poet. The letter went on to speak about Shaul's desire to "go home" to death, and his craving the certainty that would accompany it. He wrote that he didn't want to remain in the wide world, but to have definite knowledge that he would never again commit a sin. After his roommates found his body, hanging from the light fixture in the bathroom, the desk chair having been kicked away from underneath him, they gave the letter to the *rosh yeshiva*, who took it personally to Shaul's grieving parents when the rabbi accompanied the body back to the States for burial.

Despite feeling incredibly shitty after going to see a body off yet again at the airport, Wendy had an appointment, made weeks ago, with Fulbright advisor Avner Zakh, in the late afternoon. She didn't have a good excuse to break it. She was supposed to meet with him periodically over the year so he could monitor her progress. The meetings were perfunctory chats, more for his benefit than hers, to make sure Zakh was fulfilling his obligations and could continue to collect his Fulbright advisor salary, paid in US dollars. For his duties of meeting with a few students individually over the year, and the entire group once a month, he made a hefty percentage of his paltry Israeli academic's salary.

Wendy had learned not to expect much from seeing him. She had her plan for her research, and had been more or less following it, handing out surveys, then doing recorded interviews with select subjects, Shaul among them. The trouble was, at this point, she hadn't actually started writing the introduction to her dissertation. She knew that's what she should be doing by this point in the year. She had done most of the literature review; she had notes on the intro; she just needed to knock it into shape, connect the ideas, flesh it out. It wasn't complicated, but it wasn't done either. As her undergraduate writing teacher might have said, the structure is there, she just had to paint the walls and add some furniture.

For Wendy, the hardest part of anything was making decisions. If she painted the wall one color, it closed off the possibility for another. What if she didn't like it? Sometimes, it was easiest to do nothing. Her main advisor, Cliff Conrad, was not pushing her too hard to give him something written, but hinting via e-mail that he'd like to see something. He kept her apprised of the progress of her peers in the States, and let her know he expected she was in the same place, workwise. Wendy did have what seemed to be valid excuses. She wanted to work on the interviews, write them up more, to get to a sense of what the trends were so that she could write the beginning. She should have the general direction of the research first, because she'd have to rewrite it anyway if what she came up with differed vastly from what she initially thought. That was true.

There was also a deeper truth. She was scared to start writing. What if it wasn't good enough? What if she didn't have anything new to say? What if, once she wrote it, no one cared; there was no audience for her work? She hoped Zakh would not intuit how terrified she was of failing as well as how utterly empty she felt since she had heard, from Orly of all people, who called that morning to tell her of the death of another American that she heard on the morning news on the Hebrew radio station. Wendy hadn't listened carefully, until Orly told her what yeshiva he was at. Then, when she heard Shaul's name, she was stunned. Orly begged Wendy to accompany her to the airport send-off, which she wanted to report on for the Jewish News Media Service that she wrote for regularly. Wendy observed Orly taking notes on the proceedings, interviewing the sobbing mourners, and asking them for speculation on why he did it. Wendy had an inkling, but wondered: *Did any of the things she said to Shaul push him over a precipitious ledge unseen by anyone but himself?*

Wendy entered Zakh's office in the humanities section of the University, with its ultramodern architecture. There were bright colors in each of the sections: orange, green, yellow, blue. To get to the offices, one had to go up a series of spiraling staircases. There were a few offices off each landing, then one ascended more to find the next cluster. Wendy hadn't ever figured out where common space, or departmental office space, was. Perhaps professors just met in the cafés scattered everywhere in the building? The intense Israeli desire to socialize, she'd noticed, led to a proliferation of eating places at Hebrew U. Wendy thought that someone should do a sociological study on the proximity of food to academic departments in different countries. How *does* the life of the mind mesh with the life of the body? *Wouldn't it be cool to get a grant to travel all over the world to check this out? International Office/ Food Configuration Strategies—what a title,* Wendy laughed to herself. She thought, *At least something could still amuse her,* as she finally found Zakh's office.

She'd been there only once before, because the other times she met him were always before or after the group meetings at his apartment.

On hearing her knock at the open door he looked up at her and said, "Wundy, shalom." She tried not to be irritated that he still couldn't pronounce her name, even after six months. "Let me just finish this e-mail." Zakh turned back to his computer. After a minute, he finished and turned from his desk towards her.

"So I understand, you've . . . ah . . . what shall we say . . . Run into some . . . *kushiyot* . . . difficulties, yes?"

Wendy looked at him. "I . . . I don't know. I never, never expected that my research would harm anyone, that someone would die because of it. I . . ." She put her head in her hands, and tried to keep from sobbing, to hold herself together.

Zakh handed her a box of tissues. "This is an '*eretz ochelet et yoshveha,*' a land which eats its inhabitants, the spies tell Moshe in the Torah. They are afraid. You are brave to stay."

"My parents would have been happy if I'd left after Benj was killed. If I had, Shaul would still be alive."

"I saw the article on Shaul in the newspaper this morning. Did you?"

Wendy nodded no.

Zakh continued speaking, "This young man had a history of hospitalizations. This wasn't his first suicide attempt."

"Is that supposed to make me feel better?"

"This wasn't a new problem for him. You examined things that had been troubling him for a long time."

"I pushed him. I could tell he was upset, and I didn't stop asking. I . . . pressed him. I kept asking . . ."

Zakh stood up and started pacing. He looked at her, held his hand up, palm to her, and said, "Stop. I don't want to hear any more. I got a call from Cliff Conrad this morning."

She looked alarmed. "Oh, my God." She put her hand to her mouth, imagining some kind of worst-case scenario. Was she being kicked out of the program, and her Fulbright taken away? Was her career over before it started? Much as she didn't want to know, she asked, "Why?"

"You need to be careful. It is possible—he was informed by Princeton University's legal counsel—that there may be a lawsuit. Shaul's parents are considering suing the yeshiva for allowing you to speak to him, and Princeton University for enabling you to do this work under their aegis."

She wasn't sure she could keep breathing; all this information was so unnatural. She could only whisper timidly, feeling like a hunted creature, "So . . . what does this . . . mean?"

Zakh continued pacing. "We don't know. You would be called as a witness; your notes and the tape recording of your interview with him would be subpoenaed. They could subpoena all your data and notes, if they wanted. Where is that tape of you interviewing him?"

"My apartment."

"Did you coerce him to answer? Would the tape show that?"

Wendy sighed. "I . . . feel like I did. Legally, I have no idea if I did something wrong."

"Look," he said furtively, "I didn't say this, okay? Yes?"

She nodded, wondering what was next.

"If you were my daughter, I would tell you this. Get rid of that cassette! Lose it, misplace it. If it doesn't exist and there is no evidence, you can't be convicted."

"What would I be accused of?"

"Involuntary manslaughter? I don't know. I am imagining it is more monetary compensation his parents want, or some kind of vindication it wasn't their son who killed himself, but someone who talked him into it . . ."

Wendy was in shock.

Zakh continued, "Cliff doesn't think, nor do I, that there is a legal case. If the boy had a history of mental illness, there is no way to prove you harmed him. It's nonsense. You had an institutional review board approve everything; all research with human subjects must pass. But grieving parents . . . you can go nuts." He paused and looked at her. "You know we lost a son. Nine years ago already."

"I'm sorry." She paused and then asked, "The army?"

"Nothing so glorious. He was on the end-of-year trip with his high school class, and jumped, daredevil style, off a cliff. That was my Gil—first, toughest, bravest. The water at the bottom was much shallower than it appeared from above and he was killed instantly."

Wendy was silent, absorbing yet another tragedy in this land.

"A parent wants to do anything to preserve a child, the memory. We thought of suing the school for taking them to a potentially dangerous place where teenage boys will dare each other to jump. Or suing Gil's friends for encouraging him."

"Did you?"

"In the end, no. We realized it was ultimately Gil's decision to act. We needed to grieve and accept our fate. It has been, will always be . . . tremendously difficult."

Wendy wasn't sure how to ask what came next. "You don't think . . ."

The professor said emphatically, "It wasn't suicide. Just recklessness. If someone had dropped a stone, seen the water was shallower than it appeared from the top . . ." Zakh stopped pacing and sat, lowering his head to his hands.

After a few moments he looked up. "I gave you no advice today, correct?"

"Absolutely."

They sat in silence for a moment, and then Wendy tentatively said, "Professor Zakh, do you . . . well . . . did I . . . do wrong?"

"I wasn't there. I can't say. You were doing what you thought right. Others have made mistakes too."

"On a scale like this? Someone's life?"

Zakh pulled a pack of cigarettes out of his drawer and starting tapping one on his desk. "I started smoking again after Gil died. As a kid, he begged me to quit, so I did. But once he was gone . . ." He kept tapping the cigarette thoughtfully and turned to gaze out the window.

Zakh opened the window and turned from facing the window with his back to Wendy to face her from behind his desk, where he lit up and sat, ashtray at hand, smoke aimed at the open window letting cold air in. "You know the story of Rabbi Yohanan and Reish Lakish? One of the first baalei teshuvah?" he said, puffing.

Wendy nodded, "I'm familiar with it."

"The end? The tragedy?" he exhaled.

"One jumped into the Jordan and the other said your strength should be for Torah. He became a rabbi."

"That is the beginning. The end of the story is that, publicly, in a debate about weapons, Rabbi Yochanan insulted Reish Lakish, telling him, You give us the answer, ben Lakish; a thief knows his weapons. The public humiliation caused Reish Lakish to become sick, to the point of death. Even when Reish Lakish's wife pleaded with Rabbi Yochanan, her brother, he refused to budge. Reish Lakish died. Soon after, Rabbi Yochanan died as well."

"This is supposed to make me feel better?"

"Great personalities have made grave mistakes. I don't think there will be a lawsuit. Still, lose the cassette."

Wendy looked at her hands in her lap.

"I persist in expecting you to do your presentation for our March meeting. Your work is important—you do know that?' he said kindly.

"Not more important than a human life," Wendy said, rising and collecting her coat and bag.

"*Yihyeh tov*, you'll get through this," he said in a quiet tone.

As Wendy exited, she wasn't sure if she was meant to hear those words, as he remained seated, drawing the tobacco into his lungs and staring out the window in stillness.

When Wendy got home, after she sat at her table and ate the felafel and salad she had picked up from Rafi's Felafel on Rahel Emeinu Street, she decided to do something right away, without procrastinating, uncharacteristically. She cleared the paper wrappers from the felafel and put her glass in the sink. She took a towel and wiped off the table to rid it of residue. Then she moved her laptop from her desk by the window and got out the cassette player from her purple messenger bag. She opened her computer file with the interview notes from the RISE/Yeshivat Temimei Nefesh cohort and went to the spot for Shaul. She supposed she would have to delete all her notes on him—no sense using notes when she would not be able to check back with the informant later.

She started sobbing involuntarily—*Can't check back with the informant*—the finality of it, that she would never be able to speak to him again, was what got her. Shaul was totally silenced, he would never speak again, and she had here some of the last things he'd said to another person. Should she send it to his parents? Would it be precious to them as a reminder of who he was, what he thought about—just the physical sound of his voice should be something they would want to have. But there was this threatened lawsuit, whether it came to pass or not. Would she destroy the tape? Maybe she could just give it to someone else, someone who wouldn't mind complying in what could become an illicit transaction. Todd—she would give the tape to him, in the extreme case that she was subpoenaed and her apartment searched.

The thought made her shudder: someone coming into her private space and looking through her things, trying to find evidence of wrongdoing on her part. What would they find? Someone a bit untidy, maybe not careful enough with her money, a bit frivolous with her purchases, impulsively buying expensive flowers from Atelier Delphine because she couldn't resist the beautiful things she saw in the window and craved the evanescent loveliness of the blooms, even knowing they would soon fade. Were these things so terrible, her little foibles and flaws? Not in comparison with murder.

Was it really murder? Avner Zakh had told her explicitly that he didn't think so; Shaul was a person who had been ill. He had been treated for this illness and doctors had tried to help him. She was not a doctor and Shaul was not her responsibility. End of story?

Not really. *I am a human being, and imperfect though I know I am, I was not put on this earth to cause harm to others. And yet I may have. Well, one way to find out*, she said to herself, breathing in deeply and then breathing out, readying herself to listen to what had transpired between herself and Shaul. The truth? Could there *be* a truth in this case? Whatever she said on the tape, there was no way of knowing what was going through Shaul's mind. If he was so sunk in depression as to kill himself later, maybe he already had voices telling him all kinds of things, ideations of himself dead, and he wasn't listening to her at all? Maybe her voice reminded him of the voice of someone else, someone who didn't think he could change or recover?

Whir . . . the hum of the cassette, its blurred white noise began, until her own voice, sounding professional, like the plummy tones of a voice-over actor, came on: "We are speaking today with Shaul Engel at Yeshivat Temimei Nefesh. Shaul is twenty-four years old, from Larchmont, New York, right near my home town." She remembered herself smiling at him and adding the next thing: "We discussed that, right? Okay, good." So far nothing out of the ordinary, the attempt to bond over Jewish geography. He did know people I did, those with older siblings my age, that kind of thing.

Now she heard herself start, "Okay, so let's begin. First, what is the best thing for you about being religious?" Very cheerful in her diction, professional.

Shaul's reply came laconic through the machine. "It makes me feel less depressed, most days. There are still bad ones, but it's definitely better than it has been in the past."

Wendy could hear herself pausing to collect herself and decide whether to just proceed or to leave interviewer mode and give a word of comfort, some expression of human sympathy to the person sitting across the table from her. She continued.

Now listening, she groaned. *How could I not say something? In any other situation, any other interaction with a member of the human race, especially one where I am sitting with him face to face, I would* acknowledge *the* person *first, notice there is* someone in pain sitting across from me. *Why not this time?*

She heard her voice saying, "Okay, good. Next question: What aspects of your life have changed most since you became observant?"

"I . . . I don't know. That's hard. I mean, surface level, yeah, I keep Shabbos, and *kashrus*; I'm *shomer negia*—that is a challenge for sure—but really, the real self of mine, the self that most of the time just feels dead? That self is still around."

What the fuck was I thinking? Wendy yelled at herself out loud. *If that isn't a cry for help I don't know what is! I have got to be the world's biggest asshole!* She stood up to stretch and pace the room, to distance herself from the tape recorder's disturbing emanations.

She could still hear herself telling Shaul, "Right. Okay, next question is about specific observances. What is the hardest part of observance and what the easiest?"

"Easy—not eating the limb of a live animal. Did you know that?"

She could hear her voice in the background—"I've heard of it"—faint, not wanting to overpower him with a loud voice so he would continue to speak.

And then his, "Yeah, it grosses me out too. So definitely that is easiest. But hard, I mean respecting your father and mother has always been hard, but I'm so far away it isn't so relevant now. Can you come back to that?"

Wendy continued, without pause on the tape, "Absolutely. Now, can you pinpoint the particular event or point in time that made you realize you were staying the course with religion and not going back to your former life?"

On the tape Wendy could hear Shaul tapping on the desk and shuffling his feet. She realized now that this was a sign he was uncomfortable—yet another missed cue on her part. Then he said, "You know, that is a hard question. Of course, any question can be made a hard one, but that . . . I . . . no." She listened to the white noise of the tape, pausing. "I'm sorry, I really don't know. Maybe I will walk out of here today . . . But to what? I left college and I can't go back. I often think it would just be so much easier . . ." —he trailed off to a whisper that Wendy could hear clearly on the tape—"if I weren't here." And he repeated himself in a hush, "Easier not to be here, not to have to answer these questions."

Wendy turned the tape off and put her face in her hands. She wept and thought to herself, *It's worse than what they suspect me of. I didn't provoke him to question himself and then commit suicide. I didn't actually pay any attention to what he was saying.* I missed him. He was there in front of me, sitting across from me, and I could not hear what he was telling me. I failed to comprehend. *But this is not a test, some kind of exam that I should have studied for and couldn't, or an essay that I didn't understand the question to, so couldn't answer right; this is a person communicating something, asking for help, and I was completely oblivious. My vision was just totally blocked, occluded, not working, like I had some kind of compassion stroke, a temporary unavailability of the part of my brain that should be aware of what the living breathing human being right in front of me is trying to get me to hear."* The tears flowed harder as she thought that the live person who had been sitting across from her, little more than twenty-four hours ago, was now in a coffin in the cargo section of an El Al plane, making the return journey to the States. She put her head down into her arms on the desk and wept with greater force and louder sobs, stopping only to click the cassette player open and hurl across the room the plastic tape encasing the evidence of her transgression, her inability to listen and prevent a suicide. She could easily have told someone, one of the rabbis, *Keep an eye on him; he seems very sad.* And they could have protected him, called his doctor, had him hospitalized. But she didn't.

Wendy Goldberg, thinking about herself and her research and her career, missed something far more important. And now she had to figure out how to live with herself. Words from short-story writer Alice Munro came to her: "We say of some things that they can't be forgiven, or that we will never forgive ourselves. But we do—we do it all the time."

Will I ever get to that point? Wendy asked herself.

ELEVEN
Dr. Hideckel

Willing or no, who will but what they must / By Destinie, and can no
other choose?
—JOHN MILTON, *Paradise Lost*

As Wendy walked from the bus stop on Aza Street towards the office of Dr.
Daniel Hideckel at 10 Bartenura Street, in the next part of the neighborhood, she thought about how she would present herself to Shaul's psychiatrist. To make the appointment, she had merely phoned and spoken to a
receptionist. There was none of the American efficiency of taking down
information, putting forms in the mail, or questioning whether she had
health insurance coverage. The Israeli system like everything else here
seemed to be casual and friendly—Okay, you want to come over, come—so
inimical to the American penchant for advance planning.

Wendy was here in this neighborhood of buildings, with stunning lack of
complication in their angles and design, to ask Shaul's psychiatrist whether
she was implicated in Shaul's death. As she looked for Hideckel's building at
number 10, she saw an older man go into an adjacent building, his face
vaguely familiar from her trips to the Hebrew University library on Mount
Scopus. She didn't know his name or field, but assumed he was a professor.
Even though this man didn't know her, she felt shame and embarrassment at

her proximity to 10 Bartenura. Would anyone think *she* was crazy if they saw her here? She did not want to be exposed as someone visiting a psychiatrist's office.

Spotting number 10, Wendy walked in and, on the row of mailboxes, saw the name, Hideckel, unit three, second floor. It seemed to be a completely residential building from the signs with family names on the gray metal mailboxes set into the wall, large enough for bills, periodicals, postcards, and any other items deemed fit to transport via the inefficient Israeli postal service.

Wendy climbed the steps to the second floor. Even in a prestigious neighborhood in Jerusalem, there was no elevator. On the first door at the top of the stairs there was a sign, in English and Hebrew, for Dr. Daniel Hideckel, MD, licensed psychiatrist, the only indication of the nature of his profession. She opened the unlocked door and found a small waiting room, three chairs with tan faux leather covering and metal arms and legs, looking as though they were bought used from an office furniture store in the early seventies or late sixties. There was a coffee table, same provenance, holding a selection of magazines in English: *Time, Newsweek,* and the *Jerusalem Report.* Similar selections in Hebrew and German were on the side tables. She removed her purple canvas messenger bag from her shoulder and unzipped her coat. She began to thumb through the *Jerusalem Report* and came across an article about Jews and their attitudes to child-rearing. According to this survey, commissioned by a Jewish group trying to gauge what distinctiveness remained to American Jews in an increasingly assimilated society, Jews value being able to ask questions and think for oneself. This set Jews apart, for only 32 percent of those of other ethnic groups valued this, as opposed to 78 percent of Jews. Other ethnic groups valued obedience (23 percent), being well liked (16 percent), working hard (18 percent), or helping others (11 percent) most highly. *I'm glad someone sees questions as worthwhile. They certainly don't seem to have helped Shaul. I hope this doctor will answer mine,* Wendy thought.

As Wendy continued to read the *Jerusalem Report,* she heard an inner door open and the footsteps of a person walking by. She did not want to see any fellow inmates of 10/3 Bartenura, and deliberately did not look up. A few moments later, she heard another pair of footsteps. This time, they were connected to a voice, which announced pleasantly, "Wendy Goldberg?" At her nod, he said, "This way," and turned around to march back to his office. As Wendy walked down the corridor, she saw a kitchen on the left and a closed door beyond it, which she presumed was a bathroom. They entered Dr. Hideckel's office. It was filled by a dark crimson Oriental rug, a glass-topped coffee table, and a window with a view of a garden behind it. It was flanked by bookshelves containing books in English, Hebrew, and German; medical texts, novels, and sociological studies shared the space. Hideckel gestured to Wendy to sit in a black leather armchair, while he took a white legal pad and seated himself on the matching sofa. She faced him and the window to her right, while to her left was a large desk, piled with papers and medical journals of indeterminate date, maybe recent, maybe from ten years ago. There was not a computer or typewriter.

She gazed at the doctor wearing a plain black crocheted kipah, no designs on the edges. His black hair was gray around the temples, with more gray sprinkled through his head. He was wearing a white button-down shirt, gray wool cardigan, navy blue slacks, and sensible leather shoes. His brown eyes, like his other features, seemed sedate and moderate, calm behind his reading glasses. She wasn't sure what to do next, so she waited.

He began the conversation, looking at her, but with a pen in his hand. "What brought you here today? What are your symptoms? I'm here to listen."

Wendy reached into her backpack for her own notepad. "This isn't about me. I . . . interviewed your patient. Shaul Engel. Before his death . . ." She paused to take in a long breath of air. "I . . . need to know. Am I responsible?" Daniel Hideckel took off his glasses and gazed at her, a long look, something changing from his previous air of calm. "I don't know how to . . . Okay . . ." He gave a long sigh. "Shaul's medical history . . . there's no way to point a finger at a specific cause." He stopped and looked through her, adding, "Shaul's parents are thinking of suing the yeshiva. For negligence in not noticing signs of Shaul's increasingly severe depression and for letting you speak to him. I've received a call from the lawyer his parents hired. I told him there wasn't much of a case. One can't know what effect anything has on a person already sunk in clinical depression."

Wendy looked at him and lifted her body into a more upright and proud position, and said, "You don't think I'm to blame?" with a new lilt in her voice.

Hideckel placed his pad and pen on the sofa and looked at Wendy. "You asked about changes he made in his life. When he responded, he started to feel that he hadn't changed and he wasn't the righteous person he wanted to be. He mailed me a copy of his suicide note, apologizing that he just couldn't keep trying." Hideckel paused to wipe the tears from his eyes and replace his glasses. "He wrote that it would be easier to be dead than to keep struggling. He just wanted to say 'good night' to everything, to let it end."

"If I hadn't asked those questions, would he still be here?"

"Impossible to answer." He looked at her. "Legally, you should be fully exonerated. You didn't intend harm to him; your questions haven't had a negative impact on other subjects. I don't think he would have made it this far had he not become religious. There is a phenomenon, research shows, among baalei teshuvah; the turn to religion can stave off symptoms of mental illness for three to five years. After that, religiosity has a negligible affect, and the illness returns with the same potency. Another thing about suicide is that, often, the time when the patient seems to be improving is a time greatest danger. The patient has an awareness things are better, but once improved, he begins to grasp how far there is yet to go. That awareness of the distance to optimal health seems to propel some patients to suicide."

"You don't think I'm guilty?" Wendy said, surprising herself when the words left her mouth.

"There is a saying in Judaism: 'Innocent in the eyes of man; guilty in the sight of heaven.'" In a human court, you've committed no crime. And, fortunately for you, Shaul's parents are divorced and can hardly agree on anything, much less a lawsuit."

Wendy breathed comfortably. "I hope you're right." She added, "What do you mean 'guilty in the eyes of heaven?'"

"There are higher standards than human ones. If you feel you've done wrong, atone."

"Dr. Hideckel, I am feeling vulnerable now and I don't want to get drawn to . . . some . . . religious thing. I . . . I . . . didn't expect that from a medical doctor, person of science."

"All I am suggesting is that if you feel responsible, it could help you to atone. You will also pay if you do nothing. Guilt has a cost."

Wendy looked at him, steadily. "Point taken."

"I know you're under stress now, and I'm just making suggestions, not forcing anything on you," Hideckel said in sympathy. "These are ways Jews repent: giving tzedaka, doing deeds of loving-kindness, praying, studying sacred texts . . . Doing any one of these might help you feel you are atoning."

"Maybe. I'm not a super-religious person. I go to synagogue here sometimes on Friday night; it's social. I don't have much money to give to charity. What else?"

"Study of sacred texts and deeds of loving-kindness. Study might be a good place to start; you're a student. My wife, Atarah, teaches a class on the Torah portion. She has a PhD from Chicago in Social Thought. That's where we met. As a religion grad student, you'd like her; she's read all the religious phenomenologists—Eliade, Levi-Strauss, Geertz . . ."

Wendy looked at him with a surprised expression. "Really. Most of the religious people I've come across here are either hostile to academic thought or positively anti-intellectual. This is new," Wendy smiled, intrigued.

Hideckel continued, "Atarah knows traditional text study and modern literary theory. She meshes them. Her book is coming out this fall, Oxford University Press."

Wendy sat up. "Impressive. Maybe I *will* try her classes. It will help me understand my subjects better." Then she added, half jokingly, "Can I come back for a prescription for sleeping pills?"

"Absolutely. Anything else?" he added kindly.

"I don't know." She stopped and paused before asking what had been on her mind: "Why is it so hard for these returnees?"

"I am sure you have heard from your subjects of the difficulty of finding acceptance in the religious community. It wasn't always like that. The rabbis of the Talmud said, 'In the place where a penitent'—the actual words they used were 'baal teshuvah'—'stands, a completely righteous person cannot stand.' What I remember learning—and this speaks to the question of Shaul and his attempts to overcome his illness—is that the reason for the relative greatness of the baal teshuvah is his ability to withstand temptation."

"I've never heard anything like this from my interviewees." Wendy continued, "Why aren't baalei teshuvah taught about the value of what they're doing instead of constantly being made to feel ignorant?"

"The yeshiva isn't at fault for Shaul's suicide. I was his doctor. I was the one who could have saved him," he sighed sadly. "'*Al ta'amod al dam rayekha,*' don't stand by your brother's blood. I should have admitted him to the hospital, to a safe place. I didn't."

Wendy asked, "Have many patients under your care committed suicide?" Wendy was afraid to pry into the psyche of this psychiatrist, yet also curious.

"Even one is one too many. Psychiatry is such a tough specialty, because each individual and each illness has its own contours. One never knows with certainty whether the patient would respond better to hospitalization, or a course of ECT treatments, or a different combination of medications . . ." He sighed and stared into the distance for a few moments.

Wendy fidgeted for a moment before responding. "I have an uncle who is a hand surgeon, and he says that surgery is inexact too. Only another surgeon, going in to the incision and looking at what was done, can evaluate the accuracy of a surgeon's work. Most of us can't evaluate whether the operation was successful because, even though we can see the surface, we can't know what went on underneath the skin."

Hideckel responded, "Right. Even the most exact of medical specialties can't be evaluated externally."

They were both silent for a few moments until Wendy continued, "Is it common for certain events to trigger a suicide? With all the interviews there seems to be a certain degree of difficulty for the interviewee in realizing how much he or she has changed, but also how the past lurks in the background, threatening to overtake the progress made towards becoming a new person."

"This physical metaphor—an old person waiting to lurch out like a panther or a ghost. Your imagery or your subjects'?"

"My subjects'. And that is why I feel so"—she paused and then said—"culpable . . . in Shaul's suicide. He had a hard time with my questions about how he had changed since he had become religious. He started saying he'd never get to where he wanted to be, that he was a failure . . . He became very emotional. I could tell it was painful for him. His eyes became almost watery. I could see that he was on the verge of tears. I didn't know how to react. I . . . didn't express . . . compassion and . . . I regret that."

Dr. Hideckel sighed. "That was Shaul. Setting unreasonably high standards for himself and then feeling a failure for not reaching them. We worked on that, but unfortunately when people become religious it often magnifies particular aspects of their personalities, rather than really transforming them, as they may hope. They focus on those aspects of Judaism that are most compatible with their personalities. Shaul had a real sense of inferiority and he used religion to reinforce it. Others, who have a need for order, will focus on the most punctilious—though not strictly necessary—observances of *halacha*. I wish I could convey to the rabbis at baal teshuvah yeshivot that individualism is not a threat to religion but a basis for it." He put his hand on his chin and added, "One of the names for God in the Torah is 'elohei ruhot', 'God of the source breath of all flesh.'" Rashi commented that, in appointing a leader to succeed Moses, God must appoint someone who can deal with each individual in accordance with his own "*ruah*," temperament. Israeli society values the *hevreman*, the group-centered person, rather than the individual."

Wendy responded, "I agree. Conformity is unhealthy."

"For baalei teshuvah, so much is new. The returnee isn't sure how to integrate new things with who she or he was before the teshuvah process. Have you ever seen a plate in an anatomy book, all the different layers of a human—the circulation system, the muscles, the vital organs, the skeleton? If you see the whole, it is coherent. If you look at one layer, it won't give you a realistic picture. Baalei teshuvah focus so much on the religious layer of the self that they often miss the others. It is difficult to reach a point of personal authenticity. That is the focus of your research, yes?"

"Yes. It isn't so much the layers of self, but what does the new picture look like? How is the present different when one sees the past behind it? There is a good visual analogue in the work of this photographer Shimon Attie— have you heard of him? There was an exhibit of his work at Princeton last year. He took pictures in modern Berlin and then found archival photos of the exact location before the war when the area was a Jewish neighborhood. He superimposed the two. The montage is . . . haunting. One can't see those places as they are now without seeing what came before. It's as though the ghosts have come back to life. My baalei teshuvah don't know how to look at themselves as a whole with these two aspects, past and present. They haven't been able to fuse the images and create a composite. Nothing coheres."

"You're right. Baalei teshuvah don't feel there is room for a crisis of faith; they see things in stark terms—religious or non-religious, Jew or goy. One needs leeway to doubt and question. You know, I've found with my patients, the ones with the most successful outcomes are the ones who come in most full of doubts about the therapeutic process."

"What do you mean?" Wendy felt perplexed by this comment that she would not have expected.

"That they . . . well if they express their fears about the process, that enables them from the beginning to admit their struggles and make our treatment more effective." He stopped and saw from Wendy's face that she was still perplexed, so he added, "Have you ever heard about the Bobover rebbe? He survived the Holocaust and had a crisis of faith after the war. He shaved his beard, didn't want to be a rebbe. He eventually returned to his role, and he was able to attract followers because of his own doubts. Everyone needs to be able to step back and question."

"Do you?"

He laughed. "I'm a baal teshuvah myself. My parents came to New York from Germany in the 1930s. They were secular and we lived in an intensely Jewish neighborhood in Washington Heights, full of Jews and refugees. When I got to college at Chicago, I took a Jewish studies class and was invited by another student for a Shabbat meal. I felt comfortable with Shabbat and the community at Hillel. I became religious."

"Oh." Wendy was silent for a moment and then asked, "Did your goals change after you became religious? Would you have done something else if you hadn't?"

"Hmm. You know, it is a general problem, how to integrate youthful ideals into the realities of life, to merge dreams from the past with one's present where they may or may not come to fruition. I always wanted to be a doctor. As a child of immigrants I was a caretaker in many ways, mature for my age. I don't know whether being religious heightened my interest in psychiatry . . ." He looked at his watch. "I'm sorry, Wendy, but I have another appointment."

She stood up and slung her messenger bag over her shoulder. She reached out to shake his hand. "Thank you so much for your time, Dr. Hideckel."

He shook firmly and said, "A pleasure to meet. Good luck with all your challenges in the next few weeks."

She added, standing, "One final question, relating to you and to Shaul. Why do some people cope with the fact that their present life and their past dreams need to create some kind of composite, and some can't let go of their expectations from the past?"

"I wish I knew. There's so much we don't know about ourselves and others," he said as Wendy exited his office.

As Wendy left the building, she gazed at the Bauhaus buildings in the neighborhood, constructed by Jews like Dr. Hideckel's parents, those who fled Germany in the 1930s. She thought about how their well-crafted minimalism negated the complications of the lives of those who escaped. The forced simplicity of the buildings—was it a necessity? The attempt to reduce design elements so, on the surface, all could appear controlled, no frilly ironwork or odd angles to disturb the purity of the architect's modernist vision. Wendy wished that she could do the same, reduce the messiness of her subjects' lives, and her relationship to them, to a particular kind of grid: these emotions here, those there, cause and effect, neatly sorted. She considered human attempts to purge their lives of messiness and what the cost was. Obviously, for Shaul it had been high. Once he allowed that untidiness to return, to see there was still much that was preventing him from being the person he aspired to be, he felt the enterprise of changing himself entirely hopeless.

Jerusalem's buildings veered from the architectural purity of the Bauhaus style and became less elegant and simple as Wendy's walk brought her closer to her apartment on Mishael Street in the German Colony, away from the Rehavia neighborhood of Hideckel's office. She had been told that *Mishael* meant "who is asking" in Hebrew. *Who was she to ask others about their lives?*

She had asked someone about his life, to learn hours later that her probing questions led him to give up trying to change, to obliterate himself.

Could she continue her dissertation research? Was her career as important as a life? Did she have the right to do work that could damage others—what if there were other baalei teshuvah who were, unknown to her or others, in Shaul's fragile condition?

Thinking about herself, was she any different from them? Like Shaul, she set high standards for herself. She had felt lost and unmoored in college until she decided to be a religion major and go to graduate school; the academic system was a path as much as a baal teshuvah yeshiva was. Being a graduate student was a way to get out of her parents' house and antagonize them a bit. But it was also a way to find answers and reach goals, to be less lonely. She wasn't so different from any baal teshuvah in what she was seeking. Her Fulbright award and being a grad student at Princeton couldn't change her status as a human with the same needs and problems as others.

Like anyone else, she had the boring and unenviable task of putting one foot in front of the other, trying not to think about anything but that for the next twenty minutes, until she got back to her apartment. She neared her neighborhood, the German Colony, settled in the 1870s by German Templers, a Christian group whose descendants were deported from Israel in

1945 by British Mandate authorities. Walking, she thought about the differences between German Jews in the 1930s and German Christians who entered Jerusalem in the 1870s.

The Christian Templars who built up the German Colony had attempted to reenact architecturally the pastoral look of the villages they left in southern Germany, though with the materials of the Middle East, Jerusalem stone instead of wood and brick. The German Jews attempted to create a modern style, to proclaim themselves a new group with new goals and ideals, living in this oldest of lands.

Which are baalei teshuvah doing? Wendy deliberated. *Reconstructing elements of America in an Israeli tempo, or building something completely new in their lives?*

The next day, Friday, Wendy met Todd Presser, from her Fulbright group, at *Caffit*. They hadn't seen each other since he'd been back in the country after a midwinter vacation week in Greece where he met a friend from the States. Wendy wanted to catch up with her pal, but hoped her problems wouldn't monopolize the entire meeting.

She began their conversation. "I went to the airport to see Shaul's coffin off, like I did for Benj. Twice already this year." She shuddered.

"What was it like?" Todd asked in an almost reverential whisper, the quiet tones of his voice reflecting his uncertainty at how to approach the tragedy.

"The *rosh yeshiva* got up and spoke, and one of Shaul's teachers. It was such . . . pablum, bullshit, the rabbi saying that we each have a role in life and some fill the role sooner than others. This other teacher told a story about figs, and how if you are worried they will spoil, you eat them even if they aren't ripe, and Shaul was taken at a young age so he wouldn't spoil. You would never have known it was a suicide from what they said—it sounded like he had a heart attack. I was sobbing loudly, and a woman walked over, put her arm around me kindly, and asked how I knew Shaul. I told her I interviewed him, and then . . ." Wendy lifted her shoulders and shook herself, "All hell broke loose. The woman took her arm away quickly, as though I were contagious, and said coldly, 'Oh. You're the one.' Then she looked at me like I was monstrous and added, 'Can you even call yourself a Jew? You don't have the right,' and walked away. She quickly whispered to the other women and they moved away from me too." She paused and breathed hard, weary. "Shit, I really screwed up. I can't believe I did this."

"He's dead. Whether you pulled those *tefillin* straps or not, there's nothing you can do now. Go on, enjoy your life, *mon cherie*." He took a large and satisfied sip from his double cappuccino. "I love the coffee here," he sighed, satisfied, looking around him at the large Friday morning crowd.

"You just like the waiters." Wendy smirked at him. He stuck his tongue out at her. It was so easy with gay men—why couldn't she get along better with heterosexual ones?

"Seriously, what am I going to do now? How can I write this thing, feeling like someone died for me to write? Do I have blood on my hands?" Wendy asked, her hands shaking as she picked up her *café hel*, coffee with cardamom, an Israeli flavor combination she had come to love particularly.

He reached out a hand exaggeratedly and picked up one of hers. "Let's see, my pretty. I'm looking." He held her hand in one of his and turned it over with his other. "I see a need for a manicure, no blood. Get them done in red. My treat."

Wendy made a face at him, curling her lip in dissatisfaction. "*I* don't get my nails done. I could never type with a manicure; I'd spend all my time gazing at my nails. Don't you have any sense of morality?"

"I'm writing on Isaac Babel because I love glorification of violence by Jews. It's the best part of being in Israel: watching Jewish soldiers act like Cossacks, nightly on the news. Next time there is some big incident, I'm going to write about the analogy, what Babel would be doing if he were alive today. Maybe I can get it in some trendy publication."

"You scare me."

"*You* provoked a man to a violent death, darling. I just write about it. Face it, academics and writers are cannibals. You've devoured your first victim. To finish, you must digest him and excrete him in writing. It's a blood obligation now to finish your dissertation."

Wendy wanted to sip her coffee but found her throat too dry suddenly. She was nauseated. "Excuse me."

She raced to the ladies room and kneeled down over the toilet. She heaved a few times, and finally threw up the cheese toast she had just eaten. Usually after throwing up, Wendy felt purged, thoroughly cleansed. Now, she still felt bloated, disgusting, as though she had ingested something entirely sickening, something she couldn't get rid of, that would stay in her system. She washed her blotchy face and dabbed on some foundation to try to cover it. She went back to Todd.

"Pregnant?" he looked at her suspiciously.

"Sadly, no chance. I'd prefer it, life over death and all that."

"Just . . . stress?"

Wendy signaled the waiter to come over, and noticed Todd elaborately smiling at him and trying to get his eye. She ordered her lukewarm coffee taken away and a fresh hot cup in its place.

"Todd, I . . . it's different now. Shaul is dead. No jokes for a minute." He gave her his best poker face in response.

"Something in me has shifted; I can't be the same anymore. I saw . . . Shaul was . . . upset, and I . . . I . . . I don't know. I kept pushing, asking, demanding. I was relentless, like I was pummeling him, ferocious. I just let this side of myself, all my anger at Noah and his betrayal of me, and my anger about the *matzav* here, it just all got knocked at Shaul. I don't know why. Even worse, I wasn't listening. He was asking for help and I heard nothing. But I have to live with myself." She reached into her purple messenger bag and removed the cassette tape. She handed it to him. "Before I forget, this is the tape with the interview. I'm giving it to you for safekeeping."

Todd took it from her and asked quizzically, "Om, sure, but *pourquoi*?"

Wendy sighed a bit of relief as she saw the tape vanish into Todd's maroon backpack with its white Harvard logo. "It's so weird. You know, Zakh isn't the most . . . communicative guy, or warm or cuddly. But he was nice to me the other day, concerned. So this is the deal—he got a call from my advisor, Cliff Conrad, saying that there could be a lawsuit for wrongful death, against me and the yeshiva. Zakh told me I'd be better off, if this came about, if the cassette tape wasn't available. Don't destroy it; just hold on to it."

"Tampering with evidence?" he raised his eyebrows and, with mock annoyance, continued, "There aren't many people I'd commit a crime for, but for you, Wendy . . ."

She laughed. "I appreciate it. There is no crime yet, only a possibility, so your conscience is, so far, safe on my account. Mine is another story . . ." She looked down at her hands, despair in her voice.

"You will live with yourself, Wendy." He stretched out his hand and put it over one of hers. "Maybe you shouldn't have pushed him; maybe you should have listened better, but you saw the newspaper article. The kid had a history. He'd been hospitalized; he was ill. The timing would have been different, but it might have happened anyway."

"I wouldn't have had a role."

"Giving up on this dissertation isn't going to help him or anyone else. If you finish it, maybe you can identify particular characteristics, things you can point out to teachers in the yeshivot, or parents, as symptomatic of the difference between healthy and unhealthy changes. That would be important." Todd looked at her carefully and patted her hand with his. "Making yourself ill over this is not the answer."

She put her other hand on top of the one he had placed on hers. "You're right. But now what?"

"You are going to drink your coffee, go into town, and do your errands. Buy your mother a birthday gift, and get on with your life. Sunday morning, you will get up and take the bus to the library on Har Hatzofim, sit in a carrel with an amazing view of the city, and work your little tootsie off. I'll find you at noon and take you to the meat cafeteria with the panoramic view of the whole city."

She removed her hands from his to sip her coffee. "I can't just pretend nothing happened. I feel like I need to . . . atone."

"You do know, *le'kapper,* to atone, in Hebrew is connected to the word *koffer,* ransom. To atone, you have to pay. When people drive drunk they go to re-education classes, and sit and listen to why they shouldn't drive drunk again. We'll trundle you off to some kind of spiritual drunk driving course where you can sit around and ask the others what they are in for." He paused. "That was good, actually," he added half to himself, pleased. "I did listen to all my abba's High Holiday sermons," he added about his father the rabbi.

Wendy smiled at him. "I'm proud of you. Maybe you can tell the waiter and he'll be impressed too." He stuck his tongue out at her, and she continued, "I want to pay; I want to *do* something, but I'm not sure what."

"Extra good deeds? Random acts of kindness? Sleep with another sinner, someone who you wouldn't ordinarily, help out a suffering Jew."

"First you see me as a cannibal and now a whore? I don't know, Todd," Wendy said, shaking her head. "You go first on that one. Maybe Noah is still lonely."

Two weeks later, also on a Friday morning, Wendy walked down the main drag of Emek Refaim towards the bus stop going into the center of town, where she had some errands— birthday cards for relatives and shopping. Perhaps she'd buy something to perk herself up.

As she was walking, she gazed down at her hands and held them in front of her, spreading out her fingers. *They don't look like they have blood on them,* she thought. *They look as they always do, ragged, the nails bitten, never manicured as my mother would like, but certainly not bloody.*

As she continued to gaze down at her hands, in her peripheral vision she saw that she was coming closer to another pedestrian. Wendy looked up to see a man with black hair with a bit of gray in it, kind brown eyes behind glasses, and a white button-down shirt, navy wool toggle button coat, khaki slacks. Something about him was familiar but she didn't know quite why. She figured she should smile anyway.

"Wendy, hello," the man said.

Quick, she commanded her brain, *place this person. How do I know him. University? Rabbi at one the yeshivas I've interviewed at? Friend of parents? Parent of a friend?*

"Hi. How are you?"

"Tell me how you are. Sleeping better?" The psychiatrist, Shaul's psychiatrist, was standing in front of her.

"The lawsuit isn't going to happen, as you predicted. I'm just so immensely relieved. But, I still feel . . . not culpable, but accountable in some way," she said, hoping her voice didn't sound too awkward.

"Hmm." Hideckel gazed at her in a way that made her uncomfortable. It was a more penetrating look than the prurient looks she got from men on the street here. She wanted to squirm away from him, but remained where she was.

Wendy was about to say, "Nice to see you again; thanks for your advice about the lawsuit, bye, Shabbat Shalom," but he started speaking.

"Let me speak as a Jew, not a psychiatrist. I don't assume you caused Shaul's death. I do think you should do something to express regret for what happened, attempt to repair it in some way. Write his parents a letter, make a donation to charity, study a Jewish text in his memory." He added ominously, "I know, from having lived through it with my wife, how difficult it is to write a dissertation. You don't need the additional burden of this guilt hanging over your head. You'll be able to function better if you do something."

"True. I just heard about the case of another American yeshiva student who committed suicide. He was at Emmet ve'Emunah, a place I haven't had any contact with, but apparently he mentioned Shaul in his suicide note and felt that Shaul's suicide gave him permission to take his own life. I feel indirectly responsible for his death. What kind of person am I to carry on with my project? On the other hand, I can't just quit. I have a fellowship and expectations from my advisors that I will finish. I feel stymied."

"Come see me in the office for a few sessions if you want to talk about it. You might also want to go to one of my wife's classes. I must have a card with her schedule." He reached into the front pocket of his coat to produce a black leather wallet. He opened it and handed her a card.

She remembered being on Emek Refaim with Noah about three months ago when the man walked out of his car to hand Noah, and no one else in the crowd, a flyer about a yeshiva. Now, she was on the same street, being handed a card by someone she had bumped into accidentally. Was there a fate in store for her as well, or was it coincidence?

Wendy took the profered card, put it in her pocket, and said, "Thanks, Dr. Hideckel."

He smiled and said, "Shabbat Shalom, Wendy. Good luck," and sauntered off without expecting anything more of her. No commitment to attend the class, no promise that she would see him for a few sessions. She appreciated that. *Did they learn this in psychiatry rotations, that sometimes you leave people alone?*

TWELVE
Meeting Atarah

Fun a kasha shtarbt man nit. (From a question no one dies.)
—RABBI CHAIM BRISKER

On a Thursday morning, Wendy went up a short flight of steps and entered a drab hallway in a community center on Sholem Aleichem Street in the Talbieh neighborhood of Jerusalem.

From the dull bracken-brown tiles on the floor to the sickly yellowish tint of the brick on the bottom half of the walls, all was in a state of heightened ugliness. The whitish-bluish upper half of the wall was painted to approximate the hair color of a matron who makes the attempt to color her white hair, but hasn't tried hard enough to make the coiffure actually look good. The feel of the place was unadorned and institutional, down to the smell of disinfectant from floors that must have been recently mopped. Wendy hadn't felt so deflated by a classroom since being in the dreary building that housed her junior high school. She wasn't sure which room on the long hallway she would find Atarah Hideckel in, but figured she would just keep poking her head into the rooms until she found her class. She would sit in the back and leave when she found whatever rhetoric this woman was sure to emit as tedious as the surroundings. Hopefully, she wouldn't bump into Atarah's psychiatrist husband again, but if she did, she could say she had attended one of Atarah's classes and had attempted to assuage her guilt.

Wendy poked her head into the first room on the right—empty. First room on the left, also empty. The second room on the left was, by contrast, full. As she walked farther in, she saw it was quite full, not yielding even one empty chair. She asked the person closest to the door if this was Atarah Hideckel's class. The woman was wearing a floppy blue velvet hat whose brim overshadowed her face, making her appear like a giant hat with a miniature face underneath. She nodded a yes and then said, "If you want a chair, borrow one from one of the other rooms. Go quickly; she's about to start."

"Oh," Wendy said. Then she asked the woman, "Is there something special today?"

A laugh came from under the hat. "No," she replied. "It is always this full." Then, looking again at Wendy's jeans and backpack, she said, "Is this your first time hearing Atarah?" When Wendy nodded in reply, the woman said animatedly, "You are in for a treat today. A real treat."

Somehow, I don't think our ideas of treats are the same, lady," Wendy would have said to her had they been speaking a few months ago. *I'm from Princeton. I regularly have the chance to hear the greatest minds on the American academic scene give lectures. Nobel Prize winners, MacArthur scholars, Guggenheim fellows. That's a treat. This? Not so much. And, what's the deal with the paint on the walls?* But now, post-Shaul, Wendy plodded out of the room obediently, to grab a chair from the other room. She dragged it back, sullenly musing, *Why don't they just hold the class in a bigger space if it gets so crowded?*

The din in the room was grating. *Do women have to talk so loudly? Weren't any men here?* She spotted a pair of male retirees in the front corner, sitting with crocheted kipot next to women she presumed to be their wives. A few rows behind them was another retired man, dapper in a striped bow tie and matching handkerchief in the pocket of his navy blazer. No one in Jerusalem dressed like that. He must be a retired rabbi from the US trying to keep up his image; he needed to preserve his identity by continuing to dress formally in a country of informality, she guessed. Wendy continued to look around at the hundred or so people who filled the room. The crowd was mostly women in their forties, fifties, and sixties with children old enough to be in school or out of the house. There were some younger women, around Wendy's age, mostly with their hair covered with fashionable scarves or bandanas or funky hats, not the drab and dowdy looking head coverings. There were also a few whose hair wasn't covered, so Wendy didn't completely feel that she stood out. Even babies were here, mostly asleep in those little carrier contraptions with handles. Wendy didn't immediately see anyone else wearing pants, but on closer inspection, she saw a woman a few rows ahead wearing maroon corduroy pants, her hair covered with a matching maroon beret. *That's a first,* Wendy thought. From what Wendy had observed over her past six months in Jerusalem, women who were religious enough to cover their hair wore skirts always, and women who wore pants didn't cover their hair. Here was category overlap, a challenge to the usual assumptions Wendy was conditioned to make about people in this holy city.

Suddenly, the din ceased.

Wendy looked up from placing her backpack on the floor next to her and saw a woman in her early fifties seated at a desk. The desk was elevated on a slight platform so that she could be seen by each student in the class. The woman sat erect and held her head, beautifully coiffed, in a pedagogical demeanor. The hair was pulled back off her face with an elaborate metal barrette, and the rest of it hung slightly below her shoulders.

As Atarah Hideckel moved her head with a slow smile, from the right side of the room to the left, taking in with her glance and nod each of the students present, the hair stayed in place, stiff. *Could it be a wig?* When Wendy saw women with wigs on Jerusalem buses, usually the ones who got on at the Meah Shearim stops halfway between the university on Mount Scopus and the center of town, it was patently obvious that the hair on their heads was not natural. The hair was the wrong color, or didn't sit quite right on their heads. Wendy felt sorry for those women—wigs seemed to go with heavy clumping orthopedic shoes and clothing that came only in hues of dark blue or darker black. The hair of these women appeared to be constantly minimizing itself, shrinking to the background, from the young girls whose long hair was always in two tight braids at the side of their heads, to the women with the stiffest wigs imaginable. By contrast, Atarah's remarkable wig was the beginning of her hip demeanor. She was wearing a loose-cut dark emerald-green velvet jacket and matching long skirt, and the shirt she had on underneath looked to Wendy like a Rubik's cube, blocks of color in orange, purple, green, and yellow, with a scooped neck attractively fitted but not tight. Her earrings and necklace were beads with a similar array of colors. She would look chic anywhere.

Atarah began tapping the portable microphone on her lapel and asked, "Is this working? Can you hear me?" To the murmurs of assent, she replied, "Good. Let's begin." Atarah pressed the button on the small taperecorder at her side, as students held pens over notebooks, expectant.

"This week's *parsha* is Yitro. Now we know, Yitro is *Hotain Moshe,* father-in-law of Moses. Is there more to him? Why does he merit the section containing the *aseret hadibrot,* the Ten Commandments, to be named in his honor?" Wendy became apprehensive, knowing, *I'll never get any of this if she keeps throwing out all this Hebrew.*

Wendy's eyes wandered the room beginning to zone out, trying to fathom what all these people were getting out of this class, but realizing it would be rude to leave now, so soon after the beginning. As she looked around, she saw expressions of rapt fervor on the faces of the students. She thought about the expressions she encountered on her students' faces when she was a teaching assistant at Princeton. Wendy had never witnessed a flicker of joy in her students' features during class. The moment class ended, their visages became more animated, alive, awakened from the stony frowns of concentration exhibited during class. Oddly, each student in this dingy room in Jerusalem looked radiant, happy.

Wendy tuned back in to hear Atarah say, "This *parsha* begins with a simple narrative, a reunion of a man and his wife and children. One would assume that here the Torah would speak of the beauty of family life, the power of love. We know from the story of Jacob and Rachel the power of romantic love, recalling Rashi's comment that Jacob wept when he met her because he saw by divine prophecy they would be buried separately in the future. That is passion, something we certainly all yearn for: to be loved so furiously that our being is missed for all time . . ." Did Atarah and her husband have such passion—was it true, as her baalei teshuvah claimed, that rules of the permitted and forbidden made sex sweeter?

Wendy listened again as Atarah spoke while turning her head slowly and gradually from side to side to see students individually, her face reflecting the seriousness with which they faced her. "The Torah does not choose to tell us what kind of reaction Moshe's wife or children had to his return, just his father-in-law's. Can anyone recall for us another story of in-law relationships in Tanach, our Bible?"

Wendy saw several hands shoot up, and Atarah nodded at the man in the bow tie and navy blazer. "Rabbi Hurwitz?" Atarah called, nodding in his direction.

He stood up in his seat and addressed Atarah: "Saul and David. Then, Lot's sons-in-law are mentioned, and Shechem ben Hamor, who wants to be Jacob's son-in-law."

"These three, yes. Two others are the *pilagesh* at Giva, the concubine that concludes the book of Judges, and Samson negotiating with his father-in-law. These relationships are all fraught with tension and violence. Shechem takes Jacob's daughter violently and then falls in love with her. It is ironic he has such passion for her since Dina is the unloved Leah's daughter, not beloved Rachel's. Saul attempts to eliminate David by putting him in a situation where he can be killed. All these relationships have incredible rivalry. More positive in-law relationships in Tanach?"

A young woman, probably Wendy's age, with a rainbow-striped scarf wrapped gaudily around her head and a baby in a Snugli carrier snoozing on her chest, raised her hand. Atarah said, "Yes?" The woman said proudly, "Ruth and Naomi have the same kind of loving relationship as Moshe and Yitro. The example of one brings the other to *gerut*, to become Jewish, in both cases."

Atarah said succinctly, "Nice, Rivky, thank you," and nodded at her. Unfortunately for Rivky, her speaking startled the baby snoozing at her chest, who began to wail. She got up to comfort the baby and began pacing and shushing in the back of the room. "Ruth and Naomi. Let's look at the frame story. Which character appears at both the beginning and end?"

Several students called out, "Naomi."

"Absolutely. So why do we read *Megillat Ruth*, not *Megillat Naomi*? The book of Ruth begins, like the portion of Yitro, with a nuclear family: father, mother, and two sons. The family is not at first separated; they stay together and move to another country, an alien land, Moav. This place is another echo of the in-law relationships from the story of Lot." Wendy was confused. What do Moav and Lot have to do with each other? Should she write down her questions so she could ask someone later or were there too many, was it too overwhelming?

Atarah continued, "The family of Naomi is separated by death; husband and sons die. Naomi is left with her daughters-in-law. She tells them she is too old to have sons for them to marry, that they should leave her. Clearly, this is a depressed woman. My husband is a psychiatrist, so I feel qualified to make a diagnosis. I checked the DSM, the diagnostic manual." The class gave a little laugh. "Naomi says initially, why do you want to be with me? The hand of God is against me. Is there anything that will lift her out of her depression? Over the course of the story, we have a changed Naomi, capable of praising God. How does that transformation occur? Before we answer for Naomi, let's see what kind of transformations occur in our *parsha* in Exodus. The first three aliyot, specifically."

Wendy saw the students flipping through their Bibles. Most Bibles were in Hebrew; some had a larger Hebrew text in the middle and more squiggly Hebrew lettering on the sides and at the bottom. She glanced around, and the person next to her, a woman in her fifties with uncovered hair, wearing a light gray cashmere sweater set with a coordinating Hermes silk scarf in orange, black, and gray swirling patterns, with a darker gray wool skirt and pearls, gently held her Bible out to Wendy and nodded. Wendy responded, "Thanks, but my Hebrew isn't that good. I'll just listen and try to follow."

Atarah's voice continued, "Preparation for revelation, the ability to hear God's teachings and be transformed. That's the purpose of standing at Sinai. All heard, yet not all were prepared to take it in."

As she listened, Wendy thought about other times she had heard some-one speak words of Torah. The last one she could remember was at Dara and Jason's for Shabbat dinner a few weeks ago. Jason gave a marvelous speech about the dreams of Joseph, and how he converted them from mere visions into something solid, with interpretation, and each of them was moved to add a personal interpretation of the story. Dr. Hideckel—what was it he had told her about the "god of the winds?" A leader needs to deal with each individual in accordance with his own temperament. That moved her too. Maybe there *was* more to Torah study than what her baalei teshuvah said: "I go to my rav. He's the expert. He tells me what to think." This kind of Torah study demanded individual thought and input. This teacher, bewigged and quoting Derrida, intrigued Wendy.

After class, Wendy decided that she would like to ask Atarah a few questions. She went to the desk at the front of the room. She waited as a long line of people spoke with Atarah. When Wendy's turn came, she introduced herself and told Atarah that her husband had recommended she come. Wendy asked whether there was a time they could speak? Since there were still more students waiting, Atarah gave Wendy her card and told her to call to set up a meeting.

A week later, Wendy walked through her neighborhood, the German Colony, to the adjacent neighborhood, Bakaa, where Atarah lived. Wendy was surprised it was so close. As Wendy turned onto Atarah's street, she thought about the descriptions some of her interviewees had given her of going to see their *rosh yeshiva*, the trepidation they felt. If only they knew the appropriate questions, he had answers to explain what troubled them. And then, the exhilarating sense they had when leaving: "Some mystery has been solved, he understood me. I am in the right place, this is the leader for me." Wendy wished she could know whether *she* would ever have the feeling they described. She had moments of elation in the library or while writing a paper—the "aha" moments when her ideas came together and she knew that she was on the right track; this bit of information or way to synthesize her ideas was the right one. She hadn't had those moments with a person, though.

The Hideckel house on Shalom Yehuda Street was a one-family house, a rarity in a densely populated city. It was set back from the street, reached by going in a gate, which surrounded the small garden area in front, and walking on a path. Though by Wendy's Westchester standards there was nothing particularly special about the house, she had been in Jerusalem long enough to know that this one was unusually nice. She couldn't even recall having been in a one-family home since arriving here.

She knocked on the door. Atarah answered and ushered Wendy past the living room, into her study through an adjoining door. The room was incrementally smaller than the rest of the house, less than the size of a single room in a college dorm; books filled every space. Shelves extended to the ceiling on three walls, with the exception of the one narrow wall at the back where there was a window and the shelves extended only as far up as the window. The window extended from the middle of the wall to the ceiling, and the books did not block its light. The titles were in both English and Hebrew, with a few shelves of French as well. Wendy was awed by the erudition encased on the shelves. Generally, when she entered a professor's office, she looked at the books to see which ones she had also; she often used a common title as an icebreaker to start conversation.

Atarah gestured to a chair in the corner for her guest while she seated herself at her desk chair. The desk was a long plank of wood, attached to the wall, with some space around it, but otherwise books were above it on the wall and on either side. There were a pile of spiral notebooks on the desk and the bound galleys of Atarah's book, along with a tangle of photocopied texts in English and Hebrew. Atarah wasn't wearing a wig today; instead, her hair was covered loosely by a yellow chiffon scarf, the color of a newborn chick's fuzz, giving her a youthful, girlish look, as though she were going driving in a convertible, ready to wave at passersby.

Once they were both seated, Atarah asked, "Well, Wendy, how has your year been going so far?"

Wendy exhaled and raised her eyebrows. "Where to start? It's just been . . . crazy? Nothing's what I expected. In the fall, I was dating someone. A man tried to seduce him, in the summer before we met, and that man was killed in a *pigua*. My boyfriend was, is, in complete turmoil about his passions, what they are. Then, I interviewed a young man—who, I later learned, was one of your husband's patients—and he killed himself after the interview. So . . . now . . . I am . . . I don't know . . . How can I keep going when my work had a role in a death?"

Atarah looked at Wendy and said, "You know, I'm a teacher," pointing to the galleys of her book, "now, I'm a writer. I'm not a rabbi. That was my father, *alav ha'shalom*, may he rest in peace. I'm one of three sisters, no brothers. When I was about eleven, my father took me to another neighborhood of Brooklyn from Sheepshead Bay, where we lived, to see a rebbe my family had known in Europe, before the war. My father was aware that this was the last time I would be able to have this kind of experience, before I was too old to mix with men. We went to the rebbe's home. There was a room full of men, but when the rebbe saw my father come in, he gestured to the seat of honor by his side. Others moved, and we sat there. The rebbe continued to teach. At the end, he made small talk in Yiddish with my father about their town, people from it, who was where in America, Israel, Australia. When we left, I'm not sure why I asked this"—she looked at Wendy for confirmation that she was still listening, and Wendy nodded, her gaze focused raptly on Atarah—"but I asked my father, 'Is this rebbe a genius?' My father didn't reply. I asked again, I guess because the veneration I saw among his followers was so different from the way my father's congregants behaved. I wanted to understand why. My father said, 'This rebbe is a great man, a leader. He is not a genius.' I asked 'Why? Why isn't he a genius?'" Atarah paused here.

Wendy responded, "What did he say?"

He said, "'This rebbe is not a genius, because to be a genius one must be challenged. When this rebbe says something, his followers listen blindly; they never question. '*Fun a kasha shtarbt man nit*,' my father said in Yiddish. 'From a question no one dies. One must be able to respond to challenges—that is the mark of genius, Atarele.'"

"From a question no one dies," Wendy wrote down in her notebook. Smiling, she added, "You don't think I harmed Shaul?"

"I wasn't in the room when you interviewed him. I can't know," she added conclusively. "It isn't you, but the system. The whole notion of the baal teshuvah yeshiva is riddled with . . . *kushiyot*, difficulties."

"How?" Wendy queried, pen poised over notebook.

"My story of the rebbe points to the problem. Often baalei teshuvah find teachers who are not willing to let them develop on their own. Teachers at baal teshuvah institutions want disciples to follow them. Students can be crippled in their development when they have a need to always ask someone else. There is a story in the Talmud of two famous rabbis, Rabbi Yohanan and his study partner Reish Lakish. After Reish Lakish died, the other rabbis, trying to help Rabbi Yohanan, sent a new study partner to his house."

"It wasn't well received. Like buying a new pet for a kid mourning the old one."

"Well," Atarah said as she smiled broadly and crossed her legs, "what irked Rabbi Yohanan about the new partner was his being sycophantic. He echoed everything the rabbi said, instead of bringing twenty-four objections to an issue like Reish Lakish had, for which Rabbi Yohanan needed to find twenty-four answers. A great rabbi wants to try to maneuver his ideas to cover all contingencies. He doesn't want a yes man."

"If that's so, why would a leader just want students to parrot him? Don't all teachers want their students to progress?" Wendy looked at Atarah raptly, pen poised over her notebook.

Atarah smiled. "That's not hard to answer. You're in graduate school. Tell me, are there professors who keep students in the program for unnaturally long amounts of time, create hoops to be jumped through for no reason?"

"Their egos, to prove the students aren't as good as they are."

"Same thing in the religious world. The fear that students may veer off course, leave the reservation as it were."

Atarah began to fidget with the papers on her desk, to signal that the interview was over. She moved them and glanced around, searching her shelves for a book.

Wendy said, "Thanks for your time; you were really . . . helpful. I'm . . . in a strange place at the moment." She paused. "I'm grappling with what it means that I feel responsible for Shaul's death. Intellectually, I know I'm not responsible, but on an emotional level I feel I am, no matter how much information I get from your husband about the risk of suicide being greatest when it appears that there has been some recovery. Your saying, 'From a question no one dies,' helps, but my human instinct is to want to be responsible for others. Shaul's death weighs on me."

"Look, one final thought I'll leave you with before I must go to pick up our daughter from her piano lesson. Have you been following the controversy swirling around the climbers who tried to summit Everest last May?"

"People who died along with their guide?"

"I read an article about those climbers. One of them was a postal worker, divorced with teenage children. He had tried and failed to summit Everest the previous season. The guide persuaded his client to try again, giving him a steep discount. The second year, again, the man turned around, not feeling able to continue. The guide persuaded him to persevere, to try to make it the entire way up. They both died in the attempt."

"Awful. But, how is it the guide's fault? I mean, he died too."

Atarah focused on Wendy as she spoke. "The guide was concerned with his own reputation, saying, 'I can do it, I can get *anyone* up.' The guide wouldn't heed the wisdom of the climber himself, to turn around. You know, no one can climb that peak for you. You need to do it yourself, as an individual, though with the support, guidance, and experience of others. The hubris of both the guide and of baal teshuvah yeshivot are similar. They both say, in effect, 'We will give you everything, all you need, and in a few weeks you will be living a life at high altitude, all spiritual peaks.' The problem is, you may not have sufficient resources to cope with the speedy ascent. When mountaineering groups go, they take time to acclimate before attempting the summit. There are many who are critical of the whole enterprise of guided mountaineering, saying that if you can't get up the mountain yourself, you don't belong. You *shouldn't* use supplemental oxygen. In baal teshuvah yeshivot they don't always allow students time to adjust to the thin air at high altitude. They won't always distribute the supplemental oxygen or other support. Or warn students they may need it."

Atarah gazed at Wendy and continued, "Like the guide and client on a mountain, the teachers at a baal teshuvah yeshivah want to prove to themselves: 'I can make anyone religious. I can get anyone up that mountain.' So far as I know, no teachers have perished in the ascent." She paused and added, "You don't know what the effect of Shaul's death will be on the yeshiva—I wouldn't be surprised if there were more deaths, maybe some teachers too. It may have been that notion that he *should* be living at the top of the mountain all the time, that total and perfect faith is possible, that was harmful to Shaul. Your questions made him aware of the gap between his ideals and reality. The worst harm wasn't from you. It was the yeshiva's suggesting to him that he could summit easily and quickly. You only reminded him of his inability to reach the heights. They were the ones who brought him to the base camp and told him he could ascend. Like guides, the teachers at the yeshiva are earning their livings this way," Atarah said, sighing with sadness. "I used the analogy because they offer tools to individuals to do things they couldn't and wouldn't get to on their own, but I'm not sure, like Everest guides, that they take the capabilities and capacities of their clients into account. One can't ascend too rapidly, no matter who the guide is."

Wendy was silent as she tried to process this. She had never heard so sharp a criticism of these yeshivot from an insider. She wrote a few notes, and Atarah added, "I have to go, but I'd be happy to see you back in class. It is important to acknowledge the places that we feel injured. Torah study may provide a glimpse of the possibilities of being whole. That is the goal of *limmud* Torah, making us more fully human, splendor and squalor alike."

"I'll try to make your class again. Thank you so much."

Atarah rose, her signal that their time was over. She walked to the door of her house and Wendy followed. As Atarah opened the front door, she added, "The writer Grace Paley said, 'The writer is not some kind of phony historian who runs around answering everyone's questions with made-up characters tying up loose ends. She is nothing but a questioner.' Keep asking those questions. I've always been fascinated by baalei teshuvah and their willingness to take on the mammoth endeavor of changing their lifestyle. That's why I married one," she said with a grin.

THIRTEEN
Purim: Until You Don't Know

The entire time he is drinking he is required to examine himself to determine whether he has reached the point where he cannot distinguish between cursing Haman and blessing Mordecai which means that when he gets to such a point he still knows so to speak what it is that he no longer knows. This is the formulation of a halachic norm, and the irony pokes out from it as though restraining the commandment from itself, by itself. A commandment of commission rolled up in a prohibition: become inebriated soberly.

—ELIEZER SCHWEID, *Jewish Experience of Time*

Walking down Emek Refaim on Purim day, Wendy saw the city of Jerusalem in a state of intoxication. Inside a bus stopped at a traffic light, she glimpsed the bus driver wearing a curly haired clown wig in rainbow colors. Kids in Superman costumes and pirate disguises yanked the hands of parents wearing masks and wigs. Those not in costume looked incongruous. Why be sober on a day when it is a mitzvah to drink enough to blur the line between good and evil, Mordechai and Haman?

Wendy walked, in costume, through the streets of the German Colony to Atarah's neighborhood of Bakaa. It wasn't far enough to take a bus, but it wasn't easy to walk either. Her skirt didn't fit well. It was turquoise and purple paisley print cotton, with varied panels, the print alternating with solid colors. She loved it, but it was too long. Wendy was a gypsy today—always an easy costume to do. Basically, one needed bright clashing prints. She had on a white cotton embroidered peasant shirt from Guatemala, her ears laden with large gold hoops, and scarves everywhere: a scarf around her hair, not covering it like a religious woman, just wound around her head, and scarves at her waist and hip as sashes. A purse slung over her shoulder that she had bought at Mahane Yehuda, in a colorful fabric with touches of gold embroidery and beads fringing it. She was wearing a series of thin gold colored bracelets on each wrist. She jingled and clanked as she walked, calling attention to herself in a way she usually found uncomfortable. When she had mentioned to Orly that she needed a gypsy costume, Orly found a red embroidered shawl from Turkey that had belonged to her grandmother. It completed the outfit.

I hope no one seeing me thinks I am actually dressing like this, that it's not a costume." As she thought this, she looked at the others on the street—almost all adults taken in by her glance were, in the middle of the day, in costume. She needn't have worried at her ridiculousness, even trying to hold up her excessively long skirt. No one she saw on the street looked quite sane, from the parents and children delivering goody baskets of food to friends, to the puking men in black hats she rarely saw in this neighborhood. That guy in a black hat and *peyos*—was it a costume or was it his usual attire? She didn't know how to tell. Even for Jews, creatures of memory, there was a one-day hold on making distinctions between categories of people. Thus freed, the city seemed to release itself from the particular tensions of the year—suicide bombings on buses, the stabbings of Jews by Arabs in residential neighborhoods of Jerusalem, economic woes, worries about the future.

Wendy felt a hilarity around her, a kind of mass emotion on the street, that she'd never felt in America. As she walked, she thought about how she liked that life in Jerusalem was lived at a more primal level, without artifice. People were nosy here, wanted to know how much you paid in rent, but also hospitable, invited you over without much fuss, and could show a level of caring she hadn't found in the States. In the weeks since Shaul's death, she had felt people really reach out to her. Todd and some of the others in the Fulbright group had taken her to coffee; Orly and Dara called every few days to check up. She felt connected in this city in a way she had never anticipated.

It was odd, only a few weeks after she had been in Dr. Hideckel's office, being invited to his home for the Purim meal. What was it called, a *Purim*

Soo-dah? She knew *se'uda* was the Hebrew word for *meal*, but still wasn't sure of the exact pronunciation. She clutched carefully the bottle of wine she was bringing, remembering that she had paid for it what she estimated was a good portion of what Hideckel would have charged for an hour. Wendy felt like she owed Dr. Hideckel for his time that day in his office. She was grateful he didn't bill her, because she didn't want there to be any record of her visit to a psychiatrist's office. If her parents learned about it, she didn't want to explain. They would tell her, "Come home immediately if you need help. We'll make sure Wendy sees the best people in New York. Can't leave anything to chance with our Wendy," she could hear her mother Sylvia saying.

Wendy had bought the wine at the fancy gourmet wine store All the Gefen on Emek Refaim, a few blocks from her house. It had only been open a few weeks and had a bar with tapas samples certain days of the week; you could sit for thirty shekel, taste wines, and nosh. She had gone once with Orly, so she went back to get wine for the Hideckels instead of going to a cheaper place in Mahane Yehuda. When she answered all the questions of the adorable salesman, who had to be gay because straight Israeli men never take that much care with their hair to mousse it perfectly into place, she looked at the wine he'd given her. It wasn't kosher. When she told him she needed kosher, he looked at her strangely. "Kosher wine is zee worse. *Worse*, you understand. Zhey boil all ze flavor out, no aroma." And to get his point across, he wrinkled up his sexy mouth as though he had just actually tasted the loathsome substance. He looked at her again curiously. "You're not a *dos*, *motek*; drink something with a taste! *Ieeecchs*," that uniquely Israeli conveyance of disgust, a more distilled form of *yuch*, with the additional guttural adding potency.

Wendy replied, "It's not for me. I'm invited by some *dosim* for Purim."

Grudgingly, he loped over to his kosher section, in the back. He found a bottle and handed it to her. "Best kosher stuff, yes? I wouldn't be embarrassed to drink *zees*. You wanted to spend 200 shekel, no?"

"Sure. Do you have a gift bag?"

"*Betach*," he said holding up her choices.

So the wine was enrobed in its finery of a purple iridescent paper wine sack and a sticker in Hebrew and English, "*al ha-gefen*" (on the vine) and "All the Gefen," in English, adorning it. Now, the bottle itself was costumed, looking as though it were a fancy gourmet wine, imported from Europe or California, when it was really an Israeli domestic product, produced just a few hundred kilometers from Jerusalem.

As she arrived at Atarah's street she wondered, did she have more in common with the salesman in the store, and his attitude to the wine, than she did with the people who would be here? Why had she accepted Atarah's invitation? Curiosity to see this teacher in a social setting? Curiosity about Dr. Hideckel? Their relationship? Daniel and Atarah Hideckel were both so polished and formal—she couldn't imagine their passion, that they slept together without wig and kipah. But both were refreshingly honest and might even be the types to talk about their sex lives when asked, in the interests of promoting married passion—at least after a few drinks. She remembered, on the subject of teachers talking about sex, one of her professors in graduate school had told them that his parents belonged to a religious sect that absolutely disapproved of sex except for procreation. So far as he knew, his parents had only had sex a few times. She was repulsed, as were the rest of the students, by being given too much information.

Being honest with herself, she admitted she was here because she'd been invited. Wendy didn't get enough invitations to refuse one.

She went up the walkway to the door and knocked. After standing on the threshold a few moments, listening to the raucous voices inside, she realized it was open, and she entered to the sight of people standing and sitting in the living room, wine glasses and beer bottles in their hands. All of them, like Wendy, were in costume.

Wendy entered, walking hesitantly. No one noticed her entrance, until an Elvis impersonator, in white polyester jumpsuit edged with gold sequins at the chest and wide bell bottoms also edged in gold sequins, red cape, jet black hair and sideburns, approached her with an outstretched hand. "Wendy, so glad you could make it. *Chag Purim Sameach*, welcome."

Who was this Elvis who knew her name?

"You don't recognize me," Elvis smiled, amused.

Wendy jerked her head back and then shook her head, quickly, twice from side to side. "Dr. Hideckel?" she queried. Laughing, she answered her own inquiry, "I would never have recognized you! You're . . ."

"Majestic," he boomed. "I'm the King."

"Your Majesty," she said, playing along with his role and curtsying. "I brought some wine for you and Atarah," she said as she handed the package to him. "Thanks for inviting me."

"Thanks for coming." He glanced at the label. "All the Gefen. I've passed there a few times. It looks like a nice addition to the neighborhood."

"A great little place. Not kosher, but they have a kosher section in the back where I got this."

"I look forward to drinking it. Let me introduce you around." He looked over at the crowd sitting and standing in the living room: a clown; an individual in a feathered mask and Mardi Gras beads; a Dead Head in tie-dyed dancing bears T-shirt, ripped and faded jeans, with a bandana on his head; a doctor in a white coat and stethoscope wearing a donkey mask; a witch; a princess; and Hillary Clinton. All were holding glasses containing various species of alcoholic libations. He called, "Josh, Uri, this is Wendy. Get her a drink and introduce yourselves."

Hillary Clinton and the Dead Head walked over to Wendy. Hillary asked in what sounded like a British accent, "What do you want? We've got beer and wine, some mixed drinks, and a pitcher of peach bellinis."

The Dead Head said, "Josh. Nice to meet you," and held out his hand.

"Wendy. Hi." After she shook Josh's hand, she said to Hillary, "What's in the pitcher looks good. I'll have some of that."

Hillary said, "It is." Wendy noticed that the peach colored liquid in his glass was at the bottom. "I'll get you some."

Josh the Dead Head said, "I'm Dr. Hideckel's resident this year. How do you know them?"

"Oh," Wendy thought. *Do I say to another psychiatrist, I went to see Dr. Hideckel after one of his patients committed suicide partly because of me? Not lighthearted Purim banter there.* "I've just started going to Atarah's classes and she was nice enough to invite me."

"Cool. I've heard she's a great teacher."

"I'm not religious, but I really wanted to learn more and she's just . . ." Wendy couldn't think of the appropriate adjective as she lifted her jingling hand to accept the drink Hillary was offering and said to her, "Thank you, Hillary. What brings our lovely first lady to Israel?"

"Taking care of our Jewish constituents," she said as she patted the bottom of her wig. "You?" she asked Wendy.

"I'm a gypsy; we wander. Can't you tell?" she said, shaking both her wrists so the bracelets made their jingle-jangle tones.

"Read my palm," Josh the Dead Head said. Before she could respond, Hillary stretched out her hand, palm up towards Wendy. "Ladies first," she said in a falsetto voice, looking at Josh pointedly. Josh got the hint and left to refill his glass.

Wendy put her untasted drink down on the table near her. "Let's see." She planted her left hand underneath Hillary's, while the right traced the patterns on the palm. "There is a line here," Wendy said, tracing the line on Hillary's palm while simultaneously looking up at Hillary's clear blue eyes underneath the mask with the politician's face. She hadn't been entirely certain of Hillary's gender; the unshaven legs under the stockings, along with the hands, confirmed maleness. Hillary's hand had fingers thick enough to have an impact, looking like they could open the lids of stubborn jars. The fingers were not fat or too large, but fleshy enough to contain gentle feeling, tender sensations.

In Wendy's experience, palm reading was a girl thing. Only women, unable to say out loud, *I want to earn money or go on a long trip or find the love of my life*, could use the excuse of going to a fortune teller and having her say, "Oh yes, this will happen to you"—and then shaping a life to match hoped-for predictions. Wendy never believed in palm reading, though at the overnight camp she attended, all campers on the girls' side feigned firm belief in it. She was grateful to remember enough from Camp Kodimoh's late night palm-reading sessions to put on a reasonable show.

She continued to hold "Hillary's" hand in hers, and heard herself asking, "First? Whether you'll be president yourself one day? What the chances are that health care reform will pass? Whether there will be an indictment for Vince Foster's suicide?" Wendy stupefied herself by being able to joke about this.

Hillary responded, "Eleanor Roosevelt's ghost told me all that with the Ouija board. I want to know whether I'll meet anyone new—Bill and I are history."

It was a strange intimacy, standing in the living room of Shaul's psychiatrist and Wendy's new teacher. They were surrounded by people, yet it was just the two of them, his trust reposing in her, hand in hers.

"Someone male or female?"

"Female, definitely," "she" said in a falsetto voice. "It was great at Wellesley. Bill has been man enough for the rest of my life."

Wendy laughed and lifted his hand closer to her face to peer at it with mock attention. "Let's see. Your heart line looks forked, so divorce is in the offing, but the forked part continues, so there will be more relationships."

"Sounds good."

"I can't tell more about who it will be . . ."

"I've met you," she said, looking fiercely at Wendy with those blue eyes behind the mask.

Wendy didn't know how to interpret this. She couldn't tell what she thought of this guy since all she could see of him were his blue eyes and his hand, which did have a nice heft, in hers. She wasn't ready to flirt—it depended on what he looked like when the mask was off, and who he was. She decided to continue in her role as gypsy chiromancer. "You've met me, and there is a good line of intuition, shows you have good judgment. Here's the travel line, some long trips in the future . . ."

"You do palm readings, Wendy? Good," said Dr. Hideckel, returning to introduce her around. "Is my resident Uri here staying in Israel or going back to merry olde England?"

"I was reading Hillary Clinton's palm. I hadn't been introduced to Uri." She put out her hand. "Uri, I'm Wendy."

He removed the mask that went over the whole head with its attached wig, revealing a face that complemented the eyes. Blue eyes, thick brown hair with no signs of receding. This was good, since Wendy hated premature baldness in men. His evenly spaced and immaculately white teeth made her picture a horse's. They weren't too big, but had a certain equine health and vitality. So stupid, she kicked herself inwardly, to be thinking about breeding qualities—baldness or its lack, good teeth—with a man she had just met. His eyes had nice crinkle lines when he smiled, suggesting sensitivity and vulnerability. Worth flirting with, and he seemed to like her.

"*Hag Sameach*," he said. When had she heard Hebrew words, especially with that guttural phlegm-filled "*chet*," sound so sexy?

"Same to you," she said, not wanting to risk butchering the throaty sound that remained slightly out of reach even after a half year of *ulpan*.

"Wendy, did anyone get you a drink?" Dr. Hideckel interjected.

"I had something. I put it down to read Uri's palm." She looked around and spied the glass she had put on the table. She went to retrieve it.

"Let me introduce you to the others," said Dr Hideckel as she returned, glass in hand. The doorbell rang, and Uri said, "Dan, I'll introduce her. You get the door."

"Take care of her."

As Elvis meandered off, Uri asked, "How do you know the Hideckels? Are you related?"

"I've been taking classes with Atarah." Wendy didn't annex an apology about not being religious.

"I've heard her teach a few times. She blew me away."

"Me too. I've really been . . . challenged . . . by her."

"What else are you doing in Israel besides studying with Atarah? Not that it wouldn't be enough . . ." Uri laughed awkwardly, hoping he hadn't made a blunder.

"I'm questioning return." He gave her a blank look. "I'm in Jerusalem working on my dissertation."

"Brilliant," he said in his clipped British accent. "Your field?"

"American religion. You?"

"Me? I work for the man, Dr. H. I'm his resident."

"You drink with your boss? Whenever I go to department parties, everyone is so awkward and self-conscious. You are trying to be clever and brilliant and ambitious, but everyone else is too, and it is supposed to be a party and fun and it isn't and you just go home with a huge stomachache. The food is always bad."

"Don't worry about that here. The Hideckels are amazing cooks."

"They both cook?" Wendy said, surprised.

"Shabbos and holiday meals are collaborative."

"Hmm." Wendy was surprised to hear a busy doctor cared to make time to cook. She didn't know what to say next. "How did you pick psychiatry as a field?" came out. Would he see her as an idiot for such a dull query?

"Picking psychiatry?" Uri echoed Wendy's question thoughtfully and took a big swig of his drink. "If you really want to know, we'll have to sit down." He did this both to see whether she would follow him and to decide what information might interest her most. Wendy liked the British tinge to his accent.

She followed Uri over to a couch in the living room. There were others there, but he didn't introduce her. They sat down and Wendy continued to sip her drink.

"I feel like I've met you before," he said. "Or maybe I've just already had so much to drink that I'm kind of floating."

"I've never been to England—is that where you are from?"

"Sort of. My parents were born here, but I've lived mostly in England, partly here. I might stay in Israel. I don't know. I like the approach to psychiatry here. I want to help people change how they think about themselves, not dispense pills. Drug companies are so *dodgy*, you know?" Again the British accent came out with the word "dodgy."

"I'm studying how people think about themselves. You could probably help me analyze the data." *Oh, that sounds so stupid. How enticing is an invitation to analyze data? Get a bit warmer, back to the gypsy role; he liked that,* she advised herself.

"Do you want me to read your palm as Uri now?" He held it outstretched towards her, and she put her drink on the floor to grasp it in both hands.

He inquired, teasingly, "Is this a sham or do you know how to read palms?"

"What do you think?"

"Don't care at all," he said, leaning his head back on the couch and smiling up at her sitting upright.

Just then, Dr. Hideckel called everyone to the table for the meal.

Atarah was sitting at the head of the table, wearing an exaggeratedly large corona made of colored cellophane paper and plastic jewels. Her garment was a *galabiyya*, a Morroccan embroidered gown, of deep purple. If not for the wig, Wendy decided, she would look like a total hippie. The garishness of the both the silver and gold embroidery on the *galabiyya*, and the homemade crown, gave her a look entirely different from the carefully selected garments that were her usual attire.

Dr. Hideckel made a mock Kiddush in Hebrew, which consisted of lots of biblical and talmudic quotes extolling the appropriateness of wine and its great qualities. Wendy got the oft-repeated words *yayin*, wine, and *gefen*, vine, but there were other places where everyone except her laughed at the sacred parody. She didn't like not getting the jokes, but kept taking sips of her drink and felt pleasantly overcome by the alcohol, in that rosy state one gets after sufficient drinking, before one is entirely drunk. The group went to ritually wash their hands before eating bread, and the meal began.

After all were sated with copious amounts of food, along with corresponding drink, Atarah spoke. "So we aren't here to have a corroboree tonight, though that is certainly part of it. We are trying to define the line between sober and inebriated. It is like an asymptotic line, coming closer and closer to drunkenness without truly approaching it."

Wendy was too awed by Atarah's wisdom to do anything beyond continuing to drink. She was rarely in such a state; now that it was so pleasant, she wasn't sure why drink had never had a whole lot of appeal for her. She had to remember not to drink like she did her first Shabbat in Jerusalem, with Donny. She would not make that mistake twice, if she could help herself.

Atarah asked everyone to go around and introduce themselves. "Now, I want names as well as"—she paused and did her signature glance at the faces of all those present—"an absurd fact about yourself, in keeping with the tone of the holiday."

When they went around introducing themselves. Wendy said, "I'm questioning return. I'm trying to see what it means for people who didn't grow up with Jewish rituals to suddenly declare this is the only possible path they could have taken, their return to religion inevitable, which can be seen as an absurd claim. What does 'return' truly mean when it is to something one has never experienced?"

Uri smiled at her from across the table.

Wendy got an e-mail from an unfamiliar address a few days later: Ushalem@ hadassahhospital.edu. She couldn't figure out what it was from looking at it—a funny name, Ushalem—sounded like some kind of play on Jerusalem. She almost deleted it, but then thought it could relate to Shaul or another one of her subjects. Uri wrote that he found her address on the Princeton religion department website, where all the advanced graduate students had postings with short synopses of their projects. He said he enjoyed meeting her on Purim and inquired whether she'd do another palm reading—he had been too drunk to remember her advice. She wrote back that she wasn't sure sobriety would improve the readings, but she'd be glad to try again. They decided to meet the coming Thursday afternoon, at five, at Uri's favorite café in Jerusalem, B'Sograim, on Ussishkin Street. He figured Thursday at this time was good because he didn't have to work on Friday. If they had a good time, they could get dinner afterwards or a movie. If not, then they'd just part. He liked Wendy but needed to set it up for both scenarios, staying and leaving, the classic single-guy ploy of leaving himself with an out if needed.

Wendy was pleased he had contacted her via e-mail—it meant he hadn't asked the Hideckels for her phone number and they wouldn't know she was going out with him. If she knew he had gotten her e-mail from Dr. Hideckel, she might have said no. But the accent, the hands that had the promise of tenderness, the blue eyes, the wiry thick hair, and her general sense that he was interesting all made Uri an attractive possibility.

There hadn't been any males on her horizon recently. She was going back to the States in three months, at the end of June, so it was sort of irrelevant anyway. Before then, Wendy needed to wrap up her interviews, fill in gaps, and actually start writing. This terrified her. What if, when she began to write things up in the States, she needed to clarify a point and couldn't find her interview subject via e-mail? What if she wanted to speak to one of the rabbis again? *Stay focused. Reply to his e-mail; don't get into a whole thing about the future just yet,* she told herself as she wrote down the meeting place in her planner. Even if she had someone to go out with for the next three months, it would be nice. Uri was appealing, cute, and a Jewish doctor in training.

The only problem was that he was religious. But he put his hand in hers and let her touch it. She knew from her baalei teshuvah that a strictly Ortho-dox man wouldn't touch her at all. Uri seemed normal, comfortable with himself, able to joke around, calling Dr. Hideckel, "the man." She would never be comfortable enough to get drunk with *her* dissertation committee. The religion thing would take care of itself somehow; being with him couldn't last longer than three months anyway so it wasn't a big deal. And, it would be a great punishment to her mother to taunt her by dating a religious Jew. Not that Sylvia was antireligious. She wasn't. Sylvia loved being Jewish—wouldn't deny it, or try to hide it—but only up to a point. Jews in any way more religious than herself went far beyond Sylvia's definition of "up to a point."

Wendy vowed not to tell Orly about Uri till after the date. She knew Orly would tease her mercilessly about *dossim* who only wanted to have sex with a sheet with a hole in it.

Thursday morning, the day of their date, was a sunny day, in the sixties Fahrenheit. Spring was finally in the air. Wendy dressed more carefully than usual, in a white sleeveless V-neck sweater and matching cardigan, paired with a blue cotton miniskirt. She wore her new red sandals, a present to herself for finishing transcribing the interviews she'd done. Every time she walked past Freeman and Bein shoes on Yaffo Street she had coveted these cherry red shoes, which were like clogs, with a buckle. She didn't usually like items of apparel that called attention to their wearers, but maybe the ways women around Jerusalem dressed, much less conservatively than in Princeton, influenced her. The thought of wearing the red shoes in Princeton, bringing a piece of the flamboyance of Jerusalem back with her, gave Wendy great pleasure. And she wore her Michal Negrin earrings, another Jerusalem find, with their bright colors—red, green, yellow, and blue enamel. They were colorful but not too big, sort of shimmery and ultrafeminine, but not too dangly and un-serious. The outfit was topped off by a light patterned scarf, also in bright red, green, yellow, and blue colors she'd found in one of the stalls off King George in the center of town, when transferring buses from the university to her house. When she went to the library in the morning she didn't put makeup on, but brought it with her so she'd be ready for tonight. She wanted to look nice, but not look like she had made too huge an effort. When she left the bathroom at the Hebrew University library before taking the bus to the center of town, she was pleased with how she looked.

She had a bit of trouble finding the place. She had the street address, but there was a parking lot to cut across, which made it unclear how to get there, so she was a few minutes late. Finally, Wendy entered the restaurant, formerly a stone house with mosaic tile patterns on its floor. It had narrow old-fashioned windows, original artwork on the walls—mostly photos—and fresh flowers on the tables. The atmosphere signaled that the food was prepared with more than usual care.

Uri was sitting in a corner in the back, reading the *Journal of Psychiatry*. There weren't that many other people inside the restaurant; most of the customers were outside on the porch enjoying the beginning of spring. There were two other tables with single occupants, and another with a young couple. Uri was the only man alone, but Wendy was still relieved to see the journal, a sure sign that it *was* him. On the table in front of the journal was a slim black segment. As she approached closer to the table, she realized it wasn't a beeper; it was a wallet that he must have removed from his back pocket and placed there. It was remarkably like the wallet her father always carried. She walked over to the table and put her hand on his arm, lightly. He looked up, confused, startled for a moment out of the concentration of his reading. She said, "Hi, Uri."

He gazed at her blankly at first. She worried, *Was this date was a colossal mistake?* As she walked to the seat across from him to seat herself, he said, "Wendy. Hi. I'm in the middle of reading a great article. I was totally absorbed. It generally takes me a minute to get back to ordinary life."

"No problem. Sorry I'm late; I had trouble finding this place."

"You didn't just walk up Ben Yehuda to Betzalel?"

"I did, but the parking lot confused me." Looking around, she added, "This place reminds me of this restaurant in Princeton, Market of Eden."

"There are kosher restaurants in Princeton? I didn't know the community there was that big."

She frowned, "It's not kosher. Why would you think that?"

He looked at her and noticed now that she was wearing a sleeveless sweater, having swung the matching cardigan over her chair when she sat down. "Aren't you religious?" he asked.

"Did you think I was religious?" Wendy said, worried. *He's going to dump me before this date has even started. I can't believe it. Did I mislead him? I didn't say I'd never studied Torah before Atarah.*

"You were studying with Atarah; you were dressed modestly . . . I ass*u*med," the stress on the "u" of the word heightened his Britishness, "anyone at their house was."

They stared at each other, she angry and bewildered, he just perplexed. "Look." He splayed his hands out, palms up, vulnerable. "Wendy, I'm . . ." He stopped, not sure how much to confess, but decided just to continue. "I invited you here; I'd like to get to know you. Order something. If you want to drink something cold, the *choco kar* is great. It's like hot chocolate, thick and flavorful, but cold, with these delicious flecks of chocolate."

"I don't know. We're both busy; maybe I should just go. Thanks for introducing me to this restaurant. It's nice." She could see herself meeting Orly here and whining to her about the "un-date" she'd experienced in its precincts as she started to gather her pocketbook.

"Wendy," he reached out for her hand and grasped it gently, but firmly, for emphasis. "I really don't care whether or not you are religious." He let go of her hand and continued, "I just assumed you were. I was mistaken. I'm not totally *frum* myself. I grew up with it, but I'm not sure what direction I'm going in. Life is too complicated to have one set of answers; that's part of my attraction to psychiatry. I'm interested in the nuances and complications of people's lives, working to untangle them."

She breathed a sigh out. "Okay." She paused and smiled. "I like complications too." She paused to tuck a strand of hair behind her ear and leaned forward, "What bothers me most about the baalei teshuvah that I am interviewing is their certainty. They think they have a set of answers that will work for everyone in all situations. That is what has been so eye-opening about the Hideckels. They are religious without that smugness. They seem to believe in complexity, that it can add to a religious understanding, not take away from it, and is actually preferable, if I understand Atarah correctly."

"I don't think we're so far apart," Uri said with a smile.

The waitress came over and said, "*Hazmanot*?" Orders?

Uri said to the waitress, "*Od daka.*" Another minute.

Wendy said, "I haven't looked at the menu but I'm not particularly hungry."

"I'll order for you? I know what's good here."

Part of her intuited that this might be an indication that he was some kind of control freak, but part of her didn't mind letting him, with his obviously fluent Hebrew and interest in food, take charge.

"Fine."

He addressed the waitress in Hebrew with their orders, and she left.

"Do I get to know what I'm eating?" she asked teasingly, trying to resume the flirtatious tone she had earlier.

"I'll let you be surprised," he said smiling.

"It's funny to be here with you as yourself, when we met in costume."

"How do you find me as a man?"

"I'm just remembering what Atarah was saying at the seudah"—did I pronounce it right?" she asked, uncertain, and after he nodded, continued—"about Jacob being most himself when he proclaimed, "I am Esau, your oldest son," because as Jacob the trickster, part of him really *was* engaged in becoming Esau . . . That in some way he was fully authentic only in costume."

Uri responded, "We met in costume; our shadow selves saw each other."

"I was only a gypsy because it is the default costume. You just need long skirts and lots of scarves. Why is Hillary your shadow self?"

"Same, default. My roommate had that full mask and didn't want to wear it. But I am attracted to power and Hillary has it. It is interesting to see how the other half lives, what women's clothes are like."

"Ah ha," she said archly.

"Not that I want to do it on a daily basis; it's just interesting to see what the differences are."

"It takes women longer to get dressed; there are many more options. I'm glad I wore something sleeveless today—it's really getting hot. Does it bother you? I can put my sweater on," she added hastily.

"No, not at all," he smiled. "You look great. I like you better without scarves on your head."

"So you don't want a wife who will cover her hair?" Wendy said, provocatively fluffing the scarf around her neck for emphasis.

He responded in kind, openly, "I want a wife who makes her own decisions. My mother doesn't cover her hair except at *beit Knesset*."

"So you're really *not* that religious. All the baalei teshuvah I interview are obsessed with that issue. A hat, a wig, do they let some bangs show, no hair, some hair under the hat . . ."

"I've no interest in telling people what to wear."

"You just want to tell them what to think as a psychiatrist?" she said. *Then*, she thought to herself, *why am I being hostile, to religion and to psychiatrists? I've got to be a bit nicer unless I'm not interested. He told me I look great, so I should at least give him a chance.*

"What do you have against my noble profession?" he teased, pretending to take notes on the notepad still lying at his side from when he was reading the article.

"Nothing. I didn't tell you yet the real reason I got to know the Hideckels, though."

He leaned forward, his hands on top of each other and elbows out. "Aaaah, there *is* more to the story."

"I may as well tell you the whole thing, now that I'm out of costume and outed as a secular woman. Then you can decide what you think." She continued, "I have been going to Atarah's classes and she invited me on Purim, but . . ." She stopped mid-sentence, deliberating about how to start. "Okay, so you know I am questioning return. I've been interviewing baalei teshuvah at various yeshivot around Jerusalem. Most of the time they craft their stories in a similar way: 'I was in such and such a place, distant from *Hashem*, but *Baruch Hashem*, I met a religious friend or a teacher. Or, traveling, I decided to stop in Israel before or after hitting the beaches of Goa; it must be *basherte*; I'm so happy I'm *frum*. You know those 'life is good' T-shirts? They irritate me; they just seem to say, my life is good; yours isn't. It seems like a taunt—I guess that is something I find in general about baalei teshuvah— they want to taunt you with how great their life is. Baalei teshuvah should have their own shirts: 'Life is *frum*.'"

Uri added, "'*Frum* is good.' With smiley face with a kipah."

Wendy laughed and continued, "In Jerusalem, you could make a fortune on those. I try to find my way into the cracks and fissures in their arguments, asking them, what do you not like about being religious, was there anything difficult to give up, how has your relationship with your family been affected? Basically, I try to get at the places where that smile of contentment is smashed and fractured."

"You are relishing making them squirm. Do all of them have difficulties?"

"Hell, yeah." She hoped he wouldn't be upset by her use of swear words; maybe she shouldn't have said that, but she was getting into her subject, getting relaxed, and that just came out. "It's just a question of getting them to talk about it."

"What's the connection with how you met the Hideckels?" he asked with a slow smile, amused at her excitement about her work.

The waitress came with their food. Uri had ordered a *choco kar* for Wendy and for himself. He had also ordered a small platter of assorted small cookies, which she put between them, and gave them each a plate. He thanked the waitress in Hebrew and she left.

"This is really good," Wendy said after her first slurp. She continued to gulp as quickly as her straw permitted. "It makes me want to trust you. You have good taste."

He smiled and said, "If you're hungry, have a cookie too. The baked goods here are the best in Jerusalem."

"Have you been to Don't Pass Me By Tea and Pie in Nahalat Shiva? Worthy competition."

"I haven't."

"Next time," she said and then realized she shouldn't so prematurely assume there will be a next time. She worried she would turn him off by assuming this.

He didn't respond, not wanting to commit one way or another. "You were in the middle of a story," he reminded her gently.

"Right," she exhaled slowly, the animation with which she discussed her work gone for the time being, "I may be a bit harsh sometimes with the questions I ask people. One of the people I was interviewing, Shaul Engel, was a patient of Dr. Hideckel's."

"Why do I know that name?" Uri mused.

She gazed at him, clueless as to what would happen after this admission. "He committed suicide after our interview. In the suicide note, he wrote that after the interview, he realized he hadn't changed as much as he wanted to. He didn't want to subject himself to more temptations, so decided to end his life. He used a verse about the day of death being better than the day of birth," she said sadly, biting her bottom lip to keep herself from crying.

"I'm sorry, Wendy." Uri looked at her carefully. "If he'd been under an excellent psychiatrist's care, surely you aren't to blame. You've interviewed plenty of others without anything"—he said it in such a British way, *an-na-thing*, she found charming in spite of the seriousness of the conversation—"so tragic occurring."

"That's true, but I was telling you about my interlocutory style. I kept interrogating Shaul. He was getting upset. I could tell from his tone of voice." She let out a big breath and added, "The worst part is that, beyond pressing him, I didn't get the main thing he was trying to express." Wendy was trying to hold back tears herself now. "I went back and listened to the tape the next day, and he is so clearly making a plea for help, saying how unhappy he is. He actually said . . ."—Wendy looked up at Uri with tears in her eyes—"he said to me, 'It would be easier if I weren't here.' And I couldn't understand that simple message from another human in pain."

Unsuccessful at staunching what was starting to become an uncontrollable flow of tears, she needed to exit before her sobbing became of notice to the other patrons. "Excuse me, I need the ladies room." She picked up her bag and retreated to find a place to cry as she wished; she quickly asked a waiter directions. On finding her refuge, she locked herself in the teeny room with a high ceiling and a toilet with an old-fashioned mechanism, the rectangular basin on top and a long pipe connecting to the bowl. Wendy put the lid of the toilet down. She sat and put her hands on her face. She cried and moaned, "Why did I do it? Why didn't I stop asking? Why can't I pay attention to other people? I wish I could go back in time and listen, and keep

Shaul alive. I'm a horrid excuse of a person." Wendy continued to wail, alone. After a few minutes of crying, she thought, *Okay, I am horrible, I know, but I can't sit here feeling that permanently. Now what? I like this guy. He's a psychiatrist but I don't know how he'll feel about a show of emotion like this on a date. Well, if he thinks I'm awful it's okay since nothing with him would have amounted to much anyway; I'm leaving the country in three months. There's always Matt when I go back to Princeton.* She didn't want to give up unless Uri had fled by the time she returned. She commanded herself, *See if you can salvage this date.*

She wiped her eyes with the toilet paper, annoyed that the sink was outside the room with the toilet, as in most Israeli bathrooms. She'd have to wash her face at that sink in public, with waiters and waitresses walking by, and lurking customers waiting to do a ritual hand washing before eating bread. Hopefully, Uri would be sitting at the table reading his journal and not come look for her and find her like this, red-eyed, looking and feeling like shit.

It was funny, the times she cried with men, she thought, splashing water on her discolored and mottled face. Usually, if she could cry, it meant she felt comfortable enough with them to really open up about what mattered—it might even be a cry of relief over having found someone who understood her. She couldn't remember the last time she had cried with a man.

What would Uri do when she returned? Wendy asked herself as she dried her face with the horribly scratchy brown paper towels still standard even in upscale Israeli restaurants. *A fortune could be made in marketing high-end janitorial supplies in Israeli restaurants and hotels, where no two-ply, much less three-ply, toilet paper exists,* Wendy concluded. There was a mirror above the sink, a small rectangle, slightly above Wendy's eye level. She was able to see her eyes by standing on tiptoe. She put on mascara, foundation, and powder, and walked, deliberately, back to the table, where she found Uri sitting, gazing around at the other customers.

"Sorry to be so emotional. I've been under so much stress about Shaul's death. Every time I sit down to work, I worry, is what I'm going to say more important than the life of another person? It's completely paralyzing. I'm always second-guessing myself. I feel so guilty—what kind of person am I to care about *my* work and not about another person's life? Or feelings?"

"You feel you were unnecessarily cruel, which may or may not be so, but

Shaul's death is *not* your fault. No one knows what triggers a suicide. Honestly. I'm not just saying that." He looked at her and tapped her arm lightly with his fingers, for emphasis. "I don't see you as a bad person. In fact, your honesty is admirable. Your attempts to get baalei teshuvah to be open about their struggles are so important. So many of us struggle with being religious but can't or won't admit where the difficulties are. I love your project. It's . . . fresh. Innovative. It takes an outsider to look and really see the religious community. I admire your need to be honest with yourself—you may have pushed and probed him more than necessary, but you are not to blame for Shaul's death."

"Dr. Hideckel also said that."

"You went to see him after Shaul died."

"Bingo," she added. "He told me, if I felt like I wanted to atone, I could pray, give tzedaka, or study. He thought that as a student I might prefer the study option."

"He suggested that you go to Atarah's classes," Uri said with a smile.

"I'm glad I didn't have to explain this when we met," Wendy added.

"You shouldn't feel that what happened with Shaul means you're an uncaring person," he said compassionately. "Academia doesn't teach you to care—or need you to care. That you have to decide on your own."

"It's frustrating. Besides Hideckel, the only other person who has listened to me is the Fulbright adviser here, Avner Zakh. My dissertation committee . . . I haven't been able to talk to any of them about this whole Shaul thing. It isn't part of what they are teaching. Just write and publish, that's their mantra."

Uri ran his fingers through his thick brown hair. "Medicine is the same way. Worse probably. You get compensated for the numbers of patients you see, not quality of care or success of the treatment outcome. That isn't for me. I will judge myself, ultimately, on how well my patients heal, nothing else. That's it."

"I hope you stay idealistic once you start practicing," Wendy said sadly.

"I hope," he said, sipping his *choco kar*. He put his hand, palm down, in the middle of the table, as if to offer a challenge. "You? How will you know you've succeeded in academia?"

A slow smile came to Wendy's lips as she gazed at Uri. She also took a sip of her chocolate drink and a bite of her cookie. She loved capacious questions, ones where a huge net was tossed out in the effort to pin down and capture something of the elusive mixture of qualities that embodied the essence of the person sitting across from you. If a person cared enough to pry, to make these inquiries, it meant he wanted to *get* you, to know who you were, *really*. There was an element of marvel, Wendy thought. *Here is an interesting person across the table; it's possible to get to know him, what he's about.* Wendy was struggling with the complexity of wanting both to put herself in the most alluring light and being honest. She finally answered, "If my work changes the field, enables my colleagues to see paradigms differently, I'll feel I've succeeded."

They each sat in silence for a few moments, sipping the *choco kar*. Wendy decided that she was not going to make the next conversational move. She would leave it to him, if he were motivated enough.

He was. "We discussed why I was Hillary. Why were you a gypsy?"

"Lawlessness, freedom? Being on the margins, outside societal restraint."

"We're getting somewhere," he smiled conspiratorily.

"Maybe. Could be my attraction to this whole subject—and why I feel so guilty about Shaul. I want to be beyond, an invisible observer no one is aware of standing on the margins, noticing, recording. As the youngest in my family, I was always absorbing things that no one realized I was able to decode."

"Decoding—what the gypsy and the politician have in common."

"How?"

"A politician has to decode what people want, know their hidden desires to craft appealing platforms. He or she has to know how to assess people's needs, so they'll vote. A gypsy also has to know what interests people in doing fortunes, to get paid."

"I like the driftless part of being a gypsy. To live a month here, three weeks there, five weeks somewhere else—freedom on the open road. I've been so focused on getting this dissertation researched and written. I've barely traveled around Israel . . ."

"Shall we stroll around the neighborhood here and walk off a few of those *choco kar* calories?"

"Sure." Wendy was pleased with the invitation.

Uri gestured to the waitress and paid the bill. Wendy often offered to split, but he had ordered for her and seemed like the traditional kind of man who'd be insulted if she offered to pay. She asked if she could leave the tip, to make the gesture, guessing it would be rebuffed. He did refuse, as she guessed, but didn't seem insulted.

They exited the restaurant to a spring day, the weather now fully temperate even as it was coming close to the crepuscular hour. All of Jerusalem's residents were relaxing into spring; even the religious male Jerusalemites they passed were wandering the streets clad only in long-sleeved white shirts, black jackets slung lightly over shoulders.

"Mmm, it's such a beautiful day," Wendy murmured.

"It is." Uri casually took her hand as they crossed the street. Wendy was a bit surprised; she hadn't expected it, but it was pleasant. She hadn't thought he would want to display affection for her after her breakdown about Shaul. And, it felt odd to Wendy to hold hands in public with a man wearing a kipah.

After two blocks, walking hand in hand, they came to Noga Frames, Noga Misgarot, the name written on the window in English and Hebrew. Uri knew this store often displayed art from students at the nearby Betzalel art school. There was a long bulletin board-type contraption outside the store, extending for perhaps twenty feet. It was covered with a sort of collage, of birds and clouds and stars, out of white paper, with a cerulean blue background. On its background decorations, it had photos and poems mounted along it at intervals. The effect of the collage seemed to Wendy to lend a new appearance to the stones on the building behind it. It made the stones seem stippled, with different shades of yellowish brown, like something natural, the colors of a school of fish swimming along in a stream, or of the water itself, undulating, the resonating patterns created by the light and its own movement. There was something alive about even the stones in this city; they too were participating in its activity, refusing to stand still, in the act of transforming themselves. The organic effect created by the variegated colors, like a fleet of horses running, fascinated Wendy.

Wendy's gaze lowered from the stones to the bulletin board, and she and Uri looked at the poems, in English and Hebrew. Some were original works by students. Some were translations of poems from other languages into Hebrew, translations from Spanish of Borges and from French of Mallarme. English was represented by Emily Dickinson.

They dropped hands and wandered to the various poems and photos as they looked at the collage separately. Wendy read out loud Dickinson's "The Brain—is wider than the—Sky."

The Brain—is wider than the Sky—
For—put them side by side—
The one the other will contain—
With ease—and You—beside—

"I studied that poem in university. I love American poets: Whitman, Plath, Auden, Robert Lowell, Wallace Stevens."

"Really? I wouldn't have expected that—poetry doesn't seem compatible with medical studies."

"No? Poetry is training for psychiatry. I'm trying to get to the essence of a person, to catch the most salient details. Then I put that distillation in front of the patient, to show them, this is the narrative you've created—if you're dissatisfied with it, let's find ways to edit and change it. Where are the places we can add a comma, change an image, extend a metaphor?"

She didn't know what to say next. "Uri, you sound like Atarah! I would never have thought of a connection between psychiatry and poetry."

"The brain is wider than the sky—my neuro-anatomy professor spent the introductory class parsing that poem to introduce us to the concept of how the brain is organized. Poetry can infuse the ordinary with such beauty. The way Dickinson uses language, she just gives words, ordinary things, a glimmer, a veneer of extraordinariness. Here we are in Jerusalem, with this poem."

"Jerusalem is wider than the sky," Wendy added. "It seems to encompass everything sometimes, casting its sheen over life, transforming it to something beautiful. Look at those stones. They seem like something organic, creating their own collage in accord with the collage underneath them."

"Like when you meet someone new, and feel things are changing in response to her presence, that poetry is everywhere when you're with her." He squeezed her hand firmly.

FOURTEEN
A New Chance

Yet even as the pilgrim thinks she knows where, and why, she's going, the beauty of every trip is that circumstances are far wiser than she is, and she seldom ends up where she expected to. Her unseen partner on the road is serendipity.

—PICO IYER, in *Traveling Souls: Contemporary Pilgrimage Stories*

"Orly, hi. Wendy," she said on the phone.

"What's up?" Wendy heard a banging noise on the other line as a pot was put down. "Now I can talk, got those noodles done."

"Oh," Wendy sighed, "Can I kvetch? I just cannot get myself to start writing this dissertation. I know I have to just begin, but every time it seems like I'm ready, I come up with a thousand excuses. And then I am tired."

"Get started. You know, what I learned about writing from journalism is that it doesn't have to be perfect. What it does have to be is *done*, on deadline. The editor can deal with it from there. If you don't finish, you won't get paid. I've missed deadlines, and lost the assignment and pay, even though I've handed the piece in. If they can't use it, it doesn't matter."

"I suppose I'm lucky then. I am still getting my stipend checks even though I haven't started writing."

"It won't last forever—won't they cut you off if you don't produce?"

"I guess. But I am just so scared that it won't be good enough. It is easier to not do it than to have to get it to the level I want it to be at. I know I'll need lots of drafts but I want it to just come out perfect, fully formed and ready to go."

Orly laughed. "Birth only happens that way in myth, Athena springing adult and fully clothed from Zeus's head. Live births are messy, bloody, painful, through the womb, with pushing. It's okay, though: all mothers say they forget the pain and discomfort once they see the baby. I'm sure it will be the same for you—once you're done and have a job, all this anxiety will be a distant memory . . ."

"I hope so. If I could just be sure it would be perfect . . ."

"Kiddo, write the damn thing. The worst that can happen is that you will have to redo sections. So what? You can handle it. Believe me, no one on your dissertation committee can possibly be as scary or weird as some of the editors I've had to deal with." Orly was in advice mode.

"I have to not be such a perfectionist, and just get that first draft out there," Wendy said, knowing it was way easier to say than to do.

"When something is finished, it looks obvious and easy; the layout and word choice and facts cited are significant, the organization totally clear. But you—and your advisors—know that you have to bust your butt to get it to seem that way. The ease is an apparition, if you will, the specter of clarity hanging over the chaos of tons of research." Wendy laughed and Orly added, "Do me a favor. Make an outline; have a sense of the narrative arc, what you want the piece to do. Then, put ass in chair. That's it."

"Amen, sister. Tell it!" Wendy concluded to Orly's invocation to productivity. "Praise the Lord, Hallelujah. Hey, speaking of praise the Lord, I'm excited to tell you. I met someone. Well, I hope I did."

"Mazal tov. Where'd you meet?"

"On Purim. I was wearing your grandmother's shawl."

"On the street?"

"At a Purim seudah. He's a psychiatry resident of Dr. Hideckel's."

"A Jewish doctor. Oy. I'm kvelling. The *nachas* for your parents . . . your own personal shrink."

"Love you too. He's part British, part Israeli, has this great accent . . ."

"I wish I could meet a nice doctor instead of a struggling musician." Orly began peppering Wendy with questions. "What does he look like, what happened, how did you know he was interested?"

Wendy sighed dreamily and lay back in her chair to luxuriate in the details of Uri, not even needing to embellish or exaggerate to arouse her friend's envy. "He has blue eyes, and brown sort of thick wiry hair, a good build, really nice teeth—they remind me of a horse's. Not in a bad way, just straight and neat and looking like there is good breeding behind them. He has these tender hands; he held my hand yesterday, on our first date. When we met, he was dressed as Hillary Clinton—a mask, women's clothes—and he asked me, as a gypsy, if I did palm readings."

"Clever line."

"I read his palm, and we talked. I told him I was at Princeton. He got my e-mail from the department website."

"Resourceful. So far, so good. I sense there's something you're not telling me," Orly's voice trailed off with a hint of suspicion.

"He grew up religious."

"Religious?" Orly intoned with a tinge of distaste in her voice as she might say "spoiled fish" or "bacteria," something awful that leaks and oozes. "What are you going to do?"

"He's not super religious now. He held my hand. The funny thing is, since he met me at the Hideckels and I was dressed like a gypsy, long sleeves, long skirt . . ."

"He assumed you were religious too."

"Yup."

"So I have to stop calling you on Shabbat? You're attracted to these religious guys. What's up with that?"

"I didn't know at first—we were both in costume. He was wearing a wig and I couldn't see his kipah. But, people who are born religious are different from my subjects. He doesn't spend every minute agonizing over what his rebbe would say. He's open-minded; he's willing to let himself have doubts."

"Do I get to meet him?"

"Eventually. I like him and he seems to like me, but I'm the first non-religious girl he's dated. I worry that he might decide he likes *me* but can't be involved because he wants someone more like himself."

"Maybe you'll become more like him. People who say that if you study religious people you want to become one can be right."

Wendy said in aggravation, "Stop! I'm so sick of everyone assuming that. Even my advisors warned me not to get sucked into the BT culture. Enough—not true."

"You're admitting you're attracted to it?"

"Not at all." Wendy was now at a decibel level just below a scream. "My dissertation is a career move. Why is it easier for people to assume that I want to be religious than that I want to have a career? It's so sexist—women can't be careerist, only religious. I can't believe Orly, the crusading journalist, is saying this. This topic made the most sense for my career. That's it; no more, no less."

"Have a career. I have one too. I have goals—get a piece into the *New Yorker* before I'm thirty. Write a book by thirty-five, have a really good job . . ."

"But if you found a nice Jewish doctor . . ."

"I'd marry him and keep working."

"So we're in agreement. I called to tell you about this guy. I didn't think you'd be so jealous—what's going on with Nir?"

"Oh, he's just depressed about his music career here and wants to move to London, and now I have this job writing features for the *Jerusalem Post* and I don't want to move because I'm doing research on my book about immigration and my family here. I don't want us to break up but I can't move to London now, so I might have to." Orly sighed heavily.

"I'm sorry," Wendy said. "Somehow, I doubt he'd be happy in London, with fewer *dossim* to mock."

"He's lived abroad; he'll be fine. But not all the band members want to; they're still debating."

"We're trading; I have a British import who likes the approach to psychiatry here, and you have an Israeli who wants to do better in the music business in London."

"That's life," Orly said laughing.

At the end of March, Wendy was ushered in to Avner Zakh's study at home by his wife. Seeing this spousal devotion, she felt a pang of jealousy for the life he led. She wished she had someone so devoted to her and her work to ensure there was quiet, and time to write, and meals on the table. Being single and doing all chores herself—paying her bills, doing her laundry, grocery shopping on her own—was getting tiring. She wanted support sometimes.

Zakh was sitting at his desk, typing on his computer. When she entered, he gave her a big smile and said, "Wendy! Just a moment while I save this file," and returned to his computer and made a few more keystrokes. Zakh had finally mastered the pronunciation of her name. She was unexpectedly pleased.

Though she had been to monthly meetings of the Fulbright fellows at his apartment, they were always in the living room. He had occasionally gone into his study to get a book, but she couldn't remember actually being in the room. It had floor to ceiling bookshelves, filled with books in English, Hebrew, Yiddish, and German. She could see some of the titles: *Tradition not Change: The History of Hungarian Jewry, After the Shoah: Ultra-Orthodoxy in Israel,* and *Dead Rebbes and Live Followers: The Success of the Bratslaver Dynasty.* There were stacks of journals on the floor and a filing cabinet. Large windows behind the desk faced the little park Kikar Magnes, Magnes Square. It was one of the quietest places in the city, like New York's Gramercy Park, a surprise of green and quiet one didn't expect in a bustling city populated with continual buses and frequent car alarms. Wendy's chair was a leather upholstered recliner. His long oak desk, probably twenty-five years old, was placed next to the newer computer desk. He could wheel his chair back and forth between the two, like toggling between the raw materials of scholarship on the desk, articles and books, and the means to transform them to a cooked piece of published work, a prepared dish redolent of details and ideas, all in their proper place, strongly flavored ingredients harmoniously melded into a piquant stew.

Wendy decided that if she had a tenured job at a university and a peaceful room like this filled with everything she needed to work, and someone to guard her from interruption, she would be happy.

Why had he set up this meeting? Wendy waited. He probably had to do some kind of yearly report on the progress of each student and needed to be sure he was meeting with her as he was supposed to. She was here, holding up her end of the deal with the Fulbright people. She was so privileged to have this fellowship, with time and freedom to research, no teaching responsibilities, but she wasn't where she wanted to be in the writing. She'd hoped to have the introduction finished by now, but was still completing the literature review. She had thought that by the time she left the country, she'd have half of it written, and outlines for the other chapters. That was unlikely now, at the end of March, when she was scheduled to leave mid-June.

"So," he said swiveling his chair from his computer screen at his side to the front of his desk, facing her. "How's your research going? I was really interested in the presentation you made to the group last week."

She looked at him and then bent down to tie her untied shoelaces. Holding her shoe and looking up from almost floor level, she said, "Do you want the good or the bad?"

"Tell you what," Zakh said, picking up a sheaf of papers. "I'll give you some news I believe you'll find good, and then you tell me about your progress."

Wendy, startled, had no more to say than, "Alright."

"I'm on the board of the Lady Touro Society. We provide opportunities for academics from abroad at all levels, graduate students, postdocs, and full professors, to spend time at Israeli universities and interact with their Israeli peers. It's a reciprocal exchange, valuable for both sides."

"Okay." Wendy, still confused, had no more meaningful reaction.

"Since the deaths of Sam Handelman and Benjamin Margolis, *Hashem yinakem damam,* applications for the position are down. We made offers to the top three applicants for the graduate fellowship. They all declined. The quality of the applicant pool dropped precipitously from there, so I have taken it upon myself to find some other applicants, who I will then go back to the board to present. Would you consider applying?"

Wendy crossed her legs, fixed her gaze on him, and said, "I hadn't thought about staying another year. I have a teaching fellowship at Princeton in fall. If I stayed, I don't know if I could do my teaching there the following fall, while I'm on the job market . . ."

"You could finish writing the dissertation here next year. Then, the year after next, work on turning your dissertation into a book. The questions you are posing are absolutely splendid. No one has asked them of the newly religious and it makes so much sense to take your approach."

"Thank you." Wendy laced her hands together and said, "I'm still not sure what to say, but tell me some more about this fellowship?"

"Of course." He relaxed his hands and handed the brochure on the fellowship over to her with a smile. "The society is generous—the stipend is quite a bit more than the Fulbright. You'd teach a course here at Hebrew University in the spring and attend monthly seminars where graduate fellows along with the postdocs and full and assistant professors present their work."

She glanced at him. "Sounds like a great opportunity, but . . . being away another year. I don't know how my parents would feel . . ." But then she thought of Uri. What was he doing next year? Even if he went back to England, Israel was closer than Princeton. They had barely started dating—should it be a factor? She added, "Can I see the application?"

Zakh handed her the application form and told her, "You need to fill this out, get a transcript from your university, three letters of recommendation, one of which will be from me, and submit an essay about your project."

She took the application and told him, "If I stayed here, I could check in with my subjects if I needed to—it might be easier to write."

"Apply. Give yourself the option of staying another year," Zakh told her smiling.

Wendy walked out of Zakh's building onto Kikar Magnes in a daze. How would it be to stay in Israel? She had been worrying about how being far from her research subjects could pose problems. What would she do if she needed more information from her subjects as she was writing everything up? What if she couldn't locate the person? Would she have to throw data and interviews out, hours of work gone because she was thousands of miles away from her fieldwork site?

The more pressing anxiety was harder to face. Though she had been denying and denying, Wendy hadn't gotten far enough in her writing. *Okay,* she thought, *to be honest with myself. I haven't started the writing. I'm finishing the literature review. It would be good for me to stay here to write, especially if I have fewer teaching responsibilities than I would in Princeton.*

Standing outside Zakh's building, she looked across the street at the patch of green in the center of a square, the protected enclave of Kikar Magnes, a park in a populous city. The difference between the elitism of New York's Gramercy Park, and the still socialist and populist inclined Jerusalem's Magnes Square was that there was no locked gate here to keep the green sward exclusively for eligible residents. The verdant expanse was available to anyone who knew it was there.

In Zakh's Rehavia neighborhood, elegant streets were named for grammarians of the Hebrew language. The language these grammarians articulated and defined with precision was entirely attuned with the exactitude of Rehavia's pristine buildings and well kept walkways. The scholars whose names were on these streets had figured out the mysteries of the entire spectrum of expression in three simple letters, the *shoresh*, the root, at the heart of the Hebrew word. They knew of the possibility of a continuum of meaning in a permutation of letters, a reconfiguration of vowels. Wendy loved the mysteriousness of the language, the complexity of meaning a mere vowel change could make. A different kind of elegance in the alphabet, she thought as she meandered up *vov*-shaped Alfasi Street. When Alfasi met Radak, becoming Ibn Ezra, she saw a pay phone next to the *makolet*, the all-purpose grocery store.

The *makolet*, neighborhood grocery, exemplified a uniquely Israeli business model. The proprietors knew the name and birthplace of every customer who came in; all comers had accounts. A six-year-old could go in, get what her mother or father needed, and leave without money changing hands. The bill would be settled later, accounts kept in a handwritten notebook. A *makolet* had pretty much anything one might need: newspapers, fresh pita, breads, milk in the Israeli *sackiot* (plastic bag containers), candy, yogurt, canned goods, coffee and tea, spices, frozen items. In the earlier times when few Israelis had cars, it was possible to shop exclusively at a *makolet*, supplemented by trips to an open air market or a fruit and vegetable store. There was a closeness in neighborhoods here, different from America where people needed to drive everywhere, which created a physical and emotional distance. A *makolet* was more fun to be in than an impersonal supermarket. Wendy liked that the proprietor could reach anything with a stick with a gripper handle that reached to the top shelf. It was such a contrast with the immense and impersonal American supermarket where no employee was ever able to determine the location of a specific item or if it might even be stocked.

A pay phone was stationed next to a jumble of mops, buckets, *smartutim*—Wendy had learned the word for rags—and cleaning supplies piled outside the *makolet* to help customers prepare for upcoming Passover cleaning. It was only a few steps from the bus stop. She could make a call and hang up to catch her bus when she spotted it arriving.

Who to call? She didn't want to call others in her Fulbright group, because she didn't know who Zakh had approached and who he had not. It could be awkward if she talked to someone who wanted to stay but hadn't been approached. Orly would just say something crude, like *you've gotten laid more here than in Princeton. Stay, and may your good fortune continue.*

Uri, she thought. *I'll call him; he'll have a level-headed attitude about this.*" She opened her bag and took out an *asimon,* a phone token, and looked up his number in her planner since she hadn't memorized it yet.

She dialed. She wasn't sure he'd be in, but figured it was worth a chance. Maybe he was on a night shift today and hadn't yet left his apartment? After a number of rings, when Wendy was just asking herself whether she could get her phone token back or not if she hung up since there had been so many rings, she heard, "Hullo?"

"Uri?"

"Speaking."

"Hi . . . ah . . . Wendy," she said rather tentatively.

"Wendy! I'm on my way out in a jiffy; I'm on call tonight," he added with his adorable accent.

"I want some advice."

"Brilliant. Go."

"I've just been talking with Avner Zakh, my faculty advisor here. He wants me to apply for a Lady Touro Society fellowship for next year but I don't know what to do."

He responded in his best doctor voice, "What do *you* want to do?"

"Apply. I'd be able to finish my dissertation, with access to my subjects and less teaching than in Princeton. But being away another year . . . I don't know. My parents and grandmother wouldn't be too happy."

"Sounds like something else bothering you."

"Even over the phone you're good, Uri. Zakh wants me to apply because the people who were awarded the fellowship turned it down."

"Okay, you have a chance at this because someone else doesn't want it. So what?"

"They're turning it down because of the *matzav.* Basically, Sam Handelman and Benjamin Margolis's deaths."

"You didn't plant the bomb that killed them. Why do you feel guilty?"

"It feels . . . false. Kind of . . . I'm . . . feeding on someone else's corpse. It's not fair that I benefit from the situation and from their deaths."

There was silence for a few moments. "You don't know yet whether you'll benefit. It doesn't hurt to apply."

"Yeah." Wendy didn't know how to bring up the next topic. But she needed to. "What are you doing next year? Do you stay here or go back to England?"

"I'm here till December. Then, I take my boards in England, finish up there. After that, unclear. I might try to stay here—depends . . ."

She blurted out, "That's motivation for making me want to stay."

"No." He paused. "I'm gla-ad"—his accent lengthened the vowel—"you want to stay, but we haven't known each other long."

Shit, I messed up. I'm pressuring him; guys hate that, she realized. Wendy backtracked, "No, no, I just meant . . . it will be nice to be in the same country you are. But . . . I'll apply because of my career, not my relationship. We don't know what will happen." She didn't want to say "us"; it would be too intimate at this point. She couldn't even put a label on what existed between them. This was it, the dreaded relationship talk. Each party thinking this amorphous thing, a relationship, should be configured differently. The endlessly labyrinthine conversation of, if we take one direction it is "this," another, it is "that"; one can never pin the thing down to the mutual satisfaction of both parties. This was not the time to morph the relationship into a recognizable mission statement like, "We're seeing each other," or "We're dating," or "We are lovers."

Wendy looked at the buckets and mops of the *makolet*. She tried to visualize what the scene in front of Uri was—they'd never been to each other's apartments.

"It would be great if you and I were in the same country a few months longer," he reassured her. "I just don't want to think you'd be doing this for me. Apply because it's right for your project."

"Right. Thanks for the advice."

"Hey, I'm almost a shrink. Good luck with the application. See you, *motzei Shabbes*, okay?" Her murmur of assent was followed with the clink of the phone announcing the finality of the discussion.

I guess I didn't screw it up too badly because he still wants to see me Saturday. Remember, no hint of pressure. I'm not even sure how much I like him.

I like him, she imagined herself telling Orly. *He's reassuring. From when I first met him, nervous about being at the Hideckels', he was a calming presence. He knows what questions to ask, to elicit the response the person needs. I love the soothing sound of his voice, knowing I'm communicating with him.*

That night, in her apartment on Rehov Mishael, Wendy decided to take a preliminary look at the Lady Touro application Zakh had given her. She had less than three weeks to complete it, so her usual procrastination mode needed to be temporarily placed on hold. She sat at the desk she'd purchased on Meah Shearim the first week she'd arrived, because someone in her *ulpan* had said that was the easiest place to buy cheap used furniture. The cab she had to take home with the desk strapped to the top cost her more than the desk itself. She laughed at the memory. She started her "beginning to write" ritual, putting a gorgeously patterned scarf around her neck so she'd feel dashing and sophisticated, an interesting person capable of writing work that people would want to read. She'd started with the scarves, ever changing in their colors and patterns, in college, after the professor of her anthropology seminar confessed to the class that she wore red cowboy boots while writing the book that got her tenure because they made her feel tough and empowered. Wendy decided then that she would similarly find a costume to help her get a jump on her writing, put her in the right frame of mind. She lay the application face up on the desk with a blank yellow legal pad next to it, and took out a bar of chocolate to nibble as she worked, rewarding herself for acting so contrary to her usual inclination to procrastinate. She wasn't a pathological procrastinator, waiting to do something until it was impossible to accomplish, but she didn't like to work on projects where there was a great deal at stake—like her whole career—until she was sure how to do them. If she stayed here or went back, it would make her life totally different. This application counted. But somehow, she wasn't anxious—maybe because the present task seemed so much less fraught than writing her dissertation.

This application was something she could do easily without making herself crazy about how much hinged on how good it was. She would figure out what had to be done, make a list, and do it. Make outlines, write the essays, show them to one or two friends for critique. Finish it. *I can do this*, she told herself, breathing out. *It isn't so complicated. I just hate being judged—what if the committee finds my project is stupid and a waste of time?* Her rational self knew her concern was irrelevant; she had the Fulbright, and a teaching fellowship to go back to at Princeton.

She didn't need this Lady Touro. That knowledge of its essential superfluousness to her life made the application easier to work on—maybe she needed to do that with her dissertation too. She could just tell herself, *This is a draft. My professors will read and critique it, and help me get it to where it should be. That is their job, to tell me what is missing, to help me find the right sources and precedents, and to make sure it passes muster on all levels. It doesn't have to be perfect from the start. I need to give myself permission to make mistakes, and accept that and just write the thing.*

She unwrapped the Swiss chocolate bar, put a small piece on her tongue, and made a note on the legal pad to e-mail Connie, the religion department secretary, for a transcript, and her advisers, Cliff Conrad and Mark Sokoloff, for recommendations. All the usual information was required: name, date and place of birth, educational history, curriculum vitae, two-page research proposal. She would revise the templates from her Fulbright application for this. No sweat. After these simple questions was a three-part essay, each response to be no more than 1500 words.

I. How do the particulars of this place shape your research?
II. Why must you do it here?
III. How do you feel about spending a year in the land of Israel?

Wendy wished she knew more about the role of these essays. *Is this an academic fellowship or a way of convincing people to live in Israel? Or of getting people who like being here to go back to the States and say how great it is? What if I want to say something critical? Like, I enjoy living here but don't understand why there is an entire people that feels itself so oppressed that individuals are willing to blow themselves up on buses? Or why, if this is a modern country and there is supposed to be universal service in the army, the ultra-Orthodox don't serve when they benefit from state services?*

She began her list by brainstorming:

I. Closer connection to lives of my subjects. Being in Israel, one lives a Jewish life, religious or not. I can continue to learn how holidays are celebrated, the rhythm of a week organized about the Sabbath rather than the weekend. Israel is more of a communal society than an individual one.

Able to keep in touch with subjects.

II. Sense of history. By virtue of being in Israel, each person here has come to reclaim something, make something that has not been in their life or their family's life once again part of what they are.

Importance of place—subjects feel a profound connection here—I seem to understand it more, the longer I am here. Yet I can still give critique of it as an outsider. (*I do worry what will happen as it all becomes more familiar to me. And Uri? What is his role?*)

III. Feeling of vitality in Jewish life—Judaism isn't confined to a synagogue for a few hours a week. It permeates all of life—there are Hebrew cows. The food, language, and rhythms of time are Jewish. It is such an expansive mode of being, not just using Yiddish words, or eating bagels, or laughing at Borsht Belt humor. Being here connects one to something larger in a way that can't happen in America. Jews from all over the world can all be on the same public bus, speaking Amharic, Yiddish, French, Spanish, German, English, infusing an ordinary activity with a biblical sense of ingathering of exiles.

Then she wrote out cons.

Con: *If I stayed another year, I'd still miss my cat. What if my advisors can't write good recommendations because I haven't been around enough? Will staying make me lose out on a career? If I delay going on the job market till the year I get back, what if all the good jobs are open next year and there aren't any the year after? What if no departments are interested in me because they think I've "gone native" by being here so long? What if I'm still not done after two years here????*

She began to write in her journal: *It would be great to be here longer. The place gives me something. I love to eat felafel, to smell the freshly baked challah scent coming from bakeries on Fridays and see people walking around with bouquets of flowers to bring to one another to greet the Sabbath. The quiet that pervades the neighborhood when I wake up Saturday morning to silence, no buses or cars. I love the simplicity of it, the peace I feel hearing birds singing, not car alarms blaring. Being a Jew is so ordinary here. I like the sounds of children racing as they wander freely in the streets and take public buses everywhere. I like the smell of pita. I like seeing names of biblical and historical figures marking the streets.*

But really I need to discuss why this is important to my project. Do I need to have these feelings and experiences in order to accomplish my goals? I need to gather some ideas about how being here will help me understand American Jews who become more religious.

I am studying people who have sought dramatic change in their lives. Having had to undergo and adjust to change this year, being an American Jew who is living in Israel, helps me understand why and how they undergo their changes. What are they gaining—closeness, community, ease of being normal as a religious Jew not some kind of oddity, sense of surety that they are doing God's will? What they may be giving up—careers, talents in the arts, graduate school, the ability to make a secure living?

Wendy put her pen down and looked up at the poster on the wall beside her desk. It was the poster announcing the lecture her advisor, Cliff Conrad, gave when he was promoted to Elias Brill Professor of Religion. There were two photos of him. One was with Oprah when she had him on TV to discuss his work with modern religion and its Puritan roots, the other of him at the head of a seminar table in 1879 Hall, teaching graduate students. Wendy admired Conrad, with his large audience, bringing scholarly ideas to a vast number of people in an interesting and relevant way. That was Wendy's goal in her scholarly work too.

Below Conrad was a picture of the late anthropologist and thinker Elias Brill. Brill had been a friend of Freud's in Vienna and fled to Princeton in the thirties, having already done the groundbreaking fieldwork in Eastern Mauritania that created his reputation. He'd had fierce disagreements with Franz Boas and Claude Levi-Strauss, but always asserted the primacy of the individual believer even within a tribal society. Brill had found that, though the tribal elders held to a certain system of belief, others in the society were less rigid in their ideology, even professing unbelief in private conversations with him, though continuing to publicly uphold tribal values. The dissonance between the formal picture of Brill in his study writing in longhand, surrounded by totemic artifacts and books, and Conrad on the set of the talk show couldn't be greater.

Now, she looked at the poster and saw transformation, the movement from Austrian Jew and rabbi's son to scholar of an African land, and then again to American éminence grise. Conrad, his heir, had undergone shifts too: son of Midwestern greengrocers, to scholar of New England Puritans, to public intellectual and individual who could communicate intelligent ideas broadly on television.

In the next generation, yet another shift. Brill's son Jonas had become a religious Jew and now taught psychology at a university in Israel. Wendy hadn't come across Brill *fils* yet, but had heard of him from people who asked if she'd met him when she said she was in the religion department at Princeton.

Smiling, Wendy tried to imagine what the images would be when it was her own picture on a poster. Would it reflect another transformation? Obviously, women in the academy, but what else? A new kind of scholarship, less theory-based than evidence-based, beginning with the research and being concerned with getting at how ideas generated and re-generated in the words of the subjects themselves.

What would you make of my work, old Brill? she asked as she scrutinized the face with the round wire-rimmed glasses of the century's early intellectuals. Brill had left his family and his village—the only one of his immediate family to survive World War II—for a culture halfway across the world. Did his work provide an antidote to the Nazism spreading over Europe and poisoning his beloved café society, showing that when individuals think for themselves they can't be swayed by an evil leader? Cliff Conrad too found himself in his work, reinterpreting the Puritans not as stuffy and awkward outcasts from the mainstream, but as forward-thinking individualists, proud to be able to express themselves freely in their new country.

And how, Wendy thought as she looked down again at her list, would she see herself in her subjects? Many of them, with their *"Baruch Hashems"* and *"der aybishters"* and *"bashertes,"* reviled her. Their certainty was so disturbing—didn't they ever speculate that they might have been better off had they stayed in the secular world? They could have been comfortable if they'd stayed in the US and gone to professional school like their parents wanted, instead of taking the uncertain career paths many encountered in Israel. The artistic types, who were struggling with modest ways to express their talents, told her, "God gave me these gifts, and He'll find a way for me to use them." *It would be great to have that certainty about anything in my life,* Wendy found herself saying out loud. *Can't I just study them, see who they are, and walk away?*

Shaul's face and last words to her popped unbidden into her mind, "You can't be certain until the day of your death," he had told her sadly. *I guess they aren't all certain; it is a pose for many of them,* she thought.

I owe it to his memory to finish this, to write something letting others out there know that certainty isn't so absolute; even when tremendous changes are made, there are numerous ways baalei teshuvah retain their old selves—keeping up skills they had in the outside world, putting on coveralls used in a job as a garage mechanic for Pesach cleaning, playing the violin for the children as they go to bed at night, singing their kids songs from musicals they'd performed in high school, and then being surprised listening at how offensive the lyrics are . . . but still singing them.

I guess coming here was a dramatic change for me as much as them. I was willing to expose myself to a different culture and way of life. I've seen how a place can influence people, how different it is to be in the orbit of a new language, the universe of alien sounds creating an entirely other experience. And away from my family, establishing a new life and relationships of my own, as confusing and terrifying as it is at times. Do I stay or go? Impossible to know till I write this essay.

She began in longhand in her journal, "My subjects have created numerous changes in their lives in order to live and study in this land, and forge their own ways of connecting to it, to put themselves into the lineage of those for whom living a holy life in the holy city was an ultimate goal. An anthropologist writes of the need not only to search out the past, but to plant oneself in it. I cannot understand the journey of my subjects without being in the places they are. I wish to conduct research here to aid me in seeing how the place has shaped their journeys . . ."

FIFTEEN
Rituals of Incorporation

In the third phase (reaggregation or reincorporation), the passage is consummated. The ritual subject, individual or corporate, is in a relatively stable state once more and, by virtue of this, has rights and obligations vis-à-vis others of a clearly defined and "structural type"; he is expected to behave in accordance with certain customary norms and ethical standards binding on incumbents of social position in a system of such positions.

—VICTOR TURNER, *The Ritual Process*

Wendy was in her apartment, trying to write, on a Saturday afternoon in April. She and Uri had a date scheduled for when he got off duty at the hospital later on, so she was trying to have a sense of accomplishment before their outing. Wendy needed to feel she had earned the right to have fun. She always felt she didn't deserve to relax unless she had earned it some way.

That morning, she had gone for a stroll, to stretch, clear her head, and enjoy the solitude of the empty streets. It was what she loved about Shabbat here, savoring the quiet of a city at rest by perambulating on boulevards laden with Sabbath hush, smelling fragrances of Sabbath foods from the windows of apartments with open windows, mixed with the aromatic pine smell of the trees in the city.

After nine months, it was still amazing to Wendy how aspects of daily existence could be re-engineered to accommodate a country's value system. There was something wonderfully comfortable about being in the majority culture. What would it be like when she had to undergo what her subjects termed "re-entry" to the US and its Christian ways? America would be even more of a foreign place were she to remain here another year.

She had her laptop turned on and was opening the introduction file. She had notes but still wasn't sure what the optimal template to organize this section might be. Open with historical material about American religion? No, maybe with psychological research on individuals transforming their religious practices and groups? Either of these decisions was a large one; it would make a huge difference to the whole. She did not feel ready to make a big decision now. What if she just finished reading the chapter from *Trends and Traditions in Religious Conversion* by James Zorro? That way she'd have a limited task and feel virtuous if she completed it, before meeting Uri.

Really, she wanted to put off the harder work of deciding how to begin the introduction, what date and details to install in a central position to her argument, what to jettison, and what to include merely in footnotes.

This dissertation was a piece of writing she'd be identified with for the first few years of her career. It was what hiring committees would read when considering whether they wanted her. With so much at stake, how could she possibly begin? It was too overwhelming: this gargantuan thing, the dissertation. She'd start one day this week, not today.

She read from the Zorro book: "It is necessary for the convert to reconstruct and redeploy his or her biographical sketch so as to accentuate the newly adopted system of values cutting across all planes of his or her life. Additionally, this redeployment and rearranging of a life highlights events that might previously have been thought minor, but are seen now in transition as the catalysts, bringing into focus a major and crucial life modification event. It is one of the most significant and life changing of the aforementioned rituals of incorporation . . ."

As she was underlining the passage, the phone rang. She heard Uri's voice: "I'm off. I'm walking out of the hospital towards the Old City. Can you still meet or are you deep in the middle of something?"

"I'm working but I'm also looking forward to seeing you. Where and when?"

"About fifty minutes? Jaffa Gate?"

"Sounds good."

Passage from Professor Zorro completely underlined, Wendy closed the book with relief. She left Mishael Street and walked down Emek Refaim in the direction of the Jaffa Gate. As she walked, she thought of Uri. She thought of the thrill she would feel when she caught sight of him from a distance. How she would watch as he drew closer, wanting so much just to give him a hug. As she crossed the Valley of Hinnom, she remembered a walking tour she'd done in this place at the beginning of the year with the Fulbright group. The guide told them its legends, that the Canaanites had slaughtered children and thrown them here, sacrifices to Molech, their god. *Could this too be one of "the dark places of the earth," as Joseph Conrad put it in* The Heart of Darkness? Wendy shuddered. Then she gazed over the vista asking, *Are my subjects also offering themselves to the shades of the dead and their way of life?*

Striding over this Valley of Hinnom, ground where there may be children's skeletons, Wendy debated internally, *Is my whole career predicated on dead bodies?* One theory about baalei teshuvah was that their souls originally belonged to children killed in the Holocaust, given another *gilgul*, reincarnation, in a new body. Wendy's current life was built now partly on the dead bodies of Sam and Benj, the violence of their deaths perhaps giving her an opportunity to remain in Israel another year. Most troubling was the death that Wendy held some degree of responsibility for: Shaul Engel's. And that without his death she would never have met Uri.

Her entire present life was built on the bodies of others, paralleling the ghostliness of this city, one layer built on top of another, the specters and shades of the earlier level of habitation still perceptible. What had been there before, the layer of civilization previous to the current one, remained. The neighborhoods of Talbieh, Bakaa, Katamon retained their pre-state Arab names. The Israeli government had created new Hebrew ones in their place, and none of the pre-1948 Arab inhabitants still dwelt there to use the Arabic ones, but the names endured, unchanged. She mused. How many Native American place names remain in the US? There had been many more Native Americans killed in the US than Arabs in Israel. No one thought about those excisions; native names for geographical places in America replaced with the biblical ones—Goshen, Salem, Zion, Canaan, Bethlehem. All over New England, Puritans bestowed their surroundings with names that originated here, with the Hebrew Bible; no one was criticizing them. She sighed, as she realized that, despite her earlier romanticizing of the city with names connected to its own history, even here in Jerusalem there was an elsewhere, a whole group of people yearning to return to homes they once inhabited. She had no solution: she knew both that Jews have a claim on the land, and that they had displaced others to create what exists now.

She had crossed the Valley of Hinnom, bodies and all, now, and was inside the Jaffa Gate. Walking through the German Colony and Yemin Moshe, she could hear only the hushed Sabbath—befitting tones of those strolling languorously. Yet, inside the Jaffa Gate was an ordinary day, Arabs and Christians carrying on regular activity. Police cars with blaring sirens pulled up to the station directly at the gate's entrance; tourists with backpacks spoke Danish and German, Swedish and Spanish. Arab shopkeepers verbally accosted all passersby within earshot with their claims to truly remarkable merchandise.

Wendy seated herself on a bench just inside the Jaffa Gate, by the side of the Tower of David Museum, with the Immanuel Church in view, to wait for Uri.

She took a plastic bottle of water out of the small purse slung over her shoulder and along her side. She hadn't brought money with her, but had her credit card, just in case, and her notepad and pen. As she swigged her water, Wendy looked across the plaza to observe a man in a black hat, white button-down shirt, and black pants approach a couple with backpacks. They gave him peculiar looks. She guessed it was because they didn't share a common language. The man smiled and backed away. The man spied another pair, two guys wearing rock concert T-shirts; she noted the listing of cities and dates on the back. The man spoke and they listened, nodded, listened more, and accepted a piece of paper from him.

Wendy knew the underside of this interaction. She saw the suited man gesture with his hands in a wide arc, a friendly, embracing-the-air motion. The man then asked the students—she knew the details from her interviewees—"if they've come to Jerusalem have they truly experienced all it has to offer? Don't they owe it to themselves to check out a Sabbath meal, have an authentic experience in the Old City? It's free, it's fun, lots of American guys just like you are there." Wendy saw the man gesture at what she now saw were Black Sabbath T-shirts, and guessed he would tell them of the performers he's heard, back in the day. Then he'd say, "You like music? After Shabbos, we'll have a concert; some of the students will be jamming, some faculty will join in; there is a guy who played guitar with Lynryd Skynryd; he usually comes. We used to have a former bassist for Eric Clapton but he's up north in Tzfas now." In response to their disbelieving faces, he'd say, "For real. Here, at the yeshiva. It's yours, free. Your Jewish heritage."

Wendy didn't need to hear the dialogue. She knew how the black-hatted man would meet any arguments, and what the outcome of this exchange would be. One-half to one-third of the time, the recruiter would succeed in getting the recruitees to go to a class or a Shabbat meal. In approximately ten percent of the cases, a student might stay up to a week. In one percent of the cases, students stay a month or longer. Those who remain after that and commit to the religious life—the topic of her dissertation.

She should be grateful to this man in the suit; without him and his ilk she'd have fewer subjects. She watched the transaction: the recruitees at first distant and skeptical, then moving closer to him, on the pavement and out of the street when a moped came zooming into the space they'd been in ten seconds before. Finally, they were standing quite close, the three of them almost in a huddle.

Wendy watched the proceedings with the same combination of fascination and disgust she would have watching a snake swallow a mouse. She felt the same horror one would feel seeing the small creature slowly become absorbed into the larger one, only the tail twitching in agony at the end, when the rest of the its body has been incorporated. While watching, one cannot take one's eyes off the process, at once both wanting to see how it's done, while totally feeling revulsion from the spectacle. Wendy wanted to yell out to the students, *You have free will; don't go; don't listen to him.* But *she* wasn't offering a free meal—what right did she have to intervene? On the other hand, she wanted to tell them that this man was getting paid for this. He was there to lure them into the world of the yeshiva. It was all a set-up and they should know that. The guys looked so naïve to Wendy, so guileless, though she assumed that as twenty- or twenty-one-year-old college students they felt themselves men of the world, sophisticated.

"Boo."

Wendy jumped up, startled out of her snake and mouse visions. When she saw that it was Uri, she looked visibly relieved.

"I couldn't resist," he said playfully, as he lowered himself to the bench to sit beside her. "What is so absorbing?"

She pointed to the tableau vivant, the boys chatting with the man in the black suit, now gesturing, pointing straight, left and right, directions to the yeshiva. "A hooker. Nice profession for a Jewish boy. On Shabbos yet? A real *shande*," Uri responded jokingly, using the Yiddish word for *scandal*. "What'll happen to those kids?" he added.

"An experience. Probably, they'll enjoy the evening, leave, and go back to their lives. One of them might stay longer, deciding he wants to be "open-minded" and give it a chance. He'll remember going to synagogue with his grandfather who's since passed away—maybe he'll recapture the experience by staying? Or, he wants to really antagonize his parents."

"Have you ever considered," he said in his clipped British tones, "that there could be more to it than easily classified motives? That perhaps, people do things because of passion, or feeling?"

"Too simplistic. Moved by the singing, maybe. They are wearing concert T-shirts, so that is probably important to them. They may like being part of a group, observing rituals together. Emotion plays a part, but I can still scrutinize and label their responses and reasons for their actions. There are always motives behind people's actions. If there weren't, you wouldn't have much of a profession."

"I try to help people understand the motives, the base notes if you will, for their emotions. I don't dismiss emotions like you."

"Who said anything about dismissal? I'm trying to see how and why individuals make choices, to see if we can understand how those individual choices fit into a larger societal context. I'm not belittling emotions. If you want to be critical of me, I'm not in the mood."

He patted her arm, "I'm not being critical, just trying to get you to see things with more . . . more nuance. Maybe those guys will go to the yeshiva, and being there, feel some kind of powerful emotional pull. It may be something they can't articulate fully."

"It's Shabbat. I am off dissertation duty. Let's walk."

"Let me switch hats," Uri said as he pulled a battered olive green canvas hat with a brim around it from his knapsack. He was wearing a blue striped oxford shirt, chinos, and leather walking shoes, a nicer version of hiking boots. He looked too tailored to be the Israeli version of tour guide, which usually consisted of white T-shirt, blue cotton work pants from a kibbutz store, and always the *neshek*, the gun. But, he had his own tour guide accoutrements. "Now I am tour guide," he said with a mock Israeli accent, after donning the *kova tembol* hat. "Come *zees* way," he added, reaching out for her hand.

Uri walked holding Wendy's hand for about twenty-five feet till they were standing at the entrance to the Citadel of David. "We are on the poet's tour of the Old City. We will be reading from my favorite poet of Jerusalem, next to King David the psalmist," he said with mock piety. Uri reached into his knapsack and pulled out a black and white paperback titled, *Poems of Jerusalem.*

"So," he said in proper tour guide form, "you know *zees*?" pointing at the Citadel.

"Fifteen different layers of civilization, one on top of another, all in their way contributing to the city." In a more excited tone she added, "It's kind of amazing to imagine all the people who have been here, things they have thought, dreamt, imagined, yearned for, craved . . ." she said staring at the stones, seeing the differences in the layers as she looked at the striations.

"Let me read you Yehuda Amichai." He opened the book:

Once I sat on the steps by a gate at David's Tower. I placed my two heavy baskets at my side. A group of tourists was standing around their guide and I became their target marker. "You see that man with the baskets? Just right of his head there's an arch from the Roman period. Just right of his head." "But he's moving, he's moving!" I said to myself: redemption will come only if their guide tells them, "You see that arch from the Roman period? It's not important: but next to it, left and down a bit, there sits a man who's bought fruit and vegetables for his family."

"Uri, this text really gets at what annoys me about these recruiters for the yeshivas. They care about students as bodies to recruit, not individuals. Amichai's approach seems more . . . humanistic?"

Uri shut the book and said, "Caring about people, in all their complexities. Both of us feel that. I wasn't trying to be critical of your work before. I was trying to get you to be honest about the range of human motivation."

"Apology accepted. What is that poem called?"

"Tourists."

He put his accent back on, "Okay *Uri's tours*. Next stop the Cardo." In his own voice he continued, "Ghosts, remain here at the Citadel of David to await the redemption, when fruit and vegetable eating Jews become more important than Roman arches. We move on."

They walked hand in hand through the narrow alleys, the sun shining on dappled and textured Jerusalem stones that were put in place less than twenty-five years ago but had the look of eternity, as though they had always been there. Wendy was reminded of Princeton, with its Oxford-imitating, artificially aged stones and leaded glass, to give century-old buildings an injection of medieval permanence.

As they walked, Uri pointed out rectangular white ceramic tiles embedded in the stone and inscribed in Hebrew, Arabic, and English. "See this? We've transitioned from the Armenian Quarter to the Jewish one. We are no longer on Saint James Street, named for a guy whose head is supposedly in the cathedral here named for him but whose body is in Spain. Now, we are at Or Ha-Hayim Street, the light of life. The Christian problematic of head severed from body, which we are still feeling the effects of in Western culture, has been converted back to a Jewish one."

They were coming to a spot with massive pillars, beginning below street level and extending up. Wendy said, "I know this is the remnants of a Roman main street but is it something else too?"

They descended some steps and Uri led her to a stone bench facing the Cardo. He gestured for her to sit. It was oddly quiet at this late afternoon Sabbath hour, as though all the residents were deep in the temporary hibernation of their Sabbath naps, their lairs the apartments here, which all had iron bars over their windows, fortress-like. The Jewish quarter seemed medieval now as much as ancient: stones, iron, fortresses.

With confidence, Uri opened his poetry book to a page marked with a yellow Post-it note. "Cardo is the Latin for pivot, the pivot around which the city turns. Here is a poem of Amichai's that reminds me of this spot." He declaimed:

> Jerusalem is full of used Jews, worn out by history,
> Jews second-hand, slightly damaged, at bargain prices.
> And the eye yearns toward Zion all the time. And all the eyes

Of the living and the dead are cracked like eggs
On the rim of the bowl, to make the city
Puff up rich and fat.

"Here we have the city, puffed up, this incredible street still standing after two thousand years, yet for a long time the Jews themselves were expendable. This was only built after Rome took over and expelled the Jews in the year 70, Common Era. Look over there," he said, pointing behind them, "See that huge arch?"

"The big stone rainbow? What is it?"

"The remains of the Hurva Synagogue. The Jordanians blew it up in '48, to rid themselves of traces of the used Jews, worn out by history. The title of the poem, by the way, is 'Jerusalem Is Full of Used Jews.'"

"Why hasn't the synagogue been rebuilt?"

"Good question. We'll discuss on-site." As they walked he explained various opinions on the ruins of the synagogue. "Some wanted to restore it to the way it was originally, some to build something new. The American Jewish architect Louis Kahn was commissioned for the design. A third group wanted it to remain as is, a reminder that, though the city is rebuilt around it, the world remains less than whole."

Wendy interrupted, "How much did you prepare for this tour guide role? Maybe you should start a new therapy, taking patients around and talking to them about how their emotions and problems can find an objective correlative in the objects around them. A depressed person comes here to a ruin, a person more in need of rejuvenation, to a rebuilt part of the city. Therapy on tour."

"Too New Age. Back to the rainbow," he added as they were now standing underneath the large stone arch.

"I'm listening," she said and yawned, like a bored student.

"Come on, this is interesting," he said eagerly. "I don't know how professional guides keep whole groups entertained. I'm boring you and you're just one person."

"No, no," she lied emphatically. "The significance of the rainbow, continue."

He got up on a stone ledge of the destroyed synagogue and leaned against the arch. "In *Bereishit*—sorry *Ge-ne-sis*"—he exaggerated his pronunciation of the English name to be sure she understood—"God makes a promise to

Noach that there will never be another flood, that water won't be used as a weapon. As a physical manifestation of that pact, God put this disabled bow in the sky. In Hebrew, 'bow,' as in 'bow and arrow,' and 'rainbow' are the same word, '*keshet*.' Some commentators say the rainbow is a symbol of the divine willingness to disarm. In a non-aggression pact between God and humanity, God tips the bow upside down."

"That sounds like something Atarah would say."

"I'll assume that's a compliment." Wendy nodded when he looked at her. "Now, Amichai's poem on "Jerusalem 1967." "Jerusalem stone is the only stone that can feel pain. It has a network of nerves."

"Imagine the pain felt at this site, stones being blown up," said Wendy.

"But here we are trying to find beauty, despite pain."

"Are we?"

"You don't find this beautiful, the starkness of the stone against the softness of the white clouds and the azure sky? The understanding that this place is enough, as is. It doesn't have to be taken back to the past or brought into the future, but just be enjoyed."

"There is a kind of resignation: we don't have to change this place, but will leave it as it is," she commented.

"Right. In any situation, coming to a mature acceptance is vital."

"Resignation is difficult. I always want to analyze, understand, fix, change. I can't just let anything be," Wendy told him.

"Sometimes it is healthy to let go, consign yourself to emotions. They have their own power—I see it every day with patients."

"Sometimes I might like to let things be. I can't though."

"Why?"

"I don't know. Maybe you can help me change?" she said, surprising herself by how girlish she sounded, surrendering, interrogative, her voice lifting and lilting, as she spoke.

"Do *you* want to?

"I think so."

He leaned towards her and kissed her softly on the lips, gently and carefully. When he pulled back to look at her, he said, "To emotions."

She leaned forward and whispered, "To emotions," as she kissed him back.

"You're an effective tour guide, Uri. I never expected this."

"Which?"

"Feeling so . . . connected. To you, to the city. Everything is becoming more linked for me. A network of nerves underneath the stone. That's what I need to feel, in my life and my dissertation. It's tough—I prefer being analytical observer to emotional and vulnerable participant. I want my dissertation to be like that—precise, rigorous, carefully etched, solid, but with reticulations of nerves and emotions running through, to keep it from being completely hard. I have such a high standard of what I want it to be. It won't be as perfect as I dream."

He leaped off the ledge to stand next to her. "Keep trying! Next stop? Uri's Tours this way," and beckoned with his hand.

They walked through the Old City, down steps, through the checkpoint, and arrived at the final stop, Robinson's Arch. Uri declaimed in good tour guide fashion, "We began this tour with an attempt to shift our perceptions, to notice the people feeding their families, engaged in nurturing matters, rather than Roman arches. We proceeded to a Roman shopping arena where we saw the dangers of overlooking the people to focus on architecture. Then we went to the ruins of a synagogue built first in 1700, rebuilt in 1856, and destroyed in 1948 and being left as it is, a demilitarized bow in the midst of the city."

He waved his arms and continued, "Now, tour group, we are at Robinson's Arch, the first interchange in history. An interchange is for alternate streams of traffic to each go where they need to, without intersecting. It was part of the Temple Mount, and this wall here is the continuation of the more famous Western Wall."

"I don't get it. Why isn't this a place of reverence rather than an archaeological park?"

"Question of questions. Why indeed? Let's see what Amichai has to say." He removed his Amichai book from his bag and opened to a page marked with a Post-It note.

Jerusalem is a port city on the shore of eternity . . .
Yom Kippur sailors in white uniforms
Climb among ladders and ropes of well-tested prayers.

And the commerce and the gates and the golden domes:
Jerusalem is the Venice of God.

He looked at Wendy expectantly. She looked back at him. "Still don't get it."

"The ways that Jews, Yom Kippur sailors, can travel is through 'well-tested prayers.' We need to tread well-worn ground to reach eternity. It can't be on newness but on entrenched places and ideas that we communicate with the divine. We use an established system, but it's harder because each individual still needs to journey, to make it his or her own."

"Just explain the poem," Wendy said, crossing her arms in frustration.

"We pray at the Western Wall because it is where we have always prayed . . . It is the accessible part of the wall. It isn't intrinsically more holy than these walls, or the tunnels underneath the *Kotel*. Jews over the years have prayed at the *Kotel* so it has been endowed with holiness."

"Human agency is enough to invest a place with holiness. So if you and I decide that the Hurva Synagogue is holy because we kissed there, it will be holy now?"

"If we can convince others. It's a dynamic process. Different aspects of the religion become important at different times, in response to different needs."

Wendy stood on her tiptoes and reached to implant a kiss on his lips. And another. She couldn't imagine anything more romantic than sitting here among the ruins of all the vast layers, imagining the criss-crossing of the pilgrims going to the Temple on pilgrimage, the emotions they would have had communicating with the divinity.

"I'm glad you took me on Uri's tour. It showed me the unexpected, the subterranean poetry, lurking at every turn. Thanks."

He kissed her back. "I'm glad you liked it. I've never done it before; it's something I've imagined, but it was actually quite spontaneous. I picked out some of the passages I liked, but hadn't figured out exactly where and how to read them. You inspired me." He smiled at her.

"Next stop?" she said.

He glanced at his watch. "When Shabbos is over, we can take a bus into town and get a bite to eat. I have my bus pass for when the buses start running."

Wendy said, "I wish I had my camera."

"Oh."

"To remember this." She waved her arms about. "To let someone else see what I do. I wish I could be a photographer and force people to look at the world with my perceptions. It's a bit of a violent desire actually—Here, you must see it like this. I will make you have the same sense of perspective and focus, and you must know what belongs at the periphery and what at the center—I've never told anyone this before."

"Why?"

"I've never met someone I thought would be interested," she said, and smiled at him.

They gazed around at the stones, pieces of friezes, columns, moss peering up from between the stones, even flower buds poking upward from the ground at this beginning of spring. "Do you want to sit for a minute?" Uri asked. They moved to find a spot where the flat stone was big enough for them both to sit side by side.

"Wendy," he took her hand and looked into her eyes, "I'm glad you're applying to stay. But don't do it for me. I'm in flux; I don't know where I'm going religiously and I want to figure it out on my own. It wouldn't be fair to involve you."

"You did all this to break up with me?" Wendy said defensively.

"No, " he said, patting her hand, "I just don't want you to get too invested in it."

"I don't know where I'm going religiously either. I like Shabbat; it's comforting, peaceful. I like holidays too. Things are so much richer when they are part of the texture of a whole country, not a few minority people, valiantly upholding odd customs. I'm not sure how or if I'd incorporate any of what I see here into my life on my return. The longer I stay here, the more of it may seep into me, oozing languidly into the rhythms of my life, so I want to continue. What I like most about Shabbat here is it doesn't feel . . . forced."

"We're all Jews by choice," Uri said.

"Huh?"

"We choose what to observe and think. It is a choice to believe in the power of *halacha* to coerce you."

"Oh."

"We're choosing each other now." He reached toward her, to embrace her and kiss her on the lips, in the midst of the ruins of the past.

SIXTEEN
Confronting the Question: The Seder

The play of the afikomen on the Seder night is a way of acting out the
question of the presence or absence of God in history, and the disposition
to confront oneself with that question which is so essential.
—MARC OUAKNIN, *Haggadah*

On the night of the seder, Wendy was staring at the painting across from her.
She was inside the dining room of friends of Uri's parents, Judy and Charles
Spicehandler, two weeks after Uri's tour. A large canvas, its dimensions
shaped by the mystical number seven, as it measured seven feet by seven
feet, to create a flowing energy field. At its center was a depiction of Sigmund
Freud; in the background, objects were in a circle, at various angles, like
meteors streaking the painting. The other floating items included his couch,
his pipe, some of the totemic statues he surrounded himself with, a pile of
his books on fire as the Germans burned them in Vienna, and a pair of his
glasses. Oddly, there were also pieces of matzah and parsley and a Haggadah, which had a bloodied flayed rabbit with tawny feet and the Hebrew
letters *yod-kuf-nun-heh-zayin* on its open pages. Freud's books ringed the
edges of the images, randomly flying as well, next to a wooden spool with a
string attached to it. The artist, Oren Laniado, titled it *(In)Query*. Wendy
couldn't take her eyes off the artwork. She was seated across from it, and its

yellows, greens, reds, and blues seared into her mind and pulled her deeper into the inquiry. There was something of the painter Chagall, yet the colors were different, pared down, reduced to the essentials, all primary colors and their close cohorts.

There were manifold objects in this Yemin Moshe home to attract Wendy's eyes. She noticed the vaulted ceilings and the brickwork above the curved windows. It was dark, but the view across to the walls of the Old City and the Citadel of David was spectacular, modern electric lights caressing the ancient stones. Each room was filled with museum quality art and elaborate Judaica—menorahs grouped tastefully together on the wall here, *tzedaka* boxes on a shelf there.

On the dining room table, the bouquet in the center was large, though not enormous enough to be called ostentatious. It contained white lilies, with their luxuriant aroma, tastefully arranged, but not too high so the guests could see and talk over them. The china had gold trim and the silver was monogrammed *S* for Spicehandler. The white damask napkins were carefully laid and pressed. Wendy hadn't ever been to such an elegantly arrayed table in a private home. The table itself was a length of glass, modern and at the same time elegant, with tall steel-backed chairs in a matching modern style, the fabric on the seats coordinating perfectly with the Oriental rug underneath. She could imagine the scene photographed for a lifestyle magazine, *Yemin Moshe Living*.

It made her nervous that Uri's parents had such sophisticated friends—what were the parents themselves like? Would their hostess, Judy, be on the phone to Uri's mother—who had been her best friend growing up in London—when the holiday ended, to tell her what Wendy was like? Wendy hadn't thought about that when she accepted the invitation. She saw a new side to Uri, at ease with the whole elegant scene, from the Laniado Freud painting across the wall to a painting by Sigmund's actual great-grandson, the painter Lucian Freud. There was a painting in the sunken living room by an artist whose work she knew she had seen at the Israel Museum. Alex Katz? R. B. Kitaj? Moshe Gershuni? A modern Jewish or Israeli artist—she knew that much if the name itself escaped her.

Wendy would have to find an excuse to get up, go to the bathroom, and poke around, exploring the magnificent nooks and crannies of the home. When she had walked around this neighborhood earlier in the year, first with Orly after the lecture at Mishkenot Sha'ananim, and later by herself, she never imagined that she would one day be inside one of these homes.

Charles Spicehandler, the investment banker patriarch, was beginning the seder by intoning the *Kiddush*. He was an investor for hedge funds and was able to live anywhere. After many years on the Upper East Side of New York, he and Judy had moved to Israel. Charles began to recite the familiar words and tune of the Kiddush prayer. Even at this distance from Grandmom Essie's New York row house, the sound of the prayer made Wendy nostalgic. She should have gone back to the States for the holiday like many in her Fulbright group. It made her sad not to be with her family on Passover, squeezed into the narrow dining room with thirty relatives, eating Grandma Essie's famous brisket and her sponge cake with sunken cheeks that was always served with strawberries on top. Her cousins were constantly joking around, kicking her under the table, changing the "He" for God to "She" with her for English readings. Family seders for the Goldbergs were chaotic affairs, older children "encouraging" or forcing—depending on your perspective—the younger ones to really sniff the horseradish since it was "so good, try some" and visiting dogs consuming the afikomen, or trotting in on key when it was time for the cup of Elijah. This was the first time her niece Margo, Lisa's daughter, would be asking the four questions. But, Wendy had wanted to finish interviews and writing here, in case she wouldn't be staying in Israel next year. And, she was excited about the trip she and Orly had planned to Eilat in a few days. Going to the beach with her favorite girlfriend or home to New York? Not much of a choice. Still, this was the first Passover she had spent away from her family. She had never seen a Haggadah without the Maxwell House imprint; at this seder each person had a different book.

The Spicehandlers' Filipino maid brought a pitcher of water, a cup, and a towel first to Judy and Charles, and then around the table to the other guests. Charles took a piece of parsley from the seder plate in front of him. The seder plate was a Lucite container that stood upright, with Hebrew words on it in sterling silver letters in a modern typeface. On the side of the box for the matzoh were three glass dishes, tiered, one slightly farther out than the next and held up by silver wiring. The Hebrew on the container read, "*Ha Lachma Anya*"—"This is the bread of affliction," Uri translated for her in a whisper and added that the seder plate had been designed by Ludwig Wolpert, a craftsman known for his infusion of modern design into Judaic objects. Wendy remembered the gallery in the Israel Museum that was filled with items intended, with their beauty, to amplify the sacredness of the rituals performed with them. Charles passed around the dish with the parsley, and the assembled guests dipped parsley in salt water and pronounced the blessing over the fruit of the earth. The maid returned with an assemblage of vegetables, plated for each person, the *karpas* course. Uri had warned Wendy that the seder would be long; eating early in the proceedings was a pleasant surprise. All baby vegetables for spring, Judy was explaining. Each plate displayed lightly steamed beets, carrots, parsnips, and frisée lettuce, exquisitely formed; a tasty vinaigrette was drizzled carefully on top. Wendy had never seen this produce in these shapes, so delicate, plattered with an attractive doily underneath, a print of a Persian rug, dark maroon with white and green designs woven in. She nervously grasped the salad fork, looking at which one the others were using, praying she had gotten the utensil right, and then whispering to Uri that the beets were delicious. She heard a clatter as another guest must have dropped the utensil first, and saw a second maid bring a new one to the Spicehandlers' older neighbor. The maid also wielded a bottle of wine, and circulated, refilling the cups of all the guests.

As they began to eat the *karpas*, Judy told the assembled, "*Karpas* is also mentioned in the book of Esther, as a tapestry. I found these doilies reminiscent of tapesty for our course, since *karpas*, as a symbol, invites us to pass between the holidays, between Purim and Pesach."

Oren Laniado, the artist, commented, "The two are so different though, Judy. Purim is . . . carnival, free, and Pesach, bound to tradition, stiff. Why the connection?"

Charles said, "To encourage us to incorporate a more free-form modality, a kind of play, into the seder. A seder has been compared to a tea ceremony, each aspect and moment designed to provoke an understanding, an emotion, with precision. But within that rigidity we need to remember the uncertainty of Purim; we can't get too comfortable in our roles. We have to glide between certainty and uncertainty."

"Are you going to throw nuts on the table now, Saba? You just said the seder was for play," a four-year-old grandson burst out while his mother shushed him. The fond grandfather gave a smile and reached into his pocket for a handful of walnuts with their shells on that he rolled down the elegant table, towards the children. The clatter of the rolling nuts was startling in the stillness of the room.

Wendy was surprised to see his goofy grin while tossing the nuts and to hear him speak of gliding between roles. She didn't expect someone so affluent and well situated to be thoughtful or profound. As they ate the salad, Judy asked the guests to introduce themselves to the group. The Spicehandlers' adult daughter, Emanuella, was first. Wendy, eating and half listening, decided "Emanuella" was a plutocratic name, the heft of its many syllables able to be hoisted only by an incredibly wealthy person, a Hebrew equivalent of lavish Victorian names like Lavinia or Cordelia. Emanuella's Israeli husband, Oded, and their three young children were next, and then the artist Laniado and his actor partner, Yehuda Dahan. Wendy and Uri were seated by a young American man who worked in Charles's office, and a post-high school girl in Israel for the year from New York, whose parents had been Upper East Side friends of Judy and Charles, before they made *aliyah*. The company was rounded out by an older couple who lived in Yemin Moshe a few houses away. A recent knee surgery had prevented the husband from flying. They had planned to spend Pesach with one of their grown children on sabbatical abroad for the year, and their other children were vacationing with their sibling, so they came to the Spicehandlers'. Prompted by Judy, each person had to bring up a question they wanted to ask at the seder.

Wendy, who questioned people for a living, felt flustered. When it came her turn, she said, "How does one achieve a state of certainty? You mentioned Passover as a holiday when we have more certainty than on Purim. How is it achieved?" The actor, Yehuda, asked whether there are any questions too dangerous, threatening, or disruptive to ask. Uri asked whether questions such as are asked on Pesach can heal. The six-year-old grandson wanted to know if he'd get a prize for a good question, which all the guests laughed at and affirmed; he looked around, surprised at so much attention to what he saw as the only obvious thing to ask.

Charles uncovered the three matzot on the table. He asked his grandchildren what he was about to do and all three screamed, "Hide the afikomen; hide the afikomen." He smiled and broke the middle matzah with a resounding crack. He waved the grandchildren into the kitchen and told them to help Graciela the maid while he hid the matzah.

Judy, taking over Charles's role as leader while he was busy finding a good hiding spot, said, nodding to Oren, "Afikomen always reminds me of the negative space in a painting; you see as much from what is there as what is not."

"Does hiddenness also enclose a form of presence?" the artist responded.

His partner concurred, "When we stage something, we have a view to maximize the negative space between the actors."

Uri said, "I was reading a Haggadah by a French rabbi, Ouaknin. He sees the play of the afikomen on the seder night as way of acting out the question of the presence or absence of God in history. Confrontation with this question is an essential task of the Jew."

Judy's daughter Emanuella, said, "I like that. The childishness of hiding the afikomen reminds us of our own childishness in sometimes thinking of God as absent in history. But God will always let himself be found."

"*Eef* we look," her Israeli husband, Oded, said. "We must to look."

Wendy wanted to add to the conversation but she wasn't sure how. She was impressed with Uri for this insight. "What would Freud say?" she said, just to say something, inane though it might be.

This was an opening for Oren to talk about his work, *(In)Query*. "You know, it is such a privilege, Judy to be here, having a seder with my painting. I think the spool and thread"—he pointed and all looked at the canvas—"zat is zee grandson's game, *fort-da*, the coming and going, like the Jews and our afikoman, and the . . . life cycle. This is the first Pesach my mother has been dead, and I thought what will I do, what will the holiday be? It would be too painful to go to my aunt, or my brother, without my mother. When you invited us I was so pleased. To be with my Freud again . . . I think, em Vendy?" and at her nod, said, "Freud would say, with your friend, confront the question; truth can only be got at if the question is, em, confronting. How did he do *hees* analysis? He asked the questions. That is the power of the seder, our willing to continue to ask. I hope I convey the fragmentary state we are all in as we make the queries, it *ees* . . . em . . . destabilizing? yes, but we must to begin somewhere. And that is the genius of Freud; he vas villing to ask."

Uri squeezed Wendy's hand and said, "Wendy's dissertation is all about asking. She is questioning baalei teshuvah about the process of their return. Questions hint at a lack, and she tries to find where that is. People don't always like her questions."

"Fascinating. Tell us about it," said Judy, her best hostess gaze on Wendy.

Wendy wanted to shoot a look at Uri that would tell him, *Why did you do this to me?* But she was proud that he cared enough about her work to bring it up in this gathering. "I am looking for faultlines in the new identities that people take on. I want to see how, even though on the outside they may appear to be totally observant Orthodox Jews, fissures exist in their belief systems. The various facets of their personality may not be completely integrated."

Oded, the religious Israeli, looked at her suspiciously. "You don't like baalei teshuvah? It *ees* forbidden to remind a baal teshuvah of his life before his return. You don't want to throw his sins in his face. It can cause his death." Wendy looked at him, surprised. "The story of Rav Yohanan and Reish Lakish, you know it?" he continued.

Wendy nodded. He continued, "Em, Rav Yohanan met this *poshea*, how you say?"

Judy translated, "Sinner."

"Ok, yes, seen-er, and he convince him, do teshuvah. One day, in the *beit midrash*, they talk weapons and Rav Yohanan say to his study partner, 'A thief knows his tools. You know when the weapons are done.' Reish Lakish, now a rabbi, say, "What good have you done me? There with thieves I was called master and here with rabbis I am called master." Rav Yohanan became ill, and Reish Lakish also fall ill, *em*"—when he hesitated, his wife, Emanuella, interjected, "Fatally."

Oded continued, "So, yes, the sister of Rav Yohanan, Reish Lakish's wife, ask him to pray, to think of her the widow, the children, the orphans; he don't listen. Reish Lakish dies and Rav Yohanan goes bee-serk, until the rabbis pray for him, for his death."

"How tragic. What an awful story," one of the guests added.

"Zees are the consequences of reminding the repentant one of his former life."

"I'm not trying to create tragedy," Wendy said in her defense. "I just want to see how people tell their stories, how the narrative unfolds."

Ernst, the older neighbor with the bad knee, said, "At the seder itself, we are narrating the collective unconscious of *am Yisrael*, how we tell our tale. Do we begin with *shevach* or *gnai*?" Uri translated in a whisper for Wendy, noticed by Judy alone, "Praise or degradation," as Ernst continued, "What is the way we wish to see our past? So, young lady, how do individuals tell their tales?"

"It depends," Wendy responded. "Some do begin with degradation, drugs or alcohol, and move to ecstatic religion. And some begin with this desire to do more, draw closer, be more religious. Tales are told both ways."

Charles returned to the table, his sequestering of the afikomen complete, rubbing his hands. "Call those kids back and let's continue. This is the bread of affliction . . ." he read.

A moment later, Netanel, at six, the oldest grandson, returned. With a broad gap-tooth smile where his top middle teeth were missing, he said, "Saba, can I ask yet?"

His grandpa smiled indulgently and turned back to the group. "And now, the *Mah Nishtanah*. I bring you," he said, waving his arms in the manner of a stage impressario, "Netanel Maoz."

After a perfect rendition and many ohs, ahs, and claps, a prize was produced, an illustrated Mishnah Pesachim, laws of Passover. Netanel, looking as though he would never be more pleased with himself than at this moment, went to sit next to his mother. His youngest sibling, not to be outdone, climbed into her mother's lap and started tugging at Emanuella's necklace and then earrings, to her annoyance. Judy shot her daughter a look, as if to say, remove the child, but the daughter ignored her mother and let the almost-three-year-old keep yanking at her.

Charles held up a Haggadah for those assembled to see. "This is a visual depiction of the need to ask."

The Yemin Moshe neighbor, Janine, said, "I can't tell what that is," screwing up her face in confusion.

As the book passed to each participant in turn, Wendy could see that the page contained four lines of text, the four questions. Each line contained a paper, cut with a word describing that question and a depiction of the side of a face in silhouette. A child's profile faced a father's, a wife faced a husband, a person alone faced himself, and two scholars faced each other. Though the book tottered gently over the wine glasses as it was being passed, a few quick saves ensured no spills, until the three-year-old almost upended one and was taken by her mother to another room.

Uri asked, "Charles, why do you think the questioning is so central to the enacting of the seder that someone must ask himself? How does one even ask oneself? It seems so ahhdd," which Wendy realized after a minute was a British way of saying "odd." Wendy was glad Uri asked this since it was on her mind also.

Charles replied, "The silhouettes are based on a passage from the Talmud in *Pesachim*, which makes clear questioning isn't just for kids—scholars need to ask each other too. It is a technique, a prompt if you will, to move the seder, propel it forward. Unless there is a question, the story can't be told." Charles nodded to the maid holding a bottle of wine behind him to refill his cup, and gestured with his chin towards the table's other empties that needed similar attention.

"If I may," Yehuda Dahan interjected, "the question pushes one to tell the story properly, even to oneself. If there are no questions, the story won't change. Indian philosophy has a concept of *satyagraha*, truth attachment. Those who are truth embodiers create small changes in society. If we want a true society, we must all be truth pursuers."

Tanya, the post-high school student from New York, said, "But can't we do that within *halachic* concepts? We don't need *Indian philosophy*," she said, screwing up her face as she spoke the words.

Wendy hadn't spoken to Tanya yet, but had a feeling she could peg her. She was from the Upper East Side; Wendy guessed that she attended the Zemer School, a hybrid of East Side prep school and Modern Orthodox co-ed yeshiva. The school was presided over by three generations of a family of rabbis who, when asked about Judaism in America, had responded that in America, New York was the only city sufficiently Jewish; in New York City theirs was the only synagogue to get things right, and of the families at their synagogue, only they themselves were properly observant. Their attitude set the tone for their congregants: total insularity. Wendy had known a few kids from this school at Columbia and always found them incorrigibly smug, unable to understand there were alternate ways to approach Judaism or the world. It was a world where all outside it was pushed away.

"Why can't we use things from other cultures to help understand our own? The rabbis of the Gemara knew Greek philosophy and science. Why can't we?" Oren defended his partner, Yehuda.

Tanya retorted, "We don't need other things. Torah is enough. *Hafakh bah, hafakh bah di koola bah.*"

Judy, a good hostess, translated, "Turn it over, and turn it over for all is in it. The Chapters of the Fathers." Wendy didn't know whether she was the only one who needed translation. She didn't notice that Uri gave Judy a big smile for that note of inclusiveness, touched that Judy was trying to translate for Wendy. What would happen next in this conversation—oddly disordered in what was supposed to be such an orderly ritual, seder itself meaning "order"—she knew from Atarah's class that week.

"We need the paradigm shifters. That is why I painted Freud. He was willing to shift the level of conversation in the culture through asking his questions," Oren said.

Oded added, "But that is our tradition; we learn from *shakla ve'tarya*, the *em* . . ."

Emanuella translated, "Give and take. Like the story you mentioned before, Oded, about Rav Yohanan and Reish Lakish. When Reish Lakish died, Rav Yohanan was upset not to have a colleague who would come and challenge his ideas, raise objections to things that he said. That's why we want Oren's Freud to watch over our seders." She smiled at the artist and he nodded his thanks back.

Judy said, "Every culture needs artists who will look beyond already constructed categories, to move things ahead to another level."

Oren put his hands behind his head, linked them, and leaned back. "You know, this *In(Query)* is in a series with some other pieces. One of them, *The Beautiful of Jerusalem*, shows Rabbi Yohanan, the same rabbi whose beauty is described as being like a silver cup filled with red pomegranate seeds, rimmed with roses. There is another story about him going to visit a sick rabbi and exposing his arm for light in the dank room. The sick man started to weep and explained that his weeping was because of the beauty of the arm, that it was mortal and would one day become rot, decomposing. My painting is in still life tradition of Western art, depicting beautiful objects along with decay. In the middle of the painting Reish Lakish is leaping toward the exposed beautiful light-filled arm of Rabbi Yohanan. The periphery is surrounded by timepieces and peonies, the fattest, most luscious roses that are beginning to fade around the edges. Then I have insects, a silver goblet, and pomegranate seeds. I wanted to visually explore what decay means, to us as humans, not just objects as in the still life tradition. If we don't have the moving ahead of questions, the necessary ones, all will deteriorate, nothing will change. The moment of Reish Lakish's risk, his leap towards the other, is the fulcrum around which everything else occurs."

Tanya said, "But the story isn't about the attraction to the beauty; it is about the change, the turn to Torah. Western art is irrelevant."

Yehuda, smiling, said, "When you're old enough to fall in love, young woman, you see if you jump to a person or an ideal."

She crossed her arms, "I'm going to love a person who *embodies* an ideal, the Torah way, as I'm trying to live."

Charles continued the telling section of the seder: "We are all here together, struggling as a group to see what the way will be for us. We have both our ways we go separately, our own areas of expertise, and those we tread together, in this group journey. To read is to comment, and in order to present this tale properly, we must all be co-authors and comment. This is a communal event." Each participant read in turn, and all were asked for their opinions on various matters, throughout.

The maid served each course of the meal and produced a booklet for all when they were ready to recite the Grace after Meals, after the grandchildren finished tracking their quarry and captured the afikomen. The booklet was a souvenir Haggadah that Judy created every year for all the guests. The cover had a reproduction of Oren Laniado's *(In)Query* on the front with the words "*(In)Query*: The 1997 (5757) Spicehandler Seder." It had a guest list in calligraphy on the first page and a menu:

> *Montage of spring baby vegetables, en vinaigrette*
> *Chicken consommé with matzah balls in three color palettes*
> *Chilean sea bass with sauce of mango, ginger, tamarind, and pomegranate juice reduction*
> *Beef roulade with shallots and creamy parsnips*
> *Vegetable medallions, individually wrapped*
> *Flourless chocolate torte*
> *Sponge cake with strawberries and parve crème fraîche*
> *Coffee and tea*
> *Afikomen*

The rest of the pages were readings and commentaries on aspects of the Haggadah text that Judy and Charles had found particularly meaningful this year, along with the text of the prayer after eating a meal. It was a keepsake that could be used to recite the Birkat Hamazon, the Grace after Meals, throughout the Passover holiday, and it had the additional value of not being *hametzdik*, encrusted all over with bits of food that might get leaven into the Passover things. Judy had made designs for some of the pages and sections; the book was an artistic outlet for her. Some years, if she was particularly proud of her work and it was done far enough ahead of time, she would send additional copies to friends and family in the States and England, to help them enhance their own seders.

After the seder's conclusion, Uri told his hosts that he would walk Wendy home, a fifteen-minute walk, and return to the Spicehandlers where he was sleeping because travel was forbidden on *yom tov*, the holiday. It was a spring evening, but there was a chill in the air as it was long past midnight. Uri had a key to the Spicehandler house, so he could return after the walk.

As they walked through the slightly cool night, Uri put his arm around Wendy to keep her warm. She felt warmed already by Uri, having been sitting near him and listening to his melodious voice make intelligent comments throughout the night. She tried to anticipate what would happen— would they sleep together? The excuse of all the refined wine drunk at the plutocratic table would convince them both that whatever happened could be boiled down to loosened inhibitions if there were regrets on either end. The wine would be a good out, either way, for performing or lack of ability to perform. Was it too early in the relationship? Probably, though she would willingly surrender anything, she thought, as she leaned into him, and his alluring smell started to overcome her, a combination of aftershave and his own natural aroma.

Uri asked as they walked, steps matching and attuned, "Did you like the seder? I hope it wasn't too overwhelming, all the people, all the Hebrew?"

"Way more intense, and thought-provoking, than my family seders. For us, seder is just family time, being together, making jokes, not this profound experience. I did find it kind of ironic that a lavish feast was spread to goad us to remember what it feels like to be slaves."

Uri laughed appreciatively and Wendy continued, "Seriously, I do love the idea of the Jewish collective unconscious being examined at a seder."

"Ritual can touch all parts of the human condition."

"That's what was best about it"—she hesitated, struggling to articulate her thoughts—"it was . . . almost . . . therapeutic for me, knowing of the essential need for a question. Does that make sense?"

"The Haggadah with the silhouettes interrogating each other?"

"Exactly. To move forward, you must question, even if you are alone."

"Even if it is difficult for people to hear those questions."

"But it isn't only for the ones being asked, it is for the one doing the asking," Wendy added, surprising herself.

Uri looked over at her face in profile and was glad they were walking side by side so he didn't have to look at her directly face to face. He could tell by the quaver in her voice that this was getting at an emotional truth for her that was intensely personal. He knew that sometimes it was better to experience empathy and listen, but not look on and witness the transaction so nakedly. He tightened his hold on her shoulder, to let her know he was supporting her, and kept silent.

Wendy continued, "Questions affect the questioner. I didn't want Shaul to die. I feel, after this seder, questions are . . . necessary. The idea of a truth embodier . . . I hope that's the ideal of most academics. To get to a new understanding through asking questions. When I hear baalei teshuvah talking about their faith, it raises the issue for me of what *I* believe in. That's the power of the question. I wish the process weren't so painful. But I feel now . . . what I am doing isn't wrong."

"And Shaul?"

"It is not only my fault. His issues and difficulties didn't come from me; he had them before we ever met. Had I not been there to ask those questions, something else might have upset him and caused his death. I still feel awful. But if I don't finish, it won't help him or anyone else either."

"If he hadn't died we wouldn't have met," Uri said wistfully.

"That's creepy. Change the subject?"

"Ladies' choice," he said with a disarming smile.

"I want to remain in this happy hopeful modality; the seder was great, the food incredible—who would have thought matzah balls could be three colors? That fish was just . . . succulent. And, oh . . . the flourless torte was the best chocolate dessert I've ever had." She sighed. "I feel good about what I am doing, asking questions of religious returnees. I will finish."

"I'm glad you're in such a good mood," he said, again a bit wistfully.

"And," Wendy added, trying to express herself without being overly ambitious in her affirmations, "I didn't say the other part of why I am so happy now." She stopped and turned to face him. "Being together."

"I'm happy with you too. You know what I liked about the seder?"

"What?"

"The discussion of the story about Rabbi Yohanan and Reish Lakish, the thief who became his student and married his sister."

"Hmm, "Wendy said and moved away from him slightly as they were coming down a curb and she wanted to avoid a pile of something appearing unpleasant to step into.

"I was thinking tonight, who is the hero of the story, really?"

"The thief, for jumping the rabbi, wanting him. Pretty gutsy to put himself out there like that, in my opinion." Wendy rubbed Uri's stubbled cheek. "I've never seen stubble on you; the five o'clock shadow is such a turn-on."

Uri laughed and gently moved her hand away, but kept holding it. "You have so much to learn, Wendy. I don't shave on *yom tov.*"

Wendy hoped she hadn't offended him in her tipsy state. She was walking a bit crooked, and Uri had to steer her onto the next curb while steadying his own body against hers.

"You don't like my answer, that the thief's desire makes him heroic. How's this? Baal teshuvah thief as hero for the leap of changing himself for another person." Would Uri take the bait and realize she was talking about perhaps changing herself, even a tiny bit, for him?

"Does he? After all he has the same status: he is a master in both the house of study and the criminal world."

"Okay. The rabbi?"

"Why?" Uri asked.

"Wanting him to change?"

"No," Uri said excitedly. "That's the point. What Rabbi Yohanan says to Reish Lakish is "*chailach l'oraita,*" use your strength for the Torah. Not change *who* you are, but transform it. Take your unique strengths and abilities and put them in service of the Torah. The rabbi admires the thief's strength, and the thief admires the rabbi's beauty. But the rabbi takes his beauty and makes it a means to encourage others to learn Torah. It is the opposite of what many of these baal teshuvah yeshivot tell people: 'Here you are; we don't want what you have, your strength or your beauty, since you are empty of Yiddishkeit. We have to take you and fill you with it.' Rabbi Yohanan says, 'Remain who you are but use your strength for Torah, instead of for crime.'"

"Uri, don't scream. Why are you so upset?"

"I feel so frustrated with the whole religious world, especially in Israel where there is this sense that it is all or nothing, you know, either/or, religious or secular. There have to be more spaces in between, like at this seder, where different kinds of people can come together to discuss things. This idea of 'your strength for Torah'—let me tell you something. When I was in ninth grade I won a poetry contest. I told my rav, and he said poetry was *bitul* Torah. Not worth spending time on. I stopped writing for a while. I had this need to express myself, and finally started writing again, but I never let myself get as serious about it as I once wanted to. I'm sad about that."

"Not being a poet isn't just a question of your desire to earn a living, but your being thwarted by the religious establishment."

"You could see it that way," he said.

"But you've found a way for yourself," she said. "You are using your talents. It may not be in literally writing poetry. Poetry is an attempt to . . . reinscribe, to legislate even, an order on reality, with a sense of heightened language. What you do, seeing patients and helping them create a healthier way to see themselves and their world, is a poetic project," Wendy said stroking Uri's hand.

"I'm still angry my rav put down my poetry."

"It made me feel angry when people told me I should stop writing my dissertation because it killed someone."

"You didn't kill anyone. You spoke with someone who was ill before and after you spoke with him."

"You have poetic talents; you can use them in a variety of ways."

"I'm probably a better psychiatrist than I would have been a poet."

They continued to walk in tipsy silence, breathing in the spring air, hearing snatches of song from those concluding their seders, floating and hanging in the air from the apartment buildings they were passing. Wendy broke the stillness and said, "I like your metaphor: be who you are, but transform it. You're a poet, helping others puzzle out and distill their lives. And I'm a questioner, using my questions to help others."

"Wendy, I want this to continue," he said, striking a balance between the desire to throw all his cards on the table and tell her he loved her, and the fear of making too extravagant a declaration without a reassurance of reciprocity.

She slurred, "Uri, I want you," and kissed him. He opened his mouth in ardent response and she reached her tongue into the crevices of his mouth, with avarice, wanting to make contact with every part, getting as much of him to be part of her as she could. Uri did not respond at first, let himself be lapped and probed, and then, after a few moments, returned Wendy's ardor with his own, exploring her mouth with his own tongue, there at the junction of Sigmund Freud Square and Emek Refaim Street.

"Uri, am I in love or drunk? Don't let this end badly; let's not betray each other."

Uri leaned in to Wendy, letting her feel his desire, his hard member against her hip, holding her at the small of her back and pressing her to him. "No, no, it won't end badly. I'll never ask you how you make your weapons. Don't change; just let mine in."

Wendy's brain stopped working and all she knew was her body against his as they made their way to Mishael Street.

SEVENTEEN
Self-Counting

Seven weeks you should count for *yourself . . .*"
—DEUTERONOMY 16:9

"I made these plans weeks ago, before I met you," a frustrated Wendy was saying to Uri on the phone. "Orly's expecting me to come. You want me to just drop her for you?" She hoped appealing to his best instincts would do the trick.

"It's only three days," she added. "I'll see you the day we get back, okay?"

Uri countered, "It's a plan"—the last word pronounced 'pla-an' in his British inflected English. "The Spicehandlers invited us for dinner next Shabbat."

"Orly bought the bus tickets and I don't know when we return. Let me get back to you?"

"Call me when you know," he said before hanging up.

When Wendy and Orly started making plans to go to the beach during Passover, it was still winter, long before she'd met Uri. They realized that winter was going to be over, they hadn't been to Eilat, and both wanted to go. Orly said she'd arrange it for Passover and Wendy agreed, glad to have a break to look forward to. She couldn't have known this was Uri's only extended vacation from his residency for the next few months. Now that

Orly's boyfriend, Nir, had broken up with her, Wendy felt she too could not abandon Orly.

Orly's plan for the trip was to lie on the beach and meet gorgeous Scandinavian tourists for a mad fling to rid her mind of Nir. Wendy had been hoping for a guy on the beach too, but now there was Uri. Still, she would be on the sand with her towel and a magazine, glad to have a chance to relax.

When they got off the bus from Jerusalem to Eilat, they put their bags in the room at the hotel Orly had booked and went straight for the waves. Lying on the beach in her one-piece suit, Wendy said to Orly, "Why didn't I do this earlier in the year?" Orly, on her stomach, the straps of her black bikini untied to give her a completely even tan, shrugged. They munched matzah, cheese, and dried fruit, and luxuriated in the tranquil beach. After they had been there a few hours, two Dutch guys, strolling, walked over to them and began to chat. Sven and Niels were filmmakers, in Israel scouting locations for new work and taking a break on the beach that day. Wendy and Orly made plans to meet them at the Maui Lounge later that night.

After quite a bit of time deliberating about what to wear, they arrived at the dance club at 10:15, fashionably later than the 10:00 p.m. they'd agreed on. They went inside the crowded and noisy room, decorated with fake thatched leaves and strings of lights in tropical colors—pink, yellow, green, orange—all designed to cater to the fantasies of what someone who has never been to Hawaii might imagine it to be. They looked around the crowded room without success. Finally, they caught a view of Sven and Niels chatting up another woman, who bore a startling resemblance to Orly—the same dark skin, thick long black hair, white teeth, and brown eyes, though a smaller nose. Wendy saw them first and nudged Orly. "They're chatting up a girl who looks a lot like you. Do you find that strange?"

"The blond boys want someone darker. Vacation conquest rule—get a native. I'll take Sven any day," she gave a bit of a tiger roar. Wendy swatted at her playfully with the back of her hand and said, "Should we go over to them or let them see us?" as Niels, with his darting bird-like eyes, made eye contact with her and gave her a big smile. He looked nice in his loose Hawaiian shirt with pictures of tropical scenes and trees, tailored tan linen shorts, and brown leather fisherman sandals, like clogs, the kind of shoe an American man would never wear for fear of being seen as too feminine. Wendy saw him gesture to Sven. Sven handed his card to the Orly look-a-like, who kissed him on both cheeks and said good-bye.

The men walked over to them and, as both Wendy and Orly had hoped, Sven greeted Orly. He was still wearing the black leather dog collar and diamond earring he had on at the beach, but now with a black short-sleeve turtleneck and black leather pants, along with black clogs, his hair more spiky than it had been at the beach. He gave Orly a meaningful glance and a kiss on the lips. Orly was surprised at this liberty, though pleased. Niels gave Wendy a more sedate peck on the cheek.

Sven and Niels looked a bit odd together, Wendy decided—Sven in black and leather not quite fitting in with the other patrons of the Hawaiian-themed bar. The more average looking tourist-guy outfit of Niels seemed the more appropriate model of dress.

Wendy herself was wearing a sleeveless gauzy dress of very thin, tissue-like material with pinks and purples shot through it, along with some silver threads. It had spaghetti straps, but was loose fitting and not low cut, which helped hide the sunburn she had gotten all along her cleavage area and her upper thighs, places that her own bathing suits always covered and which she consequently had not thought to apply sunblock to. The bathing suit she borrowed from Orly, since she forgot to pack her own bathing suit, was cut differently from anything she would buy herself. She had on flat sandals with thin silver leather straps tied around the ankle. She thought, despite her hair's uncontrollable frizziness from the desert humidity, she looked nice. Orly was wearing a black halter top with a long-sleeved white cotton crocheted bolero that snapped in the front, both pieces ending well above her midriff, and a black miniskirt with black high-heeled sandals. It was not an outfit Wendy would wear, but it didn't look out of place next to Sven. Wendy had to suppress a laugh to see the two couples, dressed to suit each other without advance planning: Orly and Sven fashionable and provocative, she and Niels more ordinary and bland.

Sven led the way outside to tables that were by the sea. There was still music out there, and, in fact, a whole mosh pit area where dancers of all nationalities were gyrating. As the path ended, there was a tiki hut where a hostess had a table with a diagram to plan out seating. Sven told the hostess something in a low voice. She beckoned to a waitress, who led them to what seemed to be a reserved round table for four on a raised deck overlooking the dancers and the water. Orly said, "Oh, the dancing looks so *fun* here," in a giddy and ditzy way that would never betray that she was actually college educated.

Instead of asking them to dance, Sven said, "Let's have a drink, get to know each other a bit." He then asked if they wanted the house special coconut rum. Wendy said, "I think I'll just have some white wine." But he said, "You must try these drinks; they are so good," and beckoned the waiter over.

The waiter, a young dark-skinned Israeli who could have been Orly's brother from the similarity of their looks, smiled at Sven and Niels, nodded at Wendy and Orly, and said, "Back again? You boys are busy. What'll it be now?" Sven glared at him in response.

After requesting four house specials, Sven quickly started an amusing anecdote about some kind of linguistic misunderstanding between himself and the Israeli maid in the hotel they were staying at. His patter and rhythm were too perfect for this to have been the first time he told it; the tale sounded canned.

Wendy reminded herself that she was willing to put up with whatever was necessary to make Orly happy. Wendy would prefer to see a foreign movie, or sit in a café reading the *New Yorker*, or to be with Uri on one of his Uri tours of Jerusalem rather than be in a club with sleazy men. Orly wanted a conquest, to prove herself attractive to the opposite sex. She wanted to send Nir a postcard detailing how great a life she was having—though a postcard wasn't truly necessary since Nir still hadn't left the country for London, as he told her was imminent when breaking up with her.

At the table, Wendy was spacing out, forgetting the point of the canned story, but laughed when Orly kicked her under the table, reminding her to.

When the drinks arrived along with an order of batter fried shrimp, the waiter put all four drinks in front of Sven, sitting between Niels and Orly and across from Wendy. Sven paid the waiter after flourishing a thin black lizard-skin billfold that had what appeared to be multiple currencies, all in large denominations. The note Sven gave him looked to Wendy like 200 shekel when the bill was probably half that. It bothered her for some reason, as did the fact that Sven insisted on stirring all the drinks himself, telling them that he wanted to make sure his guests were well treated and that they wouldn't taste as good without being properly stirred.

Wendy, not used to large doses of alcohol, took a sip of her drink and thought it bitter. After another sip, she knew it wasn't right. Niels, a cinematographer, started pointing out the possibilities for photography of the scene in front of them, waves crashing on the beach, what angles might be used and how a shot could be gotten, as Wendy furiously kicked Orly under the table, receiving only a nasty face from her friend. As she replied to Niels, she noted that the drink in Orly's cup was quickly dissipating. It was now about half gone. Wendy decided to take action. Mid-sentence, Wendy stood up and said, "Why don't we all dance now? I love this song." She grabbed Orly's hand to run to the dance floor with her and, in the process, bumped her hip against the table, spilling Orly's drink over the table and even a bit onto Sven. Sven stood up and muttered what they assumed to be a Dutch profanity.

"I'm sorry," Wendy said stupidly.

Niels said, "Never mind him; he'll dry out." Sven's cell phone rang. He answered, "Ja," and gestured with an upward tilt of his chin that the other three should adjourn to the dance floor without him, as he continued speaking on the phone.

They walked towards the dance floor together, Niels leading the women. Before they had reached it, Orly tapped him on the shoulder, and said, "Excuse us for a moment, we need the ladies room."

As soon as they were out of Niels's sight, Orly screamed, "What kind of dumbass thing was that to do? A guy buys us drinks and you spill on him?"

"Did your drink taste bitter?"

"My drink was fabulous. Go back to your religious boyfriend if you aren't having a good time. Sven will take care of me."

"That's what I'm worried about. Wasn't it odd that he insisted on stirring all the drinks? He was putting something in them; I'm sure."

Now, she looked at Wendy, wide-eyed, and then her eyes narrowed. "You think? A date rape drug?"

"Something. Their story just doesn't add up. Why can't they tell us more about the movie they are scouting locations for? Why didn't they know what the Cinematheque was?"

"They've only been here ten days. Why should they know all the art house cinemas in the country? I'm more concerned about the drugs in the drinks. Why didn't I taste something and you did?"

"Mine was meant for you? I do not trust this guy."

"Wendy, I'm not saying this again. We are here to have fun. F-U-N. It may not be in your vocabulary, but it is in mine. Don't spill more drinks," Orly said, laying a firm hand on Wendy's bare shoulder.

"Ow!" Wendy screamed in pain. "Another spot I must have missed with my sunblock. Ready to dance?" Wendy grabbed Orly's hand and led her back to the dance area directly in front of the sea. They found Niels, who was dancing alone, whether out of loyalty to Wendy, or just not being able to find a partner, being on the shortish side on a floor full of taller men, blond and Scandinavian-featured as well as swarthy and Middle Eastern. They asked, "Where's Sven?" and Niels gestured with his head up to the table where they had been. Sven was still on the phone. Orly tried to ask him if something was wrong, and he just shrugged. They danced to some Boy George song from the eighties, and then Niels said, "He's off the phone. It looks like he had another round of drinks sent." He turned his head towards Sven at the table on a raised deck forty or fifty feet away.

"Let's dance more," Wendy said.

Niels said, "No, he's waiting. Let's go back."

After they had returned to the table, Sven insisted they finish their drinks before they went back to the dance floor. This final detail made Orly suspicious, and Wendy and Orly both drank vigilantly small sips. Sven noticed and said, "Would you perhaps like another type of drink? Am I too . . . what is the word . . . Pushing my tastes on you?"

Orly smiled broadly, put her hand suggestively on his arm, and said, "No. It's fabulous . . . like you" and took a large slurp of her straw, licking her lips suggestively in the process.

He said, businesslike, "Good, good." He smiled at each of them in turn, showing his teeth, which to Wendy seemed too small for his large face and mouth. Sven put her in mind of a crocodile, mouth large, but actual teeth quite small, as he said, "Listen ladies, I have this thought. I hope you'll like it." Orly looked at him intently and Wendy waited for him to say the inevitable: Why don't we switch rooms? I'll go with Orly to your hotel and you go to ours with Niels? Wendy was trying to think ahead about how she was going to protect her friend, when Sven deviated from the script in her mind. "It would really turn us on . . . if we could watch the two of you . . . having sex."

Niels added, "And film it. It is the most erotic thing imaginable to watch two beautiful women from behind the camera and then, when they are aroused, come out and join them . . ."

Wendy crossed her arms and legs protectively in front of her and said in anger, "Excuse me?"

Sven continued, "Ah, but this is why we came here . . . to watch two beautiful Jewesses . . . together . . . the most lovely sight. Haven't you ever wanted to be with your friend . . . you know . . . on another level? When she comes out of the shower, don't you desire her glistening body? We could even find a secluded spot along the beach with the sounds of the water in the background . . ."

This time Orly responded. "I thought you liked me, not us. I'm not some porn performer." She stood up and Wendy followed. "Let's go." As she stood she added, "I'm not a prude. Sven, I'd go with you . . ." she said suggestively.

He said, "Mmm . . . I thought you'd be like that," he said, looking up from his seated position at Orly standing over him. "Not tonight. I wish we could get her on screen; look at her, Niels." Niels followed his boss's directions, but Wendy could not see anything different than the Orly she had known for fifteen years.

Sven continued, "My gorgeous, I must stay here, we have a few more scenes to cast and film before we go back to Tel Aviv. I'll call you from there—give me your number—I want you in." Was the last statement a double entendre or a reference to his movie?

Before she could warn Orly, Orly replied, "My e-mail is O-r-l-y-7-0 at hotmail.com" and began to walk away.

Wendy followed her, adding, "Good luck with your filming, guys. Sorry we're not up for your cinematic aspirations," she said with a smirk and sashayed off. She turned around to look at the scene again and remember it—for what? An anecdote? Totally failed attempt to pick up foreign men yields porn director?

Wendy could not sleep in their hotel room that night.

"Orly?" she whispered.

"I can't sleep either. Sorry I brought you here to meet those . . . creeps."

Wendy paused. "I just feel . . . grossed out, violated . . . like they were trying to . . . possess me." She shuddered under the thin sheets and blanket, though the temperature was still warm. "Why do they even have the right to imagine we'd want to be filmed? Or filmed together."

"You don't find me attractive?" the deeply insecure Orly said sadly.

"Orly, of course you're attractive. I'm not Sven though," Wendy replied. "I hate this male assumption that women always want them, whatever they do. It's just so . . . arrogant. That's what I hate, their arrogance. Even thinking they had the right to suggest it." She shuddered.

"Are you going to tell Uri?"

"I'm not sure . . . I didn't do anything wrong, but I feel like I did. I do want to tell him—I'm not sure how."

"Will he be outraged? Two guys wanted to film us? It's . . . weird." Orly added.

"It is."

"Let's just try to calm down and get some sleep. It's the season of our freedom."

"Good night, Orly."

"Night, Wendy."

As she drifted off to sleep, she thought, *season of freedom,* and remembered snatches of the discussion at the seder. Freedom from . . . freedom to. Must be a purpose to the freedom or it isn't free. Wendy thought, drifting off, *I do want more purpose in my freedom.* There was certainly no purpose, other than attempting to boost Orly's self-esteem, in picking up creeps on the beach.

By mutual consent, their next day began late—as they had both had trouble sleeping—and with strong coffee at Reshet Eilat, the Internet café. It was a spare place, with most of the furnishings budget going to the computers, which were up to date. The breakfast choices were what one would expect: granola, yogurt, various croissants, and muffins. There was also matzah with cream cheese or butter on offer. Orly and Wendy ate their granola and yogurt parfaits without saying much. They glanced at the *International Herald Tribune* a previous customer had left behind on the table and hurried over to the computer terminals when they were finished eating.

Orly sat at the screen and typed Sven's name into the Internet. A list of websites came up, and they clicked on the first one. They were brought to a website with loud pulsing music, pictures of beaches, the Taj Mahal, and the Dome of the Rock, with a caption reading "Click here to see our latest project."

They clicked and saw a montage of pictures. A scene appearing to be inside the Dome of the Rock mosque with a man in traditional Arab dress dissolved into a screen where he had removed his clothing to reveal a huge erection and the caption—"Where's the rock now?" A group of women in bathing suits with sequins and high heels stood gazing at him.

Orly said, "Could it be real? It's like, a foot long. Do they *ever* come that way?"

Wendy said, "Surgical enhancement?"

These photos then dissipated to reveal, after the caption "Love of Holiness," two young ultra-Orthodox women wearing wigs and heavy stockings at the *Kotel* giving each other soulful looks. The next photo showed them walking away from it together, in the appropriately pious backwards motion, their eyes locked not on the holy site but on each other. In a third image they were in a room going at each other in poses reminiscent of any in Penthouse. Wendy had to stifle a laugh because the whole thing was completely cheesy. Stereotyped. The obviousness of these desires—it troubled Wendy. Why were they so . . . predictable? Isn't the interesting thing about desire that it can come from unimagined odd places, from unsuitable people? The final series was titled "Peace Dividend" and showed two of the Arab women from the mosque scene with the two Jewish ones.

Wendy asked, "Where would we fit in? Two friends find love on the beach?"

Orly shuddered and said, "Ugh. I can't believe I didn't put the pieces together about who they were." She put her head in her hands. "I'm glad you saved me from being seen on the Internet. Can you imagine?"

"Don't blame yourself. There are non-creeps out there. We'll find them."

Neither of them had the stomach for exposing themselves on the beach, so instead they went to see dolphins. Wendy told Orly she did not want to be intimately near a slippery if affectionate sea creature just now, so they refrained from swimming with them. They went to the coral reefs and, though it was slightly beyond their usual budgets, Orly treated Wendy to a ride in a glass-bottomed boat to see the coral. The exquisite colors and shapes lurking beneath the sea were completely unexpected and satisfying.

They decided to take an earlier bus back to Jerusalem the next day, Friday. Wendy used Orly's cell phone to call Uri and tell him what time she'd be back. Their bus would get them into Jerusalem just as the Sabbath was starting—she wouldn't have a chance to buy any food for the weekend because all the stores would be closed for Sabbath already, and she would have to take a cab from the bus station back to her apartment because the buses would have already ceased. Uri offered to pick up some food for her and drop it off at her apartment. She said, fine, but then found herself saying, "Why don't you drop it off and stay and eat with me? Do you have other plans?" He told her that he'd planned to go to the Spicehandlers, but she shouldn't come if she wouldn't be there before Shabbat—it wouldn't be appropriate to disrupt the meal. They agreed that he could get the key from Amalia, the landlady, and bring Shabbat dinner for two to Wendy's apartment. Wendy would call Amalia to let her know. Mostly, she was relieved that he assumed she was coming back for him, not asking about what had happened in Eilat, so she didn't have to tell him just yet.

After she hung up, she felt . . . cozy and taken care of. *Here this guy was, making arrangements for her dinner, and all she had to do was get back to her house. What if this feeling, that he would care for her, attend to things, lasted longer?* She didn't want to get too far ahead in her thoughts, so she focused on the nice Shabbat they'd have. There would be challah—oh no, oops, still Passover, not this week—chicken . . . maybe he'd bring flowers. A romantic reunion. She should be grateful to Orly for creating an opportunity for absence to make his—and her—heart grow fonder.

She looked over at Orly on the other bed, lying on her stomach, legs in the air, reading *Vanity Fair* magazine.

Wendy was bustling around the room making sure that her things were, if not in her duffle bag, in its general vicinity so she'd be ready to go tomorrow. They were planning to check out of the room and leave their bags at the hotel desk until they went to the bus depot for the 1:30 bus. They had agreed to go to the beach in the morning and that they would speak to no one, of either sex, on the beach. As Wendy was reaching under the bed to see if something had fallen there, Orly sat up on her bed and said, "I have this idea. What if I contacted Sven and Niels and wrote an article about their trip?"

"Sven and Niels do the Holy Land?"

"Exactly. It covers an amazing range of issues. Besides the sex, which sells an article, it has this whole thing about European perceptions of Israel. I could very wittily describe some of the scenes they film, talk about how they picked what to film, the taboos they are trying to shatter . . ."

"Brilliant! It gets every hot category—Middle Eastern politics, sex, perceptions of porn. You could do profiles of Sven and Niels, a discussion of what makes a pornographer tick. I could totally see this in the *New Yorker.*"

"Really? I was fantasizing that, but I'd be happy with something smaller. Still . . ."

"Go for it. Imagine the cover art? Remember when Art Spiegelman did the one with the Hasid and the African American kissing after the Yankel Rosenbaum stabbing? They could get someone to do a riff on the website—you know a caricature of Sven and Niels in various obscene poses in front of easily recognizable holy sites. The controversy it would generate—I love it! Will you tell Sven and Niels you're doing it before you pitch it to editors?"

"I'm trying to strategize. Being up-front with them would work best, you agree?"

"You don't want to do investigative journalism, go undercover and see what it is like to be in this movie? What is it called—immersion journalism—live it and write it?" Wendy joked.

"Should I tell them I want to write about them or pretend I'm interested?"

"Would they really object if you wrote about them? It would be incredible publicity."

"I'd like to write about their actual perceptions of Israel, the funny stories about misunderstanding, missed cues that they were telling us on the beach . . ." Orly took out a note pad and started writing. She laughed to herself as she remembered one of the odd moments.

Orly used the hotel phone to call, since she didn't want him to have access to her cell phone number. When he answered and asked when he could see her, she said, "On camera or off," and he replied, "Either."

She told him, "I am a journalist."

He replied, "Have you and your friend changed your minds about our movie?"

Orly continued, with Wendy looking on, "I would like to write about you and Niels and the process of making your movie."

There was silence on the other line and then, loud enough so Wendy could hear, "What do I get from this?"

"Free publicity. If tens of thousands of people read about it, some of them are bound to purchase of your movies. It's a method of penetrating the

American market." Wendy, sitting on her haunches on her bed, arms curled around her knees like a little kid, fell forward onto her knees and giggled at the word "penetrate." Orly waved at her furiously not to laugh too loudly.

"No, there wouldn't be any adverse affects." There was again silence. "Why don't we have coffee and discuss it? In Tel Aviv Saturday morning, Café Fleur on Rehov Sheinkin?" Orly smiled broadly at Wendy and said, "See you then." She hung up the phone and gave Wendy a broad high-five slap. "He agreed to meet. Psych!"

Wendy did a voiceover imitation: "Our heroine, Orly Markovsky, once again proves, anything can be a career move. Picked up by the wrong guy? Write an article on him. Get depressed? Write a book. Parent with terminal illness? Write on her choice to commit assisted suicide. Orly's guide on how to improve your career with a *New Yorker* article for any scenario."

"Stop. This could really get me somewhere. You don't want to go out dancing now, do you?" Orly started jumping and leaping around the room, pumping her hands on the air, her long black tresses flying behind her.

"When you publish this in the *New Yorker* I will take you dancing. Deal?"

Orly put out her hand so that Wendy had to shake it.

The next morning, Wendy and Orly lay on the beach, each with her own sunblock, SPF 30 and 4, respectively. Wendy rolled onto her side from her back and impulsively asked Orly, lying next to her, face up, "Where do you see yourself in ten years?"

"Ideally or realistically?" she queried.

"Ideally."

"Living on the Upper East Side, writing interesting freelance pieces for good magazines, married with a kid and a nanny . . . You?"

"Tenure at a university I have at least heard of, in a reasonably large place, married, one or two kids? I feel like I am closest to door number one, tenure, though the others could happen . . ."

"Is Uri the one? Are you nervous about dating someone religious?"

Wendy raised herself on an elbow and looked over at Orly. "His allegiance isn't only to religion. He's kind of a *satyagraha,* a truth seeker, like me. You too, as an investigative journalist."

"Everything doesn't have to be so serious for me. This article about pornographers in the Holy Land is meaningful enough."

"Don't limit yourself. Maybe you will write some longer pieces that will change something, make a difference. I'd like to think *my* work will make a difference in the world."

"That's the difference between us: you think you are doing work that is not only something you are personally curious about, but will help others understand their motives."

"No, actually, what I really like about this dissertation is giving people an opportunity to talk about their journey, seeing how they put their life story together. When they fill out a questionnaire, they tell one kind of story—my family wasn't *shomer Shabbat,* or kosher, we belonged to a Reform temple and attended maybe once a year— there isn't any evidence of Jewish connection. Then I talk to them and they say, 'Oh I always had these spiritual yearnings and loved to read about Orthodox Jews,' or 'I had a grandmother who took me to *shul* with her.' The story is so different when it is actually in a person's voice."

"Of course you're attracted to a psychiatrist—it sounds like you are shrinking your subjects!"

Wendy leaned her head on her elbow and turned to look at Orly. "Maybe. I don't know, Orly; I am trying so hard to make sense of my *own* life."

Orly looked surprised and responded, "What's so hard?"

"Everything. Is what I'm doing worthwhile? Should I be in graduate school or is it a total waste of time, because when I'm thirty years old I'll have a PhD and no job and live with my parents? Will someone ever love me? Will I have kids? Will I even finish my dissertation? Am I going to stay in Israel for another year or go back to Princeton? It's all so uncertain. I hate that." She stopped and, with her next thought, felt tears come to her eyes. She hoped Orly, lying flat on her back with sunglasses on, wouldn't notice. "I just don't feel like I've advanced at all. When I arrived, I was trying to find the shared cab and Professor Lamdan asked me, 'Do you know where you're going?' I'm still not sure. I've done some research, I have a start, but I haven't started writing. I don't know how it will turn out." Wendy controlled the quaver in her voice before Orly noticed it.

Orly, still prone on her back, agreed without turning to Wendy. "It's hard. I do understand the attraction of religion for your baalei teshuvah. If everything is certain and destined, life is less unknown. But, for me, having too much certainty makes life less exciting. The not-knowing is part of the game.

When I walk into a party or a bar, will I attract someone? Will they be attracted to me? What will happen, when, how? I like unpredictability."

Wendy looked away from Orly and out to the Red Sea. "The excitement and anxiety of the unknown, the plodding ordinariness of the known and secure. There has to be something in between. I wish there were some way to know, with absolute certainly, *I should be here writing my dissertation. I will finish and get a job and have a career.* That's why," she said more excitedly, "the seder felt so important. For those moments when we talked about how you can't have a seder without asking questions, I felt, *Yes, I am doing the right thing.* Being here, asking people questions about themselves; it *is* important."

"Everyone needs affirmation, " Orly nodded. "It must be hard, doing all this writing and not being able to publish it for a long time, not having a sense of whether people will read it. It is so different from what I do: write, send to editor, publish."

"That's the thing: you know there is a point to your work. You write, get published, get paid. For me, I write, people judge it, maybe eventually I'll send it off to a journal, and perhaps, oh, a hundred people may read it."

"Why do it?" Orly asked innocently.

"I like trying to fit different kinds of information together. I like writing and I like teaching—academia will be a good career for me."

"Stop worrying and start writing."

"Easy for you to say. Don't forget, we're here for F-U-N, remember? Let me bake blissfully on the beach for the next hour."

"F-U-N sounds good. I guess you've absorbed Eilat," Orly said laughing at Wendy.

They continued to lie on the beach, absorbing the rays of the sun, each with her desired layer of sun protection, until they went to fetch their luggage and catch the bus back to Jerusalem.

On the bus, Wendy napped and attempted to read her novel, *The Golden Bowl*, begun on the plane to Israel and put aside, now taken out, a fat book in honor of the fat chunks of reading time, on the beach and on the bus, and clutching the bottle of wine she had been instructed to purchase by Orly before they left Eilat. With the reading and napping, the ride went fast, and Wendy woke, from the sun's splendor on Eilat's beach, to sundown in Jerusalem.

The only vehicles on the street were cabs, few and far between; Wendy and Orly each found one. Wendy's cabbie drove her down Yafo, the main commercial street from the bus station, past the usually-bustling Mahane Yehuda market. All was completely empty; the shops of the commercial district were shuttered and locked. No one was in the street as the remnants of daylight calmly receded and it grew steadily darker.

Wendy thought that in another place it might feel creepy to see bustling streets silent. But in Jerusalem it felt normal, restful, appropriate. After ten months here, she knew this was the mode of Friday night, *erev Shabbat*. She thought it would feel weird to go back to the States and *not* see a closing down of things, a sense of restfulness, of cessation at the end of the week. In Jerusalem, things came to a halt for the Sabbath as though by force of nature.

"HomeStore" read one of the storefronts the cab passed. How can one's home be a store? Why should a home be commodified? Comforting, that, yes, a home can be created, Wendy thought. Purchases can be made, a mood set, and *voila*, a home. But a home doesn't come from the objects, she reflected.

Progressing down Shlomzion Ha-Malka Street, she thought she could hear snatches of singing from a synagogue when the cab stopped at a light. *That is what makes a home, people to sing in it,* she thought. *Had she ever sung in her home? The one Shabbat dinner with Noah—was there singing?* She couldn't remember. Would Uri sing to her tonight? The prayer for the woman of valor?

She clutched her knapsack on her lap and felt the bottle of wine, still in one piece. She was looking forward to having whatever Uri had brought for her. Would he cook anything at her apartment? She had gotten rid of bread and cereal, but didn't really know how to clean for Passover. Even Essie didn't do the regimented cleaning Wendy's returnees described, getting every surface in the kitchen disinfected with bleach in case there might possibly be *hametz* there. Wendy's mother just told their cleaning lady to be extra thorough, and she put away all leavened products. Wendy hoped Uri wouldn't expect that she do anything more exhaustive. The idea of cooking in her apartment, along with singing, excited her. It would make it a home to have snatches of melodies and cooking smells floating through her little apartment.

She hadn't envisioned any of her apartments as homes, really, but as temporary abodes for her to eat, sleep, work, maybe bring a guy when she was lucky. None of them were places she would remain long-term. She was tired of the transience of it all—the apartments never decorated because they were short-term solutions to the problem of where to sleep, eat, and work; the friends who were people to hang out with for now because they'd all be scattered soon enough; the food that was microwaved or a powder to be transformed into something edible when boiling water was added. She was doing no more than subsisting; none of the efforts around the home were for things she was creating or building.

The cab, now on David HaMelech Street, was passing the Laromme Hotel on the right and the Yemin Moshe neighborhood of the Spicehandlers on the left. What was happening at the Spicehandler villa now? She saw people on the street turn down in the direction of the Yemin Moshe homes. Were any of them were going to the Spicehandlers'? Was their maid Graciela serving the soup?

As the cab continued onto Emek Refaim and approached within a few blocks of her apartment, she realized that she hadn't ever had anyone welcome her home. And she thought about how, in interview after interview, it seemed like almost half or more of her interviewees came from homes where their parents had divorced, and they had spent their lives searching out a sense of home, and wholeness, that they found in Orthodox Judaism and Shabbat. They were seeking this sense of home, and being loved and welcomed in it.

She got out of the cab, took the wine and her backpack, paid the driver, and returned his greeting of "Shabbat Shalom." As she fumbled for her key to enter, she thought she could smell roast chicken. When she got inside the entryway and opened her mail slot she sniffed again. Potatoes? Mounting the steps, her olfactory senses seemed to indicate soup. She also realized that, though she occasionally cooked something for herself, she didn't usually smell cooking odors wafting down while she was walking upstairs. It was comfortably temperate in the early April evening, but she felt pleasantly warm as she ascended the steps.

Uri opened the door. He was wearing the male Jerusalem Sabbath uniform: white cotton button-down shirt, khaki pants, sandals, white knit kipah with dark and light blue décor crocheted in its rim. He gave her a huge hug, which she returned, though she worried that she was sweaty and smelly from the more than five-hour bus ride. He held her at a slight distance for a minute and said with the accent she still found adorable, "Wendy, you look grand. You got some nice colour on the beach."

"Really? I got burned too, see?" she said pulling her T-shirt and sweater aside to display the sunburn on her shoulders.

"The wages of pleasure," he said with a smile.

"Being with you is much more pleasurable than being away," she said sincerely.

He took her hand and led her inside her apartment and gently closed the door. He again pulled her close to him, but this time planted his lips firmly on hers and kissed her, their lips tasting each other. Wendy prayed he would not try to French kiss her as she imagined the sourness in her mouth from the nap on the bus and the sharp-flavored Bissli snack she ate would be less than enticing. Fortunately, he didn't penetrate the recesses of her mouth with his tongue.

"Are you hungry?" he asked her after their lips disengaged.

"Can I take a shower first? Then I'll tell you . . ." Wendy said, in what she hoped was an alluring tone of voice.

"Sure," he said, sounding a bit disappointed. He'd been shopping and cooking all day in anticipation of her return, and now that she was back, she didn't seem interested in him or the food. "I hate long bus trips too. You need a transition from the rest of the week into Shabbos. Take a shower, change. I'll be reading here."

He turned back to the couch to get his book, which Wendy recognized as a *siddur*.

Then, starting to walk to the bathroom, she saw her table, which she hadn't noticed until now. Usually piled with books and papers, it presently held a white tablecloth embroidered with delicate spring flowers, a vase filled with bursting nasturtiums, and place settings for two. The settings were not the dishes Wendy had in her apartment. He must have purchased them specially for Passover.

She didn't know what to say. She'd expected some take-out food, eaten on paper plates. She hadn't imagined that he would make this elaborate effort.

"Uri, it's beautiful. I . . . I'm touched. You must have been working all day."

"Well," he said happily, "I'm pleased you like it. I was waiting for you to notice."

"I'm sorry. I didn't see it at first. It's . . . remarkable. This apartment has never looked so good."

As she looked around, she saw that the soft glow wasn't only from the reading lamp over the couch, but from the Shabbat candles that he had lit. She didn't recognize the candlesticks—he must have brought them also. Uri had lit them on the counter built between the kitchen and dining room/living room, where Wendy often ate sitting on a stool.

"You lit candles. Can men do that? Isn't it gender-bending or something?" she asked, perplexed.

"It's a symbol of home. If a man lives alone, he should light for his household."

"You light candles every week?"

"At home. If I'm elsewhere, I let the woman of the house do it on my behalf. You weren't here, so I took the liberty."

"Those flowers are gorgeous—was that vase in the apartment?"

"From the florist. Judy told me where to go, and when I told her Judy referred me, she threw it in for free."

"*Protectzia.*"

He laughed. "You're getting the Israeli way. Go shower and then we'll eat. I'm glad you appreciate everything."

She planted another kiss on his lips, assuming that he wouldn't mind any residual sour taste on her lips. She said, "You made this homecoming so special, Uri," and dashed off down the hall to shower and change. She saw that he had left the bathroom lights on but not the bedroom lights, so she opened the bathroom door, as well as the adjacent bedroom one, to find the outfit she wanted in her closet, instead of disturbing the Sabbath harmony, as she normally would, by flicking the light switch. She set her backpack down next to her laundry hamper and removed her toiletry kit. This was pretty much the only thing in the bag that didn't need laundering because it smelled of smoke from being worn in a bar, or of sunblock or sand.

In the shower, she tingled. Would he be touching her in the places she was cleaning? Unlike the uncertainty about her life course she experienced discussing her future with Orly on the beach, the uncertainty of the evening had a flirtatious and exciting instability about it. There was a connection between the uncertainty of what would happen and the palpable excitement she felt after Uri's initial kiss. She thought, *If I only had the sense, as I do now, that something good will come eventually, I could live with uncertainty of the rest of my life.*

As she got out of the shower and dressed, she heard Uri's strong and sweet tenor voice singing. Uri was chanting the Song of Songs, read by Ashkenazic Jews in the morning of the intermediate Sabbath of Passover. He had been asked to read from it tomorrow morning at the Spicehandlers' synagogue in Yemin Moshe and was practicing. She was reminded of the voice she had heard her first Shabbat in Jerusalem at *Shir Tzion,* with its melodic cadences and confident harmony. She decided, humming along, that Uri's was the most beautiful voice she knew; she would listen as long as she could.

EIGHTEEN
Forty-Two Journeys

These are the journeys of the children of Israel who went out of the
land of Egypt . . ."
—NUMBERS 33:1

The journeys totalled 42 and they are with every person from the time
he/she is born until he/she returns to his/her eternity; for the day of birth
has all aspects of leaving Mitzrayim.
—BAAL SHEM TOV on NUMBERS 33:1

These are the journeys of the children of Israel' Moshe Rabbeinu wrote all
the journeys of Israel. And the matters were in the whole Torah. Now,
Elijah is writing all the journeys, the wandering and hardships of Israel
and when the Messiah comes, *this* will be the book that all will learn
from.
—RABBI DAVID OF LYLOV, Hasidic commentator on NUMBERS 33:1

The day after Pesach ended, Wendy was climbing steep stone stairs to an
apartment off a narrow street in the Old City. She was here to interview its
occupant, Rahel Shmuely, née Rachel.

Wendy had, after much back and forth between herself and the members
of her committee, decided that to provide a bit of ballast to her project she

would interview those who had been religious for five and ten years, not just those in yeshivot now. Her guiding premise was that those who had been religious longer would view their lives differently. Wendy wanted to know how the lens of greater distance from their original lives as secular Jews had altered their views of that prior life. The biggest problem with this new task would be finding people to interview. Some returnees who had remained in Israel were in touch with the schools they had studied at, so she was able to get their names. But others were out and about leading their lives, often trying to forget there was a time before they became religious.

Wendy wanted to get a sense of what direction these interviews would go in so she could begin to orient the tone of her whole piece accordingly. As she'd done with her first round, she wanted to conduct a few preliminary interviews to help her figure out what the most helpful questions would be and how to frame her conversations.

Today's interviewee, Rahel, was a professional harpist. She had been in the middle of studies at a music conservatory when she came to Israel for a summer at the age of twenty-four. She never went back to the States. Now twenty-nine, Rahel had stayed in Israel and learned. She was married and had a child, and was currently expecting her second. The woman who answered the door was wearing a crocheted cotton beret that was light pink and cheerful, a loose pink cotton shirt that reached below her elbows and had room for her surging belly, a denim skirt, and fashionably clunky sandals with thick heels. She said, "Wendy?" with a smile and at her nod invited her in.

"Come in. Sorry for the mess. I'm still finishing putting away all the Pesach dishes."

Wendy said, "Don't worry."

Rahel answered, "No, I feel bad about the mess because I don't want you to see it as hard to be religious. I want you to have a good impression of baalei teshuvah."

Wendy tried, in her most Uri-like and psychiatric voice, to say, "And why is that?" and hoped there was enough authority in it to convince Rachel to tell her something truthful.

"It's a great way of life; you might like it if you try it."

Wendy wished she had a snappy all-purpose comeback line to these constant overtures to become religious, like, "*Goldberg is my last name because my father is Jewish and my mother isn't,"* or *"Actually, I'm a psychopath; you don't want me in your community,"* but instead she said, "I'm more interested in honesty. I judge better that way."

Wendy sat down in the small living room on a futon couch that could become a bed for Shabbos guests, and Rahel entered the tiny kitchen across from it. Rahel said, "I can't offer you much since I don't have my *hametzdik* dishes out yet. Would you like some tea and Passover brownies?"

Wendy was prepared to do what she needed to for her research, even if it meant eating unappetizing kosher-for-Passover baked goods. Did the statement "can't offer much" have to do with truth or food?

"Sure," her polite voice offered.

Rahel brought out the tea and brownies and they sat at the small dining table next to the kitchen. Sipping the tea, Wendy said, notebook out, "Tell me how you became religious." She was still trying to figure out what the best approach to this part of the interview process was, so wanted to start with a basic open-ended question.

Rahel sipped her tea. "One place to start is my frustration and disgust with the master's program in music performance. It was this culture of narcissism, people obsessed with themselves and their instruments, their careers, what kind of PR image they could project to market themselves and create a compelling narrative for audiences"—Wendy nodded, understanding the hothouse environment of graduate education—"and my feeling that I love music, and I love performing, but aren't there other things out there, which Juilliard students are vastly ignorant of?"

Wendy said, "Aha," in what she hoped was an encouraging way, and wanted to ask whether Uri had a bag of tricks, little things he did to indicate to patients that he was engaged with their stories. She'd find out.

Rahel continued, "I'd been thinking these things, and one day, my friend Natasha was crossing the street, got struck by a cab, and died."

Wendy commented, "That's . . . *awful.* I'm so sorry."

"It was. Tragic. She was an only child; her parents were immigrants from Russia. She was their shining light, their daughter at Juilliard. Then, she was gone. I started thinking more about what it was I wanted out of life after her death, and decided I needed to do something different, to get out of a rut. I had this obsessive focus on music, but I felt like I'd reached a plateau in my playing. I found this free summer program through Aishet Lapidot, Woman of the Flame. I came to Israel. I brought my harp and played. I realized I enjoyed playing more now that I wasn't so obsessed with it. Having something else in my life—Torah and then my husband, Aaron, and my daughter—gave me this . . . openness. I could compartmentalize my playing—it was important, a big piece of my life, but . . . not all there was."

"Doesn't playing music have intrinsic worth?" Wendy queried.

"Yes. This is the thing, though. If I died tomorrow, I'd prefer to be remembered as a person who lived her life with Torah values, as a decent human being, than as an outstanding musician. Part of embracing *frumkeit* is accessing those things that make us more fully human."

Wendy frowned. This was something she hadn't quite heard before. Rahel was different from some of her other interviewees in that she had retained her past in her current life. Rahel hadn't walked away from her past, the world of music, or decided that the world beyond Torah Judaism had no value. "Could you parse that, fully human, for me?"

Rahel said, sipping her tea carefully, "Music accesses aspects of being human, the need to express emotion, to create something of beauty, to be creative. In Jewish life, each holiday reflects and refracts a different emotion. Purim for hilarity, Tisha B'Av for sadness . . ." she looked at Wendy, unsure of how much she needed to explain. "You know about Tisha B'Av?"

Wendy responded, "The commemoration of the destruction of both Temples, though Jews have folded in all catastrophic historical events, like the expulsion from Spain."

"Good," smiled Rahel.

"What emotion is Passover?" Wendy asked, deviating from her prepared questions out of curiosity.

"A time of probing and questioning, the beginning of the journey to revelation at Sinai."

"To you personally, what does it mean?" Wendy continued.

"It's like when you begin a relationship,"—Rahel saw Wendy blush here, but reserved comment for the time being—"and you feel this fervent love. It says in Jeremiah, *lechtaich acharai bamidbar b'eretz lo zeruah.*"

Wendy interrupted her, "Translation?"

"'When you followed after me to a land unsown,' that the children of Israel, even though they weren't certain how it would turn out, were willing to follow God. Passover is that time, the beginning of the relationship, the proof that they were willing to embrace *Hashem* and follow him to the desert. It culminates at Sinai. To get to certainty or understanding, you need questioning and not knowing. If you don't bring up those doubts, you can't proceed beyond them."

Wendy reacted without her mask of professionalism. "I haven't heard other baalei teshuvah say that."

Rahel raised her eyebrows, surprised, "What do you mean?"

"So many seem to . . . just gloss over their difficulties. Or try to. It's that . . . they want so much to believe, and then they . . . can't allow themselves the slightest chink in the armor of their faith, because they think it will make the entire suit crumble."

Rahel said, "I've seen people like that; but we're all responsible grown-ups and have to make choices. You need to know what you can handle. I've never felt that if I just repress my doubts they will go away. I confront them."

Wendy decided to toss her professional mask entirely now. "With your husband, when did you really know he was the one?"

Rahel said, "You've met your *basherte*, haven't you?"

Wendy blushed again and stammered, "Okay." She paused, then continued, "I didn't come here to talk about myself, but," she held out her hands in front of her in the motion of a stop sign though she continued to speak, "I just started dating someone. I don't know how we'll face some of the obstacles we may have though."

Rahel took a bite of her Passover brownie and said, peering at Wendy over the pastry, "Which are?"

Wendy realized she hadn't interviewed anyone older than herself yet. This was odd—having the tables turned by someone so obviously talented and smart. "I'm American; he's British; we're both in school. I don't know where we could live and both have careers. He grew up religious; I didn't. We're not at the stage yet where we are even discussing these things—I'm just worrying for the future."

Rahel added, "Live in Israel. Neither of you will need to compromise."

"I want a university job. It's *extremely* tough to get one here."

"You never know," said Rahel, nonchalantly.

"No, you don't. Anything's possible," Wendy added. Then, shyly, she said, "Really, how did you *know* with your husband?"

Rahel smiled dreamily as she narrated. "I'd gone on a number of *shidduch* dates, and nothing clicked. Finally, I realized, 'I need someone who is a musician, who will understand me and my need for music in my life.' Not a professional musician, just someone with a commitment to it. My *rebbetzin* said, 'I'll see what I can do,' and Aaron was the next person I went out with. It was as though I had to . . . recognize what I wanted and articulate it before it could happen."

"What was it like, when you met?"

"We went to a recital, and then to eat, and at dinner we talked the whole time, very comfortably, no awkwardness. Then he said he wanted to hear me play. No one I'd met before had ever asked that. We went back to my apartment, and I played for him, with my door ajar, of course, because it would have been *yichud* otherwise. My roommates were really angry because it was late by this time and the music woke them. I barely noticed their anger because Aaron really responded to my playing. Then we left the apartment and went out for a walk—it must have been one or two in the morning—and he sang to me. I'd liked him, but the moment he opened his mouth to sing, it completely sealed the deal. I was . . . totally captivated, mesmerized." Wendy saw Rahel put her chin in her palm and a happy look in her eyes. "He makes sure I have time to practice my harp every day and I give him time to practice singing. We're committed to each other's musical growth." She looked at her watch. "He should be home soon, actually. He usually comes home around now to watch the baby from four to six while I practice. Some nights he goes back to the yeshiva for night seder." Wendy looked puzzled, so Rahel said, "Evening learning, or to finish up work in his office or make calls overseas."

"What does he do?"

"He's an accountant when he isn't singing and composing. He works for the yeshiva now, so we get this apartment free. A two-bedroom is fine for one, even two, kids, but God willing, we'll outgrow it. We're hoping to move to Bat Ayin one day."

"What's that?"

"A holistic community. Artists and musicians, organic farmers, massage therapists, and aura readers."

"Berkeley meets Israel?"

Rahel laughed. "Exactly. Except it is mostly religious, baal teshuvah to be sure, but the politics are *diametrically* opposed to the views of most Berkeley residents."

"Do you ever think of going back to the States?" Wendy was curious.

"Aaron's from Australia, so we're in the middle here. That's why I suggested it for you and . . ."

"Uri."

"Uri. My light, I've always liked that name. It was one of my choices for Shir-li if she had been a boy." Rahel continued, "In terms of living in America, I can't perform on Shabbat, so there are actually more opportunities for me here than in *hutz la-aretz*, outside Israel. Being a harpist is kind of a unique situation. You aren't needed by an orchestra all the time, but when you're needed, you're crucial. I'm in discussion with the Israel Philharmonic to tour and perform with them as the understudy for a piece in the winter. I don't want to commit because of the new baby, but on the other hand, knowing I have to perform will force me to keep in top shape. I need that push of having a performance."

"Great."

"Not exactly. I don't see how I could do it—touring in Europe and nursing a baby. Aaron is encouraging me just to accept and then figure it out. Maybe one of our mothers could meet me there, or one of our siblings, but if I have to pay for his sister's or mother's ticket from Australia, and her hotel, I wouldn't end up with much in my pocket at the end. I don't see the point, but Aaron says I should have the experience; it will open other doors. I think I'll do it . . ."

The door opened and Aaron entered. Wendy first noticed his eyes, their vivid emerald brightness reminding her of those of a cat shining in the dark. He had curly deep black hair and was wearing an olive green sweater emblazoned with navy and white argyle diamonds, and navy corduroy slacks. Wendy was surprised at how handsome he was. When she saw the muscles on his lower arms under the sweater that was rolled up a bit, she thought he looked as though he could do fifty pushups.

He nodded at Wendy and said, "Hi, I'm Aaron," with an Australian accent, and went over to the seated Rahel, put his hand on her shoulder, and leaned down to kiss her forehead. "How are you feeling today, my darling?" he asked her. Wendy saw that a thin gold band encircled a finger on the hand that rested on Rahel's shoulder. Rahel positioned her hand on top of his, and their gold wedding bands made an awkward accidental clank. Rahel looked up at Aaron and smiled in a different way than Wendy had seen her smile before. Wendy had a pang of jealousy, seeing how clearly in love they were. She wished she knew whether she would ever have that sincere and open love with someone. If so, was that person Uri?

Rahel answered him, "I'm feeling good. I was just talking to Wendy about the beginning of our relationship, listening to each other's music."

Aaron looked at Wendy with his jewel-toned eyes and told her, "When I heard Rahel play, I knew I wanted that in my life. The harp is such a treasured instrument. The psalmist says, '*Oora kvodi*,' awaken my glory—awaken the harp and the lyre. Rahel just awoke something in me," he said, squeezing Rahel's hand, still on her shoulder. She removed her hand from his and said, "Aaron, don't embarrass me."

"Rahel," he said. They all heard faint wailing and then, more articulate, "*Imma, Abba*, out, out, *Imma, Abba*. Shir-li out," from the second bedroom. Without being asked, Aaron went into the room and they heard his parental patter: "Shir-li. Good morning, honey. Do you want out?"

"Out, Shir-li out," she assented.

"Okay, sweetie. Here we go."

Wendy could hear this in the background; she and Rahel continued to talk. Then she heard Aaron sing to his daughter and stopped her own words mid-sentence. It was a nonsense song, syllables strung together. Wendy assumed he had made it up, but she found the sound of his voice astonishing, astounding.

When Aaron finished his ditty, Rahel said to Wendy, "He has an incredible voice, doesn't he?"

"Rahel, it's . . . just beautiful. If that's how he sounds singing a children's song, I can't imagine what he is like when he is really making an effort."

"It's celestial. For our first anniversary, he commissioned a composer to write a duet for us, voice and harp. It is based on Psalm 42, about the yearning of the soul for God and the need to praise him. We've performed it a few times together, for a fundraiser at the yeshiva, on Sukkot. It's an incredible experience to make music with someone you love . . ."

Aaron re-appeared now, carrying Shir-li on his hip. She had his black curly hair, about shoulder length, and was adorably chubby for a toddler, with a round face and perfectly round pinchable cheeks. She was wearing a pink long-sleeved cotton shirt; a pink, gray, and black plaid elastic-waisted skirt; and white tights on her chunky toddler legs.

When she saw her mother she waved and said, "Hi, *Imma*." Rahel waved back and said, "Hi Shir-li."

Aaron's eyes were even more green now, Wendy thought, as they gazed with admiration at the first product of his loins. "I just changed her, and if you get us a snack, *Imma*, we'll be on our way." To Shir-li he said, "Do you want to go for a walk with *Abba*?"

"*Abba* walk, *Abba* walk," she responded with enthusiasm, bobbing her head up and down, up and down, to ascertain that her intent was understood. Rahel got up and went to get a juice box and some cheese sticks from the fridge. As she did this, Wendy chatted with Aaron, "How often do you get to perform? You have quite a voice."

He looked down, embarrassed. "That's kind of you Wendy. Really." He looked back up and added, "I usually do some *hazzanus* on Shabbos, but I also write music. I have a few guys I perform with, special occasions, Purim, you know."

"I hope you don't have to spend too much time doing accounting—your talents clearly lie elsewhere."

"I like to sing, to elicit emotions from people. Music can really invigorate a person's *neshama,* you know, inspire someone to get closer to *Hashem*. It is an important tool."

"I imagine," Wendy said, she hoped calmly, while swooning inwardly.

Rahel reappeared with snacks securely packed into a reusable purple nylon case with pink and white flowers. Shir-li looked ecstatic at the sight of it. "Shir-li flower snacks. Shir-li flower snacks," she said, giggling.

Aaron and Shir-li exited with a stroller, a bottle of a soap for blowing bubbles, and the flower snacks. Rahel took off her beret and said, "I do really need to practice. As I decide whether to do this piece for the Israel Philharmonic I need to see what kind of shape I'm in, how much work I have to do to get to where I need to be."

Wendy asked, "Why are you so ambivalent?"

"Oh," Rahel said, opening the case her harp was in and seating herself in her practice chair, "I don't want to do a poor job. They told me as part of the contract that I am guaranteed a few performances, even as an understudy. I'm not sure I can devote as much time as I need to to the music and care for a young baby. But if I don't take this, they may not ask me to do things again. If I take it now and don't sound so hot, I'll definitely kill my chances with them in the future. Either way, it's a risk."

"You have Aaron and Shir-li and, being *frum*, it's not like music is your whole life now," Wendy said, surprising herself.

"Yes," sighed Rahel, looking more than three years older than Wendy. Wendy suddenly realized that, at twenty-nine, she could be in the same position as Rahel, mother of a toddler or pregnant and deciding about which way to pursue her career.

Rahel continued, "I set out to be a musician. I want to be *frum*; I don't want music to be the only thing in my life, but I am still ambitious." She sighed. "Aaron and I are different in that way; he likes having a profession and a skill and a way to earn a living so that his music is completely *lishmah*, for its own sake. His favorite kind of singing isn't in a concert, facing the audience and looking at them, but *hazzanut*, facing the *aron kodesh*, pouring his private emotions out before *Hashem*. He likes allowing others to listen in, understanding his yearnings and passions, but not seeing his face or him seeing theirs. He prefers knowing his singing is really directed to *Hashem* and not for his own glory. I *like* performing for others, watching them react, seeing what they think." Wendy voyeuristically imagined whether this carried over to their private life, lights on or off, but didn't ask. "I care about the audience. So I probably won't turn it down."

Wendy was not sure what to say next.

Rahel added, "And then you never know. God willing the baby will be healthy and everything will be fine, but if I turned it down because of the baby and then something happened . . . it would be so much worse, knowing I didn't have a baby or a career. So . . . I *will* probably take it."

Wendy asked a final question: "How do you think being religious has affected your career?"

"If I weren't religious and was living in New York, I certainly wouldn't be playing with any Philharmonic. Too much competition. Here, there are only a handful of harpists. There is less work, but also less competition. So I'm doing okay, surprisingly. I definitely wouldn't have kids if I were in the New York music world. I'd have to wait till I was established, or be seen as not serious about my career. In that world, if you have anything at all besides music in your life, you are ranked a dilettante. In Israel, people see having kids as just part of life; you have them and then go on with the other things you want to do."

Wendy did know. "In academia it's the same way. Unless you have tenure, you don't have kids. By then you are so old; it's difficult. I don't know that I want to put everything else in my life on hold until I get tenure. But I *do* want an academic career."

Rahel said, "It's all about choices. Had I known I would have had this great opportunity, I might not have tried to have a second child so soon. But I'd like, God willing, to have a big family, so I don't want to wait so long for more children. Would you like to hear me play?" she said, beginning to stroke her harp, its strings emanating soothing sounds. As she warmed up, she said, almost methodically, "The harp has a long place in Jewish tradition. King David played for King Saul to soothe and calm his tumultuous emotions; the *cohanim* played in the *beit mikdash*. The harp is in the repertoire of the Jewish *neshama*, so I feel somehow, even before I was religious, I was beginning to connect by playing the harp. Maybe that's too mystical . . ."

Wendy wasn't sure whether she should interrupt here or not. "Many baalei teshuvah have this sense that somehow they were always meant to be religious, that it wasn't entirely volitional, but they were being guided, led along. Do you feel that way?"

"I'm bothered by that explanation. I consciously chose to transform my life when I left Juilliard. Saying, *Hashem* was guiding me, it was *hashgacha pratis* and meant to be, removes my agency. *Hashem* doesn't need little drones doing his will. I prefer to say, Here I am, a human being with all my wants, needs, desires, and there are lots of worthwhile ways to live my life. I've *chosen* to be *frum*; I'm willingly embracing it. The rabbis say, in the Gemara, if we walk by a restaurant where something *traif* is cooking and we smell it, we shouldn't say, 'That's *hazer*; its *traif*; it's disgusting.' It's better to say, 'Oh, that has the most wonderful aroma; I'd love to have some, but I can't. The *Ribbono shel Olam*, master of the universe, has forbidden it.'"

Wendy said, "What's the difference. You're still not eating it."

Rahel said emphatically, "Denying the attractions of the outside world, closing yourself and your senses off from everything to make it easier to be observant—it's tunnel vision. Most students at Julliard had it too: nothing else exists except my world view and way of being. Anything else is by definition unattractive; I can't want it. That's the *haredi*, ultra-Orthodox, mentality. The intensity of *haredi* life is easier—always knowing the newspapers you read and stores you go to will be approved—but it isn't for me. I can't have only one thing in my life. I'm much happier now that I have music, and a spouse and child, than I was when I only had music and nothing else. Hey," Rahel said, glancing at her watch, "I would love to play something for you, but then I must have my practice time."

Wendy looked up from her notepad. "I didn't mean to impose on you.

Sorry." She looked at Rahel and said, "I appreciate your honesty. This has been so helpful because of your candor. People aren't usually so open. You know, I hope to be in your position one day: having kids, trying to figure out how ambitious I want to be. It sounds like you are balancing everything."

"Why don't you listen to me play, and then judge how well it's balanced?"

Rahel tuned her harp. Wendy watched Rahel touch the harp tenderly and tilt it towards her. It was taller than her head, and, as Rahel tilted it, Wendy noticed that it was a bit off kilter to make room for her enlarging belly. The sounds began. Rahel brushed her hands across the strings and pressed the pedals with her feet. There was something ancient about the reverberations and their rhythm, each aspect of the way it was done somehow recalling an earlier time. Wendy saw the hands on the strings and thought of demonstrations she'd seen of weaving, the hands going through the strings to create something new, coming out the other side. Wendy thought Rahel's hold on the harp seemed more like an embrace of something alive, something that would draw living sounds out of itself. The sounds were like the sudden rush of water at a creek: plashing, soothing, life-giving.

As she listened she looked around the small apartment more carefully. Wendy noted a discoloration on the wall from some kind of leak, crayon marks and other scuffs from the prior generations of juvenile inhabitants on another part of the wall, linoleum tile coming up in odd spots in the kitchen, and the age of the battered furniture. How was it possible to coax celestial sounds from such earthbound surroundings? As she listened to Rahel's harp, she closed her eyes to focus on the sounds, departing mentally from her physical setting.

That evening, Wendy met Orly for dessert at Don't Pass Me By Tea and Pie. Violating their rule of not going to the same place twice, this was their third or fourth time there. The décor was lots of exposed wood, warm orange- and yellow-toned paint on the walls, rotating displays of art, and a menu that was almost all pie, both savory and sweet, with a constant rotation of varieties. It was a place that felt cozy to hang out at and gab, as they loved to do.

After they each ordered a slice of pie, Wendy started to tell Orly about Uri, and the dinner he made when she got back from Eilat.

"Have you slept together?" Orly asked.

"We've had fun."

"No details?" Orly said, disappointed.

"No divulging. This is . . . it's more personal now. I will say he knows what he's doing." Wendy smiled dreamily and looked into the distance.

Orly said, "He's read medical books. They learn the bodily functions."

Wendy felt annoyed that Orly was so willing to reduce something so transcendent and ethereal as sexual desire and the satisfaction of it to cold facts, a student's ability to absorb and regurgitate the locations of bodily sources of pleasure and stimulation. Wendy said, with a closed-mouth smile and her eyebrows raised in an attempt to look mysterious, "Uri is a skilled clinician."

"What are his faults?" asked Orly, looking for a realistically unhappy angle, the other side of the story she knew must exist.

Wendy sighed. "Religious differences. I can't believe how much I can mess up even when I try."

Orly smiled, her journalist's training letting her know she'd found her lede. "Oh?"

"I bought some beer for him, actually *ale*," she said, exaggerating the British pronunciation, "and put it in the fridge before the seder, hoping he might come back to my apartment. Friday night, we drank the wine you told me to buy, and I asked, when we'd finished the bottle, whether he wanted a beer. He looked at me and said, 'I can't break Pesach. How could you have *hametz* in your house? When I saw it in your fridge, I poured it down the sink.' I looked at him, confused, and he said, 'Beer is *hametz*. You didn't know?' Did you know, Orly?"

She nodded in assent. Wendy continued, "Well I certainly didn't learn that in Hebrew school. How would I know?"

"What happened?" Orly asked, sipping her cappuccino.

"He looked at me queerly; he couldn't believe I didn't know. It was . . . embarrassing. I wasn't *trying* to offer him something not kosher. I even went out of my way not to use *one* light switch all night," Wendy continued.

"He was there all night, I see?" Orly raised her eyebrows.

"Plead the Fifth," Wendy rejoined.

"This thing about the ale—was he angry?"

"He was . . . surprised I was so ignorant. He said, 'I just don't know if I can be with someone who has *hametz* in her house on Pesach.' And *I* don't know if I can be with someone who gets so freaked out about the contents of my fridge.' I don't even like ale—I bought it for him."

Orly looked at her. "So what's next? Does love conquer all? Or is he an arrogant Orthodox jerk?"

"It isn't so simple. I can adapt, and he can accept me. He was upset to find the ale, but was willing to give me the benefit of the doubt. And he told me a story of a friend of his from London who was at Wisdom of the Heart yeshiva and had grown up fairly traditional. The friend went to Wisdom to learn more, and for the co-ed aspect, he *didn't* want a traditional male yeshiva. He started dating a woman who was also studying at Wisdom and trying on different observances. They'd been dating a while, and he usually davened at a *shul* near his home. One morning, Rosh Hodesh, they had a minyan for the whole school and he came and saw her and some other women putting on *tefillin*. He broke up with her that day, just telling her, even though things had been great between them, that he couldn't date a woman who put on *tefillin*. It was like a primal scene for him, crossing some kind of line to see a woman in black leather straps."

"Putting on *tefillin* doesn't seem like a deal-breaking offense."

"The rest of the story is that she married another friend of theirs, and the guy who broke up with her is still single."

"The guy shouldn't have acted so rashly?"

"Well, Uri was upset about the ale, and hoped this wasn't a 'dealbreaker' in terms of our relationship. He thought his friend was totally foolish to say his girlfriend's doing this one thing meant he couldn't date her. Uri thinks we can live with compromises. We may not be entirely satisfied with every aspect of them, but hopefully we can work it out. I don't want to be forced to be religious in a certain way because he is. Whatever I do, I want it to be my decision. He respects that and doesn't want me to feel like anything is being forced on me. I'll respect things that he finds important, even if I don't care about them that much myself."

"You're in a relationship," said Orly, softly chewing more of her lemon meringue pie. "I wouldn't mind ceding autonomy for companionship," she continued.

Was the tartness of the lemon meringue pie was still pleasant in Orly's mouth? Wendy couldn't ask.

"I'm hoping for a relationship of equals," Wendy continued. "Really what I want is a creative partnership, someone who loves me and wants me to go as far as I can in my career, encourages me out of love, you know? I interviewed this woman today. She's a harpist and her husband watches their kid every day so she can practice. It is a little thing, but it shows that as a couple they are both committed to her musical growth. That seems so rare. I don't mind some give and take—you see the movie I want, I'll go to your lecture, but when I look at my sister and brother and their marriages . . . Ugh. My sister was on the board of the *Law Review* at Penn, and now she takes orders from my brother-in-law. Her life is, 'Take my shirts to the cleaners; call the plumber; get your car washed it looks like shit; I hope you get to the gym.' I feel so embarrassed for Lisa when Craig speaks to her like that."

"I think you *like* Uri but don't feel secure enough in your identity as an academic to feel that you can pursue the relationship? You're afraid *his* religion and *his* career would take over?"

Wendy dug into her purse, "How much do I owe you for this therapy session, Dr. Markovsky?"

Orly laughed, and Wendy said, "You're right. I like him but I'm not ready to be with someone if I might have to surrender part of my identity, or my career."

"Has he said, I don't like women who have careers; I must be with someone who will stay home?"

"No, but he's said his mother stayed home and was devoted to him and his siblings. I have a sense that he would assume that a spouse would play a traditional role, or at least have that as an ideal."

"Isn't he supportive of your work? You've told me he asks penetrating questions."

"True. I like a sense of intellectual companionship that I have with him. I like the way Uri thinks and asks questions because he's been trained so differently than I have . . ."

"Being with him is a career move?"

"Not that, just . . . Uri is . . . very different from my *idea* of a person I could fall in love with."

"Why?"

"He grew up religious; he's not American. I've never thought about living somewhere besides America. I've never dated a medical student; I assumed they were all boring grade grubbers, people capable of lots of rote memorization, without much thought beyond that."

"Well," said Orly sanguinely, "you'll just have to see what happens."

"Let's talk about you—how are Sven and Niels?"

"Still filming. I have seen some kooky things, Wendy."

"Kinky?"

"Sven and Niels think they are, but I don't know. The sexiest thing to me is an intimate touch. A guy who knows how and when to give a hug or stroke my hair. That's what I want."

Wendy got out of her seat and went to the other side of the table to give Orly, who stayed seated, a hug. Wordlessly she went back to her seat on the other side of the table.

Facing Orly, she told her, "You'll find it one day, God willing," she surprised herself by saying, and they both chortled.

"You're going to have to come with me to see Sven and Niels—you're spending too much time with your returnees."

They giggled again and ate their pie.

When Wendy returned home that night there was a message on her machine from Connie Budow, the religion department secretary, asking her to get in touch as soon as she could about some administrative details she needed Wendy to take care of. Wendy looked at her watch: 10:00 p.m. Israel time, 3:00 p.m. in New Jersey. The message had been left a few hours ago but Connie should still be in. Her anticipatory worries began—is the whole issue of Shaul and the lawsuit that never came about being opened up again? Did she want to ask about the courses Wendy would teach next year—she hadn't started that at all, a syllabus and reading list for the two first-year seminars that she would need to teach each semester as part of her fellowship? She hadn't done anything with that yet—though she had her ideas and knew she could easily throw a reading list together—because she was hoping now, improbably, to be able to stay. Zakh had told her she should hear before Shavuot, certainly, and he hoped sooner. That must be it: they got some kind of correspondence from the Lady Touro Foundation and wanted to find out what was up with her plans to stay in Israel another year, to be sure she wouldn't try to transfer and get her degree from Hebrew U., not from them? Part of her just wanted to put the call off, avoid it till tomorrow, not wanting to hear bad news if that is what it was. But, she knew, ever the good and obedient girl, if called, she would call back. She decided not to put on her pajamas but to wash up and brush her teeth, evening preparations, and then make the call. She couldn't just do it right away; it was something she had to ease herself into, not a procrastinating but a slow readying for a task, she reassured herself as she walked to the bathroom.

Readied by the firm scrubbing of her face with the apricot exfoliant and the furious flossing of her teeth, Wendy reentered the living room and sat on the couch to dial the series of numbers on the calling card she had from her parents' phone company. The multiple digits she needed to input and the mechanistic feeling that pressing the correct numbers in the correct order gave her calmed her rapidly beating heart. Anyway, she told herself, at least it was Connie she got to talk to, a person who was so kind that, even if it were bad news, she would have a reassuring voice and a nice way of telling her. Connie always brought personal touches to the department office to cheer others—hot apple cider on a warming tray in the fall, lemonade in the summer, candy corn for Halloween—and took time to ask students how it was going and whether she could help them. When former students came back to visit, they sometimes spent more time visiting Connie than their former professors because she was so likable and approachable. The number of Christmas cards she got at the office from former students was astounding.

"Department of Religion." Wendy heard a familiar voice over the phone.

"Is this Connie?"

"It is. Wendy?"

"I'm glad I caught you; it's so hard to coordinate with the time difference."

"How are you, Wendy? Every time I hear something about Israel on the news I say to myself, I hope Wendy is okay. You've had some brushes with danger this year, haven't you?"

Wendy smiled to herself, thinking that she had come a long way and wasn't afraid of things she might have feared in the past. "Israel is an interesting place, the good and the bad. Yes, I was near a bus that exploded, and someone from my Fulbright group was killed. But oddly enough, I can't say that my overall feeling about this year is that it's been tough or unhappy; I don't know why. Not that these things aren't upsetting but . . . I don't know, I just really like being here."

"Stay safe, that's all. So, Wendy, I called just to let you know about the deadlines you need. I'm sure you know that to register as a fifth-year student you have some forms to hand in?"

"Okay, what?"

"Well, the declaration to graduate form, which you'll want for next May, says that you need your literature review approved by your committee before they can sign off for you to have fifth-year status."

"I've been working on it; it's almost done," Wendy lied. She hadn't neglected it—just thought it was better to concentrate on the interviews and collecting and transcribing the material she would need for the rest of the manuscript while in Israel, and knew she could finish by the end of the year or over the summer, no big deal.

Connie could be heard typing in the background, "Oh good, honey. I'm just entering that in my new graduation tracking software. Wait, I'll put you on speaker," she said, the typing growing louder now. "There are only thirty-five or so students in our department at any time, and I think I've done this job pretty decently on my own for almost twenty years, but the university just got this new software for all the departmental administrators. We had to do a three-day training—it's the same technology used by Boeing for when they have multiple teams working on an aircraft. There is a checklist for each team and then the final person, that is me, who makes sure all the parts are where they are supposed to be."

"This sounds complicated. You could have written the program yourself, I'm sure, Connie!" Wendy joked.

"You know I could!" Connie laughed. "I did fine without it, but there are other departments where things fall through the cracks sometimes if you know what I mean—people don't do their jobs right. So instead of finding better people or training the ones they have, they get this software. Hang on a sec, dear. Okay, are you the *Religion Ethics and Politics* track or *Religion in the Americas*?"

"*Religion in the Americas*," Wendy responded.

"That's right, of course you are, working with Cliff. Now, are you ready?" She typed more. "The deadline for those forms is May 20, the last day of finals. Can you mail a copy or should we try e-mail? Big files sometimes create problems though."

"May 20? Are you serious? That's in, like, two weeks. I . . . can I get an extension?"

Wendy wasn't sure if she should say that she was thinking of staying in Israel next year if she got the Lady Touro, so maybe they could just list her as on leave before she re-registered the next fall. But she didn't know if it would upset them to have her stay, and there was no sense bringing it up unless she actually got the fellowship.

Connie typed. "Let's see, I don't think so; it looks like that is a pretty firm deadline if you want to walk in May 1998."

"Oh, well, yes, I mean I want to go on the job market in the fall, but . . ." *Oh shit, how can I do this?* Wendy was thinking, *and I really need a polished chapter if I'm going on the market. And some more articles. I haven't gone to any conferences and schmoozed any senior scholars in the field; this is hopeless unless I get this Lady Touro. I am not far enough along at all right now. Shit, shit, shit.*

"Hold on, Wendy. You know the chair can sometimes override these things, particularly given that you've been abroad. I can ask, but you know we've just brought this new chair from Vanderbilt, and he doesn't really know the ins and outs of everything here yet."

"But if May 20 is the last day of finals, there is still a grading period. Can't I have till the end of the grading period?"

"I wish it were up to me, Wendy. I'm just the messenger. Do me a favor; just do what you can on it and I'll see if I can get you an extension, alright?"

"Thanks for keeping this on track, Connie. I do appreciate it, even if I'm feeling stressed out right this minute."

"Oh, Wendy, you'll do fine. You told me yourself you were almost done. Don't be a perfectionist; remember: better something turned in and not perfect than something perfect that misses the deadline. Believe me, I am telling the truth here!"

"You always do, Connie; you always do. Thanks for my chain. I will be glued to my desk and computer for the next two weeks."

"But you'll be on track to graduate."

"Yes, I will; that I will."

Wendy hung up in a panic. *What am I going to do? I will lose my fellowship if I can't register for next year. Even if I stayed in Israel with the Lady Touro, I probably wouldn't be eligible if I'm not an officially registered student at Princeton. Cliff Conrad did keep e-mailing me that he wanted the lit review, that the other students my year—Matt, Veronique, Granby, and Asuka—had all turned their stuff in. Only me.*

Stay calm, she repeated to herself. *It will work itself out. I will finish or I will get an extension—something. I've come this far. I can do this. But how can I get it done?*

Wendy paced around, opened her fridge, didn't find much to her liking there, thought about whether any food store would be open now—only restaurants, and she felt way too guilty about not having gotten done what she was long ago supposed to have done to allow her to treat herself like that. No—no food now either. Then what? A walk to clear her head? Maybe, but would it help?

I need to talk to someone, a person who can help me think this through. Not Orly; she will just be a clucking Jewish mother: "*I told you so; I knew you needed to get that done; what have you been waiting for? Of course it was going to come back to bite you.*" No, someone sympathetic. Todd? He could be, but he too, much as he was able to joke about some things, was absolutely serious about his commitment to his career and deadlines. He wouldn't understand that she hadn't been able to finish the chapter because she wanted so much to impress her professors, wanted it to be so good.

Uri. She would call him. Part of her was nervous to let him see her at less than her best, anxious and flipped-out, whether this would drive him away and make him want to disappear from her life. But part of her wanted to see whether he'd try to help her through this . . . salvage mission. That is what she needed—someone to come in, do search and rescue, see whether this situation can be helped, paper finished in a monumentally short time?

Wendy hoped he was home because his roommate never seemed to deliver messages. "Hullo?" The reassurance of his jovial British accent reverberated over the phone lines.

"Oh Uri, oh my God, I'm so glad you're home. I need help." She didn't know how to put it except to state the obvious.

"What's wrong? What can I do?'

"First, listen; then we'll figure out if you can help."

"Easy peasy; I always fancy our chats."

"Well, you'll think I'm a total idiot after this, which I completely am."

"Stop it; you're not some kind of gormless whinger. I am fully sure that you're not an idiot, rest assured."

Wendy took a deep breath and started telling him about Connie's call, trying to keep her tears from loosening themselves from her eyes and coming out, and trying to keep the sound of the impending tears out of her voice.

"Okay, so I am in my fourth year of graduate school. In order to advance to my fifth year, I need to hand in my literature review."

"What's the problem?"

"The problem is that I've known all year that I had to do it, and now, the secretary just told me, if I don't hand it in by May 20, I won't be able to register as a fifth-year student, I'll forfeit my scholarship, I'll have to withdraw, and I'll have wasted these last four years." The sobs broke through now.

"Wendy, would you rather I came over? I'm off tomorrow. I can get a cab and come right now. I hate to hear you so upset."

"Really Uri? You'd do that. Yes, okay, come."

While she waited for him, she decided to print out what she had so far and assess it. Well, the books had all been read—that was good; nothing to do in that department. There were sort of groupings of books, not exactly as she wanted; the organization was out of whack. She needed some kind of organizing principle, some way to get things on the page in a sensible way. It would come; it had to. There were definitely books that, though she'd read them and taken notes on them—her note files on her computer were extensive—still needed more explication, a selection from them to show what they did and how they related to her work. Oh, it broke her head just thinking about it, so many decisions to be made . . .

The bell rang and she went downstairs to let Uri in. His physical presence, his enfolding hug, was cheering already. She felt so much better by the time they had returned to her apartment from the main door.

"Shall I make you a spot of tea?" he asked.

She smiled, wanting to be taken care of. "Please."

He went to her kitchen and plugged in her electric hot water heater. As the temperature of the water rose to a boil, he found two mugs in her cabinet and put a few different teas, lemon ginger, green Moroccan mint tea, and chamomile, on a plate. He opened her cabinets and found an unopened bag of veggie crisps that she had forgotten was even there in the recesses of the shelf, and opened the fridge and freezer to see what was available. He found some brownies that she and Orly had made before Pesach and wedged in the back of the freezer, also forgotten.

Thus equipped with tea and food, he gently moved Wendy's laptop over from her desk to the dining room table and cleared a space for the two of them to sit at the table.

As she sipped, he stoked her hair gently, as one would do with a child, and let her breathe gently. "So you've been faffing around about writing this chapter, eh? What will it take to get it done?"

She looked at him, "It's so nice of you to come help me. This whole thing is my own fault, and only my own; that's what makes me such an idiot. I knew it had to be done and I kept finding excuses not to. I had interviews, wanted to do things that could only be done here . . ."

"We all make mistakes; it's part of life," he said. He kissed her forehead. "I don't care for you any less because you shived your responsibilities a bit. Our flaws showcase our humanity. Let's see what you can do to solve this."

"How can you help? It's not like you know anything about Religion in the Americas." She named her departmental track in a mocking tone of self-important jest while putting up quotation marks with her fingers when she intoned its name.

"True enough; but I know about writing and papers and organization. Do you want me to read it? Or read your outline and see how the piece conforms to your outline? I'm happy to do that."

"Really? You would? That would help a lot. You know in Princeton, we always shared work among each other, but even though the Fulbright group is supposed to be that, it really hasn't been because our fields are all so different. I learn from everyone's presentations—don't get me wrong—but it just doesn't help me to share my work with someone doing modernist poetry in Hebrew or images of Enoch in the Dead Sea Scrolls and apocryphal literature."

"So let me see it."

"Now?"

"Why not now?"

"I don't know; its late; we should go to sleep."

"How's this? Why don't you describe your main points to me? I will write them down and we'll see if we can work up an outline. Then I'll read it over in the morning."

She smiled at him and took his hand in her own. "I've always wanted a boyfriend who would encourage me, who didn't see what I do as taking away from him and time with him, but as central to me and who I am and want to be."

Uri passed her a piece of frozen brownie, and she opened her mouth. He placed the first edge of it in her mouth, and stroked her cheek lightly with his hand, as though it were a delicate object, fragile and precious. "You know what will help you now? We've got to make you fall in love with the craft of writing. If you immerse yourself in the beauty of language and are excited about having command of your self-expression, you'll be more motivated to write. We'll read poetry together and take pleasure in the words."

She started becoming emotional, but knew she had to finish what she needed to tell him. "Have you seen the movie *Babette's Feast*?"

He nodded no, "Don't think so. What is it?'

"It's based on a story by Isak Dinesen, a Danish writer. The movie came out in the late eighties and it was just here in the fall at this *Food on Film* festival at the Cinematheque. Anyway, it is about Babette, a woman who is a great cook, exiled from her native France because of a regime change. She arrives penniless in Jutland, in the middle of nowhere in Denmark, and works as a servant for two sisters, daughters of the founder of a religious sect. One day, Babette wins the French lottery and asks the sisters if she can use some of her earnings to make a special meal in honor of the hundredth date of the birth of their father. She goes to the main city to make preparations and order supplies. The week of the feast, wheelbarrows of supplies begin to roll up to the house, and the sisters are shocked, particularly when a live tortoise arrives."

Uri laughed, appreciative.

"It was funny. Anyway, the sisters tell their father's followers that whatever kind of witches' Sabbath the papist Babette is preparing they will eat, but not enjoy or taste the things of the senses, preserving themselves for higher things. The day of the banquet, the followers all arrive, including the nephew of one of them who has dined at the finest restaurants of Paris and is by coincidence visiting his aged aunt. He can't believe what he is eating because it tastes like the food cooked by the female chef at the Café Anglais, Paris's most famed restaurant. Each course astounds him more than the last. Finally at the end it is revealed that the simple servant Babette is that great chef. She tells her mistresses that she has spent all the money from her lottery ticket. They can't understand—why would she do such a thing? She explains that she is a great artist and that as a great artist she did this both for her diners, to make her diners perfectly happy, and for herself, because a great artist needs to do her utmost. And then at the end, when she and one of the sisters realize that Babette will never cook a meal like this again, and her mistress, a talented singer, will never have a large audience, her mistress tells her, "In Paradise you will be the great artist that God meant you to be."

Wendy looked at Uri. "Not that I'm a great artist, but I'd like to be a great scholar. I want to do my utmost always. I'm not like Babette and her mistress, who are able to forego the rewards of having a large audience and the right tools to work with. I'm not going to wait for heaven; I want my life here, both as a scholar and a person. I want to have a career and a life, and I just"—here she did start crying—"I never thought I'd find someone like you, that you even existed, so caring, and considerate, wanting to help me"—she looked up at him and smiled through her tears—"and cute, of course, that goes without saying. I just . . . I'm so blessed that you are in my life, Uri." Wendy was fully bawling now, and he took a napkin from the napkin holder on the table to dry her tears, and then, when he used that up, took his shirt-tails and awkwardly pulled at them to rub her tears away. She smiled, pleased with his gesture.

"So I'll go over what I want to say and you write it down. Then in the morning you can read what I have and help me with an outline." She looked at him and smiled, tears beginning to dry. "I don't think it will really be so hard once I have the outline. I can get it done if I just keep myself focused and write it one book at a time, one section, one idea. It's not that it is difficult; it just requires making decisions and putting things in place. I'm making the whole process harder than it needs to be because I want it to be so good." She breathed out. "You brought your *tefillin*?"

"Have toothbrush and *tefillin*, will travel," he replied gravely.

"Okay, I have to wash my face get these tears off. Let me wash up first, then you."

"Ladies first."

"And Uri, I'm glad you came tonight, but understand, I just want to hold you and sleep next to you, nothing else."

"Perfect."

A few days later, Wendy was sitting in Atarah's Tuesday evening class at Wisdom of the Heart. When she came in, she spotted Judy Spicehandler sitting alone and went to sit next to her. It was a nice feeling for Wendy to have a connection to someone in the class. Odd that she should know someone Judy's age when most of the people here were closer to her own. They were mostly Wisdom alumni who'd made *aliyah*, and in between earning a living and raising kids, wanted to keep up with their studies. They would be good material for her second stage of interviewees—Rahel's cohort, she realized. But they weren't all strictly Orthodox. Should that matter? How to take in all the gradations of religiosity? Wendy jotted some notes down.

Judy hadn't looked up from her knitting when Wendy sat down. Now she looked over to her side. "Wendy, hello. Nice to see you. I'm sorry you weren't able to join us last Shabbos."

She wanted to be sure to praise Uri to Judy. Wendy said, "Uri was so sweet. He brought all this food for Shabbat dinner, his own pots, and a tablecloth. The gorgeous flowers were from your florist. Thanks for recommending her."

"They were nice? Delphine *is* the best florist in Yerushalayim, you know."

"Absolutely. Just stunning."

Atarah placed her hand gently over the microphone and called out, "Testing, testing. Okay?"

The class responded, "Yes," with their usual enthusiasm. Wendy remembered hearing Atarah say that she refused to teach classes which were compulsory because she wanted the students to attend of their own volition.

Atarah began, "Our *parsha* this week is *Emor*. I want to begin with a linguistic peculiarity in the enumeration of the holidays. Leviticus 23:15 reads, '*usefartem lachem*,' and you should count for yourselves. I want to explore the idea of why this is a commandment directed to the individual. Here, the counting is in the plural, but in Deuteronomy it is singular. We know that in terms of *halacha*, counting is an individual obligation. If one of us were to cross the international date line and go to Australia during this period of the *omer*, one would need to complete the *sheva shabbatot temimot*, seven full weeks, the latter part of the verse emphasizes. If a person misses a day by crossing the dateline, he or she would individually still count the full forty-nine days and celebrate the holiday according to his or her individual experience of time, even if it is not the same as that of the rest of the community."

Wendy raised her hand, and Atarah called on her by name. "Maybe I am missing something, but if holidays are communal celebrations, why would an individual celebrate at a different time? It doesn't make sense."

Atarah responded, "That is the paradox. Our holidays are called '*mikra'ei kodesh*,' holy times of gathering, but without the individual performing the commandment we can't have those gathering times. The significance of the individual is overwhelming in our tradition—one is never compelled to give up one's life for another, which is why having children is only a mitzvah for men, not women. Birth is risky, and no one can be compelled who doesn't wish to take the risk. Or, there is the case of an accidental murderer who goes to a city of refuge to keep the family of the deceased from taking vengeance. Even if the murderer is needed by all of Israel, like the case of King David's chief of staff, Yoav ben Zeruyah, the individual shouldn't give up his life for the collective, according to Maimonides. The final word on this is the Mishna in Sanhedrin, which teaches that every person is obliged to say, 'The world was created for my sake.' We need strong individuals to have a community."

Judy leaned over to Wendy and whispered, "I'm so glad you asked. I didn't fully understand it either." She gave Wendy a big smile, which Wendy returned.

After the class, Wendy went up to Atarah's podium at the front of the room and waited behind the other students, a cluster of ten or so, who also wanted to speak with their teacher. When it was Wendy's turn, she said, "Thank you for answering my question."

"Glad you were satisfied with my answer; it's a recurrent problem. How was your Pesach? I heard you and Uri were at the Spicehandlers.'"

Wendy blushed at the mention of Uri's name. "The Spicehandlers were such gracious hosts and it was a wonderful seder. Do you know their painting *In(Query)* by Oren Laniado?" Atarah nodded yes, and Wendy continued, "It set the tone for the whole seder. The artist was there and his partner, and we discussed the power of questioning and truth embodiers, satyagrahi, in a society . . ." Wendy paused in her description when she saw that another student was trying to get Atarah's attention so she stopped speaking.

Seeing the three other students in line behind Wendy, Atarah said, "Why don't you give me a call if you want to have a longer conversation."

Wendy added, "I'll look forward to that. Before I go, I wanted to share some good news I got today. I got a Lady Touro fellowship for next year. So I'll be continuing with your classes."

Atarah gave her a beatific smile and said kindly, "There are other reasons to be in Jerusalem besides my classes! Fabulous news for you, Wendy. Mazal

tov!" She added, "Call me so we can speak more," before turning to the next
student waiting to ask a question.

Wendy decided it was her turn to plan a date to celebrate the milestone of
handing in her literature review, with Uri's help. She didn't want to do something ordinary, like a movie or dinner, but something different, that Uri
would appreciate, that would build their relationship. A date that was the
equivalent of his Uri tour of the Old City. Strolling away from the bus stop in
the center of town, where she was switching buses from one that originated
at the university library to one that could return her to Mishael Street, she
saw a poster in English and Hebrew for a free outdoor dance performance.
The municipality of Jerusalem was sponsoring an outdoor dance performance at the Sultan's Pool on Lag B'Omer, the thirty-third day in the period
of seven weeks between Passover and Shavuot, a time of counting to heighten
the anticipation of the Torah's being given. The first thirty-three days of the
omer period, beginning from the second day of Passover, are for mourning;
then on the thirty-third day weddings and public celebrations like live musical performances were permitted by Jewish law. The municipality always
sponsored some kind of large public event to compete with the bonfires and
barbecues held by citizens in every open space. When she called to ask about
it that night, Uri was free and amenable to the plan.

The evening of the performance, Wendy packed up a picnic supper and
found a blanket in the apartment that looked already grungy enough to be
suitable for sitting on. She had procured hummus and pita, some bourekas,
a small assortment of olives and cheeses, potato chips, an Israeli salad, a carrot salad, and some cookies from the extravagantly expensive take-out store
on Rahel Emeinu Street near her house.

She put all the provisions in her backpack, along with paper goods and
water, and walked over to the Cinematheque near the Sultan's Pool. Uri
would meet her here and they were to walk down to the performance area
together.

"I hope you're not expecting anything as good as Uri's Tour of Jerusalem," she said greeting him with a hug. "I'm no professional tour guide. I was
actually nervous about planning this date since you set such a high standard." She looked at his blue eyes, wiry hair, and beautiful smile with those
great white teeth, the detail she'd noticed about him first, even in costume. *I*

really like him; actually, I'm totally smitten, she admitted to herself. Just getting a glimpse of him walking down the hill to see her had lifted her spirit.

He took her hand and gave it a squeeze. "Nothing wrong with amateurs. I won't hold it against *you* if the performance is no good."

"I packed a nice picnic, so no matter what, we'll eat well."

They walked down to the performance area and spread out their blanket, making a claim on their space. Wendy set out the food. Uri clinked their ales together and said, "To picnics," and took a good swig. Putting a fresh boureka in his mouth, he added, chewing, "I like the uncivilized aspect of a picnic."

Wendy looked at him, puzzled.

He continued, "Food is one of our great civilizing elements. To take away the table, and the manners, and the fussiness, just to eat, on a blanket, what could be better? It's so *basic.*"

"That's what I like about dance, its essentialness. No external props, just the unvarnished human body, contorted like a sculptural form."

"I didn't know you were such an aficionado."

"I'm fascinated with how bodies tell stories. The way a man holds himself, the way a woman walks, convey meanings beyond language. It's amazing to see how different cultures use dance to access some aspect of . . . the beyond, whether that means divinity or something else. Or just to create a spectacle."

There was movement on the stage, as though the performance was going to begin momentarily, but the audience did not pay attention; they were eating, talking, and shelling sunflower seeds and pistachio nuts. They were enjoying being outside on a nice day at the beginning of summer, when the weather remained entirely pleasant, before the searing heat of the summer. A spotlight was on the open stage, without a curtain, and the dancers trooped out and arrayed themselves across the stage. They were all wearing sleeveless leotards in jewel tones with footless tights that covered the entire length of their legs and emphasized the musculature of their physiques. The dancers were clad in sapphire blue, topaz yellow, emerald green, ruby deep maroon, coral orange; the featured dancer in the center wore an opalescent shimmering garment with many hues reflected in it. Each leotard had an arrestingly strong hue; together they were a fiery combination. Wendy wondered how these disparate colors would create a harmonic collage of motion.

The music began and the once-boisterous audience was now hushed. The dancers circled around each other and finally paired off, each male holding a female. The women appeared to soar around the stage in the arms of their partners. Wendy wasn't sure why she was so drawn to the stage. It could have been that the dancers' trained bodies were so lithe and graceful; even in movements that were intentionally jerky, the bodies created their own kind of poetry. She was moved by the beauty of using the body to create art, the most ordinary of vessels elevated so stunningly, with such careful training.

After a few minutes of intermission, a man appeared on stage alone, his hair closely cropped but most of his gleaming pate bald. He was dressed in well-pressed khakis and a white button-down shirt, wearing loafers. He looked like he just stepped from a high-end clothing ad featuring dancers who leapt and whirled in their chinos. He began to address the crowd, in Hebrew, so Uri simultaneously translated.

"*Erev tov, shalom.* I am chief choreographer Adir Mekarker. We are so pleased to be able to produce for you tonight a work of my troupe, the David Troupe. Thank you to the municipality of Jerusalem for sponsoring. There are a number of other sponsors I won't mention now, but they are listed in your program and we extend our utmost thanks to them.

"Our troupe is based in Tel Aviv in the winter and spring, and New York in the summer and fall, though we perform throughout the States and Europe. We will be leaving Israel in a few days; this is our last performance of the season here.

"Our troupe is named for King David. Not David the warrior, fighting Goliath with a slingshot, or David the harpist playing for Shaul, or David the psalmist. We represent the David who went dancing before the ark of God, naked, cavorting and leaping in a holy whirl with all his might. There is a paradoxical modesty in David's movements—he stood before the ark dancing alone before his God, though witnessed by throngs.

"The next piece we will be performing is called *Forty-Two Journeys*. It alludes to the forty-two stopping points the book of Numbers mentions for the children of Israel as they wandered in the desert. This time between Pesach and Shavuot contains forty-nine days. Absenting the Sabbaths, that includes forty-two weekdays. The forty-two spots on the trek from Egypt to Israel are also correlated to stops in the life of the individual. So, we have in our dance both the journeys of the communal and the individual.

"Though you can see I am not a *dati*, the choreographer said patting his bare head, "I look at this dance as a cultural exploration of the ways we move and transform ourselves, from the questioning of Pesach and the unknown of the departure, to the shimmering possibility of glimpses of revelation on Shavuot. In a secular key we can call this revelation 'knowledge,' 'understanding,' or even 'wisdom' perhaps.

"Dance is a way of getting access to this wisdom because movement betrays truths that the more conscious functions of our bodies, such as language, cannot. I present to you *Forty-Two Journeys*."

He left the stage, and though there was no curtain, the dark made it impossible to see anything on stage. Then, the lights shone on forty-two crouching bodies. They were all in leotards of a deep carnelian red. Were they were blood vessels? Wendy wasn't certain of the symbolism. She watched as they went through the stages of a human life: immobile, rolling, sitting up, crawling, walking, strutting in front of others like cocky teenagers, pairing off, giving birth, raising children, and aging, moving less gracefully and agilely. Finally, they collapsed and died, going back to their original positions. What was fascinating to watch was how each individual dancer moved differently and looked different. Yet, they comprised a collective, acting in concert, with a visual harmony. Within the large picture, each dancer had to act as an individual to get the look of the group to work.

Watching the stage, Wendy thought back to her first Shabbat in Jerusalem, at *Shir Tzion* hearing that beautiful male voice soaring above the other voices singing the Kabbalat Shabbat prayers. She had wondered whether, rather than being absorbed into another, it would be possible to have a love that was a partnership, a commingling of two voices that would maintain separate identities but together create a new, united sound. This dance seemed the visual equivalent of that. Wendy had been afraid of being incorporated by something outside herself, swallowed up, her individuality destroyed. Watching the forty-two dancers, she saw that the group wouldn't exist without the individual bodies and motions.

It was dark by this time. Wendy and Uri had moved closer together, foodstuffs gathered up and stowed to the side of the blanket. Uri had his arm around Wendy; she leaned comfortably against his frame. When the piece was over and it was wholly dark, Wendy continued to lean on him; they comingled in the dusk, creating their own harmony in the crowd.

NINETEEN
Teiku

Teiku. 1. An acronym for *Tishbi Yetaretz Kushiot uba'ayot*, meaning Elijah the Tishbite will come and resolve all difficulties and problems. 2. In a game, of sport or chess, or in negotiations—checkmate, a situation in which there is not one victor.
—*Even Shoshan Hebrew-Hebrew Dictionary*, Volume 4, 1449

It isn't easy to live always under a question mark. But who says that the essential question has an answer? The essence of man is to be a question, and the essence of the question is to be without answer.
—ELIE WIESEL, *The Town beyond the Wall*

The sun shone in on the mass of egg whites clustered in the bowl, bearing a resemblance to foamy soapsuds. The egg whites were ignoring the repeated ministrations of Wendy and her hand-held eggbeater. They remained as liquid as they were at the beginning, entirely resistant to the efforts she was making to get air into them and cause them to froth. She was in her kitchen on Mishael Street this May morning, trying to make chocolate mousse for the lunch for friends she and Uri were hosting on Shavuot tomorrow. Wendy liked to think of the festive atmosphere to come, with friends, food, song. Her apartment hadn't been the site of a communal meal since the ill-fated attempt with Noah.

Even if this takes an impossibly long time, I do know these eggs will eventually become a solid mass. They will *thicken if I just keep at it*, she said to herself, switching the hands performing the holding and the beating position, so each hand would be a bit less taxed and sore from repetitive motion. Yet, manual soreness was welcome, a tangible mark of her exertions. The pain was physical proof that something had been accomplished. She wished she could have the same tangible proof of accomplishment with the abstract work of her dissertation.

As her hands continued to turn the whipping implement, she thought of the fantasies many graduate students and professors harbored about the satisfactions of manual labor, the beauty of accomplishing things with toil and sweat, of seeing the object one is constructing take shape beneath one's eyes. Connie Budow, the religion department secretary at Princeton, had a number of carved wooden objects on her desk that had been made by a faculty member, his artistic escape from the life of the mind.

But escape could go too far and one could become entrenched, immured, wholly enmeshed in the world of the physical, without possibility of escape out of it into a realm above, where one could reshape things of the tangible world and transform them. And that was what had Wendy worried. Not counting the time she'd spent shopping for ingredients, it had taken an hour already to produce this mousse, melting the chocolate and whipping the eggs and cream and combining them. She still had to make a main dish; the other guests were supposed to bring side dishes and salads. And then cleaning up the apartment for guests, setting the table, making sure there was a clean tablecloth, and borrowing chairs from her landlady, Amalia—all of it took time. Time that was spent away from her work. The worst part was that Uri hadn't asked if she wanted to host this Shavuot meal when everyone returned from the *Kotel* in the morning; he had just invited people and informed Wendy. The presumption galled her—would this continue to be his mode of operation, taking for granted that her time was his own to infringe upon as he saw fit? If so, that would be it for the relationship, Wendy would make clear to him. She hoped it was a one-time oversight, maybe resulting from a discussion with one of his friends—Your girlfriend's place is closer to the *Kotel*, so why don't we go there to eat?—and Uri's agreement with the plan.

On the other hand, Wendy recalled the words of her heroine, Jane Eyre, that she was going to be "solemnizing" the "culinary rites" in such a way that "words can convey but an inadequate notion to the uninitiated like you." Was she solemnizing culinary rites in her Jerusalem kitchen? On the other hand, Wendy remembered Professor Van Leeuwen's feminist analysis of the text for Contemporary Civilization: Jane gave up the possibility of being an artist to care for her blinded spouse. The novel, Bronte's last, embodied the tension Wendy was feeling about love versus career. *I'm not going to think about that part of it, since I am enjoying the scent of melted chocolate lingering in the air, and the taste of the mousse in my mouth,* she said licking her fingers one more time. There was something to domestic and culinary rites, Wendy didn't doubt it, but she wanted Uri to share jointly in their pleasures, and to be sure that they didn't detract too much from the intellectual work that was her chief goal right now.

The fascinating thing to Wendy about making this mousse was transformation. To take a puddle of egg whites, an off-color blob, not yellow, not white, just gelatinous, and craft them into a lovely foam which combined with chocolate, cream, coffee, and a bit of liqueur for flavor gave her a certain amount of power. Making mousse, she could transform reality. In her dissertation too, she could take a mass of stories, quotes, lives, and, along with some good flavorings, put them together in a new way, create for them a new substance and existence as they are reformulated and restructured into a coherent written document. It was a kind of sorcery, infusing the ordinary with meaning. It might not have the heft of a craft like wood carving, but when done properly, it too had solidity.

The phone rang as she was tearing the plastic wrap to make a cover for the bowl of finished mousse she was placing in the refrigerator.

"Hi. It's Noah."

"Oh." *Why was he calling her?* She hadn't heard from him since she bumped into him at the Hebrew University library before Passover.

"How are you? I heard you've been going to Atarah Hideckel's classes, and I wanted to hear about them. I might go to hear her at the *tikkun* at Wisdom."

Wendy slammed the refrigerator door shut and walked over to the sink to begin the cleanup process. "What can I say? She's incredible. It's . . . she can lay a finger on my soul when she speaks. I've been inspired by teachers, had crushes on them, been in awe of their brilliance, but . . . it's not just intellect; there's more with Atarah's teaching. You *should* come. Definitely."

"I'm glad you've found a teacher. It's important to have a guide," Noah said, a faint trace of wistfulness in his quiet voice.

Wendy brightened. "I haven't changed, you know. I'm still me. One of the things I like most about her is that she doesn't offer spoonfed pablum to make things easier to digest. She discusses difficult things. She makes me want to know as much as she does, to learn more."

"Just to learn? What about practice?"

"Turn the tables; give me a survey," she said as she continued rinsing out the other bowls she had used, carefully holding the phone cord above the water with her elbow. Noah laughed.

"Sure," he assented.

"You'll never guess this! I'm dating someone who grew up modern Orthodox. He didn't know how clueless I was when we met."

Noah was quiet and then said, "Where'd you meet him?"

"Atarah's house, on Purim. He's with her husband, a psychiatry resident."

"Wow."

"That's how I feel about him too. You? Love life?"

He sighed. "Still not sure where my passions lie. I'm waiting to see who's next."

"Will you let yourself be guided by passion or are you still afraid of it?"

"Not so afraid."

"Do you consider yourself gay?"

"Some questions are *teiku*."

"Asian food? Do you want that with *teiku* sauce?"

"No," he said with laughter. "I'm glad you still don't take anything too seriously. It's an acronym for *tishbi yitaretz kushiot ubayaiyot*. It's a way to say the issue can't be resolved; it stays on the table till Elijah shows."

"So basically, the question is important but we can't answer it now." Wendy continued, "I like the idea of not having to resolve questions. For me, I want to be part of Jewish history. I want to do things out of tradition and peoplehood, in a sort of Reconstructionist way, I think, from what Dara tells me. I'm going to be listed in the Jerusalem phone book next year."

"Oh?"

"I got a Lady Touro fellowship. I'll be here another year. What's next for you?"

"I'm not sure. If I want to continue in grad school, I should go back. But it's probably not for me."

"You can say *teiku* on that too!"

"You're lucky, Wendy; you're so certain."

"No, Noah, *you're* lucky, actually. You are willing to wait to receive a glimmer of something, passion or understanding."

"Since I was with Sam, and he said to me, 'I've had the kisses of God's mouth,' I've been puzzled. Is that life, some kind of summation, which may appear truthful, but actually be entirely false?"

"Why is it false? Can't humans be agents of God?"

"It's hard to think of myself as an instrument of the divine. Sam was deluded if he thought my kisses were those of God's mouth. I'm glad if it brought him comfort. Maybe knowing that I forgave him for lying to me about the inscription he wrote in the book, he felt he had received some kind of divine favor."

"Don't use this *teiku* as an excuse to do nothing," she said, beginning to dry the rinsed bowls with a towel, phone precariously perched on her ear.

"I want some kind of intense passion that tells me, 'It must be this way,' a kind of inevitability because I am surrendering to this incredible idea or great love. But if I go through my life without ever feeling it, then what?"

Wendy decided to try to provoke Noah to some kind of response, so asked him the purposefully provocative question, "What if Sam was the one love of your life and now you've lost your chance?"

"I can't know. Is Uri the love of yours?"

"We haven't been together long enough." She thought, *Is Noah Lazevsky really the person I want to discuss this with? Hardly.* "Is passion only something that happens all at once or does it build up over time? Shavuot is a culmination of leaving Egypt and preparing to receive the Torah; it doesn't just happen in one burst of light. That's Atarah."

But she still didn't have the answer to her question about Uri. She did like him, but was still mad at how this Shavuot lunch had been handled. He invited people to her place without letting her know how many and what she needed to do. He basically wasn't doing any of the work since he was spending the week taking extra call, covering hours for others so he could be off for Shavuot. He just assumed she'd be able to do all the shopping, cooking, food preparation, cleanup without seeing whether she'd wanted hosting duties in the first place. He presumed it would be fine with her since the people being invited were those they owed invitations to. The whole thing felt unfairly thrust upon her, and she felt like he was being an insensitive jerk, not being considerate of her time, assuming he could make any demands, whether she had time to do this or not. It was a hugely, hugely chauvinist thing. But she wouldn't give Noah the satisfaction of obtaining details about Uri's less than immensely perfect nature . . .

Noah ended, "Sounds like I should go hear her. *Hag Sameach*, see you there, then."

"If I see you. Get there early if you want a seat. It will be crowded."

A few hours later Wendy found herself in a gymnasium, much like the one where she spent her first Shabbat in Jerusalem. Inside it was dank and gloomy with a bit of a mildew smell; now at the end of May it was beginning to be humid. Small windows—not much outside light, though it would be dark in an hour. Her friend Dara Glasser had been so excited by this radical innovation, a service that would be strictly Orthodox yet as egalitarian as legally possible. She told Wendy that it would be a good compromise for her and Uri. Uri had gone to the Israeli Reform movement's Hallel Yah *shul* with her, but didn't feel totally comfortable there. Wendy had gone to synagogues with *mehitzas,* but hated the feeling of being a second-class citizen, in the back of the bus. The many justifications she had heard over the year for separation of the sexes during prayer continued to sound hollow and contrived, and she didn't like being in the segregated atmosphere.

Wisdom of the Heart was enabling this new prayer group by paying for the space; they hadn't wanted to offer their own building for fear that it would be too controversial. This gym was not in the gym of a school, like *Shir Tzion*, but the gym of a community center, built with private money unconnected to the many state-sponsored venues for religious expression. Wendy didn't get the point. Women lead some parts of the prayers, not others? Why not go to a Reform or Conservative *shul* where it was completely egalitarian? She had come tonight because Dara asked her to, not out of willingness.

She entered the space and walked to the left, the women's section, picked up a prayer book from a pile on the table in the back, and found a seat. As Wendy joined the congregation in singing, she was struck by the beauty of the woman's voice leading it. The leader's voice was an expressive contralto, thrilling. Not in a sexual way as she felt hearing the voice of Aaron, the husband of the woman she'd interviewed in the Old City, or the man leading services her first Friday night in Jerusalem at *Shir Tzion*. Hearing this woman's voice, she felt glad this woman could sing for an audience, let out the private emotions, yet not in an exhibitionistic way because her face was unseen, towards the ark. The congregation was giving the woman recognition as a prayer leader, someone they wanted to represent their community before the Kaddosh Baruch Hu, the Holy Blessed One.

The woman leading the service, wearing a long all-white tallis and a white cotton beret, sang out, her voice soaring above the rest of the congregation, joyously, triumphantly. Listening, Wendy realized that, like at the Spicehandler seder, she felt like a full person here, the different parts of her equally nourished. At this service, women were treated as equals, and all the participants were praying seriously and intently, unlike at Hallel Yah, which, Wendy reluctantly conceded, did fit Noah's critique. He pegged it as a *"davening* club," people coming together, liking to sing, but with no real seriousness about their individual prayers. Even if Wendy herself wasn't as serious as those around her tonight, she felt a groundedness and commitment in the atmosphere that she liked.

After the woman concluded, there was a *dvar Torah* by Jonas Brill. He was the son of Elias Brill, the man whose chair at Princeton was the one Wendy's advisor, Cliff Conrad, occupied. The younger Brill had come to Israel after the Six-Day War and was a psychologist at Bar Ilan University, well known for his studies of the role of memory in prior events.

Professor Brill's *dvar Torah* was in English, fortunately for Wendy. He spoke of Freud's idea of *Nachträglichkeit*, memory traces being subjected from time to time to a re-arrangement in accordance with fresh circumstances—a retranscription. He discussed how British psychoanalyst Adam Phillips used the idea, and connected it to Shavuot. He spoke of Phillips's formulation that "memory is a way of inventing the past" to describe the process of earning Torah, earning the right to stand at Sinai and receive it. He quoted Geertz and Levi-Strauss, Rashi and Ramban, Durkheim and Levinas. He spoke of the need for complexity, to understand and incorporate a variety of points of view as the most important index of future happiness, and then applied this to the rabbinic notion of the seventy faces of the Torah. All of Wendy's knowledge base, from her academic studies to her classes with Atarah, prepared her for this talk. She had heard Brill's name all year and couldn't believe that now she was finally getting to hear him speak. She liked the idea of the necessity of constant rearrangement, and how continually studying and understanding Torah can help with this.

Wendy wasn't sitting with anyone she knew, though she could see Dara a few rows ahead and felt certain that must be Judy Spicehandler and her daughter Emanuella, with elaborate feathered hats, to her left. And there, a few rows up on the right, was the wife of Avner Zakh, her Fulbright adviser. Odd, how people from different parts of her life could be here in this one room. Suddenly, Wendy felt an overflow of emotions, a joy she hadn't expected. *I am happy*, she realized. Tears began to flow out of her eyes unbidden, as she sat and wept quietly, allowing the sounds of the women's singing to cascade around her.

After the service, she walked over to the men's side to find Uri as they'd planned, and was surprised to see Jacob Lamdan. Lamdan didn't notice her, but she went over to greet him.

She stood in front of him and said, "Professor Lamdan? Hi, Wendy Goldberg You were on my plane on the way over."

His usually sharp blue eyes seemed cloudy as though he couldn't place her, but then he said, "Cliff's student, Wendy? *Hag sameach*. How has your year been? I'm back for the summer already."

"My year has been . . . complicated. I've really mulled over all the things you said to me on the plane."

He smiled cryptically. "Yes?"

"The power of text study, the pulsing of the light. I felt that in Dr. Brill's *dvar Torah* tonight. I've been going to Atarah Hideckel's classes."

"You're fortunate to study with her. Do you remember the Gemara we learnt on the plane?"

"There were two rabbis, one who helped the other become religious, by telling him, 'Use your strength for Torah.'"

"Have you?"

"Have I what?"

"Used your strength for Torah?"

"I don't know. I feel strengthened by this service. There was no need to park my academic self at the door for spiritual nourishment. Everything seems to be coming together. The different parts of my life, different people I've met this year . . ." Then she said, confessionally, "I started weeping."

"Me too," Lamdan almost whispered to her.

"I'm glad it wasn't just me."

"In Jerusalem, it is impossible to remain detached. New York . . . it's all about intellectual distance. I've never wept in *shul* in New York, not even . . ." He paused, stopped in mid sentence. He composed himself and continued, "Being in Jerusalem, hearing a woman's voice, singing . . . I think of my sister, *Hashem yinakem dama*, may *Hashem* avenge her death. I wish Hitler hadn't taken her, that she had been given a chance to see this."

Uri walked up and gave Wendy a Shabbat Shalom kiss on the cheek. "Professor Lamdan, this is my boyfriend, Uri Shalem. I met him in the course of my research." They looked at each other and smiled. "He is finishing his psychiatry residency with Daniel Hideckel, Atarah's husband." She turned to Uri and said, "This is Jacob Lamdan, the Talmud person in the religion department at Princeton. We were on the same plane on the way over here."

Uri put out his hand. "*Hag sameach, naim meod*, nice to meet you" in his clipped British accent. "You are working with my friend Jay Epstein, then?" he said.

"My favorite student. How do you know Jay?"

"We were together at Yeshivat Shalvei Olam here, before university."

"Very nice. Rav Amittai, the *rosh yeshiva*, is a good friend of mine. I'll be with him next Shabbat."

Uri smiled. "A special man, Rav Amittai."

"The name he chose for himself, *Amittai*, truthful, does him justice."

Uri added, "He gave a *sicha* to us, on Yom Hashoah, about his name. He said that the Gemara teaches that worship of God is built on truth. *Hakarat hatov*, acknowledgment of God's goodness, isn't possible for someone who has just lost an entire world as the survivors did. But even in times of *hester panim*, of God's face being hidden, we need to continue the relationship with God, still speaking truth. I'd never seen him look so exerted; articulating those words seemed to physically strain him."

Lamdan looked saddened also. "*Rosh devarkha emet*, at the head of your words is truth, Amittai's motto. He wanted me to take the name Amittai also, that there should be many of us teaching truth. We both changed our names in the DP camp after the war. I knew *Lamdan*, learner, was a name I could live up to. I wasn't sure about Amittai."

Lamdan's son, a teacher at Wisdom of the Heart, walked over and greeted the group. "*Abba*, you've already got a crowd of students. They always find you!"

"Akiva, this young woman is from my department at Princeton. She's been here for the year writing her dissertation on American baalei teshuvah. Her friend knows my student, Jay Epstein. You remember him?"

"Yes, yes, nice to meet you. We need to get going, *Abba*. There is a group meal over at Wisdom." He directed his comments to Wendy and Uri. "If you care to join us, there is plenty of food."

Wendy spoke up, "We're going too, so we can walk together."

After the dinner, Atarah Hideckel's Shavuot *shiur* was in the same building where Wisdom of the Heart held most of its classes. It was an old stone building, on a lot by itself, in Katamon, a neighborhood adjacent to Wendy's German Colony apartment. It was evident from the moment Wendy and Uri entered the room where Atarah would be speaking that it wasn't large enough for the crowd. There were chairs set up in rows facing a table where Atarah would sit at the front of the space. Wendy and Uri snagged some of the last chairs in back, and the people filing in now were sitting on the floor in the front between the first row of chairs and the teacher's table. The windows were open to let air in and Wendy could smell a late May flower. Lilacs would be in bloom in New York now; the Middle Eastern equivalent of lilacs, a flower with a lovely perfume, was wafting through the room with each breeze from the window. Now people were sitting in the aisles, the only open space. Wendy looked over to the window on her left and noticed faces. People were standing outside the room, looking in the windows, so they would be able to hear Atarah speak. She looked around at the crowd, mostly people her age and Uri's age, about half the women wearing berets or scarves on their heads and half not. Almost all of the men were wearing kipot. No, there was a bare-headed one, she saw, and there another. She saw a woman in pants to her left. She looked at Uri, seated next to her, and took his hand and squeezed it gently. He smiled at her, and Atarah entered the room.

As soon as she entered, those in the back stood up, and then those in front of them, each row rising as she passed, like plants shooting up from the ground, as though Atarah was sprinkling seeds and seeing them grow instantly. When Atarah seated herself at the table, all those who had sprouted up seated themselves.

Atarah turned her face to see each person in the packed room. Wendy remembered her speaking about the importance of personal transmission in teaching, how the sense that one is not alone can bring joy, and this can only be communicated by seeing the face of another. Atarah did not know there were people outside, faces pressed through the window to hear.

Atarah started her class, "'The Book of Ruth: My Book of Transformations' is my title tonight.

"I want to open with a quote by George Herbert, the seventeenth-century English devotional poet. He wrote, 'When one is asked a question, he must discover what he is.' I'm going to speak on characters in *Tanach* who are asked questions. In response to the questions, the characters have moments of recognition and transform themselves. I want to compare these characters to one unique individual who has confidence in her identity, her ability to transform both herself and those around her, and who has become quite significant for our holiday and our understanding of Torah.

"I'll start with the most obvious example. She is a woman who has the capacity to act, to change her situation, but needs to be asked." Atarah paused here and spoke each word slowly and deliberately, "Who knows if you have arrived at this position to do something about the situation of the Jewish people?"

After she stopped speaking, Atarah smiled with closed mouth like the Mona Lisa, signaling mystery in her question. She arched her eyebrows and looked around the room packed with students. She waited for a response, adding, "It isn't so late yet; surely you are all still awake?" and continued to wait in silence.

"Queen Esther. She needs to be asked to do something and then she finally goes to the king, but not before?" came from the middle of the room.

Atarah gave a bright smile, showing her teeth this time, and responded, "Esther is queen before and queen after she is asked the question 'who knows' by Mordechai. Nothing in her status has changed. Yet, after his question, she has a new capacity to act. She perceives now that she has agency. She can petition the king and ask for her life and the life of her people. When she does this, nothing has actually changed in her status or her abilities, only her understanding that she is capable of taking action. If you notice, the text calls her 'Queen Esther' only after she begins to act."

Atarah flashed her ready smile at the group. "Who else in *Tanach* is asked 'who are you?' I'll give a hint, an impersonator, someone who is acting like someone else."

A voice from the back called out, "Yakov answered his father's question 'who are you' by saying, 'I am Esau, your firstborn.'"

"*Yafeh*, nice. Our ancestor Jacob, in response to his father's question, changes who he is. No longer will he be a simple man who dwells in tents. Now Jacob embraces the complexity of being that his brother Esau, a hunter and man of the field, embodies. Jacob becomes a different person, living his life in a more complicated way, a new self underneath the artifice of being his brother. Unlike Esther, something does seem to change in his status when he decides to incorporate this new identity into who he was before. One more, another impersonator, who costumes herself and in the process changes her future . . ."

A female voice, sitting near the front of the room called, "Tamar."

Wendy whispered to Uri, "How do these people know so much?"

He responded, barely audible, "They've been learning all year." Wendy shrugged in response; she couldn't imagine being able to guess answers to these types of questions so quickly.

Atarah's grin was satisfied. "Yes, thank you for that quick response. Tamar in Genesis 38 is a character who creates a plot for herself. No one needs to ask her who she is or tell her what to do. She goes to the place called *petach eynai'im*, the opening of the eyes, a metaphor clearly. Once there, she costumes herself so her father-in-law will assume she is a prostitute. Tamar has this moment of understanding that she must take matters into her own hands if she is to have any satisfaction from this family. In the process, she educates Judah, teaching him what it means to make a pledge and to take responsibility."

Another female voice from the middle of the room spoke out. "Would Yehuda have become a leader if Tamar hadn't educated him?"

Atarah again looked around the room, acknowledging the eager faces of the students she saw. She continued, "What is special about Tamar is both her demand for recognition, and that it is acknowledged. She is able to create a situation in which Judah must acknowledge her. More than that, he confesses Tamar is righteous; the child is his, and he should have given her to his son Shelah, whose name sounds like the possessive 'hers' in Hebrew, though that is probably not its etymological origin. What I've always found most impressive about the character of Tamar is the 'breakthrough' nature of her story. She is able to assess her situation, realize that there is a way out of it, and act cleverly, creating a breakthrough in her life. Isn't that something we all yearn for, that breakthrough? I'm using this terminology straight from the Torah, right? Tamar's oldest son is called 'Peretz' or 'breakthrough.'"

Atarah continued, speaking slowly now, to be clearly understood. "There is another character, also in Genesis, who has her eyes opened. She is on the verge of death, in a seemingly hopeless situation, and suddenly, *Hashem* gives her a new sight . . ." Atarah was quiet, expectant, in awaiting a response.

The room remained hushed until a male voice in one of the rows near the front called out, "Hagar? An Egyptian handmaid?"

Atarah said, smiling, "Isn't that the point of these stories? *Hashem* can communicate with anyone, when and how *Hashem* wants. *Hashem* opened Hagar's eyes. Tamar may be the ancestress of King David and the messianic line, and Hagar a handmaid, but Hagar has a special contact with *Hashem* and even acts as a theologian, naming *Hashem* in a way no other characters do. The name Hagar gives to God is 'El Roi,' the God of seeing. Isn't that one of the things we all seek from *Hashem*, and others as well—to be seen, to be recognized for who and what we really are, not who or what we may seem externally?"

Wendy turned to the man she hoped she was in love with next to her and saw his rapt attention to Atarah's words. She'd have to explain to him that she needed to, as Atarah said, be seen for who she really was, a serious future professor, not a caterer who can be hired at will for a particular time slot. And who was Uri? A doctor who loved poetry and using narrative to heal? She would have to work on seeing him as he too wanted to be seen; he *had* been overworked this week, but it still wasn't an entirely valid excuse for inviting people over without consulting her.

Wendy's gaze went back to Atarah, who looked around the room at the faces of the students and continued, "If we look at the characters we've discussed so far, we see that they are all, at their core, vastly different from what they appear to be outwardly. Esther appears to be a gorgeous Persian queen, passive and perfectly assimilated. In fact she is a tremendously loyal Jew, willing to act and risk her life for the sake of her people. Jacob appears to be a simple man, following his mother's commands, yet he is a hunter below his surface, tracking down two wives and two concubines, getting the flock of

Laban to yield its best sheep to his possession. Tamar appears to be passive about her fate, when in fact she is a woman of tremendous resourcefulness and initiative, who will not allow herself to remain a widow in her father's house forever. Hagar appears to be an Egyptian handmaid; however she is an exceptionally gifted seer, who communicates with *Hashem* on the highest of levels."

Atarah paused and took a sip of water from the glass in front of her, saying a blessing over it quietly first. She did her visual sweep of the faces in the room and continued, "Now, our final character who is asked a question and gave a response that changes her life."

"Naomi?" a female voice called.

Atarah tilted her head to one side and said, "Naomi is asked, 'Is this Naomi,' and responded, 'Don't call me pleasant; call me bitter.' I don't see that as life changing. Still awake? Anyone?"

A male voice called out from the far back, "Ruth and Boaz, on the threshing floor."

"Okay!" said Atarah, firmly pleased. "Boaz says to Ruth, '*mi at*,' who are you, the same words Isaac asked Jacob. Ruth appears to be a Moabite on the surface. The Moabites are a people, the Bible tells us, who are ungenerous, inhospitable, and fight unfairly. They are objects of suspicion. Yet, Ruth is not like her ancestors. She is a loyal foreign woman, in the model of Tamar, Rahab of Jericho, and Yael the Kenite who act in unexpected ways to show loyalty to the Jewish people. Ruth the Moabite is not truly a Moabite at all. In fact, she is an ideal Jew, a person whose sense of what is appropriate goes beyond what any kind of legal framework would suggest is binding.

"There is a peculiarity about the book, in its very name for Ruth. Ruth is the protagonist in many senses, but the *megillah* is really the story of Naomi. It begins with Naomi's loss of her biological family and ends with the proclamation, 'A son is born to Naomi.' Ruth's declaration to Naomi that she will cleave to her, and go where she goes, seems to be an affirmation that she is ready to form a family with her, to remain with her. Naomi doesn't completely accept Ruth's definition of family, but stops arguing with her. It is the moment Naomi orchestrates between Ruth and Boaz on the threshing floor that creates the chance for a legally plausible family. That begins when Boaz asks Ruth who she is.

"The quotation I began our *shiur* with is apt here: 'When one is asked a question, he must discover what he is.'

"Ruth doesn't need that question, as so many characters do, to know who she is. Ruth knows all along she is a Jew and belongs to this family. It is Boaz who must be reminded of what he is. Ruth's answer defines not just herself, but Boaz. She tells him, 'I am Ruth your handmaid.' Straightforward enough, but the second part of her answer is not related to the question. She says, 'Spread your robe over your handmaid; you are a redeemer.' She gives *him* an identity as 'redeemer,' which he isn't quite sure about. She is the only character that I know of in *Tanach* to give an identity to another when asked about her own.

"Ruth, like Tamar, has a particular kind of self-confidence, the ability not only to know who she is, but what she needs from people around her. And, unique to Ruth, her ability to intuit the needs of others and help them with unbounded kindness makes her unlike any other character. Her relationship to Naomi seems, from her declaration, full of passion and substance, what one would want a lover to declare extravagantly: 'Where you go, I will go.' When Boaz speaks to her, it is all about legal matters: who is a nearer relative, what kind of ceremony needs to be done. He seems devoid of emotion. Ruth is completely emotion—she performs kindnesses and creates relationships that are entirely beyond legal bounds and is praised for that.

"What I find most fascinating about Ruth is her lack of a need for an external question. Her internal compass is sufficient. She does what is right in her own eyes, without being told. And that is really what getting the Torah is for, isn't it?" Here she paused and did a visual scan of the faces in the room. "So that we act with *hesed* continually and unceasingly, like Ruth. That is one of the strongest purposes of the *mitzvot,* to create a possibility for us to act with unbounded kindness."

"That, friends, is why we need Torah: to transform ourselves from cruel Moabites to kind Jews. Ruth the Moabite doesn't need any prodding; it is the Jews around her who can't see the necessity for their own recognitions and transformations. Naomi must learn to recognize the worth of Ruth, that Ruth is better for her than seven sons. Boaz is a redeemer, yet he can't decipher his role until Ruth propels him to fulfill it.

"I will end this *shiur* with a story and final bit of poetry. There were two men, Rabbi Yohanan and Reish Lakish. One day Rabbi Yohanan was bathing in the Jordan and a man leapt in after him. He told the man, 'Use your strength for Torah, *hailech la'oraita.'* The man replied, 'Your beauty should be for women.' Rabbi Yohanan daringly said, 'Do teshuvah and you can marry my sister who is more beautiful than I am.'

"A beautiful and simple fable—the man, Reish Lakish, repents from his position at the head of a band of thieves and gains wisdom and the hand of a beautiful woman. The two greatest conundrums of life, work and love, in Freud's formulation, have been solved. Case closed. But the Talmudic story, like life itself, is more complex than that.

"One day in the house of study, there was a discussion about when a weapon is complete. Rabbi Yohanan asked Reish Lakish whether he had an answer. In asking this, he reminded Reish Lakish of his origins, saying, 'A thief knows his weapons.' This man, who elicited the transformation of another, who saw in him the next chapter, the possibilities in his book of transformations, was now insulting him publicly.

"Reish Lakish became sick and died. After his death Rabbi Yohanan could not be comforted, couldn't find a partner who would find all of the twenty-four refutations that could sharpen a problem when he wanted to examine an issue from all sides. Actually, Rabbi Yohanan lost his ability to learn Torah, to use *his* weapon of choice in confronting his world. Finally, the rabbis prayed for a merciful and quick end to Rabbi Yohanan's life. He too died.

"I tell this story as a *pharmakon*, a supplement, to remind us of the dangers of connection. Rabbi Yohanan saw a unique strength in Reish Lakish and asked him to channel it wisely. Yet, he himself severed that connection, insulting his friend, cutting them both off from the world. In the argument about when a weapon is finished, perhaps the question really was: is there ever an endpoint, a moment at which one is utterly certain that something is entirely complete?

"There may be pain and difficulty in making those connections—yet it must be done. Some need a question—'who are you?' or an instruction 'your strength should be for Torah' to enable them to change and transform. Others have the confidence and awareness to tap into the *kesher*, connection, with the Holy One of Place and the decoder of dreams, the begetter of kindnesses and restorer of souls.

"In his poem 'The Layers,' the American poet Stanley Kunitz wrote,

> Live in the layers
> Not in the litter.
> Though I lack the art

To decipher it
No doubt the next chapter
In my book of transformations
Is already written
I am not done with my changes.

We are *amailim ba'Torah*, laborers in Torah. It is not simple or easy, but necessary. May we all be privileged on this holiday to find the art to decipher the next chapter in our book of transformations and to be aware that we are never done with our changes. *Hag sameach.*"

Wendy had never been in a room where such silence reigned. It was as though the breath of each individual in it, and those at the windows outside, was tied to the words of Atarah, and they wouldn't let themselves exhale until she had finished. No one wanted to break the power of her words with the banality of their own. There was a hush for a few moments, as people absorbed Atarah's words, let them penetrate their souls. The room remained silent as people began to collect themselves and rose to leave, stunned by the power of her message.

Wendy and Uri's plan for the evening was to go back to her apartment after the midnight class to rest as much as they could before rising at 4:00 a.m. to walk to the Western Wall for morning prayers at the first possible dawn hour. Praying at the dawn hour was a Shavuot custom instituted to make up for the sluggishness of the Jewish people, who remained slumbering instead of waiting up eagerly for Moses to return with the tablets of Revelation on that first Shavuot. However, someone in Wendy's group had written an article about how the availability of coffee in the sixteenth century popularized the custom of all-night study sessions; no records of all-night Jewish learning exist before widespread consumption of caffeine. Wendy loved those quirky scholarly pieces of information that enabled one to see religious customs not as given from on high, but part of an evolution, a response to specific realities of the physical world.

When they got back to Mishael Street, Uri, who had logged long hours this week so he could be off tonight, went straight to sleep on the couch in Wendy's living room, not bothering to make his way to a bed.

Wendy wanted to sleep and knew she should, so she'd be alert to walk to the Wall and then to host the friends coming over for a Shavuot meal later. But she was restless.

She opened her journal, somewhat neglected in the last few busy weeks of interviewing the older returnees in the cohort of Rahel the harpist, going on dates with Uri, writing the essays for the Lady Touro fellowship, finally finishing the literature review by the deadline to register, and attending Atarah's classes. She started writing, jotting notes about the things that Brill had said; she would see if she could e-mail him and get that piece on the idea of *Nachträglichkeit*. She thought about Atarah's teachings and how she still hadn't resolved in her mind that Naomi was more heroine than Ruth. Ruth is the one who takes the risks and makes the biggest changes, but on arrival in Bethlehem she does Naomi's bidding, becomes more of a surrogate womb and less of a speaking person; it seemed unfair that her child was taken from her by Naomi, deserving of a son or not. Desultory thoughts were attempting to organize themselves on the page. These were not what she was after.

Mid-sentence, it came to her. She stopped writing in her journal.

Her first sentence—she had it. She had already violated a strict observance of the holiday of Shavuot by writing in her journal, yet turning on the computer seemed like more of a violation. No matter, she had to do this.

Wendy went to her desk by the window, turned on her computer, and went to the file with the same title as her dissertation, "It Was *Basherte*": Narrative and Self-Identity in the Lives of Newly Religious American Jews." She opened a blank document and began to type.

"Do you know where you're going?" A simple question can lead to unexpected places. For the population of newly religious American Jews in Jerusalem, a journey to a new life, a new sense of self and connection to other people and to God, begins with a question like this. It may be from a recruiter for a yeshiva, or a friend who is already religious. However, the impact of a question, and its importance, can never be understated. A question can open new possibilities and disturb past realities.

In this dissertation, I have asked questions of this population, at different phases of their return. The responses have been varied,

from the predictable to the completely shocking. The outcome of
the questioning, as well, has been multifaceted.

She looked over at Uri's sleeping form, stretched out behind her on her
couch. She smiled at him and walked over to stretch a blanket out on top of
him. She kissed his forehead. A gentle look came over his sleeping face in
response to her tenderness.

She returned to her computer, "This population is both similar to and
different from other American populations of the newly religious." Here, she
would need some footnotes; she could hold off on those till she'd had more
sleep.

She looked at the clock at the bottom of the computer, and saw that it was
almost four. She pressed save, backed the file up to a disk, ejected it, and
triumphantly switched the machine off. She'd done it. She had started writing the actual dissertation.

She stood up and turned around to see the still-sleeping Uri. She had
tidied up her apartment in readiness for the holiday, so that was done. The
table was cleared, with a cloth on it already, but needed to be set. Wendy got
out dishes; she had counted: there was service for eight, just enough for the
guests even if it was all mismatched. She remembered, as she put the dishes
out as noiselessly as possible so as not to wake Uri, the first Shabbat she was
in Israel at Shani and Asher's apartment, setting the table, like a little kid put
to a task. Now, she was setting the table in her own apartment, for guests
including Shani, Asher, and Amalia. She got out the glasses and wine glasses
as well, for one of Uri's friends was a wine aficionado and had brought a few
bottles over earlier in the week. She placed the ones that didn't need to be
chilled on the table.

Most of the food had been dropped off earlier so Wendy would be able
to heat it up to serve. There were blintzes, and *pashtida*, a leafy salad, a
roasted vegetable tray, a sweet couscous made with yogurt and butter for the
dairy eating holiday, and Wendy's chocolate mousse, sure to be a triumph at
dessert time. But the most striking element on the Shavuot table, apart from
the flowers provided by Atelier Delphine flower shop, was the challah Uri
had made.

He had come here to do it, since his kitchen space was limited and he
didn't want it to get "bungled" in transit. He spent an evening making the

dough and letting it rise, punching it down, and then, when it had risen again, shaping it very particularly and baking it. It was a beautiful creation, all golden curves and arcs, an elaborately woven shape that was braided then pulled together in a round. The lustrous crust glazed with honey and egg wash and drizzled with toasted sesame seeds. It had at its pinnacle a key. Wendy had watched Uri in awe, as he took the strips of dough and shaped them gracefully. She recalled happily that it was much more pleasant to watch him at work than it had been to watch Donny since they were together in an actual relationship, not a meaningless flirtation. Thinking back on the early part of her year, she understood that things really had worked out, finally—difficulties and setbacks, all in the past. In fact, when Orly asked her recently what she thought the biggest obstacle to finishing her dissertation would be, Wendy had responded, "I don't think there will be any more, since I've already had so many."

Wendy found the cutting board for the challah and brought it to the table. She gently lifted Uri's creation, and as she hefted the large loaf to the dining area she gazed at the key on top. He had told her that the recipe was something he learned from a friend in yeshiva, whose mother was Moroc-can, when he spent Shavuot with them. Jews from her community in Morocco, influenced by the medieval mystic Rabbi Isaac Luria, the *AR"I ha'kadosh*, placed a key-shaped piece of dough at the top of their loaves on Shavuot, he explained, because they were hoping with this meal to use the key to access the gates of heaven.

As she deposited the loaf in its place, readied to be cut and consumed, she wondered: Would what happened at this table effect those partaking like the meal in *Babette's Feast* that transformed aging contentious sectarians into young vital people, leaving the feast to gambol in the snow outside like young lambs, able to acknowledge truths about their lives, both in love and in deceit, that had gone unspoken for decades?

What had the meals she'd had this year, and other experiences, allowed her to access?

A fuller sense of myself. I am an intellectual, a future college professor, I hope, but I'm also someone who wants to enjoy the sensual delights given to us as humans. I've learned to cook a bit, and to value it. I need to be able to nourish myself, not cut myself off from sources of sustenance. I'm not afraid of sexuality like Noah, that my appetites will lead me somewhere forbidden;

I've found the right person to be with for now, I hope for longer, but won't get too concerned about the future before it happens.

Enjoy what you have now, she told herself, pleased with the survey of the table. The cloth napkins placed in the glasses looked white and crisp, the mismatched plates had their own charm—*Jerusalem flea market twee*, it might be called—and the flowers were a harmony of colors and shapes in a low bowl so they wouldn't interfere with conversation. The setting of violets was boldly dark against the green leaves, with another flower, hollyhock maybe, ringing the outside of the arrangement. The hollyhocks had yet to unfurl, but Delphine at the flower shop assured her that their resplendence would be evident in the morning, that first daylight was when they displayed their full coloration at its best. Gazing at the flowers, Wendy thought that she too was like one of them: all her colors had been there before but spooled up in a way, not yet unreeled and present in the world. The pink and white colors could be seen curled up in the bud, not yet ready to unleash their beauty on the table. Wendy too, had found this year her chance to give of her utmost, like Babette, in so many realms. In her relationship with Uri, who had single-handedly salvaged her life by getting her to finish that literature review, and making sure she was able to complete her task without being paralyzed by perfectionism. They were here on earth to do things as well as they could, even in the small details of cooking the intricate multistep recipes.

Judy Spicehandler's table it was not, but it was hers and Uri's, hovering in expectation of serving its purpose and giving them a meal that would transport them to a spiritual realm through their corporeal senses and appetites. Despite his crazy hours this week, and not asking her first about having people for this Shavuot meal, he had stepped up and made the time to produce this incredible-smelling loaf, to which he'd even added, off-recipe, a pinch of cardamom, because he knew it was her favorite Middle Eastern spice. She leaned into the bread and inhaled happily.

It was time to wake Uri up, which she did, with a gentle kiss on the cheek and a rub on his back, "Come, Uri, let us go now."

Wendy and Uri walked through Jerusalem streets that were beginning to grow light with day. They held hands, and suddenly Uri asked, "We're leaving Mishael Street. Wendy, who is asking?"

"Someone with a sense of possibility. I don't know if I'll ever have a decisive moment, an exact lens through which I can filter everything else. I don't know when I'll finish my dissertation, or the chapters in my own book of transformations. But I won't let uncertainty stop me from beginning."

Glossary

Abba. Father. Hebrew.

alef-lamed-vov-lamed. The letters of the Hebrew alphabet that spell the name Elul. Elul is the last month of the Jewish year, the month before Rosh Hashanah.

aliyah. To go up. To go up to the land of Israel. Also, being called to the Torah is going up. Hebrew.

aron kodesh. Holy ark. Place where Torah is kept in a modern synagogue. Hebrew.

Baruch Hashem. Blessed be the name. A pious response to a question, meant to demonstrate that the name of God is fluent in one's mouth. Hebrew.

basherte. Fated, meant to be. It can be said of a romantic partner that he or she is basherte; or an event can be basherte. Hebrew.

beit Knesset. "House of assembly." Word for synagogue in Hebrew.

beit midrash. Study hall. Hebrew.

beit mikdash. Temple. There were two Temples built and destroyed, the second in 70 C.E. Hebrew.

benched licht. Literally, "blessed light." Yiddish term for lighting candles at the onset of the Sabbath.

b'ezrat Hashem. With the help of God. Hebrew.

bitachon. Confidence. Hebrew.

bracha. Blessing. Hebrew and Yiddish.

b'tzelem Elohim. In the image of God, quoted from Genesis 1:27. Hebrew.

cohanim. Priestly class, forbidden from coming into contact with a dead body. Descendants of the biblical Aaron. Hebrew.

dati. Religious. Hebrew.

davening. Praying. Yiddish.

der aybishter. The one above. Name for God in Yiddish.

Dossim. Religious people. Singular form is Dos—a term used by secular Israelis to mock the religious, with the soft "s" pronunciation instead of the "t" that is standard in modern Hebrew.

dvar Torah. Word of Torah. Hebrew.

Elul. Month before the new year of Rosh Hashanah in the Jewish calendar. Hebrew.

emunah. Faith. Hebrew.

Eretz Yisrael. The land of Israel. Hebrew.

farbrengen. Gathering. Yiddish.

fort-da. "Gone" and "there." German. Also a section of an essay by Freud based on watching his grandson play. http://www.encyclopedia.com/doc/1G2-3435300522.html

frum. Religious. Yiddish.

galus. Exile. Yiddish.

grogger. Noisemaker used to drown out the name of the evil Haman during the liturgical reading of the biblical book of Esther on the holiday of Purim. Yiddish.

GR"A. An initialism for HaGaon Rabbi Eliyahu (1720–1797), a rabbi renowned for his erudition. He placed special stress on the Jerusalem Talmud and taught Rabbi Chaim of Volozhin, who went on to found a yeshiva and spread his methods.

Hag Sameach. Happy holiday. Greeting used on all holidays. Hebrew.

halacha. Literally, "the path." Jewish law. Hebrew.

hametz. Anything made with leaven, hence not kosher for Passover. Literally, "fermented."

Hamotzi. Literally, "Who Brings Forth." The prayer over bread. Hebrew.

Hashem. Literally, "the name." A name for God. Hebrew.

Hashem yinakem damam(hy"d). God will avenge their blood, meaning humans have no right or ability to take revenge on other humans. Term used for victims of terror attacks. The phrase's implication is that justice is left only to God not human interference. Hebrew.

hashgacha pratis. Divine providence. The idea that God is looking out and guiding each individual. Hebrew.

(the) Hassam Soifer. Moses Schreiber (1762–1839), Hungarian rabbi, opposed to modernity, best known for statement that "chadash asur min haTorah" (the new is forbidden from the Torah).

hassana. Wedding. Yiddish.

havayah. Experience. Hebrew.

hazzanut. Cantorial music. A "hazzan" is a cantor. Hebrew.

hesed. Loving-kindness. The ability to act with hesed is of the highest value in Judaism. Hebrew.

hutz la'aretz. Outside of Israel. Used by those in Israel to indicate that they are inside.

Imma. Mother. Hebrew.

karpas. Green vegetable. A stage of the seder ritual, which is made up of fifteen stages. Hebrew.

kashrus. The Ashkenazic version of kashrut.

kashrut. Dietary laws prescribed by the Torah. Hebrew.

Kiddush. Sanctification. The prayer said over wine or grape juice on Friday night. Hebrew.

Kindertransport. Trains taking Jewish children out of Nazi occupied areas to freedom from 1938 to the start of World War II. Almost 10,000 children were saved in this way. German. http://www.kindertransport.org/

Kotel. Literally, "wall." Used to refer to the Western Wall. Hebrew.

lashon hara. Literally, "evil language." Gossipy speech. Hebrew.

Lecha Dodi. Literally, "Come Bride." A medieval encomium to the Sabbath Bride, sung in stanzas, the high point of the Friday night service to welcome the Sabbath. Hebrew.

Levi. The class of those who assist the priests; the tribe descended from Levi in the Bible. Hebrew.

limmud. Learning. "Limmud Torah" means learning Torah.

ma'aras ayin. Appearance of impropriety. Hebrew.

matzav. Situation. Hebrew.

mehitza. Partition, used to separate men and women in Orthodox services. Hebrew.

metoraf li'gamrei. Completely insane. Hebrew.

Moshiach. The Messiah. For Jews, the appearance of this being happens at the end of days. Hebrew.

motek. Sweetie. Modern Hebrew.

motzei Shabbes. Literally, "going out of Sabbath," meaning Saturday night. A way of continuing to orient the week around Sabbath even when it is over. Hebrew.

Naim meod. Nice to meet you. Hebrew.

neshama. Soul. Hebrew.

Niggun. Tune. A wordless tune, used to set a mood. Yiddish and Hebrew.

Nofe Tzedek. Literally, "views of righteousness." Fictional Jerusalem neighborhood.

omer. Literally, "sheaf." Counting of the omer is counting of the forty-nine days between Passover and Shavuot. Hebrew.

peyos. "Corners." Locks of hair that religious men let grow on the sides of their faces. Hebrew.

pigua. "Attack." As in terrorist attack. Hebrew.

protectzia. Literally, "protection." The idea that if you know someone who knows someone, they will assist you. Hebrew.

narishkeit. Nonsense. Yiddish.

Nu. "So?" A way to urge someone to do something: "Nu, tell me already." Yiddish.

parsha. Portion, as in the Torah portion of the week. Hebrew.

Poolhan. Ritual. Modern Hebrew.

rosh (plural: roshei) yeshiva. The title for heads of the yeshiva. Hebrew.

shaharit. Morning prayers. Root is from shahar, meaning dawn in Hebrew. Religious Jews say these prayers each morning.

shalem. Whole. Hebrew.

Shalom Aleichem. Literally, "Peace to them." Song to begin the Friday night meal. Hebrew.

sheitel. Wig. Yiddish.

shidduch. Match. A shidduch date is one where the couple has been matched by others. Hebrew.

Shir Tzion. Literally, "song of Zion." Name for fictional synagogue.

shiur. Class. Hebrew.

shomer negia. Literally, "guarding of touch." The practice of unmarried men and women not touching each other. Hebrew.

shomer Shabbat. Keeping the Sabbath, i.e., not performing any prohibited actions. Hebrew.

shuk. Market. Mahane Yehuda is the name of the biggest Jerusalem market. There is also the Arab shuk in Jerusalem.

shul. School. Used to mean synagogue. Yiddish.

sicha. Conversation or lecture. Hebrew.

siddur. Prayerbook. Literally, "order," meaning order of prayers. Hebrew.

talleisim. Prayer garments. Yiddish.

Tanach. Hebrew Bible. Acronym for the three sections of the twenty-four books of the Bible, Torah, Neviim (prophets), and Ketuvim (writings).

tefillin. Scrolls that Jews wear to pray with in the morning prayers. Hebrew.

Teshuvah, tefilah, and tzedaka. Repentance, prayer, and charity. Actions specified to improve one's fate before the High Holidays.

tikkun. Literally, "correction." A tikkun is an all-night study session, common on Shavuot.

tov. Good. Hebrew.

traif. Not kosher. Literally "torn," since the lung of an animal that is torn and not "glatt," smooth, is rendered not kosher. Hebrew.

tremp. Ride. To get a tremp is to get a ride or to hitchhike, depending on context.

ulpan. Intensive Hebrew language class geared to new immigrants or anyone who wants to learn the language in a short period of time.

yichud. Being alone with one of the opposite sex. Hebrew.

Yisrael. Ordinary Jew, not of the priestly class. Hebrew.

yiyeh tov. It will be good. Hebrew.

Acknowledgments

For years, I have been reading the acknowledgments of the books of others with envy, wondering where these writers find the incredible friends to bring them soup night and day, permit them use of amazing writing spaces, or give helpful feedback.

And now, it is my own turn. I don't want to cause envy in others but I do feel blessed for the support I have gotten over the years of writing, from so many many sources, not all of which I will succeed in acknowledging.

Robert Mandel, thank you for saying yes—twice! I am so glad to be working with you at Mandel Vilar Press. Miriam Holmes, thank you for suggesting Robert Mandel at Texas Tech in the first place, and Jay Neugeboren, another Mandel Vilar Press author, thank you for suggesting that I submit a second time. Mary Beth Hinton was a wonderful copy editor; I'm glad her attention made sure all the details were right.

My former agent, Jacob Moore, made this all happen. Jacob really helped get the book to a level I could not have gotten it to on my own. Thank you for working with me, for getting the novel as the perspective of a young person, and outlining what the arc of the action in the novel could be, to let me revise it and make it the book I am ready to share for publication. I knew it would work out with you when you told me you were born in Raleigh, North Carolina, the place this novel, too, was born, oddly enough. I am so grateful for your belief and persistence.

Steve Albert and Robin Karlin I thank for graciously allowing me the use of a writer's studio in their lovely Pittsburgh home when I needed space to write. I will always be grateful for your kindness and generosity. Having a place to go and write each day has made a huge difference to my writing life. Now my thanks go to Dr. Bernie and Esther Klionsky and to Daniel Klionsky for giving me a writing space in the Klionsky home; and to Gail and Joel Ungar for giving me writing space during the copy edits; and to Naomi Oxman, for suggesting that I find myself a writing studio—I will be forever in your debt.

I am so fortunate to have met writer L. E. Miller at Lan Samantha Chang's summer writing seminar at the Tin House summer program in summer 2011. Laura is a fantastic writer, and a wonderful and generous reader and critic. She read the manuscript and gave countless suggestions that truly helped the manuscript reach its full potential. I cannot thank her enough for her contributions and discussions with me.

Shimon Adaf, an incredibly brilliant writer and poet as well as a wonderfully astute reader and editor, gave me a number of valuable suggestions on the seder chapter, confronting the question. His small tweaks, thoughtful questions, and deep comments made a big difference. He also read the last chapter and articulated places where the text was getting too closed—I hope I found in my revisions ways to keep it open. Shimon, I am grateful for and enjoy all your challenges that prod me to think more fully and carefully than I ever would be able to on my own.

My writing group in Pittsburgh—Jane Bernstein, Marc Nieson, and Lynda Schuster—has been a great support system and fun to hang out with! Though they didn't help with this novel directly, they provided much needed moral support and a forum to kvetch. Jeff Rubenstein, Talmud professor and friend, read and understood the novel at a late stage, which was very gratifying.

When I was writing a description of the novel for the catalog, I had great assistance from Ron Krebs, Miriam Holmes, and Yitz Francus, talented wordsmiths all, who forced me to make it punchier! Valuable input also came from Dan Iddings of Pittsburgh's great Classic Lines independent bookstore.

In Minnesota, I was fortunate to take classes at the wonderful institution that is the Loft. More than anything else, having a community of writers to discuss my work with helped me move forward in a way I could never have on my own.

I appreciate the assistance of Rabbi Michael and Tracey Bernstein and Rabbi Alexander Davis and Esther Goldberg-Davis for sharing their memories of the funeral send-off for the coffins of Matthew Eisenfeld hy"d and

Sarah Duker hy"d, which shaped my writing of chapter 7. Ron Krebs read a portion of the novel on a plane to Israel; it thrilled me no end to think of my words being read in the air.

Aryeh-Lev Stollman, yet another fantastic writer, gave me early and wonderfully supportive feedback on one chapter and helped give me permission to create a gay character, which I wasn't sure I could do successfully. Melvin Bukiet was also kind enough to read that chapter, after I met both of them at a Bar Ilan conference on creative writing in 2003.

Jacob Press, my first and for a while only friend in the exile of North Carolina, shared stories of being a gay American man in Israel, which inspired both Noah and Todd. Jacob's book *Independence Park*, on the lives of gay men in Israel, was also a very helpful source for both of these characters.

Brian Morton's summer fiction class at Sarah Lawrence was extremely helpful in teaching me many things and providing great feedback.

Nancy Reisman and the Fine Arts Work Center class let me know I had the structure of the novel in place, but I needed to paint and put up furniture.

Thank you to the Virginia Center for the Creative Arts in Amherst, Virginia, for giving me a residency at just the right time for revision. So glad to be finishing up in the South, where I started this work, yearning for the East and Jerusalem. While writing this novel, I also had residencies at the Corporation of Yaddo and the Ragdale Foundation, which deserve my thanks.

Before I left Minnesota, I gathered a group to read the novel and discuss. Judy Victor, Dori Weinstein, Paulette Donath, Beth Gendler, Ed Rapoport, Louise Ribnick, Naomi Oxman, Judy Marcus, Judy Snitzer, Judy Shapiro, Tamar Marmor—I knew that even if it wasn't published I'd succeeded in reaching some readers. Discussing the casting for a movie version—who would play Noah and Uri?—helped me realize that I could create a new world in my writing.

Ann Pava read, liked, and believed in this novel at an early stage. I have always wished I could have an older sister just like her, but she is a great substitute for the real thing!

Rabbi Gershon Sonnenschein told stories during weekly Talmud class about his time as the student assigned to Rav Joseph Soloveitchik one year, and a visit they made to the Lubavitcher Rebbe that made their way into Atarah's reminiscences.

The writing of Daniel Boyarin and Rabbi Steven Greenberg generated ideas about Rabbi Yohanan and Reish Lakish.

Sheva Zucker has been the greatest friend I could ever hope for; she listens patiently to all I confide in her and knows all my secrets. Thank you for being so supportive for all these many years, though I have not always taken your mostly-sage advice. Thanks for all your great stories and for being a great reader.

Aharon haviv—Jon—helped find me a literary agent through his insistence that we all that attend that twenty-fifth Yale reunion. You've supported and encouraged me all these years. Though at the outset of this novel I had conceived of Uri as a psychiatrist who creates healing narratives, it is truly marvelous that, over the years of my writing, you, my love interest, have moved into a similar line of work as a chaplain. I love you and am looking forward to many more years of creating the narrative of our family together, on the page and in real life. Though we have been arguing whether literature or life is more important from the time we met, I hope we continue to have large helpings of both!

About the Author

Beth Kissileff is a fiction writer and journalist who spent two years studying in Jerusalem and continues to visit Israel regularly. She holds a PhD in comparative literature from the University of Pennsylvania and has taught English literature, writing, Hebrew Bible, and Jewish studies at Carleton College, the University of Minnesota, Smith College, and Mount Holyoke College. Her fiction and nonfiction, on Israeli, cultural, literary, and religious topics, appear regularly in a variety of publications including the *New York Times*, *Slate*, *Haaretz*, the *Forward*, and the *Jerusalem Post*. She also edited the anthology *Reading Genesis*. She has received fellowships from the Corporation of Yaddo, the Ragdale Foundation, the Virginia Center for Creative Arts, the Lilly Endowment, and the National Endowment for the Humanities.